Praise for
JALAN JALAN

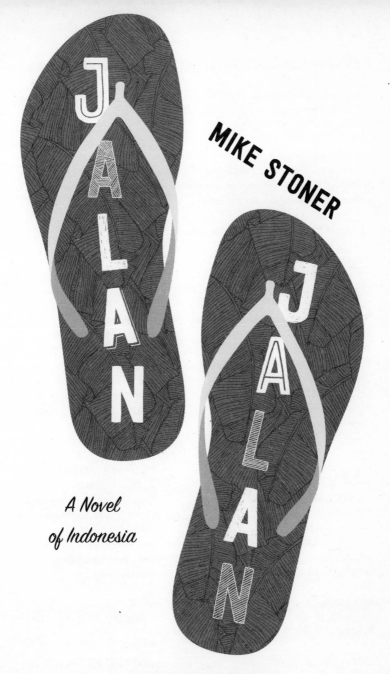

JALAN JALAN

MIKE STONER

A Novel
of Indonesia

TUTTLE Publishing

Tokyo | Rutland, Vermont | Singapore

Published by Tuttle Publishing, an imprint of Periplus Editions (HK) Ltd.

www.tuttlepublishing.com

Library of Congress cataloging is in process.

ISBN 978-0-8048-4629-5

Distributed by

North America, Latin America & Europe
Tuttle Publishing
364 Innovation Drive
North Clarendon, VT 05759-9436 U.S.A.
Tel: 1 (802) 773-8930
Fax: 1 (802) 773-6993
info@tuttlepublishing.com
www.tuttlepublishing.com

Asia Pacific
Berkeley Books Pte. Ltd.
61 Tai Seng Avenue #02-12
Singapore 534167
Tel: (65) 6280-1330
Fax: (65) 6280-6290
inquiries@periplus.com.sg
www.periplus.com

Japan
Tuttle Publishing
Yaekari Building, 3rd Floor
5-4-12 Osaki, Shinagawa-ku
Tokyo 141 0032
Tel: (81) 3 5437-0171
Fax: (81) 3 5437-0755
sales@tuttle.co.jp
www.tuttle.co.jp

Indonesia
PT Java Books Indonesia
Jl. Rawa Gelam IV No. 9
Kawasan Industri Pulogadung
Jakarta 13930, Indonesia
Tel: 62 (21) 4682 1088
Fax: 62 (21) 461 0206
crm@periplus.co.id
www.periplus.com

First edition
20 19 18 17 16   10 9 8 7 6 5 4 3 2 1   1510CM
Printed in China

TUTTLE PUBLISHING® is a registered trademark of Tuttle Publishing, a division of Periplus Editions (HK) Ltd.

For Dad, Andy, Linda,
and everyone else who is still there,
living in those moments.

CONTENTS

'And I asked myself about the present: how wide it was, how deep it was, how much was mine to keep.'
—Kurt Vonnegut, *Slaughterhouse-Five*

ESCAPE

A chilly late-spring day on the seafront in a preseason coastal town; a few couples meandering hand in hand, hatted grannies on Zimmer frames, granddads in electric carts tied to black Labradors, kids wobbling on Rollerblades, wearing fingerless gloves. People trying out the sun's weak warmth for the first time of the year, looking through winter-softened eyes at a cold calm sea. The blue-white pier tinged with the brown-orange of rust and rotting wood, is dipping its toes in the spring-tide water. Small waves whisper as they curl in on the pebbled beach.

Drinking tea with a tiled counter between them. The young man and the young woman, leaning into each other. Hands almost touching. Two people who have just met, talking about everything like best friends. All early uncertainty and awkwardness gone, evaporated in the steam of half a dozen cuppas. She steps away every now and then to let an elderly lady buy her own tea, or a young mum with pram and toddler buy the first ice cream of the year; a mini-milk, it's too early in the season to turn the Whippy machine on. And then she moves back in, leaning across the counter further, until finally she takes that first kiss, rips it right off his face like a plaster and he's left there, licking his lips, feeling for damage, wanting more.

The sun is now midway between midday and sunset.
'I need to go,' she says.

'And I need to close up,' I say.

We look at each other. She is back-lit in silver with ebony hair tumbling from under a green hat onto a green scarf. Green eyes blink once from under thick black lashes. A smile appears briefly at the corners of her lips.

'Well?' she says.

'Well,' I answer through a mouth of dry, crumbly clay.

'The tea?'

'The tea?'

'The tea.'

'Oh the tea.'

'Yes. The tea.'

'On the house. Free.'

'Thank you.'

She raises one eyebrow. I smile not knowing what I'm supposed to do in response, not sure what she even means with this gesture. Why is she raising her so very fine and utterly black eyebrow at me?

'So?' she asks.

'So,' I reply. I move straws and spinning windmills and a postcard rack carrying pictures of cliffs and lighthouses and gardens full of flowers off the counter.

An afternoon has passed too quickly and now my mouth has reached a point of immobility. My mind races to think of what I should say to her now, before she goes, so that this is more than an exceptional afternoon, so that it is to be repeated. I must think of something and force it down and along the muscle of my tongue.

'Eight o'clock,' she says with an eyebrow raised once more.

'Yes.'

'In front of the pier,' she tells me.

'Yes.'

'Good.'

'Good.' I smile. I reach across. I put my hand into the softness and warmth behind her neck and guide her forward. I kiss her. She kisses me. We kiss.

It is...

It is...

Beautiful.

It is Painful.

It is Hurtful.

Mean.

I open my eyes and a tear falls, landing on the back of my hand. I wipe it on my trousers.

Oh, you hurtful bastard, taking me by surprise again. Why do you make me relive it? It's done. Laura's dead. Forget it.

I blink and look from the window and through rain that batters the car. I see night, and that is all. Darkness and water stick to the glass like oil, thick and viscous.

You will not get in my head anymore. I want you gone. Enough of you and your pain and pathetic sentimentalities. You and her stay down in my gut where it's dark. Be quiet and be forgotten. Lie there, cuddle up and wrap yourselves together in your self-pity. Sleep next to the beating of my heart and leave me be.

My hand scrunches the front of my shirt, wishing it could reach under, through the flesh, and rip them out forever.

'Is first time in Indonesia?'

I look to the man driving this four-by-four. His name is Pak Andy and he has just collected me from Medan's airport on Sumatra. He's a Chinese Indonesian with a swirl of thinning hair and a large mole under his lip. My new boss.

'Yes.' My blunt answer does the trick and doesn't lead to any more questions. As he was late in meeting me at the airport and his voice hints at boredom, I don't think he cares anyway.

The silence returns. I try to focus on and imagine where I'm being taken; an apartment, a house, a hostel, a hovel? I haven't got a bloody clue where. I haven't got a clue about this country. And I've just signed up for a year. The first year of the new millennium and I'm here, lost mentally and geographically. How messed up is that?

After five minutes of more silence the rain has stopped and billboards appear along the roadside, lit up in the car's beams like TV screens being switched on; happy Indonesian faces drinking condensed milk, coffee, driving Nissans, smoking cigarettes without health warnings.

Then the city starts coming at us. First little roadside shacks appear, made of bamboo with blue plastic tarpaulin roofs and young shirtless men frying food under them. I open my window to let in the after-rain air. The bittersweet smell of soy sauce and chilli rushes through the car and the boomph boomph of music increases, decreases, increases as we pass various roadside sound systems. Behind the shacks houses start appearing: low white buildings with white perimeter walls and trees sprouting over the top of them. As the houses increase in number the smells start to vary and mingle. Old rubbish, fried chicken, rotting fruit, dust from the already drying roads, coffee.

'Close your window,' says Pak, 'we are coming to traffic lights.'

I wonder why an open window should be a problem, but I close it anyway.

The flight from England via Singapore is finally taking its toll on me and a yawn escapes. Through watery eyes I see traffic lights ahead trickle from green to red. In front of us two lines of three or four cars are coming to a stop. We pull up behind them. I'm looking to see what it is that worries Pak Andy so much when there's a tap on my window. A boy stands there, face pressed up to the tinted glass and hands cupped around almost-black eyes trying to look in. At first his eyes move and flutter like a blind man's while he tries to focus on the inside of the car. Finally they find me and a big toothy smile appears like a cleaver's cut through flesh to the white of bone. His hands quickly shape themselves into a bowl and I hear muffled words through the glass, 'Please, *bule*. Please, mister.'

I look at Pak Andy and he is just staring straight ahead while waving his hand and shaking his head at two young boys tapping on his window.

I shift in the seat and slide my hand into my front pocket and feel around. When I touch the hexagonal sides of a fifty-pence I remember I only have some English change in my front pockets and large Indonesian notes in the wallet in my back pocket. The boy has his face pressed to the glass again. Shrugging my shoulders at him I show him empty hands. I feel like a cheap bastard sitting in this monster of a car, pretending I have no money. I wear skin the colour of—and thanks to the air-conditioning, the texture of—uncooked chicken. He must know I'm no poor man compared to him. He cups his hands again, tilts his head and stares so pitifully from under his lowered eyebrows that I can't help myself. I pull my wallet out from under my bony behind. As I fumble out a crisp, clean, not sure how many rupiah note, the car starts pulling off.

'No. Wait,' I say.

Pak Andy steals a quick sideways glance at me and looks forward again. The car doesn't stop. The boy is jogging beside us, still trying to get his face back against the glass, and manages a glance at the note in my fingers. He's running and alternately tapping at the window and pointing to my hand. Pak turns the car right and the boy loses the race. I look over my shoulder and see him in his shorts and button-less open shirt raise his hands to the black night sky and shake his head.

'Very bad people. Always asking for money. They should get a job. I have a job. You have a job. They should get a job.' Pak is shaking his head. 'Very bad.'

I return the note to my wallet. I just hope my bed isn't much further. I don't want to sit next to this man for any longer than I have to.

'We will be at the school very soon,' he says.

I turn my reddening and tired face towards him.

'I will give you your timetable for classes before I take you to your house.'

There is a little smile touching his mouth. It isn't warm.

I close my eyes. Try to make my mind wander to irrelevant places. Ignore the fact that I've taken a dislike to my new boss, that I've made another glorious fuck-up in my life. My stomach grumbles. Lack of real food? Or the two additions to my innards?

The pair of them, muted and gagged. Shoved down in my gut and not allowed to interrupt my 'new' life until I'm ready for them, which I might never be. Old Me isn't as clear-cut as New Me. I can push moments of life aside. He can't. He dwells and sobs on the things which I try to ignore. He's pathetic. He wants to share his moments in time. Relive them like they're still now. Well he can just shut up about his moments with Laura and the times that the two of them want to regurgitate.

I've had enough. That's why I've got rid of him, of them. She is dead and he needs to shut up about the past. Shut up saying that it is still there. That those moments still exist. That if they happen in the first place then they must still be there, like an object to revisit. He needs to stop telling me that if those moments still exist, then, maybe, so does Laura..…

Just stop.

There is no point. Not to his questions and not to her constant amateur philosophising. Her quotes from head-fucks like Einstein. Stupid fucking gems like, '… the distinction between past, present, and future is only an illusion, however persistent.' Blah blah blah.

She messes her hair up like Einstein when she does it.

Bullshit.

He drives me fucking mad with his hope. She drives me mad by showing up in my head, talking her rubbish. So stay in the dark, both of you. For good. You, Old Me, are as dead as her. A ghost. Stay with the ghost of her.

I rub my eyes and look at the outside. We are now moving slowly through traffic. The city has enveloped us. Cars and motorbikes spew black smoke and edge along on either side of the car. Then we pull off of the road and onto the forecourt of an ugly building.

'We are here.'

I look to Pak Andy, and something in me wants to hurt him.

HUNGER

The school is green and white under flickering floodlights. It is three storeys tall. Above it a green and white sign spells out 'English World'. In front of the building stand about ten people, smoking, talking, but mostly just smoking. They are older teenagers, some dark-skinned Indonesians, some Chinese, all holding books under their arms. Others walk out of the glass doors: attractive dark-haired girls; Chinese boys dressed like James Dean popping cigarettes into their mouths as they flick back their amateur quiffs; younger kids, about fifteen in white-shirted and grey-trousered school uniforms. They cross the two-car-sized forecourt we have just pulled into, passing by my window, and disappear into the mayhem of the road we've just left.

'The classes have finished,' says Pak. He turns off the engine, opens his door and is gone.

'Righto.' I stare after him, open my door and climb down from my seat.

I enter an airless outside; the smell of diesel and two-stroke engines sticks to the atmosphere like a greasy film. I look behind me at the road. Motorcycle taxis putt-putt and leak black fumes, car taxis beep at them to move, bicycle taxis ring their bells for lazy pedestrian attention and nothing moves at more than ten miles an hour on the constipated road.

'Hey. You. Hello,' one of a group of four sitting in front of the school shouts.

I smile back, but am too tired and too unsure how to reply. Confidence and energy are dripping from me like oil from a sump. It won't be long before I seize up.

'You are the new teacher?' He is strutting towards me, a Chinese boy in leather jacket, white open-neck shirt and a bouncing quiff.

'Yes. I am.'

'I am Johnny,' he announces as if he is the MC at his own concert, all stress on his name. Pulling his collar up around his neck, he flicks a white filtered cigarette between his lips.

'Nice to meet you.' I wonder if I've accidentally flown Time Machine Airlines and travelled back to the '50s. I half-expect him to start singing an Elvis song and the people on the forecourt to start jiving.

'What's your name, man?' he asks, looking at me from under his quiff.

'I'm...' A piercing two-fingered whistle, louder than the noise of the traffic, kills my introduction. Pak Andy is standing in the door to the school waving his hand for me to go away. I look about, trying to work out where he wants me to go to. I point a finger at his car. He shakes his head and waves his hand some more.

I point to the street, lost by his directions.

'No, man. He wants you to go in,' says Johnny.

'So why's he shooing me away?'

'I don't know what "shooing" is, man, but what he does means come here.' He waves his cigarette at a scowling Pak.

I point to my chest and then to the school to get confirmation from Pak. He nods and waves for me to go away like he's trying to lose snot stuck to his hand. Even unspoken language is foreign here.

'Thanks. Maybe see you later,' I say to Johnny.

'Yeah. See you, man. Watch out for Pak Andy. He'll take your last rupiah.'

I step from the heat and stench of the street into the skin-prickling coolness of the school reception, all green and white with plastic plants gathering dust. Pak is standing with an elbow on the reception counter. Seated behind it is an overweight Chinese guy of about twenty-five. Even with the fridge-like air conditioning there is a wet patch spreading out from under each armpit. He studies me through long thin eyes that are hardly there.

Pak introduces him as Albert the receptionist. Albert hoists himself off his stool and lays his hand in mine like a piece of wet fish which lies there for a second before sliding off.

'You are hungry?' Pak asks me.

Am I? My stomach rolls and turns, but I'm not sure if it's hunger or him trying to throw some more Laura my way.

What does she think of me standing here now in a completely foreign place trying to be not me? Probably raising an eyebrow and poking me in the side and saying something like, 'Nice move, numbnuts.'

And I laugh or poke her back and try to lick that irritating, sexy, ebony caterpillar over her left eye.

'Yes or no?'

Oh, well done, you crafty bastards. I swallow down on them and the broken fragments of pain they've left. Perhaps I do need to throw some sort of foreign food down me to stop the heartburn.

'Yes. Food would be good. No meat, please. I'm vegetarian.'

He snorts and is then yelling out something that sounds like 'Eepooo.'

From down the corridor that runs off next to the counter comes hurrying an Indonesian in matching brown shirt and trousers. He is as high as my chest, with a long dark-brown fringe that hangs over his eyes.

Eepooo stands in front of Pak with his head slightly bowed through either respect or fear. Pak doles out some foreign words which have the clipped tone of instruction, and a couple of notes from his back pocket. Eepooo, if that is his name, shoves the money in his shirt pocket, looks at me from under his fringe and flashes a set of impressively white large teeth in such a way that I can't help but smile back. I think of Mowgli: Mowgli ripped out of *The Jungle Book* and put in the uniform of an errand boy, no doubt Baloo having been captured for his dancing skills and placed in a cage somewhere to amuse simple and mindless tourists.

I must be getting tired. My mind is going all over the place.

Still smiling, Mowgli goes out of the front door and boogies across the road, probably singing to himself, 'Be doop doop do, I wanna be like you-oo.'

Knackered. I want a bed.

'Food is coming. Come. I'll show you the staffroom and give you your timetable. You will start at nine tomorrow morning.' Pak walks off down the corridor.

Nine? Tomorrow morning? I look at the clock hanging behind the counter to make sure I haven't crossed fewer time lines than I think I have. Fat boy behind the counter smiles in such a way that I don't return it.

I follow Pak down the corridor and into a room on the left. A very tired New Me is about to take control of the situation and tell Pak there is no way he's working tomorrow. As Old Me would say, there are moments different to this. Moments when he thinks very strongly about saying no to things he doesn't want to do, but never actually does. Probably because he's a gutless wimp of a piece of shit. So I am impressed and proud when New Me, being the opposite of his nemesis, opens his mouth and says, 'No. Sorry. I'm not working tomorrow.'

Pak is standing next to a desk against the wall, one of about ten lining the room.

'You will sit here.'

'OK. But I'm not working tomorrow. Sorry, Pak, but I'm jet-lagged and need to sleep.'

'But I have you on the timetable for tomorrow. There are students.'

Old Me almost surfaces, but I swallow him down.

'Sorry. Wednesday alright, but not tomorrow.'

'I will have to ask another teacher to cover. He won't like it, but…you are tired. I am always being told you Westerners are different, not used to work, and I need to understand. OK. You can start Wednesday. Class J1. Here is all the information you need.' Red-faced, he picks up a folder on my desk, waves it at me and drops it again.

'Thanks.'

'And please, do not call me Pak. It is Pak Andy, like you say Mr Andy in English or Andy-san in Japan. Please show respect.'

'Oh. OK, Pak Andy. Sorry.' I guess I've pissed him off. Never mind.

'Wait here. I have some work to do in my office. Epool will bring you food in a minute.' He is gone from the staffroom. I look at the green folder and think about opening it. I can't be arsed. I sit in my new chair and hope I can stay awake long enough for the food to arrive.

So Eepooo isn't Eepooo but Epool. I prefer Mowgli.

Looking around, the room feels like an academic *Mary Celeste*. Papers and open textbooks lie arrayed on most desks, some pinned down by coffee mugs.

What has happened to the teachers? They must have made a rapid exit if the classes have only just finished. Perhaps there are no teachers. I am The Replacement. The Teacher.

I'm too tired to consider the god-almighty cock-up I might have made in coming here. What sort of idiot takes a job after a five-minute phone interview, in a country he knows nothing much about and on the other side of the world, in a school he's never heard of? Me idiot. That's who. But that's what I'm about. I don't care anymore. Or at least I try not to. I'm supposed to just do it. New Me just does it.

I lean my head on the desk, turned a little so I can feel the desk's smooth cold on my cheek. Sleep. Need sleep. Sleep tonight. Relax tomorrow. I'll be fine.

The air conditioning hums a lullaby on the wall above me, wafting cool air across my aching neck. My eyes close, open, close. Soothing on my neck. Laura gently runs her fingers over my nape and up into my hair; she rests her hand on the back of my head, fingers softly massaging my scalp while she gently whispers,

—*Don't worry, baby. Don't worry.*

Her breath sways the minuscule hairs in my ear back and forth like meadow grass, meadow grass that I'm lying in, the sweet smell of it in my nose. Her hands on my cheeks, she kisses my eyelids, my nose, my lips…

BANG.

I open my eyes, my hand clasps my mouth trying to hold her there but she is gone. I look around, not sure of where I am. Epool stands in the doorway, a bag of something in his hand, the smell of chilli swirling around him.

'Food for you, mister.' He makes a rotating hand movement in front of his mouth.

'Thanks.' I blink away any fragments of Laura and the meadow and hit my chest to silence the dead. Epool eyes me with the caution of a small, nervous child.

'It's OK. Very hungry,' I say, and instead of my chest, I pat my gut. 'Very, very hungry.'

'Oh, gooood.' The big toothy smile is back. 'Good food here.' And he brings over the bag and plonks it on the desk in front of me.

'Noodles.'

'Thank you Epool.'

'No. Not Epool. Epool.'

'Epool?' I can hear no difference.

'Wait, please.' He takes a pen from the desk next to mine and pushes it down hard on a piece of paper. He starts moving the nib slowly and carefully across it.

I look at the finished piece, a little scratchy and wobbly but a word, a name, has made it out of the pen.

'Ah, Iqpal.'

'Yes, yes.' He slaps me on the back and then double slaps his chest. 'Iqpal.'

'Nice to meet you, Iqpal.' I offer him my hand. He looks at it as if he's being given a present and then shakes it like it's made of porcelain.

'Iqpal.' Pak, sod the respect, is back talking Indonesian to my new friend. Iqpal smiles and nods at me, then runs off to do whatever it is Pak has just told him to do.

I wonder what time they finish working here. The clock on the wall clicks to nine fifty-one, which is two fifty-one in the afternoon back home. I yawn. I haven't slept in over a day and a half.

'Come. I will take you to your house.'

House? That sounds promising. I pick up my bag of noodles and the folder off my desk and follow Pak back to his car.

'Where are the other teachers?' I ask as I climb back in, placing the food between my feet.

'The driver has already taken them home. They left directly after class.'

'A driver? What time does he pick up in the mornings?'

'No pickup. Only take home. You must take a bus or taxi to work in the mornings. Taxi is safer.'

We slide off the forecourt into the slow-moving traffic. Pak starts beeping his horn and steers the car in any direction he sees an opening. Multicoloured cycle-rickshaws are steered out of the way at full leg-power by skinny men in dirty shorts, T-shirts, and sweat-stained caps. They ring their bells and shout while taking hands off handlebars to shake fists.

'How will I find the bus?'

'You are sharing with Kim, another teacher. Kim will tell you how to get to work. Don't worry.'

Don't worry? I put my head back against the rest and pretend I'm not worried. I look sideways at Pak, something dark and ugly is just under his skin, almost invisible. My gritty, weary mind slips sideways for a moment and anxiety soaks into the marrow of my bones like blood through a bandage.

We go to sleep.

His is surprisingly long and deep and dark. Nothing flashes behind his eyelids, no beautiful woman dances across his retinas, shedding clothes as she moves. Just sleep, like a taster of death.

And I sleep too, down in the snugness of his chest. But my sleep is fitful, broken and full of images, because that is what I am: a record of a life like an old cine film in a can, curled in on itself so frame lies upon frame upon frame, image doubled over image, from the outer edge of the spool to the tightest curl in the centre. A whole life stored away, but always available for late-night showings. Always ready for curtains to open on one of the countless moments of now.

Swoosh, almost silent, the curtains part to keep me from sound sleep. A short, but a classic, keeping me occupied while he snores.

I watch the scratchy lines move up and down and across the screen, the black-and-white numbers flash in countdown, focus the lens and there it is…

Her apartment: she stands with her back against the open door, one hand on the handle and the other ushering me in, as if she is showing me a portal to a magical land.

'Here we are,' she says.

I am gently spinning from alcohol and the closeness of her. I walk past as she holds the door open, aware of the sparks that jump from her to me and me to her. We are a Van de Graaff generator on heat.

There is a smell of patchouli and coffee in her apartment. A sofa, a rocking chair and small portable TV occupy the room. A rug keeps the wooden floor warm, and off to the right I see a kitchen hiding behind a wall and off to the left a bedroom winks.

'Take a seat. That seat.' She points to the sofa with its pair of big red cushions and caress-me fabric. I do as I'm told.

'Whisky?' She pulls off her hat and scarf and coat in a motion that is so quick it baffles me. Am I that wasted that time is playing its tricks with me?

'It's all I have, so it's all you're getting.' And she is sucked into a flashing white light in the kitchen.

I watch my fingers play an invisible miniature set of drums on the arm of the sofa. Then a glass is pushed into my hand. An inch of light-golden liquid sloshes drunkenly around its base while a fat and half-melted candle on the coffee table is lit. A body falls onto the sofa next to me and my shoulder is touching hers. Static builds. I run a hand through my hair to make sure it's not standing on end. The warmth from the whisky runs down my neck and through my stomach.

'So?' she says, curling her legs up under her.

'So?' say I.

'It was a good day.'

'It was.'

'Thank you.'

'Thank you.'

I swirl my whisky around the glass and then my mouth and then my head.

I look at her and she is staring at her knees and the teacup of scotch which she holds there. Her eyes are glazed and flicker in the candlelight and she is smiling.

'A very good day,' she says and looks at me and my heart detaches itself from its veins and arteries and tumbles down into my stomach, where it lies stunned, before jumping back and reattaching all its life support.

She looks like she saw it happen.

'Kiss me,' she says.

I kiss her.

She dances across my eyes, shedding clothes as she moves.

HELLO GOODBYE

When I awake at some point before dawn, there is a voice nearby, its song undulating, growing stronger with the changing light. From further off another two voices travel across the city to me, melodies added to the main theme. It is a human dawn chorus that rises from nothing to something beautiful. It winds its way around my senses and holds me to my bed. I don't expect it. I have never considered it and its appearance surprises me. I am just here, without expectations or any real knowledge of this country. I have come only out of the need to be rid of my past and with no thought for where that expulsion has taken me. That is why, when the muezzin starts, and other voices join in and fall across the city with the rising sun's light, I cry. I cry due to the unexpected and simple beauty of the song.

There again it might not just be the call to prayer that makes me cry; it could partly be due to the close call to vomiting from a few hours ago. Maybe too much beer on spicy noodles in an unsteady stomach, maybe too much grass. That could the reason for my tears—strong, strong grass. This is yesterday:

Pak takes me to my new home. He introduces me to Kim and Kim to me. Kim is a man. A Californian man, mid-thirties, tall, in a brown flower-patterned shirt. Pak leaves as soon as he can. He has to be somewhere else. Kim closes the door behind him. My new house is open-plan and cool, white tiled floor, big-cushioned armchairs with wooden armrests, a muted TV showing a small and chubby Asian-American beating up four men in suits with swift and precise movements of an umbrella. There's a kitchen along one wall and a dining table in front of a window and door to a concrete garden. Four more doors lead off the main room. This is my home.

'Fuuuuuucccckk. That man is such a fucking fuck, man.' Kim sits in a chair and puts his long legs out over the small table in front of him. He hits the volume on the remote. 'Make yourself at fucking home, man.'

I drag my travel-tired rucksack across the tiles, opening doors until I find a room that isn't a toilet, a shower or a bedroom with Kim's dirty underwear sniffing the floor. In my room are two single beds; only one is made up, the other still has a plastic cover on the mattress. I lay my rucksack on the unmade bed. Fumbling deep inside one of its pockets I find the pebble. It is smooth and comfortable in my palm. It's the only thing I've allowed myself. The only memory I've brought. No photos, no other souvenirs of her, just this pebble. I turn it in my hand, swallow down hard on the two of them who stir at the feel of it and return it back to the pocket. I give my bag a pat.

'Sleep well.'

I go back and flop in an armchair next to Kim.

The chubby Asian-American on TV is now giving life-changing advice to a small blond American boy, while Indonesian subtitles translate along the bottom of the screen.

'Yeah, go Sammo. Tell that white boy how to be good. I fucking love Sammo. Beats the shit out of people with toilet rolls and fucking bananas and things like that and is sooo fucking wise.'

I nod. Sammo does look wise.

'Do you smoke?' Kim asks me.

Not much. Not recently. Not since Laura.

How much pain have I been in? Too much to remember I'm an addict. I have never once thought about smoking again. Now I remember I am an addict, I want one.

'Yes. Are they Marlboro?'

'No, not these, man.' He waves his brown cigarette under my nose, and for some reason the pungent smell of it makes me think of apple pie. 'But you can have one if you want.'

'Cheers.' I take one and light it. The return of a forgotten comfort, long-time banished. Too pissed off and demented to remember the deadly old habit. It hits my throat like a saw and I cough. Smoke swirls around us like a mist. The sweet smell of scented tobacco hangs in the stillness of the warm and humid evening.

'Kretek cigarette, man. Strongest cigs in the world.'

'Tastes like it.' I know why the smell reminds me of apple pie. Cloves. The taste is surprisingly strong and it's suddenly soothing my throat, taking the teeth off the saw. My coughing subsides. 'But very good.' The clove coats my tongue while the tar slides into my lungs.

'Anyway I didn't mean smoke man, I meant smoooke. Do you smoooke?'

I look blankly at Kim.

'Smoke smoke. Smo-o-o-ke?'

'Ah. Yes.' Comprehension arrives as I look at the roll-ups mixed in with normal butts in the ashtray. 'Sometimes.'

With this Kim pulls a Frisbee from under his chair. It overflows with dangerous-looking green-brown foliage.

'I don't usually share, man, but as you're new.'

Kim rolls, no tobacco added, and we smoke.

And now I lie in my bed crying, listening to men singing out across the rooftops, welcoming me to the first full day of my new life. Men who may never have met, yet their voices interweave with the others to harmonise as though members of the same choir; which I guess they are. The voices stop and the silence is sudden.

I am lying with my head to the mosquito-netted open window. There must be a hole in it somewhere as a small lump on my thigh asks to be scratched. From where I lie I can see the top of a wall and a thin strip of sky. Day arrives quickly. The room changes from dark to light as the night is edged out. When the arrival of day is complete, I'm surrounded by varying off-white shades of the walls and floor tiles. I look at my watch: quarter past six. I've had maybe six hours' sleep. I try to recall the conversation with Kim, but nothing comes. A moment of life lost to magical foliage.

I wonder why Laura hasn't made an appearance yet and then push the thought aside. I get off the bed and busy myself with finding my pants. My bed cover is in a ball on the floor. The sheet I was lying on is damp with my sweat. Something small and bloodthirsty buzzes by my ear, close enough to make my spine shiver. This place is hot. And I want a cigarette. That is a morning need I haven't had for a while. I must have smoked everything to hand last night. The nicotine needs topping up. Re-infected already. Easier to catch than a cold.

I pull on dirty clothes that stick to my body like gritty cling film and leave the room.

The lounge stinks of overflowing ashtray and a sweet smell of burnt exotic plants. Kim has left a packet of Indonesian cigarettes on the table. I accept my re-addiction and take one. There's a lighter down the back of the chair. I go out the front door. A small tiled garden, hemmed in by a white wall and black metal gate, separates the house from the small and traffic-free road. The sun has risen quickly and the sky is white-blue. Lines of silver sunlight pour between the leaves and branches of a tree that holds yellow-green fruit. Mango, maybe. I pick one, roll it over in my hands and take a bite. Whatever it is, it isn't ripe. I spit it out, put the cigarette in my mouth and light it. The taste of clove and bonfires. I'm not keen on clove, it ruins apple pies, but the bonfire is OK. It sets fire to my lungs and the coughing rattles the dope hangover out of my head.

'Keep it fucking down, man. Fuuck.'

The voice comes from the window behind me. Kim must be in there somewhere behind the mosquito mesh. There's still more coughing to come so I open the gate and step onto the street where I let it out. I look at the cigarette.

'You evil bastard.'

Putting it back in my mouth, the cloves do their job. The back of my throat is numbing and the cough rolls over and goes to sleep.

Noise is still dormant in this street of white walls and small houses and trees. It is a cul-de-sac that stops at a wall to my right.

The sun is already blanching my face and the air is stuffy. Sweat bubbles up on my forehead. I'm going to like this heat. It's going to bake me into something new. I close my eyes and tilt my face to the sun. New Me is going to be brown and sun-bleached and blond-haired and careless. He's going to smoke and drink and argue and live and Laura will not have anything to say on the matter. Nothing.

—*Nothing?*

—*Nothing.*

—*Well that's not nice*, she says, ignoring the fact that she's dead.

—*Sorry, but me and you were one. We were one and you've gone. What does that leave? What am I supposed to do? What am I supposed to be?*

—*I don't know.*

—*Exactly. So be quiet. Please.*

I open my eyes before she can say more, go back in the house, pull a towel and bag of toiletries from my backpack, take a pee, shower under cold water, dry myself, put on a pair of pants, smoke another of Kim's cigarettes, go back to my bed, lie down, watch a pale-green lizard no bigger than my little finger crawl across the ceiling. I sweat, sleep, wake up, sweat some more, sleep some more, wake up, tell Laura to be quiet and go back to sleep, sweat, go back to sleep.

She dies. Nothing is linear, everything is flat. Nothing continues in perfect expectation and succession; there is no beginning, middle or end.

She dies, and the moment that lies nearest to this amongst the countless moments laid out like photos on a bed is the bus stop, the farewell. I pick the photo up and turn it so the whole moment is made clear. Studying it, I see that a little gathering of hair has come out from behind her ear and hangs against her cheek. The scent of the sea and fish and chips is being blown from the seafront down through the streets to here. A little white speck of cotton is caught on an eye-lash. I remove it with my thumb. She smiles, but there is awkward-ness between us that feels alien. She turns away and checks the time-table on the post again. Around us people walk by, unaware of the importance of this moment. Cars carrying families with picnics and buckets and spades roll up and down the street sniffing out parking spaces. At her feet is a suitcase with a shoulder bag sat on its top. In the top of the bag a passport, tissues and her camera taunt me. She is wearing cut-off jeans with straggly white threads hanging over the tops of her calves. A thin ivory cotton top shows a half-moon of her back with lightly tanned skin pulled tight over vertebrae and delicate shoulder blades. My hand goes there. The backs of my fingers stroke gently down between them. She turns and throws her arms around me. Like a fly-trap I close around her.

'Tell me not to go,' she says into my ear.

'Don't go,' I say into her hair, breathing in the scent of fruit and bottled freshness.

'I have to.' She puts her nose to my neck and I hear her breathe in.

'You smell like shit. I'll miss it.'

Through wispy hairs that tickle my face I see the white National Express coach waiting at a set of lights down the road, waiting to come and destroy me.

'Don't go,' I say again. 'I mean it.'

'I'll be back. It's not exactly far. And you go enjoy yourself too. Go find yourself somewhere.'

'I don't need to. I'm happy with me. I'm happy here, with you.'

'Well, no doubt you'll sneak a visit out to see me, even if I say you can't. You lovesick puppy.' She holds me tight to her, arms reaching far around my back.

This will probably happen. I can't believe I'm letting her go. I will have to see her somehow. I will have to. After more than three years together, I can't understand how I'll go for so long without seeing her, listening to her, watching her.

The lights have changed to green and the bus is moving towards us. My hands pull at the base of her back, pull her nearer.

'I guess that means you can see my bus.'

'No. It means I've got a boner.'

'Sicko.' Her hands grab my buttocks and her nails dig in. She grabs a piece of my neck with her teeth and pulls.

'Ow. Hurts.'

She releases.

'Don't forget me.' She leans back in my arms and locks my eyes with hers. 'Do not forget me. I'm doing this for me, but I love you. And I am not leaving you. You're just a yappy puppy going into kennels and I'll be back for you soon.'

I howl at the approaching bus.

'Calm down, Rover.'

'Nine months isn't soon.'

'Nine months is this,' and she snaps her fingers at the end of my nose. 'And anyway, I know damn well you're going to come and find me, because you'll miss me too much and you won't be able to resist it.'

'We'll see.' I do see. I see me pacing around the flat sipping malt whiskey, sniffing her old cushions and the one pair of knickers she leaves on the bed as a farewell present, looking from the phone to the clock to the phone to see if I can call her yet. I see this as a nightly routine until I finally break, get on a plane, a bus will be too slow, and go and grab her by every bit of her I can.

'I can't just leave. You know I can't. I can't pack in the teaching already.' I kid myself and am not really sure why I say it or why I'm doing it. Of course I'll leave. 'You've made it clear you don't really want me there. Not really.'

'Yes, but you need me, numbnuts. You won't cope. Don't deny.'

I read VICTORIA COACH STATION on the front of the bus as it pulls up beside us. It stops and lets out the airy fart noise buses make when they stop.

'I deny. I don't need a woman, for god's sake. You're never any good at cooking, or cleaning. So be gone.'

The door opens and suddenly everything is going at hyper-speed. How have we come to be here already? Why is she lifting her shoulder bag up and sliding it over her arm and looking at me like that? And her eyes are sparkling with wet. Her eyes never do that. And she becomes blurry because mine are doing the same and I'm a man and I don't do that. Then as the driver is putting her suitcase in the luggage compartment under the bus we're hugging and then kissing and then she strokes my face and says something and I nod and she climbs on the bus and my insides fall out and splash across the road and the bus pulls off, squashing them under its wheels.

And she is waving from the back window and I stand there with my hand in the air unable to move it, shocked by the speed of everything. The bus flashes an orange light at me and it turns. And it's gone.

And I throw the photo of this moment back amongst the others; a lifetime of snapshots mixed up and in no order, demanding that I look at them, from here, in this place he's shoved me, with his life, hoping I'll be forgotten.

PEBBLES

'You can't just get on any *sudako*, man. You'll end up in fuck knows where and you don't wanna do that 'cos you'll end up fucked knows where.'

'*Sudako*?'

'Those little yellow buses. *Sudakos*. We want number 23 or 34. Then we get off and get number 65.'

'What about taking a cycle-rickshaw?'

'They're called *becaks* here. Nah, not today. The buses are more fun and dirt cheap.'

I look at the traffic coming down the road. Yellow minivans and *becaks* overtake, undertake, swerve, pull over and slow down just enough for people who flag them down to jump in the back. Horns beep, buses and *becaks* spew black smoke out of broken exhausts. People stand along the street looking for their buses. We stand with them but I can't see any numbers on them.

'Here comes one. Watch and learn.' With this Kim steps onto the edge of the potholed road and waves his hand at a minibus coming down between two other buses. The one nearest swerves towards us and Kim shakes his head at it. The middle bus speeds up, cuts across in front of the inside one and then pulls up beside us. I see a small number 23 taped to the bottom of the window on a scrappy piece of paper.

'Get the fuck on, man. I prefer sitting up front with the driver, but for you, new boy, we'll do the back today.'

I follow Kim through a doorless opening at the rear and into the back of the minivan. Nine people turn sideways to look at us. They are seated on two benches attached to the inside of the van facing each other. A row of windows runs along each side. There is room left for about a bum and a half on the seats. Kim aims for a space furthest from the door. We are both hunched over and now being thrown against the other passengers' legs as the bus pulls off.

Kim sits down and the people on the bench opposite him wiggle about a bit and make space for me. I slide into it between the end of the compartment and a grumpy-looking man with a wispy chin. There is a letterbox-sized hole that shows the inside of the driver's cab and the road ahead. It also allows the driver a look at us with his rear-view mirror.

'Eh, *bule*. Where you go, mister?' His clove cigarette smoke swirls through the slit as he asks his question.

'That, my friend,' Kim says to me, 'is a question you have to get used to.' He then lights his own super-strength smoke.

My right thigh is on intimate terms with the grumpy man. The rest of the passengers sneak sideways and sometimes blatant looks at us, whispering and laughing while they do.

'Fucking celebrities, man. That is what we are. Only a few *bules* in this city and for us to be on one of these buses is a real fucking treat for these guys.'

I raise my eyebrows, indicating Mr Misery to my right.

'Well, some of them hate us of course,' Kim says without lowering his voice.

I turn to smile at Grumpy, to let him know he doesn't need to hate me, but as I do so he puts his hand on my thigh and pushes himself out of his seat and makes a wobbling dash for the back of the bus, banging the metal side as he does. The bus stops for a second to let him off and three more men on. They all somehow manage to get their arses on the benches.

'Eh, where you go, *bule*?' comes the smoking question from the driver again.

'Work. Teaching.' I shout through the slit.

'Ah, English teacher. I speak English. David Beck-haaam.' The driver laughs.

'Manchester United,' Kim yells through the hole and the whole of the bus yell it in agreement.

'Manchester United.'

'Fucking Beckham,' shouts Kim.

'Fucking Beck-haaam.' They're all laughing and slapping each other and me and Kim on the thighs in praise of Beck-haaam.

Kim is giggling.

'I fucking love these guys.' Kim pulls his pack of cigarettes out of his shirt pocket and hands them around the bus, ending with me.

'*Terima kasih*,' say some.

'Thanks,' say I.

We continue the first leg of our journey to work in this bouncing, close and friendly moving sauna that spews clove smoke out of the back doors like the world's slowest dragster. The rest of the conversation consists of 'Beckham' and 'Manchester United' said at various pitches and decibels with accompanying laughter.

When we get off the bus some ten minutes later my shirt is stuck to my back, my linen trousers are stuck right up my bum and my second cigarette of the journey tastes good. We hand the driver about three hundred rupiah each through the slit. Kim says '*Selamat tinggal*' to everyone we're leaving behind. I guess its meaning as goodbye, and say the same.

We're off the bus at another mad and busy road that appears to be the connecting stop for many different buses. They are pulling over, doing u-turns, beeping, and swerving in every direction. The street is lined by coffee, sugar-cane and coconut juice shacks with rusting corrugated roofs. We're also surrounded by about a hundred kids in the white shirts and grey trousers or skirts of school uniform. They line the road for about thirty metres.

'We just got to walk a little way up here to the next junction. We can stop a bus there,' Kim tells me.

We walk along the edge of the road. Every other teenager says, 'Hello mister,' or 'Where are you going?' or both.

Kim just keeps repeating the same answers, 'Hi,' or '*Jalan jalan*.'

Once we've passed all the kids we stand at the street corner where it's a little less manic. We squint eyes for the number 65.

'What does *jalan jalan* mean?' I ask.

'Just fucking walking, man. Out for a stroll. Going no-where in particu-fucking-lar.' He runs his hands through his dark hair and breathes in noisily through his nose. 'Comes from the verb *jalan* meaning to walk. It also means street and about a dozen other similar meanings. It's the answer they wanna hear and it saves you having to explain yourself and say what you're really fucking doing.'

A *becak* pulls up next to us and the rider points to his empty seats. Kim waves it on.

'And you'll hear, "Hey mister, where you go?" so many fucking times a day you'll wanna buy a gun and kill yourself or them or both. But you get used to it, man.' Kim throws his head back and stretches his arms out to the sides, as if worshipping the sky. 'Fuuuck it's fucking hot, man.'

'It is. Fucking hot.' I look up to the sun burning a hole in the cloudless sky. I close my eyes to it.

Bake me new. Bake me new. I can feel the ingredients starting to cook, standing here on this street corner where no one knows me and I know no one and a thousand different people travel past me in little yellow buses and on motorbikes and *becaks* and in the occasional black-windowed four-by-four.

'So why you here, man?' Kim asks.

I look at him. He's also turned his face to the sun with eyes closed.

'*Jalan jalan*,' I say. 'That's what I'm doing. Just strolling, minding my own business, trying to get on with nothing. Going nowhere in particu-fucking-lar.'

'Good fucking answer, man.'

'And you?'

'Me? Fuck, I dunno.' He opens his eyes. 'I don't seem to fit in back home. I may be American, but all those flags flying outside every fucking house. Too much nationalism. All that "'American People'" shit the government has started using. Brainwashing us into believing we're in a great nation together. Leave me out of your generalisations, fuckers. I'm just me and great on my own, thanks. And it's only gonna get worse if Bush gets in.' With that he steps off the pavement with his hand in the air. 'Here's ours, the 65.'

It pulls in at a diagonal, wobbling stop, ignoring anything else on the road. We climb in. This bus is quieter but the other passengers still steal glances at us. A couple of young guys give us big white smiles.

'Why do you say that about Bush?' I'm not even sure who he is, but I'm guessing a candidate for Presidency.

'Fucking nationalist loon, man. Scares me what he'll do to keep the '"American People"' happy. Probably declare some sort of war to boost the economy.'

'And he's the reason you're here?'

'Nah, not just him. It just wasn't my country, man. I feel more at home here. Different sets of values here. That's all.'

We all hold on as the bus lurches to a quick stop and two more men get on. They squeeze in as close to us as they can and nod at us in greeting.

'Where you go, mister?' asks one.

Kim looks at me and smiles.

'*Jalan jalan*, my friend. *Jalan jalan*.'

Fifteen minutes later we're at the school and I'm being introduced to the other staff. Their names are told, they enter my ears and are lost in the melee of muck that swishes around between them. I forget everyone's in admin as soon as Pak says them, although I remember fat Albert from two nights ago. I also forget everyone's in the teaching department a second after being introduced. Considering there are only four of them here this morning including Kim, my mind is being extra feeble.

I've got two classes this morning and then I'm back in for a six p.m. class. Split shifts are the newbies' tough shit, according to Kim. 'And you're the fucking newbie.'

It's eight thirty and my first class is at nine. I'm feeling uncertain of myself and anxious about the parasites in my gut. I've had a day of relaxing, sleeping, looking at my teaching file and settling into the house and the heat, but things still stir within me. I will them to stay sunk while I sit at my desk and look at the array of weird names on my first class's register. The teachers in the room throw random questions and bits of information at me.

'Where you from?' Australian accent with a beard.

'Why the hell did you choose this shithole?' English thirty-something with big breasts, frenetic fingers and wide eyes.

'The little kids are fun. Don't bother teaching them anything, just fucking play games with them.' Kim.

'How's your jet-lag?' Manchester with deep worry lines etched around his eyes and across his forehead.

'Pak's a cunt. Tell him to fuck off if you don't want to do something.' Big breasts again.

A second warning about Pak. I force optimism; from previous job experience, slagging off your boss isn't that unusual.

'Where's my class exactly?' I ask the room in general as a way of ignoring more questions.

'Which one you got?' asks bearded Australian.

'Dickens.'

'That's on third, next to Austen. Come on, I'll show you.'

As I follow Australian up the stairs, course book and pens in my hand, Iqpal is coming down with a mop and bucket in his. He shows us his wide toothy smile.

'*Apa kabar*?' asks Australian.

'*Baik-baik*. How are you, Marty?'

'*Baik-baik*.'

'How you doing, Iqpal?' I say.

'*Baik-baik*. You? Good sleep?'

'Very. Thanks.'

He smiles and rests his bucket on the step as we walk past him.

'Have good day with students.'

'Thanks. I will.'

We trudge up the next flight of blue-tiled stairs and away from the air-conditioning, footsteps echoing as we go.

'He's a happy little bloke, young Iqpal,' says Marty. 'Pak treats him like shit, but he keeps smiling,'

We're on the top floor and the air-conditioning is a long way behind. I wipe a bead of sweat from my temple.

'Here we are. You're in that one and I'm next door. Come give me a knock if you have any problems. Not that you will. These little kids are bonzer.'

'Thanks, Marty.' One memorised. Laura always says I'm rubbish with names; she'll be impressed.

No she won't. Quit it, you, and learn to shut up.

I open the class door and flip on the lights. They flicker and buzz and finally light up my green-and-white windowless room. Chairs sit on top of tables like swimmers lined up on the edge of a pool. On my desk is a remote control for the AC. I press buttons on it until at last the machine on the wall starts moving up and down and blowing cool air across the muggy room.

I'm expecting thirteen kids any moment. All I know is they range from eight to fourteen. Should be interesting. Probably be embarrassing. Probably be painful. Probably be horrible.

Turn and run.

Get to the airport.

Go home.

Pull a duvet over my head. Cuddle pillows. Sniff them, try to get a hint of her. 'Shut the FUCK up.' I whack my chest with a balled fist.

'Sorry sir. This Dickens?'

The boy is about three feet tall, ethnic Chinese, in a red, blue and yellow stripy T-shirt and trousers that reach just below his knees, where they meet pulled-up white socks with red stripes around the top. I'm guessing he's the eight year-old. He looks more uncertain than I feel.

'Hello. Yes it is. And you are?'

'Sorry, sir?'

'Your name? What is your name?'

'Dennis, sir.'

'OK Dennis. Come in and take a seat.'

He pulls one of the swimmers into the pool, just as a procession of little people comes through the door. I stand back and wait for them to choose their seats. Once they've sat, put their pads and pencil cases on the tables I start.

'Good morning. I'm your new teacher.'

'Good morning, sir.'

'Does anyone want to ask me any questions?'

Dennis puts his hand up. I nod for him to go ahead.

'What does "fuck" mean, sir?'

'Time isn't successive.'

'Explain, please.' I place a little pebble in her navel. It fits almost perfectly.

'I mean this moment doesn't follow the previous and doesn't precede the next.' She lifts her head up and holds her sunglasses above her eyes for a moment, inspecting the jewel in her tummy button. 'You want me to belly dance?'

'Later maybe. So how does time work in your highly superior mind then?'

She replaces her sunglasses and rests her head back on the pillow made of her clothes.

'Everything is side by side. Now is next to my birth and your birth and Napoleon's birth and Hiroshima and Christopher Columbus taking his first poo in the New World and the moment I said time isn't successive.'

I suck the pebble out of her and spit it onto the beach. It bounces off a stone and then another and settles into its own little crevice. I dig a little hole in the beach next to us and find a smaller one. This drops neatly into the oval dip in her stomach.

'Humans have created the concept of time moving forward, but it's never really been seen or proved. We could have taken another concept on board just as easily.'

'Perhaps we haven't, because other concepts are wrong.' My finger traces a circle around the grey gem in its pink setting and her stomach quivers.

'Einstein didn't believe it.'

'Doesn't mean he's right.'

'Doesn't mean he's wrong, but all right.' She sits up and my pebble disappears in the fold of her stomach, 'Look at this beach.'

I look. It's packed. Little children run in and out of the waves where the sand is just making an appearance at low tide. Groups of foreign students show off their continental tans and husbands stare from behind sunglasses at breasts of Scandinavian-looking girls who light cigarettes and glance sideways at Italian boys. The pier is cooling its front legs in the water, skin peeling and old frame creaking.

'How many pebbles?' she asks, using her sunglasses to hold her hair back.

'Seventy-two billion, three hundred and twenty-three thousand and four.' My eyes scan the length of the beach again. 'Maybe five.'

'Exactly. And they all sit next to each other going off in every direction. Now imagine that each pebble is a moment in time.'

I realise this is going to be an explanation that requires attention. I sit up and adjust my position so I'm sitting comfortably.

'Right, now watch.' She picks up a stone and drops it. 'This is now.' She picks up the stone next to it, it drops. 'This is now.' She does it again.' This is now.' She does it again. 'This is now.'

I consider not interrupting just to see how many times she's going to do it, but my question wants to be heard.

'So where is yesterday?'

She picks up the stone next to the one she's just dropped.

'Napoleon's birth?'

She picks up the next, drops it.

'Or maybe,' she turns around, crawls up the sloping beach two feet and picks up a stone from there, 'maybe this one.'

I look at her bottom raised in the air towards me. One half of her bikini is being eaten by it, exposing a pale half-moon of flesh. It contrasts to the golden brown of the rest of her. I think about biting the over-exposed backside. As a small boy with ice cream dripping off his mouth and hands is watching us, I decide it's probably best not to.

'The point,' she says, as she slides back down onto her towel, her feet prodding my chest as she moves, making me back away, 'is that I could move the pebbles around, or maybe they get kicked about or the sea jostles them about, and all those little moments get jumbled up *and suddenly this moment isn't next to the moment it preceded or succeeded and suddenly, whoosh.' Her hand slices the air.*

'Whoosh?'

'One moment we're on the beach and the next moment we're watching Napoleon pop out of his mum's cannon, and the next we're back on the beach. Time gets jumbled.'

'Don't you think if that was possible, more people would have experienced it? More people would be having glimpses of the past and the future?' I grab her red-painted toes and want them between my teeth, ice-cream-covered boy watching or not. I suddenly have a hunger. She yanks her foot away.

'Perhaps they have or perhaps the moment is so quick we don't notice it. How long is a moment, how long is now?'

'You're a head fuck.'

'I'm going for a swim. I need to think about if what I just said makes sense.'

She stands and pulls her bikini out of her cheeks, lays her shades on her towel, leans down and kisses me.

'I love you,' she says and tiptoes across the little hard and uncomfortable moments of time to the water.

I hold a stone in each hand and decide the one in my left is now and the one in my right is next month, when she plans to pack up and move to Prague for nine months. I put now in my bag, hidden under my jeans, and weigh up next month. It's heavy and misshapen and feels wrong, so I throw it and just miss a dog chasing a Frisbee.

VISAS AND VINYL

We're sitting in Mei's bar. Seven of us around pushed-together tables. It's Thursday evening and the first week is over. Mei is perched on a stool behind the counter, smiling at no one. She's Chinese and doesn't say much. She only comes out from her smiling place to clear bottles away and to deliver a full one to a Canadian with big glasses at the table next to ours. He stares at Mei almost without pause. The rest of us help ourselves to bottles of Bintang beer from the fridge when we like. She makes a little note on the piles of paper in front of her every time we do it. In front of me is a Bintang and my newest addiction: *kopi susu*. It's thick dark coffee in a glass mug with an inch of condensed milk in the bottom. I slide my spoon down the side of the glass and scoop some of it up through the coffee, trying hard not to mix the two together. It's the best coffee and the best thing to happen to coffee in my lifetime.

Mei's is open on three sides to the warm night air, allowing the noise of crickets to play background music to conversation. It's at the end of a small parade of shops in the housing estate where most of Medan's expats and well-off seem to live. The housing estate is more like a guarded ghetto for the wealthier of the city. It is full of detached and semi-detached white-painted houses, all with little front gardens and fences and placed in quiet roads and cul-de-sacs. There are security guards as you enter the estate on the main entrance, but there are plenty of little cut-through alleyways that take you out into the real mad Medan, which is deceptively close.

Here in Mei's where the traffic can't be heard and Europeans, Antipodeans and North Americans sit and chat, the relentless noise and fumes and overcrowded city seem a continent away. I'm not sure I like it. I feel naked, open to questions, open to reality. I've been New Me for over a week now, on and off, but Old Me and Laura still like to poke their heads up every now and then, wanting some attention.

'So, what d'ya reckon? Staying?' Marty is sat opposite me in a tattered and stained grey T-shirt, swigging the last froth out of his bottle.

'Yep. It's all OK so far. Takes some getting used to though.' I stir the remaining centimetre of condensed milk into my coffee and take a mouthful.

'You never get used to it. Always something weird and bizarre every day.' This is Julie, the English teacher with big breasts and wide eyes from my first day in the staffroom.

'Good. That's what I want.'

'It wears thin sometimes,' she says as her fingers dance on the table, doing some sort of twitchy can-can. Her eyes dart around looking for agreement from the others in our group. She doesn't get any so she nods in self-agreement.

'I fucking love it here,' says Kim, who's sat next to me. 'We'll take you out and show you the night life later, man. Fucking unbelievable. Ain't that right, Jussy-boy?'

Jussy-boy is sat on the end of the table in a white shirt done up to the collar and a Donald Duck tie. He's another teacher, in his early twenties. He's from Montana or Virginia or somewhere.

'Oh yeah,' says Jussy-boy, 'just the way Kim tells it.'

I'm not sure I'm ready for a night out yet. Daytime Medan has already given me enough to think about. It almost completely lacks personal space and is rich with poverty. It bears no resemblance to anything English whatsoever. But I'm going to go with them. I've got to let New Me be free before Old Me gets control of things and turns the pair of us into a self-pitying blob. I wish I could hold Laura's hand under the table.

—*Well, I can't do that because of these odd-jobs sitting either side of you, but how about this?*

Laura puts her arms around my neck from behind and nuzzles behind my ear.

—*You're not real. Get off.*

I twist my head.

—*Well, I feel real and I'd like a cuddle.*

I try to shake her off again.

—*You're just my sick mind messing with me, now OFF.*

A sudden head jerk. She lets go.

'You OK, man?' asks Kim.

'Yeah. Stiff neck is all.'

'Just wait 'til you get out to the jungle. We're planning on going in a couple of weeks. Go and see some real monkeys instead of drinking with these ones, eh?' This is Naomi. She is sat next to me. Naomi is twenty-three, Canadian, beautiful, blue-eyed with light-brown dreads. She works at another school somewhere in the city. Her knee keeps knocking mine.

—*I can see what she's doing down there. Watch it, mister.*

—*Not there.*

—*Am.*

'Yeah. Get out to Bukit and see the orang-utans. Eh?' Kim walks over to the beer fridge.

'Yeah, eh?' says Jussy-boy.

'Fucking eh, eh?' says Julie.

'Eh?' says Marty.

'Leave the girl alone, you racist twats,' says Geoff, the worried-looking Mancunian, sat at the other end of the table.

'Who wants a Bintaaang?' Kim yells from the fridge.

We all examine our bottles and answer 'Yes.'

'What is it with the "eh" anyway?' I ask Naomi.

She twists towards me in her chair and smiles.

'It's a Canadian thing. Have you never heard it before? We have this habit of finishing sentences with an "eh." Eh?' She smiles, all thick lips and straight white teeth.

—*God, those teeth. Bleaches her bloody teeth. Get over yourself, girl.*

'Didn't know that.' I gulp down half my bottle of beer, willing Laura to shut up. My head swims a little.

'Yeah, same as septics say "fuck", we Canadians say "eh?"' She looks at Kim when she says this.

'Fuck. Now who's being racist? I fucking hate being called a septic.' Kim slides into his chair and slams two fistfuls of bottles on the table. White froth erupts out of their necks.

'You started it, Kimbo.'

'Alright you lot,' says Geoff, 'let's change the subject.'

'Septic?' I whisper to Naomi.

'Septic tank.'

'Fucking Yank, man,' says Kim. 'Geoff's right, let's leave it.'

Silence follows for a few seconds and I wonder if, and what, the rest of the people around this table have run away from. I can feel some sort of tension from nearly all of them: Julie with her twitching fingers, Geoff with the worry lines of a bomb-disposal expert, Kim with his overuse of sexual adjectives, Marty seeming almost over-relaxed, Jussy-boy with his dodgy taste in clothes and even Naomi with her starting-to-get-annoying overzealous knee-knocking.

—*And shiny bright teeth, don't forget her shiny bright teeth. They're annoying too.*

—*Yes, and those.*

If she insists on being here, I might as well let her for the moment. I quite like her little show of jealousy.

'Anyway, has Pak asked you to teach his mate's kids yet?' asks Marty.

'He has mentioned it. Sounds alright.' I answer.

'Don't trust him.' Julie's fingers pause in their dance. 'I've said it before and I'll say it again: Pak's a cunt.'

Geoff sighs. 'Julie, do you have to swear so much?'

She ignores him.

'He asked me and I went 'round this guy's house and there's armed guards and dogs and cameras as soon as you get through the gate,' explains Julie. 'I walked straight back out. If Pak's got friends with places like that, he's a cunt.'

'I taught them for a week,' says Geoff, 'and it's true about the guards but the kids are lovely. Fitri and Benny, lovely kids. Pak paid me cash for it too.'

'Pak pays cash for everything, man. That wasn't anything special,' says Kim.

'It was extra. Paid my beers for a week.'

'Yeah, but the kids hated you.' Julie swallows a mouthful and coughs half of it across the table. 'Said you were a boring tosser or something similar, I heard.' She wipes her mouth with her sleeve.

'It is true, Geoff. That's why Pak asked Julie to go.' Jussy-boy dabs his brow with Donald's beak.

'Anyway,' I say, suddenly wanting peace and quiet, 'I'll give it a go.'

'It's bad news. Any friend of Pak's is bad news.'

'Let the newbie fucking find out for himself.' Kim sticks a cigarette in my mouth. 'Welcome to Mei's and welcome to the Friday night gang. Bunch of freaks that we be. Anyone who ain't here ain't worthy of our company.'

—*Oh, I am honoured.*

—*But you aren't here.*

'Where are all the other teachers?' I cut across her before she has a chance to reply. I've met the rest of them at work, but not everyone is here.

'Scared,' Kim answers. 'At home watching TV and talking long-distance to the people they miss. Or, in the case of some, spending their money on pretty girls or ladyboys. They keep themselves to themselves.'

'Scared?'

'Of this country. Realised they made a mistake. Wanna be home watching whatever shit it is they watch on TV back home.'

'So why don't they go home?'

A glance is passed around the table. Julie sniggers, Marty scratches his beard and Geoff's lines deepen.

'You haven't checked your fucking passport, man?' Kim takes my nearly finished cigarette from my hand, lights another with it and sticks the newly lit one in my mouth. 'You need to check your fucking passport, man.'

'Why?' I draw on the cigarette. It goes well with the beer.

'Single-entry visa,' says Julie. 'Methinks you haven't noticed.'

I'm silent. I smoke. I swig.

'Pak only gets everyone single-entry visas. Check the small print on the visa you got. Means you need his permission to leave, and you need about a million rupiah to pay the exit. And if you leave early he doesn't pay your flights.' Kim laughs. 'That's why half the people aren't here drinking, they're saving or crying. They didn't realise they'd been screwed over 'til they got here. Bit like you.'

'I said it before, I'll say it again, Pak's a cunt.'

—*Ha ha. Stuck here then, numbnuts.*

'Oh well,' I say, 'fine with me.' I take a deep drag on my kretek and smile. I'm here for the year. A long time baking in the oven.

—*You'll be well-baked.*

—*Shut it and leave.*

—*OK, OK. I'm going.* She leans over me to give me a kiss but I turn away.

—*Bye.*

'So who's coming on tonight?' asks Kim.

'Me and Donald. Donald wants to dance, don't you, Donald?' Jussy-boy holds the end of his tie up to his face so he can ask the upside-down duck.

'Not tonight,' says Geoff, 'I'm getting up to go camera shopping tomorrow.'

'I'm up for it,' Julie.

'Me too,' a knock to my knee.

'Yeah, why not?' says Marty.

'I'd better try out this night life,' say I.

So we finish our beers and queue up to pay Mei.

'Where are you faggots off to then?' The Canadian with the big glasses shouts across from his table. There is no humour in his use of the noun.

'That's nice, Barry. Nice turn of phrase.' Kim shoves his roll of notes into his front pocket, having paid for his beers. 'Why? You hoping to come, man?'

'Not with you faggots.'

'That's good, 'cos we didn't fucking ask you.' Kim heads off to the street. 'Thanks Mei. Take care.' He throws Mei a smile and a wave over his shoulder.

'Have good night, Mr Utah,' Mei replies.

I throw a glance at Barry the Canadian and he stares back without smiling.

'Enjoy your night, new faggot.'

I say nothing, but immediately wish I had as I walk away. The confidence of the late thinker is always a gallant yet futile thing. Even New Me can't think quick enough. But now a choice of responses flows into my mind as I step into the sticky night air; 'Will do, arsehole,' or 'Better than staying here with you, dick-wad.' Anything similar would have been better than nothing.

Geoff waves us goodnight and walks off in the other direction. We head toward the main gate to flag down a taxi.

'Why'd she call you Mr Utah? I ask Kim.

'Thinks I look like Keanu in Point Break. Johnny Utah.'

'You look nothing like Keanu.'

'I know, but I still take it as a compliment.'

'And what is it with that guy back there?' I ask.

'He's a wife-beating dick.' Julie pulls a lipstick out of her jeans and applies it quickly as she walks. 'He's here to escape jail back home. Broke her arms, allegedly.'

'He's been hiding out here a few years. Thinks us teachers are just passing tourists and that he's the real expat. He does some wheeling and dealing dodgy business and is sniffing after Mei.' Kim nods at the security guards who are almost asleep at the gate.

We leave the estate and step out onto the bustling main road, where minivans, *becaks* and cars are still avoiding each other by inches; back in the real Medan.

'Let's not talk about him. Let's just get stoned. I say we start at Hotel Garuda.' Jussy-boy licks his hand and runs it across his hair.

So that's where we start.

The taxi pulls up outside the hotel. Kim is in the front and the rest of us are squeezed in the back. Naomi is straddled across Marty's and my legs. She wiggles and adjusts herself a little too much and I'm finding it more annoying than alluring.

Kim pays and we all fall out the back of the taxi. Before we've taken two steps away from the car, two boys with trays covered with various makes of cigarettes and lighters hanging around their necks come up to us. One of them is about eight years old and the other maybe ten. The eight-year-old has big black rings under his eyes and his shoulders sag as though he's ready to be carried to bed. The others try to sidestep around them, but the boys move from side to side trying to block them. They look like they're practising dance steps.

'OK. Give me twenty kretek,' Kim says to the smaller boy, but the bigger boy is there first with a packet. Julie also gets a pack as Marty and Jussy sneak past.

'Please mister, buy my cigarettes. Marlboro, kretek, menthol, Davidoff.' The young one is in front of me, banging my thighs with his tray, looking up with child's eyes that have lost their wonder.

I ask for a pack of Marlboro and a pack of kretek. The older boy is suddenly there, jostling the younger one out of the way with his shoulder.

'Eh. Back off. I'm buying from him,' I tell the bigger one. He tuts and heads off to another taxi as it pulls up.

'Thank you, mister, thank you,' says the young boy. 'And a lighter? You need a lighter?' He is following us across the street to the hotel.

'OK. Yes. How much?'

He tells me and I pay him with some notes and tell him to keep the change. I want to give him the contents of my wallet, but hold back. We go up the steps to the over-lit building. I still want to turn back and give it to him. I'm not sure if the reason I don't is because of wishy-washy Old Me or 'don't give a shit' New Me or just because I know that it won't really help the boy.

The hotel is glass-fronted, alight with sequenced flashing bulbs, decorated in fresh paint and attended by a doorman in full London Mayfair Hotel doorman garb. The rest of the street is peeling and crumbling colonial Dutch facades, rubbish piles and potholes. The hotel looks as out of place as a diamond in a cowpat.

'Those kids always put me in a downer,' says Julie as we enter the hotel. The reception hall is large and wide with a marbled floor. An antique *becak* and a grand piano are centrepieces, reflecting expensive lighting in their polished surfaces.

I too feel on a downer, although I haven't exactly been off one.

As the group of us climb a curving staircase to the first floor, taking two steps at a time, I ask, 'Does that always happen?'

'Fucking mafia-run kids, man. Always on the streets, all night.' Kim leads us along the corridor towards the sound of Bon Jovi coming from behind double doors at the end. 'Forced into selling cigs and then the older kids hide around a corner somewhere, take all the cash and hand it to the local mafia errand boy. He then probably hands it to his boss who then probably gives it to the Godfather or Big Boss or whatever the fuck they're called in this country.'

'Kids are abused all over the place here. It's depressing but you have to get used to it.' Naomi is walking at my elbow. Her closeness is making me uncomfortable.

'No one should have to get used to that,' I say and take a longer step to get ahead of her.

Kim pushes the double doors open and we enter yet another world: smoke and drums and guitar solo and a packed room of about three hundred people. They sit around tables and stand in groups facing a stage. A guitarist kneels on one leg while his hands dance up and down an electric guitar. Three girls with cleavage and skirts that stop where their legs begin swirl their orange-dyed hair in perfectly timed circles to their version of 'Livin' on a Prayer'.

We walk through the smoke-filled room and a waiter comes to us. He takes us to a table right at the front. It is already occupied by a group of Indonesian men. He says something to the group and they nod their heads and smile at us and leave the table.

'Please, please sit,' shouts the waiter.

We're right in front of the stage. The lead singer smiles down at us.

'Us *bules* always get the best seats,' Julie says through cupped hands over my ear.

'Why?'

'We're good for business apparently. Get white people in or sitting next to you and everyone's happy. We're like status symbols. And they think we're loaded of course. Everyone wants a *bule* as a friend.'

I'm not sure everyone would want us as their friends, if they really knew us, but I nod anyway.

'What is a *bule* anyway?' I shout over last bars of the song.

'Albino. They call us albinos,' she yells back.

'Cheeky bastards,' I laugh.

We order drinks and light cigarettes and watch and listen as the band starts a perfect intro to Guns N' Roses' 'Sweet Child O' Mine'.

—*The best rock intro ever,* Laura shouts from my left. I look, expecting to see her eyes wide and alive and head moving to the music, but Naomi smiles back.

Now you're happy; now you're not. Music: the magician of nostalgia and emotion.

The first two or three notes are sometimes enough. The needle is placed on the record, the crackling starts and the notes line up and form their clever little refrain of a moment of life. Another track from Old Me's Greatest Hits. Rock on.

She runs back into the room, all naked white flesh, and jumps in beside me just as Slash starts playing, a little scratchy, a little worn, but still impressive. She presses her body against mine, throwing a leg over my thighs and an arm across my chest and around my neck. My arm around her back pulls her even closer.

'Strange choice of music for waking up to, Appetite For Destruction?'

'It is and it does just that, wakes you up.' She kisses my chest and we lay there silent for the duration of the first track. I smile at the

ceiling. I'm lying in bed with a beautiful girl who I don't know, yet I feel as relaxed with her as I would when I'm alone with myself.

'You haven't even asked me what my job is,' she says.

She's right. What the hell we have been talking about?

'You've known me all of a day and not even interested in what I do.' She flicks my nipple.

I ask her what she does.

'I pick up ice-cream salesmen, shag them and get a lifetime's supply of Mr Whippys, Mivvis and teas.'

'Well sorry. I'm only selling ice creams for the summer, then I'm hoping to train to become a teacher. Your Mivvis will dry up.'

'Oh well. You can leave now.' She makes no attempt to get off me. 'No Strawberry Mivvis, no more rumpy-pumpy.'

'If you like Mivvis, I'll buy you one every week.'

'OK, in that case you can stay.' Her hand rests on my abdomen and the warmth of her touch spreads across my stomach and down to my thighs and everywhere in between.

'So what do you really do?'

'Let's get all coincidental. I teach. I work in a language school teaching English.'

'Let's get married.'

'Not yet. Give it another week, don't want to rush things.' She presses a finger to my lips. 'Silence for the best intro in the world coming up.'

We listen to the opening of 'Sweet Child O' Mine'. I don't disagree with her, mostly because she's strumming along on my penis. Slash's fingers dance up and down his instrument while Laura's dance up and down mine. When the song's finished and all strumming is over, we kiss.

'I think we need to see each other often,' she says, once her lips have separated from mine.

'You haven't even asked if I've got a girlfriend.'

'Have you?'

'No.'

'Want one?'

'If you're offering?'

'I am.'

'Cool.'

She rests on her elbow and looks so deep into my eyes and for so long my vocal cords seize up.

'Do I scare you?' She leans her face in close and our lips are nearly touching again.

I shake my head, although I am scared, but not for the reasons she's asking. I'm not scared she's a psychotic stalker or scared she's moving too fast. I'm scared because I don't do this. I don't fall for girls I hardly know. And I'm scared in case it goes wrong and in case it breaks me. I'm scared because I'm scared of all that and I've only known her for about twenty-two hours. It's scary shit, being scared.

'Don't think I'm a slut for sleeping with you on the first day?'

Shake my head.

'Not worried I'm rushing you?'

Shake.

'Believe in love at first sight?'

Shake. Nod. Shake. Not sure how I should answer.

'I don't either, but you do make my heart very, very fluttery, and I've never had that before.'

Smile.

'And I've never ever slept with someone so quickly. Normally he'd have to swim the Channel or climb a metaphorical Everest to get in my sheets so easily. So what's going on, Mr Whippy Man?'

I shrug my shoulders, kiss her lips, hug her. I haven't a clue what's going on.

'How about we just go with it,' I whisper. 'It feels, it feels…'

'It feels good.'

An understatement, but I say, 'Yes. Good.'

We lie there, skin on skin, legs intertwined like ivy, strands of her hair in my mouth, my hands on her back. I sense her life moving around her body and can feel it seeping through her flesh, her breasts, her hands, and every part of her body that touches me, into mine.

Into mine.

Into mine. A scratch. A jump. A moment stuck.

ALBINOS AND ACTION MEN

Kim and I drink *kopi susu* under a blue tarpaulin at a lean-to made from a few pieces of wood. We sit at a wobbly bench watching the owner of this fine establishment pour boiling water into something that looks like an old sock. From the bottom of the sock comes very good coffee. There are three men also sitting at the one and only table in this roadside shack. Two are playing chess and the other is watching intently through the haze of smoke that pours from the cigarette hung from his lips. Traffic passes by just a few feet away. Blown exhausts and horns mean conversation has to be turned up a little. And it's bloody hot. Kim keeps picking his shirt up at the front and shaking it. Each time he does this he says, 'Fuuuck, it's fucking hot. Whoa, it's fucking hot.'

I'm enjoying the heat. My shirt sticks to my neck and back and every now and then a little trickle of sweat runs down my temple. The heat makes me know I'm somewhere different, it confirms I've changed my world, that I'm being different. My old life has gone.

'Fuuuck, it's fucking hot.' A shirt waggle.

'I know, Kim, I'm sat here next to you.'

'But fuck, I know this country's supposed to be hot but this is fucking hot.'

'You hot, my friend?' asks the chess-watcher.

'Fucking hot, man.'

'Hot is good,' he laughs. 'Is my country. Is good country. Hot is good.'

'Yeah man, good country, very *bagus* country, but fucking hot today.'

'Where you from?'

'Canada. You?' asks Kim.

'Ha. You not American. Good. Me from *disini*, from here, Medan, my town.' He throws his cigarette out onto the street. 'And you, my friend? You Canadian?'

'English.'

'Ah, David Beckham, you know? Very good footballer.'

'I know. Yes. But I don't like football.' Not bloody Beckham again.

'Manchester United? You like?'

'No, I don't like.' I smile at him and sip my coffee. A drop of sweat plops into it from my nose.

'Shame. Very good team. David Beckham very good.' He lights another cigarette and his eyes focus on the chess board again.

Kim waggles his shirt and opens his mouth.

'Don't say it.'

He looks at me mid-waggle as if I've just told him I'm sleeping with his sister.

'But it is fuc...'

'Kim.' I raise my eyebrows at him. 'Anyway, I've been meaning to ask, is it true *bule* means albino?'

'Around this part of Indonesia it does, apparently. We're albinos to them. All white and sickly and albinoish.'

'Racist buggers.'

'Yeah I know, but I bet you're racist to them too.'

'No.'

'Confident answer, man.' He scratches the side of his head. 'So you don't generalise and think they all want to talk about Man United and are all a little simple when they ask "Where you going, misterrr?"'

I pause to think of a response that doesn't confirm I'm something I never want to be. I can't think of one.

'Fucking racist, man. We all do it. We all are. We all make generalisations about everyone we meet. I bet you even did when you met me for the first time: fucking dope-smoking Californian who says fuck a lot. Bet you fucking did.'

He has a point, but I choose not to answer.

'And why did you tell him'—I lower my voice and nod towards the chess fan—'you're Canadian?'

'Just in case. Americans aren't always popular with these guys. Like I said, everyone generalises. Ethnic cleansing; major bad-ass generalisation.'

I tip my coffee cup up as far as it will go and drain the last of the sweet milk from the bottom.

'Plus I don't consider myself to be American.'

'Why not?'

'I was adopted. Rumour has it I was a Vietnam war baby. Guessing my old man was out there. Met a woman, left me in her, then split.'

Now I see there could be a slight Asian look to Kim. Olive skin, dark hair and eyes.

'I put up with some shit when I was a kid. Always been a bit bitter about the great old US of A.'

A silence rides the heat between us for a second while Kim stares at the chessboard.

'So why did you disappear so early the other night?' Kim asks, changing the subject. 'I thought you were enjoying the music and you were on for some filth with Naomi.'

'Music was good. But I'm not interested in Naomi. And I'm still tired too. Getting used to the culture change is knackering, I suddenly needed sleep.'

—*You wanted to be alone with me, tell him.*

I shake my head and hope she'll rattle back below to keep *him* company.

—*Alone with me and my sexy little body and not so shiny bright teeth.*

'You guys have a good night?' I ask, ignoring her but also enjoying the thought of her sexy little body. I then fight the bitter sickness that fizzes in my stomach. I can't ever have that body again.

'Yeah. Jussy ended up with some whore from Top Club and went off to some hotel. Julie did some E and danced like a frenetic chimp all night, while Marty sat and watched her. Naomi and me got a taxi back at about three.'

'Jesus. Is that a normal night?'

'Yep. Pretty much. Julie's become a bit of a drug fiend recently and Jussy-boy loves these Indo women. I do too, but wasn't in the mood.'

I nearly ask if anything happened with him and Naomi, but it's not my business and I'm not interested. Kim's opened up enough already. I don't want to get any closer to him. I'm not ready for good friends.

I smile when I suddenly think of my old friends back in England reading books, going to the cinema, drinking Bacardi-and-Cokes and even, in extreme rebellious moments, smoking the occasional spliff. If they saw New Me now, hanging out with these guys, all of whom seem to be motivated by hidden demons, they wouldn't recognise me. Just how I want it to be.

—*Is it?*

—*Yes it bloody is.*

'We better go, man. Only half an hour 'til the next class.'

We pay for our coffees, say bye to the chess players and duck out from beneath the canopy and its shade into bright white daylight. The sun lays its weight on us as soon as we're under it. The stench of the piles of rubbish that lie up side streets and on corners is ripe. Exhaust fumes stick to the inside of my nose. We zigzag through the traffic to get across the road and go into the school. Albert is at the front desk. The sweat patches on his shirt are bigger and wetter than ever. We nod at each other.

'Pak's little ass-licker,' says Kim as we make our way to the staff-room.

'I did wonder.'

Fifteen minutes later I'm in class looking at twelve students aged between about seventeen and thirty. They are male and female, mostly Chinese-Indonesian. This is a level seven class, second to top because they've completed all of English World's homemade course books. Their English is pretty good when they actually speak. This is my second time with them; the first was long and quiet and painful, but today I have an extra face sitting before me.

'Johnny, isn't it?' I ask.

'Yeah. How are you?' asks the leather-jacket-clad Jimmy Dean from my first night. He is sitting slouched in his chair, which is up on two legs and leaning back against the wall.

'I'm OK. Good to see you.' I stand behind my desk and open my course book. 'How are the rest of you?'

Silence. I look at today's chapter: Exercise 1 – Reading – Swimming With Dolphins.

Jesus, another long day ahead.

'Right. What's this?' I draw a rough likeness of a dolphin on the whiteboard.

Silence.

I turn back to the board and sigh.

—*Stick with it, numbnuts.*

I close my eyes and rub my chest.

—*Laura Laura Laura. Not now please.*

—*Teaching is easy. Make 'em smile.'*

—*How can I make 'em smile when you're talking to me? Please be quiet. Stay down there with him like you're supposed to.*

'Have you ever kissed a girl?'

'What?'

'Have you ever kissed a girl, sir?'

'Oh. Yes, sorry, Johnny, yes I have.' I turn and come back into the room. Every pair of eyes is on me, suddenly interested and paying attention, something that hasn't happened so far. Johnny is still leaning back in his chair, twirling a toothpick or something in his mouth to perfect the image.

'For how long?' he asks.

'Sorry?'

'How long did you kiss her for?'

'I kissed her more than once, Johnny, and more than one girl.'

He falls forward, his chair banging down onto all four legs.

'Really?'

I look at him to see if he's trying to wind me up. His face is dead set and eyes wide. He's being serious.

'Yes, really. Now, this is a dolphin.'

'How many?'

'I don't know. A few.'

'Three? Four?'

'Maybe more. Why?' I put my board pen on the desk and sit down. 'Have you kissed a girl?'

'Yes, of course.' His complexion reddens and he twirls his toothpick between his fingers.

'How many?' I ask.

'Many. Many.'

'You liar,' says the girl next to him, Jennifer, if I remember right.

'No I'm not. Many.' He shifts in his seat. He's lying, so I try to help him out.

'I kissed about five,' I under-exaggerate.

'Was it good?' he asks, leaning forward.

'It was ok, some better than others. Now shall we get on with the lesson?'

'We don't kiss here,' says a woman on the opposite side of the room to Johnny. She is about thirty, the oldest in the class and one of only two ethnic Indonesians. 'Not often.'

'I saw my mother and father kiss once,' joins in Yenny, a small girl in the middle, 'but they didn't know I see.'

At least they're talking. I close the course book.

'Only once? Don't your parents kiss in front of you?'

'Never. It is bad to kiss in front of people,' says Yenny.

'In England it's OK. Many people kiss in public.'

'Really. What sort of kissing?' Johnny is leaning right across his desk now. The students who haven't said anything yet are sitting more upright and adjusting their backsides.

'Well, you know, all sorts.'

'With, with, this,' Johnny sticks his tongue out as if showing it to a doctor.

'Tongue. It's a tongue. Yes, sometimes.'

'In public?'

'Yes.'

'I want to go to England.'

The class laugh.

'What about holding hands in the street here?' I ask. 'Is that allowed?'

'No. Not really. Some people do it now, but many people don't like it,' answers Jennifer.

'It must be difficult for boyfriends and girlfriends'.

'Do you not think your country is too free?' This is a new voice, Franz, the other ethnic Indonesian. He is about seventeen and serious.

'Shut up, stupid,' says Johnny, 'if you can kiss when you want, what is wrong with that?' The class laugh, except Franz and the older woman.

'Johnny, please don't be like that here. Don't call people stupid,' I say.

'Sorry sir, but these Muslim ideas are…'

'Johnny, shh.' I'm just starting to see the mix of religious backgrounds these students come from: Muslim, Christian, Buddhist, possibly others. As I have none, which according to Kim is an inconceivable idea in Medan, I don't want a heated religious debate in my class.

'Too free, no. There are many things in England, Europe and the US that stop us from being free. Also sometimes I don't want to see young teenagers kissing and touching each other in the middle of a street or on a bus.'

'They touch each other?' Johnny is virtually climbing onto his desk.

'I think it is disgusting,' says Franz.

'I think it is nice,' says Jennifer, 'to show you love someone when you want. To be allowed to love someone so all can see.'

Other girls in the class nod. Some of the boys' eyes seem to have glazed over and I wonder where I have sent their fantasies; probably snogging on the top deck of a double-decker with Cameron Diaz while cruising around London.

'Well, anyway.' I stand up. 'We're here to learn English, not discuss my sex life. What's this?' I tap the dolphin on the board.

'A shark, sir?' This is a girl whose name I can't remember, sitting on the end.

'Yes, thank you. A shark, sort of. Now do sharks, or dolphins, live in the sea?'

I can't believe I'm actually about to teach this stupid lesson, but the class, or most of them, are with me now. I've just given them the slightest insight into another world and they've woken up. Now I want to impart all my knowledge of dolphins, aka sharks, and a bit of the present perfect tense while I have them.

—*Well done. You've just corrupted a whole generation. They'll all be holding hands and getting beaten by their parents in a week.*

I ignore her.

'No.' says Yenny.

'Sorry?' I say.

'Dolphins do not live in the sea.'

'Of course they do,' says Johnny. 'Want a kiss after class?'

Yenny blushes and moves her books around her desk.

—*Told you, says Laura.*

—*I miss you, I tell her.*

Each present is wrapped in different paper.

'This one first.' She holds up one of the four gifts which sit on the bed between us. She hands it to me and pulls her legs up under her, her dressing gown rising up over her thighs. My eyes wander from the present to her exposed skin and my mind wanders a little further.

'That one first.' She pulls her gown over her legs, only a little. 'You can have this later.'

'OK, OK.' I squeeze, prod and sniff the gift. It has a familiar weight to it.

'Open.'

I tear a little strip of paper off and see a small hand inside. A gripping hand. I rip the rest off and he lies across my palm in his khaki camouflage and fuzzy hair: an Action Man.

I look at her and she is smiling, like she's just been given the perfect present, not me.

'It's the right one, isn't it? Isn't it? From about 1976. I checked.' She rocks backwards and forwards with her arms around her stomach. 'Isn't it?'

'How, where did you get this?' I hold him up to my face and run my finger across his head.

'It doesn't matter, but you like it, don't you.' This isn't a question but a statement. She knows damn well I like it.

'Yes, I like it.' I'm ten again. He feels so right in my hands. I want to send him on a mission across the floor immediately. Have him climb some stairs and parachute off the banisters. Make him ride the cat and shoot some plastic cowboys.

'I used to have six of these, real Action Men, with life-like hair and gripping hands, not like the crap these days.'

'Yes, I know. You've already told me.'

'It's perfect.'

'Good. At least there's one perfect man in this room.'

I blow her a raspberry.

'Do that again, bum-wipe, I dare you.'

I blow another one and she wraps her lips over my tongue and pushes hers into my mouth. I lean into her but she pulls away.

'Uh-uh. Not yet.'

She hands me the next present. This is rectangular and thin. I can tell it's a book, and again it feels familiar. I sod the anticipation and pull the paper off in one go.

'Asterix the Gaul.'

'Check the date.'

I do. 1969. First English edition.

'I'm speechless.' I am. She knows what I want better than I do.

'You've got the set now.'

'I can't believe you've got me these.' I scan my eyes over my two new prize possessions lying on the bed. 'These perfect presents. I'm a very happy little boy.'

I lean across and give her a hug, slide my hands inside her dressing gown where it's warm. I kiss her neck. My hands move to the top of her thighs. She pushes me away.

'Two more to open. Then I might let you.'

The next present is also rectangular.

'What is this, Book Week?' *I free it from the paper.* 'Oh.'

'Not a first edition. Couldn't quite stretch to that. Twenty p from a charity shop'

'The Time Machine.'

'By you-know-who. You don't sound excited?' *She pokes me in the belly.* 'Sound excited.'

'You know I hate science fiction. My dad's craziness for it killed mine.'

'I know. But I love all that stuff. So read it, Bucko. Open your mind to all those mad ideas.'

'Mm. One day.' *I put the book on the floor.* 'Asterix first though.'

'Bad boy. But I'll let you off as it's your birthday.' *She ruffles my hair.* 'OK, last one.'

The fourth present is bottle-shaped. I open it. It's a bottle: Glenfiddich.

'Ah, whisky. Your favourite drink,' *I say.*

'And yours.' *She grabs the bottle off me.* 'But I thought I could have a treat too as I've been so good to you.' *She tears the seal off the bottle and pulls the stopper out with her teeth.* 'And after a couple of shots of this,' *she slurs with it still between her lips,* 'I might be even better to you.' *The stopper is spat across the room. She takes two gulps from the bottle, then hands it to me.*

'Happy birthday, you old fart.'

'It's a bit early for booze, isn't...'

'Shut up.' *She slips her dressing gown off her shoulders and arms and sits in front of me naked.* 'We're not going anywhere today.'

'Well, OK then.' *I take a big swig, pull my T-shirt over my head while she wriggles my pants down my legs. We sit naked opposite each other, looking at the other's body. Hers leaves me tongue-tied.*

I'm pushed onto my back and she straddles my thighs.

'Ow. Action Man. Under my bum.' *I raise my backside.*

She pulls him out and looks him in the eye.

'So, Mr Action Man, my boyfriend here likes you because of your gripping hands. Well, you may well have a firm grip, Mr Soldier, but I think mine is better.' She slides him to safety under the bed and grabs hold of me to prove a point. Her grip is better. Much better. I close my eyes and the day is perfect and for once time doesn't fly, because she is so slow with me and I'm so slow with her and every moment, every touch, every sensation, word and promise is individually gift-wrapped and put in a box marked Best Presents Ever. A box which slides around in one of the many rooms in my soul and sometimes knocks into the walls, reminding me it's still there.

INSPECTION AND APPROVAL

I stand in front of a two-metre-high wall. A camera, mounted next to a large, solid metal gate, is pointed down at me. I check the address against the piece of paper that Pak gave me. It's the right place. I go the gate and press the intercom, put my mouth next to the speaker and look at the camera.

'I'm the English teacher.'

The gate slides open just enough to let me through. I enter and nearly do the same as Julie, turn around and walk back out. In front of me is a large Chinese man with some sort of gun slung over his shoulder. I have no idea what sort of a gun, only that it is big and long and it makes my sphincter contract.

Stay calm, New Me. New Me is 'don't give a shit', remember. New Me is after strange and exciting experiences, and this is one. Just smile and walk to the house.

I smile and walk to the house. I say a house, it's more of a mansion. All the ground-floor windows are shuttered up. There are another three men with similar weapons hanging off their shoulders, playing cards on the bonnet of a shining black Range Rover. Another armed man is walking around the side of the house looking up at the top of the wall as he goes. In front of the house is a large wired enclosure with three Alsatians imprisoned in it. They attack the mesh with teeth and slobber as soon as I pass. I step away to the right.

Stay calm. These things don't worry you. Nothing worries you. OK?

Got it. Nothing worries me.

One of the guards opens the polished solid-wood front door and shows me in. Once I'm in he goes back out, closing the door behind him. I stay where I am and take in the room before me. The house is all open plan and marble-tiled floors. Straight ahead is the kitchen area. Three Asian women with Jackie Onassis hairstyles, dressed in '60s miniskirts and breast-hugging roll-neck tops, are preparing ornate plates of food. Next to the kitchen area is a table which could seat sixteen at a sit-down meal, but which is now covered with a buffet of dishes I can't make out from here by the door. The smell of garlic and chicken and saffron and a dozen herbs whose names I've never known fills the air.

On the opposite side of the room, four near-middle-aged Chinese men sit in front of a large TV screen watching Manchester United, maybe, versus a team in blue. On the coffee table between the men is a pile of money. As I watch, one of the men throws another five notes onto the pile. He yells something at a blond player on the screen, who from here looks like the ever-present Mr Beckham.

At the end of the room there is no internal wall, just three wide marble steps up into an outside area. Reflections and light ripples dance on the far outside wall, telling me there is probably a pool just up those steps.

'Ah, the new teacher.' This is one of the men at the TV. 'Fitri, Benny,' he shouts, 'your new teacher is here.'

He comes over to me, but keeps an eye over his shoulder at the football.

'Good to meet you. I am Charles.' He offers me his hand and takes his eyes away from the game to inspect me. He doesn't let go of my hand, but instead holds it tight while he looks deep into my eyes. Unblinking dark, narrow eyes search mine as though he's trying to find something. The intensity hurts. I try not to blink as some sort of defiance to his ocular rape of me, but don't manage it. The intimate examination lasts only two or three seconds, but I haven't been breathing. As he lets go of my hand I suck in air.

He is about forty-five, my height, neatly side-combed hair, thin lines around his eyes—probably from all the examinations he carries out—and despite his red and white Hawaiian shirt, no sense of humour about him whatsoever.

'Come.' He leads me to the buffet and waves his hand over the food. 'Eat what you want. Drink the wine, it is flown in from France, the cheese too.' He slices a piece of Brie and takes a bite. 'The other food is also from Europe and Australia and the States. All good. Please eat what you want.' He is already walking back to his seat. 'The children come soon.'

He lowers himself slowly into his chair by the TV, where, sitting upright and regal, he returns his attention to Mr Beckham and friends.

The old adage of there being no such thing as a free lunch troubles me a little, but sod it. I pick up a plate from a pile on the table and cut myself some Stilton, perfectly soft Brie, a slice of crusty white bread, avoid the king prawns, lobster and plates of ham, beef and chicken, take a spoonful of mixed salad and another of garlic mushrooms, a slice of some sort of white fish and then pour from a bottle of Châteauneuf-du-Pape into a crystal wine glass. The lesson is going to be worth doing for the food alone.

I stand with the plate in one hand and the wine in the other and am wondering what to do next when a teenage girl and young boy come out of a door near the gamblers. They come straight over to me.

'I am Fitri,' says the girl, about fifteen and about to become beautiful.

'I am Benny,' says the boy, about ten and about to become chubbier as he grabs a plate and piles on most of the beef and five tiger prawns.

Their father says something to them in Chinese without looking away from the TV.

'My father says we should go to the games room. Please, this way,' says Fitri as she leads me and little brother towards the steps. At the top of the steps I swig a large mouthful of wine as I take in the pool, which is half covered by a roof and half open to the blue sky. It's about twenty-five metres in length and surrounded by the rest of the building. There are five doors which go off from it into other parts of the house.

'Bring your shorts next time,' says Fitri, going on ahead down one side of the pool, 'we can swim.'

Benny sucks the internal workings of a prawn into his mouth.

I follow them through a door at the far end of the pool and enter a large games room containing a full-size snooker table, dartboard, ping-pong table and jukebox. In the corner is a pile of beanbags, which is where Fitri leads us. She slumps onto one, Benny falls backwards into another, losing his remaining prawns over his shoulder. He picks them up off the floor and puts two onto his plate and one into his mouth. Fitri slaps him across the head.

'My brother is a pig.'

'My sister is a bitch.'

I place the wine and plate next to my beanbag and flop into it.

'First English lesson: bitch is a bad word.' I wriggle around until I'm stable and then pick up my wine. It tastes better than anything Sainsbury's back home has to offer.

'But she called me a pig,' says Benny, as he pulls the remains of prawn number three from his mouth. He wipes his lips on his arm.

'Well pig isn't exactly polite, but sometimes it is suitable for little boys.' I shove a handful of mushrooms into my mouth. 'And for grown men.'

Benny laughs, opens his mouth wide, tilts his head back and slowly lowers the last crustacean into the chasm.

'Oh great,' says Fitri, 'two idiot pigs.' Then she laughs.

'So,' I say, 'I think your English is already very good. Why is that?'

'My father speaks very good English and he often takes us to Australia and sometimes America,' Fitri says with a tone of superiority. 'He goes there on business.'

'And what is his business?'

'He owns discos. Also he does import and export.'

'What does he import and export?'

'I don't know.'

'Oh.'

'He is very important,' adds Benny.

'I'm sure. So what should I be teaching you two expert students?' The wine is very good. My glass is already nearly empty.

'You are the teacher. What do you think?' asks Fitri.

'OK. Why don't you just ask me questions about anything you want and I'll try to answer. Any mistakes you make I'll try to correct and explain.'

They both agree and we start a question-and-answer session.

'Do you have a girlfriend?' asks Fitri.

—Good start, says Laura, what are you going to say to that one?

—You're my girlfriend.

—Oh am I? I thought I'm dead and you were trying to forget me.

—Don't remind me.

The wine suddenly turns bitter in my stomach.

'Well?' interrupts Fitri.

'Well?' adds Benny.

'Yes. No. I used to have.'

'Was she beautiful?'

'Very.'

'Do you miss her?'

'Very much.'

—Oh, get over me. You know you want to.

—I wish I could.

—What happened to New You? I thought he was supposed to be shot of me.

'Why did you break?'

'Break up. The proper way to say it is break up.' My voice crackles.

'Why did you break up?'

'She left me.' Barely audible.

—Liar. Face the truth. I'm dead, numbnuts.

'She died.' I drain the last of the wine from my glass and smile at the two children in front of me. 'She died,' I whisper. I swallow. I blink blurriness from my eyes. There is something big and painful ballooning in my chest.

—Well said.

'That is sad. Are you sad?' Fitri curls her legs under herself on the beanbag.

'Yes. Sorry. Where's the toilet?'

It's growing and pushing on my lungs. I need it out or I won't be able to breathe.

'Outside this room and two doors on the right.'

'Thank you.' I push myself up and out of the beanbag and lunge for the door. I am using every muscle in my stomach and chest and face to keep it in. My vision is tunnelled as I focus on door handles and my feet and the pool sparkles beside me and then I'm closing doors and fumbling locks and I turn and sit on the closed toilet and my head is in my hands. It bursts out. Sobs and tears and snot rise up through my throat and nose and eyes. I'm stunned there's so much in there. I'm like a shaken can of lemonade just opened.

Finally, after I don't know how long, and with stinging eyes and burning cheeks, it's all out and I'm empty. I blow my nose, splash water on my face, look at my red eyes in the mirror, try to out-stare myself.

'Stop it. You're hidden. You don't do this. You don't throw that shit up at me. You don't remind me or tell me or tease me. I'm not listening. I'm not interested.'

No answer. Good.

I throw another handful of water over my eyes, look at New Me and nod my head.

'Sorted.'

And this weekend I'm going to get wasted, get stoned, do anything and everything I have to do to get my new self on the road to reckless completion.

I dry my face on a soft, laundered towel that smells of lavender, unlock the door and step out onto the poolside, where Charles is waiting for me with a lit cigarette in one hand and an unlit held out to me in the other.

'Are you alright?' he asks. 'Please.' He holds the cigarette closer to me.

'Thank you.' I take it and he lights it with a solid gold Zippo. 'I'm fine, thanks.'

'Fitri told me you didn't look well and she's worried she made you unhappy.'

'It's OK. It wasn't her fault.' I feel his eyes watch every movement of my face. 'You know, memories jump out at you sometimes.'

'Yes. I know.' He drags on his cigarette and the examiner's eyes soften as he looks down into the light blue of the pool.

'This is a very nice house,' I say, not knowing what else to say.

'Thank you.' His eyes focus on me again. 'If you don't want to keep teaching today, it is no problem. I understand.'

'No. I can teach. This isn't a very good first impression. I'm sorry.' I draw heavily on the cigarette. I read the banner around the filter: Davidoff.

'Don't be sorry. Life likes to surprise us at the most inopportune of times.'

'You have nice children.' Nice, what a crap word.

'Thank you. They are a little hard work at times. I worry about them, living here, in a house that looks more like a prison.'

'Why do you have such security?'

Charles smiles and nods.

'I am a businessman who sometimes does business that creates enemies. Since the riots I don't take risks anymore. I don't trust people.' He drops his cigarette and kicks it into the pool. I don't think I will bring my swimming gear next time.

'Riots?' I feel I should know what he's talking about.

'You don't know? You English, you are only interested in your royal family and the weather.' He puts a hand on my elbow and starts leading me back along the pool. 'It was 1998. Just two years ago. Economic and race riots. It was a very bad time for us Chinese living here. I will not put my family at risk again of these fucking people.'

'What people?'

'Maybe I tell you about it one day, but not now. I must return to my football. I hope Beckham will score and make me more money. You must return to your students.' He starts walking away. 'Perhaps we will talk another day. Please use my home like your home.' He waves his hand in the air as I watch him disappear down the steps and into the main room. I flick my cigarette into the water.

'That's not nice,' says Fitri standing by the door to the games room. 'My father does that all the time and I get angry with him.'

'I'm sorry. Come on. Time you asked me some more questions.'

I head back to the beanbags.

It's dark in here, but I can still see her; I am surrounded by her in every way and moment I know her.

Supposedly faces blur when you try to recall them, you cannot ever remember them exactly as they are. Well, that's rubbish. She is forever there, whole and clear, in the half-darkness of his insides, next to me.

She sleeps in this moment that appears slowly in the gloom, like a stage light slowly coming on, lighting the players. I can see her head, resting on the back of her hand. Her hair a black halo to her face.

I lie beside her, the glow from the bedside lamp lighting her mouth, her cheeks, her small, slightly pointed nose, her closed eyes. Around us night waits to fill the hole created by the light, but I'm not ready to flick the switch and let it in. Not yet. My book lies face down on my lap while I watch her. She breathes quietly through slightly parted lips, her eyelashes still with dreamless sleep. The top of one shoulder almost glowing with its paleness, while her hair is as dark as the ring of night that surrounds us.

The building creaks and clicks as it cools from the heat of the day. I put the book on the side. As gently as I can, I shuffle down under the covers until I lie facing her. I can feel the warmth of her body in the sheets and her breath on my face, little puffs of life that smell of mint and garlic. I touch her cheek and it is cool and soft. She doesn't stir. I smile and battle the urge to wake her up so I can be with her, listen to her, watch the way her face moves as she talks. I turn and flick the switch and let the impatient dark fall over us. In the blackness she is burnt onto my retinas. I close my eyes but her image stays until I fall asleep, which takes time, as my impatience for morning keeps me awake.

MILLIONAIRE GURU

Pak counts out my first month's wages onto the desk. 3,800,000 rupiah. A millionaire at last. But only a little over two hundred quid in real money.

'Thank you, but shouldn't there be more?' I ask.

He looks up at me. His tongue licks the mole under his lip.

'No. I think that is all. As agreed in your contract.'

'I haven't had my contract yet.' My voice is calm, despite a little anger cooking in my chest. 'But yes, it's the right amount for teaching here. And what about Mr Charles's children?'

'Oh yes. I'm sorry. You have been once?'

'Twice.'

'And he is happy?' He starts counting off some more notes from the pile in front of him.

'I think so. I've only spoken to him once but the kids seem to like me.'

'Good. It is good. Here you are. Tell Julie she can come now.' He hands me more cash which I count to be two hundred thousand.

I leave the office without saying more and go to the staff room. Julie is drawing squiggles across a nearly completely squiggled-on piece of paper.

'In you go,' I say.

'Great. Hope you double-checked yours. That Pak's a cunt.' She gets out of her chair with such speed it spins twice after she's left it.

'She's got such a way with words.'

'She's losing it,' says Kim, sitting at his desk, counting out small chewy sweets from a bag. 'Gonna bribe these little fuckers today. One sweet for every time they use irregular past.'

'She never had it to lose.' Jussy-boy is adjusting a Tweety-Pie tie. 'Bribes won't work. I've offered them money just to make a noise, even a fart would be welcome.'

'Justin, you've got low-level little kids. They're never going to talk. You've got to get them moving, get them active to enjoy learning.' Geoff is bent over the photocopier, trying to pull a jam out of the front. There's a sweat patch in the middle of his back.

'Whatever. Why do you insist on calling me Justin?' He sips from a mug of black coffee.

'Isn't that the name your mum gave you?'

'Yes it is, Geoffererey, but things evolve, Geofferererey.'

Kim and Jussy giggle into their drinks. I smile.

'Nob,' mutters Geoff as he slams the front of the copier shut and presses start. The machine whirrs, clicks and then triple beeps. It's still jammed. 'Bastard.'

I sit at my desk and look in the course book. The last lesson of the week: a brief history reading about the Beatles. The Beatles? Jesus, I'm sure there've been other groups since them.

'So you ready for the jungle, Newbie?' Kim gives the side of his desk a kick and fires himself and his chair across the staff room to me.

'Now I'm paid I am.'

'Early start tomorrow, but me and the gang are still thinking about hitting the town for a bit tonight. What do you reckon?' He spins in the chair. His coffee sloshes on his shirt. 'Fuuuuck.'

'Why not? It's payday and it's the weekend. I'm up for it.'

'Fucking that's my boy. Give me five.' Kim holds his hand in the air.

'No. I don't do that high-five stuff.' I step away from the hand. 'We should never have given you lot Jerry Springer and all that'—I twirl my closed fist in the air—'whoa-whoa shit.'

'High fives are pre-Jerry, man. And what do you mean? Jerry's a fucking homeboy.'

'No. He's English,' I say as I move some bits of paper around my desk.

'No fucking way.'

'Way.'

'Way,' says Julie as she comes back in. 'Born in Highgate tube station during a bomb raid in the war. Everything you boys have got was British first.'

She slumps into her chair and flicks her wages across her face. 'Tried to diddle me two thousand. Cunt.'

Geoff kicks the front of the photocopier.

'I second that. He hasn't even given us a working copier. Cunt.' Geoff screws up whatever it was he trying to copy and throws it against the wall.

We all look at him.

'What?' he says. 'Well, he is.' With that he picks up an armful of books and heads to his class.

'There goes your catchphrase, Jules,' says Kim, while sucking coffee from his shirt.

'Never liked the word anyway. Far too rude.'

I laugh with the others. My laughter is genuine and real, and I'm surprised by its appearance. Perhaps I'm finally getting over things, finally moving on. But somewhere, deep inside, there's a hope I'm not. There's a little whisper saying I don't want to move on. I'm not ready to forget.

We watch and listen to more rock covers at Hotel Garuda. We drink beer. Kim rocks from side to side and finger-drums on the table, Jussy swivels his head in near three-sixty turns to eye up the female customers, winking and twiddling his tie like Oliver Hardy. Marty strokes his beard and holds his beer to the light every now and then, as if examining an antique. Unusually, Geoff is here tonight, sat forward with his chin on his hands, examining the guitarists' fingers for missing notes and fluffs. Julie shuffles on her chair like she's sat on a pile of thistles and looks as if she wants to be somewhere else. Naomi knocks legs against mine; this time I don't mind. My head feels like it's on the verge of floating. Beer and the heat work well together, drunkenness seems to thrive in these conditions.

More Bon Jovi, more Guns N' Roses, the Final Countdown, even some Clapton. Orange hair twirls, guitarists kneel and wank guitar necks while a packed room smokes and claps and sings along. The music and noise fill my ears. I'm smiling.

The day rolls over into the next without the blink of an eye. Time passing isn't noticed, or perhaps it never passes and this is its natural state—uncertain and unrestrained. The moments continue to pile up or lie down side-by-side or do whatever they do, but no one is counting. Not tonight.

'I hate this song. Come on, let's go.' Julie stands and moves from foot to foot. She tips the last of her bottle of Bintang down her neck.

'What's the rush, Jules?' shouts Kim over a slightly sped-up version of 'Wonderful Tonight.'

'This song's shit. Come on, let's go to Ghekko. I want some *obat*.' She's poking all of us in succession, as though trying to turn us on. 'It's the weekend. This is shit. Come on.' She's moving about like she's about to wee herself.

'I think the lady wants some rave,' says Jussy, who is also standing, 'and that's not a bad idea.'

Naomi moves one up in the body parts contact game and puts her hand on my leg. 'Yeah, come on. Let's get stupid.' Her voice stabs through the music into my ear.

—*She already is stupid.*

—*Back again?*

—*Not leaving you alone with this man-eater.*

—*Nothing to worry about. I'm not interested.*

—*Right.*

'But what about the jungle?' I ask. I want to get wasted, clear my head of impossible conversations and impossible people. But I also don't want to screw up my first trip out of the city. New Me versus sensible Old Me. I'm getting annoyed he's still hanging on in there.

—*Leave him alone. At least he'd never have fallen for Bright Teeth there.*

'We'll still do it. Sleep on the bus.' Naomi is pulling my hand. 'Come on.'

—*Sleep on the bus, sounds good.*

'OK. That suits us.' I stand.

'What?' she shouts over the cacophony of noise.

'That suits me,' I say. 'That suits me.'

We arrive at Ghekko in two taxis. Julie's is there first, and by the time we pull up she's yelling at a confused-looking taxi driver. Geoff is standing slightly back from the scene looking worried as always and Marty is rubbing Julie's back trying to calm her down. The rest of us drop out of our taxi; I'm the only one who actually falls onto his hands and knees.

'Whoa there, Newbie. You OK?' Kim helps me up.

'Yes. Thanks. Not used to the drink.' I brush myself down and see Julie throwing three notes onto the bonnet of the taxi.

'And fuck you, you fucking racist,' she says as she walks away, shaking her hair back and sticking her chin up in the air. The driver pounces on the notes before a warm breeze can float them off his car.

'What was that about?' Kim says as we all try to catch up with Julie. She's already going through Ghekko's doors.

'Taxi quoted ten thousand and then charged twenty. Said 'cos we were white we could afford more,' Marty explains.

'Then?' says Kim.

'Well Jules didn't like that. Said he was a racist and she wanted the Indo rate.'

'Driver's got a point.' Naomi is now knocking elbows as we go into the club.

'Has he?' I ask. 'Shouldn't we all be treated the same? If it happened back home…'

'But we have got more mon…' Geoff's voice is lost on the other side of the door as deafening sound and blinding darkness engulf us.

I feel a flutter of panic in my chest. I wonder if it's because of Old Me or the place, but Old Me stays quiet and keeps himself to himself; it must be the place.

We're huddled together like worried sheep until our eyes adjust and a waiter comes to us with a torch. We follow and are shown some near-invisible tables and chairs that appear every now and then in the minimal disco lights. I grope for the back of my chair and lower myself onto the plastic. It feels like it's been nicked from a classroom. I try to blink the darkness from my eyes and it works a little. There are only two sets of disco lights and a neon strobe in the corner of the room, which gives us all glowing purple eyes and skin and surreally bright white teeth. Naomi is sat next to me again and her face is suddenly covered in freckles unseen before. I give her a wide toothy grin and she laughs.

'You look freaky,' she says.

'So do you. You've got so many freckles you've got a pizza face.'

Her smile falters for a second but then comes back, albeit less confidently.

I'm not too bothered. So what if I hurt her feelings. Get in there, Newbie; time to not give a shit. Even if I have to force it.

Drinks come. My eyes get used to the dark and people start appearing at the tables around us and in gloomy corners like beasts coming out of a mist.

Julie tugs on the waiter's sleeve and says something in his ear. He nods and walks off.

'Sorted,' she yells across the table.

'Good girl,' Kim yells back, but I see the words more than hear them above the thump of bass.

'What's she asked for?' I ask Naomi.

'*Obat.*'

'What's that?'

'Medicine.'

'Medicine?'

'Ecstasy.'

'From the waiter?'

'It's how it works here. All these clubs push their own drugs.'

The waiter returns and hands Julie something. She hands over some money then offers pills out around the table. Geoff shakes his head and pushes his chair away from our circle. Jussy takes one and pops it in his mouth, Kim and Marty also. Naomi shakes her head. I shake mine; so much for not giving a shit. Wimp.

Julie gets up and comes round behind me, leans down and yells in my ear.

'Go on. They're good stuff in here.'

I shake my head again.

'Go on. Chill out.'

I shake my head again.

'Maybe later,' I mouth at her.

She shrugs her shoulders and dance-walks her way back to her chair, little white bits of fluff glowing in her hair under the UV.

'Never done it?' asks Naomi.

Shake and point back at her.

She nods and says, 'A couple of times. Not tonight though. Don't want to be too stupid. Want to enjoy tomorrow.'

Julie and Jussy are now on the dance floor. There are three girls in tight jeans and a man dancing together and that's it. Jussy has his eyes closed and is mostly dancing with his arms and Julie is spinning in circles, interweaving her hands above her head like some hippy chick in an old Woodstock documentary.

Kim rolls his head around on his shoulders while tapping along on the table. Marty is smiling to himself, watching Julie. Geoff gets up and raises his hand to us all.

'You off?' I shout.

He says into my ear, 'Not my thing. You want to share a taxi?'

I squeeze a little don't give a shit out and tell him I'm staying, even though something or someone in me is desperate to get out and go home to a safe bed.

'OK.' Geoff pats my shoulder and leaves.

One song, if that's what they are, melts seamlessly into another, the same beat continuing from tune to tune. Beers become whiskeys and the taste stirs up the unwanted.

—*You enjoying this? asks Laura.*

—*Sort of.*

—*You should take a pill. Be really stupid.*

—*I will if I want.*

—Be a big boy. Shag old Freckles here later.
—I might. Can't exactly shag you, can I?
—Think of me while you're doing it.
—I probably will.
—That's not very nice for Freckles, is it?

I get up and nearly knock my chair over, staggering away to leave Laura to her jealousy. I trip out onto the dance floor. Julie is still spinning but her eyes are now open. She sees me and smiles and runs her fingers through her hair, lifting it and letting it drop down over her face. She looks relaxed for the first time since I've met her.

My body parts move in no particular order. By luck one or two of them find a beat to follow. Naomi dances next to me and moves the right parts to the right time. Julie turns me back around to face her and her finger is between my lips, pushing something in. It's small and round and sits on my tongue for a second seeping bitterness until Julie pinches my nose and I swallow.

'Take your medicine,' she yells into my ear. 'Relax. Go with it.' She ruffles my hair and spins off across the floor, bumping into the man with the three girls. They all laugh and Julie is part of their group now.

I turn back to Naomi and she is only inches away. Perfume and fresh body odour waft around her. Laura gets up and leaves.

Yeah, good. Bugger off.

The moments are flying around like leaves caught on a breeze; circling, rising, falling, circling, rising.

I catch one and me and Laura are running in the rain, laughing. I squint to try and see where we are. But the moment is blown from my hand. I go to grab another and I miss. There is only me and these moments flitting around, out of my grasp. I am reaching out in all directions but I can't get hold of one, no matter how high I jump or how fast I move. I don't want to lose them. I need them.

I finally close my fist over one and open it. I see her holding a melon to her nose in a supermarket. Then that too is lost, impossible to hold as a gust picks it up. It swirls off and joins the others spinning around in front of my eyes. The beating of his heart is loud and fast in my ears. I want to block it out, I want to be left alone and gather all these pieces up in my arms and hold them close so I can never lose them. I only manage to get my fingers on one sole moment: we watch James Stewart running up a street in the snow yelling, 'Merry Christmas, merry Christmas everybody', and she is curled up under my arm with her head on my chest. She says the lines along with Jimmy. Dampness through my T-shirt.

'Are you crying?' I ask.

'Aren't you?' she says.

And I touch my eye and there is a drop of moisture in the corner.

The moment flits off. Darkness. I can see nothing, but I hear crisp little sounds around my ears, near and far, like bats circling in the night, audible in the blackness even though the drum of his heart is so strong I can feel it vibrating through me.

I grab out blindly, hoping to find something to hang onto, to fill this void. What am I without these moments I've guarded and kept and cherished? What is my reason for being if I haven't got them? How is he doing this to me? Why is he doing this to me? Does he even know what he's doing?

I manage to get another and the darkness falls away. It's squashed in my palm and I turn away from the wind and open it up, keeping it in my hand with my fingers pressed down hard against it. I watch as it shows me the moment, a lump in my throat, feeling small and stupid again.

'Why were you kissing him?'

'I wasn't, I was hugging him.' She shakes my hand off her shoulder and yanks open the taxi door.

'Hugging, kissing. Why were you doing it?' I push myself in beside her before she has a chance to shut the door on me. She slides across the seat until she is elbow, hip and knee against the far door. The gap between is full of ice.

'Because he's a friend. And I don't have to explain it to you, but I will if it makes you shut up.' She pulls her skirt down over her thighs. 'I've known him since I was ten. I haven't seen him for about a year and his sister died six months ago.' She shrugs her shoulders. 'So I gave him a hug.'

I say nothing. An embarrassed blush heats my face.

'Where to, mate?' asks the driver.

'I'm sorry, you know,' I say, ignoring him, 'I just came back into the room and you were hugging. I didn't know. I'm sorry.' I go to touch her leg but she somehow makes herself even more compact against the door.

'The meter's running. Where to?'

I find myself looking at the driver's eyes in the rear-view mirror. I can even feel him accusing me.

'Beacon Avenue,' answers Laura.

'I'm sor...' and I lose it. My fingers haven't the strength to hold it anymore. I'm back in the darkness, my arms swirling around me, feeling for anything, hoping for the rest of that moment to fall into my fingers so that it is resolved, or for a moment of laughter or love or intimacy. But I'm flailing, like a man without his parachute, falling through a vacuum.

A LITTLE
PIECE OF CAKE

The lights whirl and spin, and when I close my eyes they leave pale pink, blue and green trails behind my eyelids. The music is numbing to my ears, it is just a beat, a tempo that speeds up and slows down and echoes in my head. I am dancing and dancing and smiling at Naomi and anyone who dances near. Every now and then Naomi asks me if I want to leave, but I say no. Kim, Jussy and Marty have already left. I don't want to. The dancing is the most important thing; I don't want it to stop, the drug does exactly what it is designed to do. I am the dancing brain-dead. But then I see her, sitting there, in the place where moving lights meet darkness, and I think she smiles at me, and her eyes are so large and dark and her long, thick hair falls over her shoulders and her lips part so slightly with her smile, that I have to sit near her, just two empty seats away. I do not talk. I just look at her profile and I am hooked.

'She's lovely. Looks Indian.' Julie has appeared from some dark part of the club and sits on my other side. She puts her mouth almost over my ear so I can hear. 'Talk to her.'

'What do I say?'

'Ask her if she's a prostitute.'

I look at Julie and she twitches her eyebrow and then the corner of her lip and then nods. 'Go on.'

'Of course she's not a prostitute.' Prostitutes are not like her. Prostitutes are…I don't know what they are, but she certainly isn't one.

'Just say hi. She probably doesn't speak English anyway. Then ask her.'

As Julie finishes saying this, the girl looks at me briefly and then back to the dance floor with that almost indiscernible smile; Mona Lisa on the pull.

I move across two seats without any thought of rejection or worry or any sign of Old Me whatsoever and say, 'Hi.'

'Hello,' she says.

'Can I get you a drink?'

'No. Thank you. I am Eka.' She offers her hand and I take it. It feels like a mix of satin and sand; hard work softened with moisturiser.

'Are we leaving?' Naomi has left the dance floor and is now leaning across Julie and shouting in my ear, her eyes on Eka. 'Early rise tomorrow.'

'No. I'm staying. You go. I'll meet you at the bus in the morning.'

'Oh. Fine.' Fine, short and curt; the word that hides so many meanings. But I'm not going to worry about the meaning of that one. Naomi fades into the darkness like a body sinking in a lake.

Julie is laughing.

'Nice one. You just don't care, do you? Always thought she was a stuck-up cow anyway,' she says. 'Ask prozzie how much,' a whisper-shout with a light thump to my arm and then she swirls her way back onto the dance floor.

'Your girlfriend?' asks Eka.

'Just a friend.'

'You want to leave?'

'What?'

'Come. We go.'

'Wait. Stay there.' I pause. I look at her. 'Can I ask you something?'

'Please?'

'Are you a prostitute?'

Her hand lights up in the beam of a random spinning disco light as it cuts through the air. The sting of the slap is intense.

'Sorry. It was a stupid question.' I curse Julie and look back to the dance floor where she is punching one hand and then the other into the air. The slap tingles down my cheek. 'Very stupid.'

'You are very stupid. Very rude.' She pouts for a second then her face relaxes again. 'But OK. You say sorry very quick and many prostitutes here. But please do not ask again or I go home. You make me angry, but you are drunk, so I forgive you one time.'

I sit in silence next to her, savouring each little pinprick feeling on my face that her hand created. I also feel her eyes studying me, creating their own little prickling sensation.

'You say stupid things, but I think you look like nice man.' She stands up. 'Come. Let's go.'

I'm too surprised to say anything, so instead just follow her through the near-darkness and out into the humid night where boys sell cigarettes and taxi drivers yell, 'Hey mister, hey mister.' She leads me to a taxi and we climb in and she asks where I live and I tell her and she tells the driver and she puts a hand on my leg and a silent twenty minutes later we are outside my house and I'm paying the driver too much but so what. We enter the house and then my bedroom and we lie on the bed and she rolls away and says, 'I am very tired,' and falls asleep with her back to me, long black hair falling across the pillow. Her shirt rises two inches up her back revealing smooth, perfect skin the colour of light chocolate. I run my tongue over my lips. We stay like this, her asleep, me watching. As time dances around, fast then slow then fast, I come close to touching her flesh, but I don't; it's enough just to look, to savour the beauty.

'Look at the arse on that.'

'I'd rather not,' I say.

We're following some bloke along the high street. He's all broad shoulders, thick neck and biceps pushing out of a T-shirt that he probably bought too small deliberately. His rear is hugging the inside of a pair of Levis. Laura's eyes are fixed on it.

'He's fresh from the gym. No one's ever that toned all the time.' I try to keep the whinging tone of jealousy out of my voice.

'Jealous,' she tells me. 'Don't be. It might be a nice rear but the rest is just far too hard. It'd be like holding a lump of concrete.' With this she yanks my hand and pulls me into her favourite 'olde worlde' tea room. 'Time for a cup of tea and slice of cake.'

'I'm not jealous. Looking is fine. Coffee and walnut?' I point through the display cabinet at one of the homemade cakes coated in thick buttercream.

'Looking is fine. You do it enough. No, carrot cake. You?' She swings her bag around and fumbles around the clutter for her purse.

'I do not. Carrot for me too.'

'No, you'll have the Pavlova, so I can have a bit too.' She smiles her overwhelming smile at the girl behind the counter. 'And a pot of tea for two please.'

The girl smiles back, then looks at me and does the same. It's natural and charming and her light-blue eyes sparkle.

'You're doing it now,' Laura says as the girl turns her back to make the tea.

'Doing what?'

'Looking.'

'I'm being polite. That's all.'

'I'll bring it over to your table,' says the waitress over her shoulder. I notice she also has a nice arse and my eyes stay fixed on it as my body turns.

'Saw that.' Laura squeezes behind a wooden chair at a wooden table with real flowers in a glass vase in the middle.

'OK, so I look. We both look. As long as that's as far as it goes, we're alright.'

Laura adjusts her top and pulls it down a bit, exposing a little cleavage.

'And as long as I always see that look in your eyes when I show you a bit of flesh, we're definitely alright.'

A pot of tea, two china cups and saucers and two large slices of homemade cake are put on the table.

'There you go,' says the girl with twinkling eyes. 'Enjoy.'

'Let's set some ground rules,' Laura says as she forces her fork into my meringue, sending splinters of white onto the table. Her eyes look at it as though they are still looking at Muscle Man's butt. 'I fancy your cake, and I'm going to have some of it. I admired that man's butt, but I don't want it and would never have it. I know this cake looks good and will taste good because I've eaten here so many times before.'

She slides the fork into her mouth and her tongue licks slowly around her lips afterwards. Her lips and mouth are the only things in the room. I lick mine.

'And it's the same with you. I know you're a nice bit of cake because I've been with you so long.'

'Only three weeks.' I take a piece of her carrot cake. She slaps my hand and it drops off my fork.

'Long enough. You look good, you taste good and you are nice bit of cake, mostly. I might look at cakes in other shops, but I'm not going to risk it, because the cake here doesn't get any better. This is cake heaven.'

I'd agree with her if I could at least taste some of the non-metaphorical cake. As I move a fork of meringue to my lips she twists my hand around and directs the food to her open mouth. I let her do it without comment, as the watching is better than the tasting.

'So, anyway, you can look, I can look, we can tell each other that we're looking and we won't be jealous, well maybe a little, but we never taste. We never eat that other bit of beautiful cake that's actually going to taste bloody awful.'

She cuts into her carrot cake and slides the forkful into my watering mouth.

'You're only tasting what I give you. Got it?'

'Got it.' Crumbs fall onto my chin and I watch as she leans in and kisses my cake-covered lips. I watch her eyes come close to mine and look into me. I look into her. I look. I look and I can't get enough.

I hear Kim showering and coughing. I don't know how long it has been daylight; an hour or maybe two, a minute or maybe two. I don't know how long I have been staring, living in the visual garden of her flesh. Everything is precise and super-real, except time. It has stopped dancing. It has gone. Time lives outside of this chemical state. Time is banished, leaving only the senses. Whatever the pill is that is going through its final stages of transformation in my stomach, it works precisely as advertised by the news and documentaries and the partygoers of the parties I never go to.

My arm is stiff where I've been resting my head on it, looking at Eka. I stretch it out and shake life back into it. She stirs and moves and straightens out on her front. Another inch of skin. I hold my breath and my hand hovers just above it, but I still don't touch. My eyes see and feel all for me.

I stare and stare and marvel at that strip of skin between her shirt and the band of her cotton-white underpants which pokes over her skirt, and now day has come, I am blissful and satisfied and new. And I haven't even touched her.

And Kim bangs on my door.

'Hey, you there, man? Fucking get up.'

She stirs.

'I'm up,' I call. 'Give me a minute.'

'Got to get to the bus by ten. Shift your ass if you're coming.' I hear him barefoot-plop back across to his room.

She turns and looks at me, big brown eyes a little confused at where she is. She pulls her shirt down to close that magical gap.

'I must go.' She sits at the end of the bed, slides sandals on her feet. Her hair hangs over her face and nearly touches the floor while she slips the straps over her heels. 'Please show where is road.'

'Yeah. Sure.' I pull my shoes on. She is already out of the door. I follow and check for Kim as we cross the main room. He must be in his bedroom.

We leave the building and I lead her up the passage beside the house and follow it towards the main road. She stops when she can see the traffic going by at the end.

'It is ok. I can find my way.' She pushes hair behind her ear. It reminds me of someone.

'Are you sure. We're a way out from the centre.'

'*Tidak apa-apa*,' she says.

'Sorry?'

'No what what. No problem. But please give taxi money.' She holds her hand out and tilts her head. Black hair falls across one eye, the other glints at me. I am caught by it for a moment. Beauty. She is beauty.

I pull out my roll of notes and offer her ten thousand, which is enough.

'No,' she says, 'more.'

I laugh and hold out the notes for her to choose. I am still a little high or on a comedown, I'm not sure which. She takes forty, not too much, but enough to pay for a taxi, a meal, another taxi and maybe another meal. I don't care. With her sliver of perfect flesh the colour of which I never knew existed, I don't care.

'*Terima kasih*,' she says and kisses my cheek. 'See you at club next week.' And off she goes, one ankle crossing in front of the other, catwalk-walking to the road, calf muscles flexing in the day's light. I watch until she turns the corner and then watch a little more at the space she left behind. My head spinning, lips smiling, under the whitening sun.

Kim and I are squeezed in the back of the *sudako*, thighs intimately squashed against strangers' thighs, leaning forward on our elbows, watching the world pass out of the open back. A scooter follows us and the helmetless rider smiles and waves at us. We smile back.

'So who was in your room last night?' asks Kim. 'Naomi?'

'No.'

'Thank Christ for that, man. She's a bunny boiler.' He slaps my thigh. 'So you had your first taste of Indo girl.'

'No.'

'Fuuuck. Not Julie?'

'No.'

The rider waves again and swerves off to the right. The smells of the city seem stronger today; the sweet sickly scent of durian fruit and spices almost hiding the smell of rubbish. I lean my head out of the back and look up at the sky. It is bluer than normal. The world is a vivid and bright place this morning. I have a tingling warmth inside me that feels like a child's Christmas.

'Will you stop smiling like a fucking dick man? You did E last night, didn't you?'

'Yep.' I smile at Kim and it does feel a little gormless, which makes me smile even more.

'First time?'

'Yep.'

'You're still spaced.'

'Yep.'

'So?'

'I think she was Indian.'

'Hope you wore your hat.'

'Hat?'

'Condom. Pre-fucking-caution.'

'Didn't need to. Didn't do it.'

'I hope you didn't pay the bitch then.'

'Only for the taxi home. And she wasn't a bitch.'

'Noooo. You paid her and didn't even get your dick wet.'

'Didn't want to. She was nice. Didn't want to.'

'You Brits are weird.'

I say nothing. Just smile.

'Weird.'

We arrive at Pinang Baris bus station, which is more of a lay-by than a station. Multicoloured buses pull in and pull out with horns honking and passengers in multicoloured clothes climbing on and climbing off. We get out of the back of the minivan and Kim leads me to the bus office. It's packed with people and cigarette smoke and noise. For a change people are too busy to pay us *bules* much attention. Marty, Jussy, Julie and Naomi are waiting for us.

'Hey, you made it.' Julie is still wearing the same clothes from the night before. Her eyes are wide and her hands don't seem to want to stay still. 'I'm still fucking high. Ha haa.' Not a laugh, a 'ha haa'.

'Ha haa,' I say back.

'Jesus Christ, I knew we should have taken them home with us when we left,' says Kim.

Naomi just shakes her head and pulls the sunglasses down from her hair to cover her eyes. There's some sort of invisible shield around her, warning me off.

'Come on, guys, let's find the bus.' We follow Jussy up the road and through the crowds. He looks at the front of a red, blue and yellow bus and then says something to a man standing by the side who might or might not be the driver. The man scratches his stomach, which pokes out of a too-small coffee-splattered T-shirt, and nods.

'This is the baby,' yells Jussy.

We get in the bus and it's surprisingly empty compared to the claustrophobic outside. I get a window seat and Naomi sits next to the window on the opposite side of the aisle, shoulders turned away. I tell New Me I really don't care. Julie sits next to me. The others sit along the back seat like naughty school kids.

'You looking forward to this?' Julie puts her knees up against the back of the seat in front and nods her head in time to the music coming from a portable radio on the dash.

'Yep. First jungle time. Can't wait. Me and Laura always wanted to see orang-utans.'

'Laura?'

Laura?

The Christmas feeling drops out of me like pine needles shaken from a dead tree and the gormless smile does likewise. I find myself examining the blue-red pattern of the seat in front.

'Yeah, well. Anyway. Take it Laura wasn't the prostitute from last night.'

I'm vaguely aware of Julie's head now wobbling left and right.

—*Are you never going to leave me alone? I ask.*

—*Left you alone last night, didn't I? Actually I couldn't even get in your messy head. Didn't want to.*

—*I wish I could take a pill now. I was happy. I was happy.*

—*Perhaps if you'd shagged someone, I'd be leaving you alone today.*

—*I don't want to shag anyone.*

'Have a smoke. You look like shit.'

How is Laura waving a cigarette under my nose? Julie pushes the side of my head.

'Hellooo. Smoke.'

'Oh, thanks.' I take one and the bus starts pulling off. Laura shuts up but I can sense she's sitting somewhere, probably on Old Me's lap down there, watching. I drag hard on the cigarette and force a smile back onto my face, wobble my head to the music.

'That's it. Dance. Shake that drug back up.'

It's Julie talking. Just Julie. She's the only one here so relax. Fucking relax.

'Love this *dangdut* music.'

'*Dangdut?*'

'Indonesian music. Love it.' Head wobbles. Wobble wobble wobble.

We wobble together and the drug does a final burst for me and then I'm whirling my hands above me along with Julie while the others behind us and a handful of locals hum, sing and hand-dance along. Naomi stares out the window and Laura and Old Me swirl around in my gut.

—*Fuck you all,* I say to the three of them, *fuck you all and let me live.*

Wobble wobble.

Forced gormless smile.

A pile of pine needles between my feet. Christmas feeling gone.

The grass sways above us and above that a near-invisible plane silently cuts the sky like a surgeon's scalpel.

'Have you ever noticed how those really high, nearly invisible planes seem to cut the sky like a scalpel?' Laura twirls a long blade of grass with her lips.

I'm too off-balance to answer. My brow creases while I try to work out if thinking the same things at the same time is scary or romantic.

'If they could keep that white incision going all the way across the sky from horizon to horizon, do you think it would tear and all the sky's innards would fall on us?'

My hand finds her naked thigh. For some reason the coolness and smoothness of it makes me sad for an almost unnoticeable moment.

'Where does your brain get these things?'

'Dunno, but can you imagine it? I bet there would be colours unknown to man inside the sky's guts. And beautiful things that fall down on the earth in soft plops and they'd be so squashy and gentle we'd be able to climb out from under them and say, "Look at that. The sky fell on our heads and it was alright and actually quite nice."'

'You've been reading my Asterix books. Vitalstatistix is always scared of that lot falling on his head. I think he shouldn't have worried.' *Something small lands on my cheek. I brush it off.*

'Do you worry about it? About everything falling in on you?' *Her hand strokes the back of my arm.*

'Not really. In the words of the chief, "The sky might fall on our heads tomorrow, but as we all know, tomorrow never comes."'

'Optimistic, those Gauls. But it does fall sometimes, you know.'

'Well if it's all soft and lumpy and colourful we shouldn't worry. And even if it's hard and painful and grey, it won't fall on us.' *I get up on one elbow and smile at her dishevelled state: her T-shirt up over her breasts and her knickers around one ankle, shorts caught up in the long grass.*

'Oh yeah, why not?'

'Because I won't let it.' *And I kiss her on her forehead.*

'Oh, my hero the ice-cream man. You'll protect me, will you?'

'Yes.'

'How are you going to do that with your trousers around your ankles?'

'I'll do it, don't you worry.' *My finger runs along the inside of her thigh. Somewhere high a skylark watches and sings.* 'And you best make the most of my free strawberry splits, because in two weeks I become a manly trainee teacher.'

'Oh, I can't wait. We can compare board pens.' *She pulls me down by the neck and kisses me and then pushes me away.* 'Come on, we're supposed to be having a walk, not spending the day shagging in the long grass and debating mortality.'

'Is that what we're doing? OK. Let's forget the mortality and just shag.'

'Uh-uh.' She pulls up her knickers and shorts and straightens her T-shirt. I lie there watching. The only sound is the skylark and the grass bowing in the light breeze. 'Walk, drink, food and then maybe, just maybe, I'll let you protect me some more.'

'I will never ever let the sky fall on our heads, whether it's soft and fluffy or hard and deadly. We're too good together to have anything happen.'

'Pull your pants up, Mr Romance. Let's get off this hill and find a beer.' She walks away with the sunlit grass kissing her naked ankles. I watch with a smile on my lips. I look to the sky and will it to stay up there, high and beautiful and untouchable to all but the chirping birds.

I crane my neck and look back into the bus. A young group are watching and giggling and the older woman with the chicken on her lap tries to hide a smile. I'm sure they can't see my bits. I hope. I change my angle to make sure.

Don't give a shit. Don't give a shit.

Close my eyes.

Don't give a shit. Come on, New Me. You can do it. You don't give a shit. No penis shyness.

And there it is. I look down at it arcing out and then being turned into spray by the speed of the bus. It is liberating. I lean to my hand holding the beer and manage to pass the cigarette to my fingers and get the bottle to my lips, then I put the smoke back between my teeth; nothing spilt or lost.

Pissing, smoking, drinking arsehole.

When I'm empty and he's back in my trousers, I stay there on the step, watching trees and ferns as tall as me go past and I smile. I'm actually about to see my first jungle. I'm not on the Number 11 going to work. I'm not in the developed world of consumerism and rules and profit and fashion and who's got this and who needs that and my car's faster than yours and what's on TV tonight.

I sit down on the step and wallow in my epiphany, knowing that to pee free is to be free, until the bus slows a little and the road disappears and becomes something I only thought existed in adventure films: a rickety bridge with great gaps between pieces of old wood and rusting metal. About fifteen metres below it a fast-flowing and shallow river is visible through the holes as we pass over. I lean out of the bus, holding onto the handrail, and look behind. The bus is following carefully placed planks that aren't much wider than the wheels. They rattle as we go over them. I smile. Life is better when death can nearly reach out and grab you. I almost wish it would. A morning of epiphanies.

We rattle off the other side of the bridge and I watch it disappear as we go around a bend. I sit back on the step and take in every leaf, every tree, every pothole, until the bus slows. We pass by bamboo and wood huts and houses and stop at the end of the road. A sign tells us we've arrived at Bukit Lawang, our destination. We blink our gritty eyes, stretch our arms, pick up our little shoulder bags and get off.

'This way,' says Kim. We follow him to a path that leads up between wooden shacks and stalls selling all colours of sarongs and batik-patterned shirts. The jungle is green and thick and high behind the buildings. In a few seconds the river is on our left, wide, fast and shallow; it flows back in the direction we have come from and then falls quickly over a weir. There is a restaurant partly on stilts overhanging the river on the other bank, and on this bank wooden-and-bamboo-constructed bars and eating places interrupt the view. Bob Marley posters and Rasta colours decorate the walls of a lot of them and occasional reggae music mixes with the sound of the river. The buildings are nearly all open on at least two sides. Cushions, bamboo chairs and tables furnish them. An occasional owner or barman says hello or tries to get us to come in for a drink or food. My stomach is rumbling, but Kim keeps us going.

After five or ten minutes of following the uneven path past the stalls and buildings it climbs into trees, but still follows the river, which flows a little way below. The jungle is becoming more imposing and trees tower over the river valley on both sides. The green is all-encompassing and surreal after the city and a night in a darkened disco.

We pause to watch half a dozen Indonesians shoot down the river on giant inner tubes, laughing and spinning and bouncing over white frothing rocks as they go.

'Who's up for tubing later?' asks Jussy.

'Nah, not me,' answers Julie, who now looks pale. She blinks about six times in quick-fire succession.

'Maybe tomorrow. I want food and beer and swimming,' says Kim.

Naomi, who hasn't said anything since Medan, mutters, 'Maybe.'

'Beer,' says Marty.

I say nothing. I'm happy just to stare at the immense green that looms over and around me. I wonder how far the jungle goes once you're in it and what's in it. I'm not even sure if it is officially a jungle or a forest or what. My lack of knowledge astounds me.

We start walking and I'm sweating again. The path dips back down and we're amongst some more bamboo stalls, shacks and bars. These too lean out over the river on one side of the path and line the jungle on the other. There is mostly only one row of buildings, except for a few add-on constructions behind, and behind them is a slope going up and up, covered in vegetation.

Kim leads us into one of the restaurants on the right. It's all open and covered only by a wood, bamboo and leaf roof. Everything inside is made from the same. It's cool in the shade.

'Hey, hello, my friend,' says a shirtless guy of about twenty, with dark-skin and lean muscle and long straight hair down to his cut-off trousers. 'Good to see you again.' He knocks knuckles with Kim. 'You want rooms?'

'Yeah, man. We all want singles?'

We answer in the affirmative.

'OK.' The Indonesian goes into a back room and brings out five keys, each hanging off a number carved from wood.

We arrange to meet back in the restaurant in thirty minutes and go off to find our rooms. Mine is up a path that runs behind the bar and then up a few steps. I climb the stone-made steps. An aquamarine-and-black butterfly the size of my hand floats in front of me and lands on a leaf by the path. I kneel to look at her, wings quivering as she rests. She seems too delicate to fly, so delicate that if a raindrop were to land on her it would tear her wing. Suddenly she is afloat again and rises into the jungle foliage. I climb a few more steps to my door, wondering at the fragility of things.

I unlock the wood-slatted entrance. It creaks open. Inside are cool shadows and basic comforts, but better than any hotel room I've stayed in; no neatly folded towels, no yelling TV, no smell of fabricated fresh air. Here is real air with a scent of damp timber and earth. Within wooden walls, a double bed with only a sheet and thin blanket, a rotting wooden cupboard and a bamboo chair welcome me. I can hear the sound of running water. I lick around my dry gums. There is no window, but daylight falls through the gaps in the wooden walls. There are two more doors. I open one. It leads onto a balcony.

I catch my breath.

The rickety and gnarled wooden platform has a roof of banana leaves and overlooks a small stream. This tumbles away from a small waterfall which pours out of the forest undergrowth a few metres away. The brook bubbles over rocks and down the hill from the forest where it disappears into darkness under the back wall of the restaurant a little below. Fern leaves and large red flowers bend over the stream, and the trees of the jungle loom above leaving only a small gap of blue sky. The smell of moisture and damp dirt mixes with the scent of flora unknown. I stand there, taking it in, when three more butterflies of different vivid colours—yellows, reds, turquoise—float across my private little valley.

I don't want to meet the others. I want to stay here. New Me almost lets me, but for the fact that there must be so much more to see, and he wants to see it.

Back inside there is a bathroom which consists of a toilet, a bucket of water, a scoop beside it and a shower. It is all open plan, with no shower curtain, and the floor is concrete. The toilet doesn't flush and I have to throw water down it from the bucket to clear it, and the shower is icy cold. I stick different parts of me under it one by one until finally all my body is acclimatised and ready to stand under it at once. I stand upright under the flow and gasp. It is so cold that it must be straight from the stream and is probably purer and cleaner than any chemical-enhanced water back home. It is the best shower in the world. I haven't felt this alive since…

since…

—*That time*—

—*Shut up, Laura.*

I spin the taps off. I towel my head so it hurts.

I want to see more of this place. And that's all I want.

I dry myself. I dress. I go to meet the others.

Since…

That time under the waterfall. I remember it, Laura. Down here, with you, I remember it. We follow the stream up from the lake, climbing over rocks, up and up and away from the road and people.

The waterfall drops from about ten feet into a pool of dark, calm water before the stream continues its journey down the hill. You lift your shirt over your head as soon as you see it, unclip your bra, step out of your jeans and underwear. Your body so pale, untouched by sun. Your black hair shining in the spring sunlight which spills through the trees lining this secret little valley. You step into the shallow water, drawing in breath and yelping at the coldness. I watch as you feel your way into deeper water, stumbling and giggling, hobbling over hidden rocks and stones. God, you look gorgeous. You throw cupped handfuls of freezing water over your hair, your nipples hard from the shock of it; your body seeming even whiter against the dark of the pool that surrounds you. You reach the waterfall. Shivering, you stand there, letting the fine spray cover you before you step under its foaming power. You scream and the scream becomes a laugh and the laugh becomes a yell.

'Come in,' you shout. 'Come here.'

I pull my clothes from my body. I trip as I step out of my pants. I come to you. The water is numbing to my feet. Goosebumps break out across my body. But I come to you. You still laugh and hold your arms out to me as the torrent runs over you, blurring your face. I must be a blur to you too. I stumble, I stagger, I feel my way over hidden obstacles to be with you under the waterfall. Then I am there and I can't believe the coldness of it. But it is life-giving; it is invigorating. It beats us, it wallops us, it pushes down on us, but we are alive. So alive. Your arms wrap around me and we kiss, fresh water pouring into our mouths, between our bodies pressed close to each other. I feel your breasts against me, your skin so soft, your nipples press hard against my chest. I am hard against you. Your legs wrap around me and I nearly fall, but we are against the rock under the waterfall. We hold on. You are warm around me. I am warm inside you. Cold outside. Shivering. Making love. Kissing. Swallowing and drinking purest water. My hands trying to hold us up, grasping at slippery rock, then grasping you. Wanting more warmth. Wanting deeper warmth. The water pounds us, massages us, makes us.

I have never been so alive. Together we are so alive. So alive.

IN YER FACE

On the table is a pancake covered in pineapple, mango, papaya and banana, drizzled with condensed milk. The table we sit at is by the river, in an open area in front of one of the restaurants. The sun is gentle on us, still hot but comfortable. I feel fresh after my cold shower. All drug and alcohol after-effects have left me. I'm relaxed, loose. Facing the river, I watch it drop in a white block over a shelf of rock into a calm black pool, where it gathers speed and bubbles off into shallower waters.

'Dig in, man. These are the best fucking pancakes ever.' Kim puts a forkful in his mouth. 'Oh yeah.'

The six of us are there, dressed in a varied array of T-shirts, shorts and sarongs. I have my first taste. The fruit tastes like fruit should, juicy and full of flavour and nothing taken out or added or preserved. 'So did you have a good night?' This is the first time Naomi has spoken to me since before we got on the bus. She pulls at a scraggly dreadlock. Kim laughs and raises an eyebrow.

'Yes. I did, thanks.' I look to the river where three Indonesians have just jumped in from the far side and are splashing each other.

'So, was she a prozzie?' asks Julie.

Kim laughs again.

'Well, I didn't sleep with her, so I guess not.'

'She took your money though, man.'

'Shut up, Kim. I didn't sleep with her and it was never on offer.

104

I just paid for her taxi back.' And why the fuck do I have to explain myself?

'She went back with you, then,' says Naomi, separating mango from her pancake and leaving it on the side of her plate. 'She was very pretty.'

'Look. Nothing happened. She was a really nice girl.'

'Seeing her again?' asks Naomi.

I'm starting to find her questions and designer dreadlocks annoying, dangling down the side of her face like ivy twine.

'No. Don't know. Probably not. Maybe. Don't really care,' I say. Muscles are tightening in my back.

'Somebody's jealous.' Kim's smile is so wide I can see mashed fruit roll around the inside of his mouth.

'Don't be a prick, Septic.' Naomi flicks a slice of mango across the table at him.

'Let's all just leave it. What I do is up to me, OK?' Tension is prodding between my shoulder blades. I should have stayed on my balcony with the butterflies.

'Nothing wrong with an occasional whore,' says Jussy. 'Me and Bugs don't mind admitting it, do we boy?' He pats Bugs Bunny on his t-shirt.

'Jesus. Men.' Naomi's hand reaches for her beer and she swallows from it as though she's just escaped the desert. Dreads swing with the sudden movement.

'Orangs. Look.' Julie is pointing across the river. Two long-haired orang-utans are on the opposite bank, sitting on a rock outcrop where the swimming men have left their shoes and shirts.

I blink to make sure what I'm seeing is what I'm seeing. It is. They are only about fifteen metres away, but don't seem nervous of people at all. One of them hunch-walks to the pile of clothes the men have left there and picks up a shoe. Two of the young men in the water laugh as the third realises it's his shoe. He stands up in the shallow water near the far bank. He shouts and splashes at them. The apes stay where they are. The one with the shoe sniffs it.

'Idiot people shouldn't even be on that side. It's all reserve over there,' says Julie.

I'm amazed at my first sight of the orang-utans. I haven't got a camera. Sightseeing and happy memories aren't my priority in Indonesia. But right now I wish I had one, right now I'm not feeling self-pitying and pathetic, right now I'm feeling awed.

'How come they're not scared?' I ask.

'They've probably not been back in the wild long. Most of the orangs around here have been rescued from somewhere and slowly reintroduced to the jungle,' Marty answers as he pulls a big Nikon from his bag.

The guy gets out of the river and climbs up onto the rock. The orang-utans slowly move nearer the trees. With each step the man takes forward they take one back. One of them still holds the shoe and starts waving it in the air.

'Cheeky buggers,' says Julie, 'they're taunting him.'

As if to prove Julie right, the ape with the shoe lollops forward holding it out to the dripping-wet man. As he reaches for it the orang-utan moves back, still holding the shoe. The two in the water are laughing and yelling at their friend, who makes a sudden dash forward. The shoe thief shoots halfway up a tree and looks back over his shoulder, while the other orang-utan ambles to the farthest point on the rock and sits down on his haunches to watch the show. He's probably as amused as we are.

The man stands at the bottom of the tree, reaching up and waving his hands, begging the orang-utan to give the shoe back. The ape leans down and waves the shoe within a few inches of the man's reach. He jumps up to snatch it but the orang-utan swings its arm back up and holds the shoe above his head.

'Fucking great show, man,' says Kim.

I wish Laura was here. I push the thought back down and shove it in Old Me's lap.

—You're not ruining this moment.

He says nothing.

The man is now putting his arms around the tree and trying to pull himself up. The orang-utan climbs a little higher and dangles the shoe again. The man reaches and the orang-utan raises it high again in one long swooping arc, the look on his face non-committal and unreadable, just pouting mouth and calm eyes.

The two in the water are pointing and shouting at their friend to go higher. He looks uncertain but pulls himself up until he is about six feet up the tree and three feet from the thief's long toes. He looks awkward, clumsy and stupid compared to the primate, who dangles the shoe yet again. The Indonesian reaches up with one hand while holding on with the other.

—*I hope the idiot falls.* Laura is here.

—*Me too.* I am actually happy she's here for this one, sharing this moment with me.

But he doesn't. His fingers are just touching the end of the shoe and he stretches to get it while the ape leans down to him, almost helpful. He's grabbing and he's going to get it, but just as his hand opens to take it the orang-utan flicks his wrist and the shoe flies off through the air in a long slow arc. It plops into the water, floats for a second, then sinks.

We're laughing, the two in the river are laughing, a group of teenagers who have gathered just behind us are laughing, Laura laughs and strokes my cheek and then leaves, knowing conversation is about to start. The orang-utan on the rock turns and ambles off into the trees. The other turns and climbs up to the branches and then is lost in a rustle of leaves and shaking boughs. Gone without so much as a titter or a bow.

The man climbs-slides down the tree, scraping his chest as he goes, and says something rude and angry-sounding to his friends, picks up the remaining clothes and shoe and clambers off along the rocks.

'Beats the shit out of TV,' says Kim, who realises he hasn't smoked for a few minutes and puts a cigarette in his mouth.

'I never knew we could get so close to them.'

'Hey, man, you can take a trip up to the feeding platform in the jungle and get even closer. They're so tame here,' says Jussy.

'Feeding platform?' I ask.

'God, you really know nothing about this place,' says Naomi. 'Most of the orang-utans around here aren't completely wild, they still need looking after until they find their feet. The reserve guys take them food everyday in case they can't find any.' The condescension in her voice grates.

'I'd like to see that.'

'Yeah, but not today, Newbie. It's beer o'clock and then I want a swim,' says Kim.

There's a general agreement with the plan, so three minutes later the table is decorated with Bintangs. The group of teenagers approaches us. They push a pretty but podgy-faced girl in a *hijab* forward.

'Excuse me please. Can we make a photo with you?' she asks.

'Here we go,' says Julie, 'celebrity time.'

'Of course you can,' says Jussy, smiling at the girl.

The group gather around us at the table and we all smile at each of their cameras, then they thank us and go.

'What was that all about?' I ask.

'Always happens,' answers Naomi. 'They can show their friends and family that they met the lesser-spotted white person. Probably frame the photos and put them on the wall like we're presidents or something.'

'You're joking,' I say.

'Nope. It gets a bit tedious after two months. Get it enough in Medan without having it ruin my weekend.' Naomi puts her sunglasses back over her eyes.

'I think it's nice. It's adding to my weekend rather than ruining it.' I watch the group walk away. They're giggling and waving goodbye to us.

'Me too,' says Kim.

Naomi snorts.

There is a silence while we sip our beers and watch the river carry another group of inner-tubers bouncing past.

'Scientists spend millions trying to prove apes are intelligent. So far it's cost me a pancake and a beer to see it proved. Scientists are idiots.' Julie takes a long swig from her bottle and lets out a sigh after. 'Love it here.'

'Me too,' says Kim.

'Can't beat it,' says Marty.

'I'd rather be up to my nuts in guts,' says Jussy, 'but this'll do for the moment.'

'Why are you here, anyway?' Naomi asks me. 'You here for the sex and disease too?' There is a definite hint of something bitter in her voice.

'No. I'm just here because I am.'

'*Jalan jalan*, eh, man?' says Kim holding his bottle up for me to chink mine against.

Chink.

'Yep. *Jalan jalan*.'

'Why you here then, Miss Canada, eh?' Kim asks. 'Dirty sex with long-haired jungle boys?'

'No, you idiot. I'm here because of this.' She waves her hands at the trees that tower above us on both sides of the river. It seems false and acted.

'Bollocks,' I say and smile at what has just popped into my head. 'You're here because you think it's a cool thing to do and you get to act the part of cool hippy chick world citizen with skanky dreads so you can rabbit on for the rest of your life about all the things you saw because back home people probably think you're boring and up yourself.'

There is a moment's silence while Naomi fingers her dreads. Marty and Jussy sip their beers and look anywhere but at Naomi. Kim openly smirks and takes a noisy drag on his cigarette while looking from me to her and back to me. Julie twitches and coughs and shifts in her seat.

Naomi adjusts her sunglasses, gets up, picks up her bag and walks back across to the guesthouse without another word.

I wait for guilt to surface from somewhere, but it doesn't. I'm more surprised at myself for having said it than sorry.

'Newbie, Newbie. A surprise-a-day.' Kim offers me a cigarette, which I take and light.

'Swim, anyone?' I ask, changing the subject before it ignites discussion.

'Good idea.'

And swim we do.

I float on my back, watching the sky and branches of unknown trees and wonder if I like New Me. What was that about? Why was I that way with Naomi? Was it me? Was it Laura? Was it me on Laura's behalf? I should apologise. But why? She is too intense. She's jealous. My night with Eka has nothing to do with her.

The branches are speeding up in their passing above and then a rock scrapes my buttock. I sit up and see I have floated downstream from where the others are diving and swimming. I swim back to the others in the deeper water and roll onto my back again. They leave me be. I like the noisy deafness the water makes in my ears.

Should I apologise?

—*But why?* asks Laura.

—*Why are you always here?*

—*Because this is where you wanted me, down in your skinny body, locked away. But you know me; no keeping me quiet.*

—*I just want to forget you.*

—*Tough. And to answer your question, no, you shouldn't apologise.*

—*You're jealous.*

—*Of course I'm not. I'm dead and jealousy is for the living. You're just scared of annoying me. Oh, and the river is carrying you back to the shallow bit again.*

I look around. She's right as usual. I roll and swim back, lay my head back in the cool water and rotate my arms to try and stay in the same place. I focus on one green branch and try to keep it in my eyeline.

—*I'm not interested in her.*

—*So you thought it was a good way to get rid of her. Piss her off and make her feel like an idiot?*

—*No. I don't know. I just wanted to piss someone off and she was an easy target.*

—*The New You. Heartless and an arse. Well done.*

—*That's what I'm after, then silly bitches like you don't destroy me by looking the wrong fucking way. You only had to get across the road and you couldn't do that right. All over for you in a millisecond, but I've got deal with it for fucking ever.*

My hands are moving faster under the water, my chest suddenly feels tight. Rivulets run down both sides of my face.

—*Oh.*

—*I'm sorry.*

She doesn't reply. Suddenly something large and fast bounces off my leg and then my shoulder rolling me over into the water. Water goes up my nose and down my throat. I right myself. I'm coughing and spluttering and through stinging eyes I see five people on inner tubes bounce off down the river away from me, spinning and twisting.

Kim is at my side, treading water and holding my arm until I stop coughing.

'You OK, Newbie? They could have knocked you out.'

I cough again and wipe my eyes.

'I'm fine. I better go apologise to Naomi.'

'Oh man. Don't wimp out. You said the truth.'

'Maybe. But I shouldn't have said it.' I swim across to the bank and clamber up to the table to get my clothes. Old Me is in control for the moment. The wimp never says a bad word to anyone. But as I pull my T-shirt over my head Naomi comes over, dressed in trousers and shirt and holding a bag. She ignores me and yells down at the others.

'I'm getting a bus back today. Bye.' She turns and heads back to the path which leads through the shacks and down river. She doesn't even look at me.

'Naomi, wait.'

She holds a closed fist up in the air and flicks the middle finger without even turning, then disappears out of sight behind a stall.

'And the same to you,' I mutter. 'Silly bitch.'

New Me takes the T-shirt back off and picks up a cigarette from the table. He sits down, swigs beer and lights up.

That's the last time I attempt to apologise.

'Eh mate, can I sit here?' A strong Liverpudlian accent belonging to a man of about twenty with sunburnt, tattooed arms and badly shaved head cuts the air like a low-flying jet. He sits down before I answer.

'Eh mate, have you ever fuckin' noticed how these Indonesians are always in yer fuckin' face?' His face is about six inches from mine.

'No. I haven't.' I look to the river hoping Kim or one of the others will come and rescue me.

'Always in yer fuckin' face.' His voice trails off and I make no attempt to talk to him.

'You're not a doctor, are ya?'

I look at him. Old Me wants to get up and run from this nutter and New Me wants to whack him. They both sit and wait undecided.

'Only I got these spots all over me dick. I slept with some bitch in Bangkok and come down here two days ago and these spots have come up all over me dick. Dirty bitch.'

'No. I'm not a doctor.'

'What about yer friends in the river? Any a' them doctors?'

'No.' I look up the river and at the trees and question if I really just saw the orang-utans and if now this nightmare from England is really sitting here.

'You couldn't take a look, could ya?'

And his hands go in the front of his shorts and fumble about and I stub out my cigarette and say, 'Sorry, no,' and get back in the river as quickly as Old Me will carry me while New Me shouts in my head, 'Deck the freak.'

I dive in under the water and come up next to Julie, who is pushing a breast back into her too-small bikini top.

'Got rid of that boring Naomi for us then. Well done. Thank god she doesn't work at our school. She'd do my head in.'

'Yep. She's gone. But now there's a Scouser up there with spots on his dick and he wants to show me.'

'You're joking. Urgh.' She looks over my shoulder. 'Tell me you're joking.' Her lip twitches.

'Nope.'

'Well he's showing all of us now.'

I turn and see the Liverpudlian, stark naked, clambering down the bank into the river. He's stumbling over the shallow rocks, smiling like he knows us. He waves.

'Everybody out,' shouts Julie.

Kim, Marty and Jussy pause from their diving competition and look at her.

'Out. Now,' she shouts again, and it's done with such authority no one hesitates. We all swim-wade-splash past the naked Liverpudlian, who's just entered the water. He looks at us, mouth open, as we go. I can't help but glance down at his penis and see the spots. He's not a well man. I pull myself up and out of the water, grab my clothes as the others grab theirs, and find it very hard not to run as we go across to pay at the restaurant. I notice the Indonesians standing nearby are looking at the Liverpudlian, wide-eyed and tight-mouthed.

One of them shouts, 'Eh man, don't be naked. There are Muslim here.'

I feel embarrassed by my skin colour and pull my T-shirt on. I tell the others I'm going back to my room. I've had enough of company. I'm tired of conversation and questions and idiot *bules*. I'm already thinking of the quiet of my balcony and little valley and want to be sitting there, listening to the water flow.

I hurry up the path to my room, shut the door behind me and go straight to the balcony. I stop still as soon as I've opened the door. Sitting on the wooden top rail of the balcony, just two feet in front of me, are three monkeys. They are dark grey and white with long tails that hang under them and curl up at the ends. They have little black sprouts of hair on their heads with white on either side and black moustaches that are curled up like an eccentric Victorian gentleman's. I expect them to jump off at the sight of me, but they just sit there, heads moving from side to side while they look at me and then peer behind into my room. I pull the door gently shut behind. I stay very still, hoping they won't leave. Somewhere in my head lies a concern about bites and scratches and strange jungle diseases. But this moment is worth a scratch, a bite, death. It's a moment just for me.

We stay there. I am perfectly still while they check me out, eyes flittering up and down my face and body. They take turns to walk up and down the length of the railing, one paw crossing the other as though on a tightrope. I hold out my hand to one of them, it bares its teeth at me and screeches, and then the three of them jump off, two into the foliage and one onto a nearby branch. They disappear up the slope and into the trees. Standing there, looking after them, I'm vaguely aware of a grin across my face. I sit down on a wobbly bamboo chair and wait, watching the jungle, hoping they'll return. I stay there watching my valley, scratching at mosquitoes, thinking of nothing but the beauty that surrounds me and making the most of the absence of others. Of all others.

'To zoo or not to zoo, that is the question.'

'Not to zoo.' Laura stands between me and her mother, Jane, while we watch the huge silverback gorilla just three feet from us. The gorilla passes us an occasional condescending glance from his pile of straw in the corner of the enclosure.

'But if we didn't zoo them they'd be more endangered than they already are,' I say as a toddler-sized gorilla chases another down a slide in the middle.

'But if we looked after them and didn't take away their habitat we wouldn't have to zoo them.'

'My daughter, the eternal dreamer and believer that people can be good.' Her mum ruffles Laura's hair.

'No, I know the human race is an arse, but I just wish it'd change. Just like you do, eh, big boy.' She blows the gorilla a kiss and starts walking off. 'This place depresses me.'

Her mum links her arm through mine and we start walking while Laura speeds on ahead. Somewhere a monkey howls and a blackbird chirps.

'If she doesn't like zoos, why did she suggest we come?' I ask.

'Because she loves getting herself worked up. Haven't you noticed that about her yet?' She looks at me and smiles. 'I think you've noticed virtually everything about her, haven't you?'

I don't answer but feel my face go warm.

'How long have you two been together now?'

'Two months.'

'A good two months?'

'The best.'

'She's mad about you.'

My stomach does a spin. It's good to hear it from someone else. It means they've talked about me. Laura has told her mum how she feels about me.

'She'll do your head in, though. You know that, don't you. She's done mine in since she learnt to talk. Questioning everything, but understanding everything at the same time.'

She holds me back so we don't catch up with her daughter, who has paused by the capybaras. Laura leans on the railing, chin resting thoughtfully in hands and peachy rear in short white dress stuck out behind her.

'I lie awake some nights trying to work out what she means by what she says just before she falls asleep. I'm sure she does it deliberately to mess with my mind.'

'She does.' Jane laughs and surprises me by putting her head against my shoulder. 'But don't ever try to zoo her.'

'I wouldn't dream of it.'

'She'd bite your arm off. You can trust my Minnie Mouse. When she puts her heart into something, it's there for good. Never doubt her and never stop her being her.' She tugs on my arm. 'Got it?'

'Got it.'

'Good. Because she will drive you nuts and there'll be times you want to tell her no, but don't even bother trying, because it'll hurt.'

Laura is skipping back towards us, kicking her legs behind her and hair swinging around her face.

'Mummy, me want ithe cweam. Pwease can me have ithe cweam?' She stops in front of us and pants like a dog, tongue hanging out. If her mum wasn't here I'd grab it with my mouth.

'Of course you can, little girl. And would little boy like one too?'

'Yes, pwease,' I say.

Jane links her other arm through Laura's and we swing legs wide and 'follow the yellow brick road' to the nearest ice-cream kiosk, before getting happy-sad at seeing more caged, bored animals who must be wondering what the hell life is all about.

HYPOCRITES AND IDIOTS

I'm flopped in the corner of the bar on cushions and leaning back with arms draped over a low rail. Behind me I can hear the river splashing and gurgling as it flows just a few metres below. My legs are out in front of me and crossed at the ankles. I'm wearing light, white cotton trousers and sandals and a batik shirt from one of the stalls. It's airy and cool. I feel relaxed, fresh from another cold shower. In one hand I have a rum and Coke, in the other a joint that's just been passed to me by an Indonesian who asked if he and his friend could join us. Kim is talking to him. Julie is nodding at their conversation and joining in the occasional laughter. Marty and Jussy are playing chess at the next low table along. The darkness behind me is stroking my back while the bar is gently lit by coloured lights and candles. I listen to nothing but the water and the occasional noise from the jungle, crickets and, somewhere over the hills, thunder, as yet unaccompanied by its partner.

I puff on the joint and my head swims. I don't want my mind to wander and I don't really want the joint. I'm annoyed at myself for taking the thing in the first place. Still feel pressured by peers, I must do something about that. I lean across and pass it to Jussy.

I stretch my head out into the darkness behind me and look up into the sky. The rumbling is getting nearer but still no flashes.

'Big storm is coming,' says the Indonesian who made the joint.

'Yes,' I say.

'And I must go to work.' He stands up from his crossed-leg position.

'Work? What sort of work do you do at night?' asks Kim, who grabs the joint back off Jussy. 'Pass around, man.'

'Me? Am policeman.' He pulls his ID from his back pocket. 'Look for people smoking drugs.'

Kim freezes with the joint two inches from his mouth.

'No fucking way.' He laughs an uncertain laugh.

The man laughs too and holds the ID close to Kim's face.

'Do not worry. I not work now, but in ten minutes I do. In ten minutes if I see you with ganja, I arrest.'

He is now holding the ID in front of my face, but my eyes are doing some jiggy little dance and can't focus.

'Now we are friends, but when I am police, I am police. Long time in prison for smoking ganja here.'

'But you've got some on you, man. How can you put people in jail when you smoke it?' asks Jussy, nibbling on the end of a pawn.

'Is my job. Smoking with you is my relax.' He puts his ID back. 'If you see me later, do not say hi. I am undercover in bars and clubs here.'

'OK. You're a fucking dude.' Kim takes a drag on the joint and stubs it out. 'Thanks for the smoke.' He offers his hand and the cop shakes it.

The policeman and his friend leave without paying for their drinks. They just nod at the barman, who sits at a chair by the bar watching his customers while plucking at a guitar.

'Jeeesuus. I fucking love this country. Hypocrisy and corruption. What a place,' says Kim.

I lean back in my corner and look out at the sky again. Nothing is visible. The trees and sky merge in blackness.

'Did you hear about that girl who taught in Surabaya?' asks Julie.

'Nope,' says Kim.

'Got caught with three joints on her and got three years in an Indo jail.' Julie picks the dead reefer from the ashtray and flicks it over the railing into the river. 'Her parents paid a twenty-million-rupiah bribe to get her out and then they didn't let her out. Took the money and kept her in. I'm not smoking around here tonight and I don't trust that copper.'

Lightning finally flashes behind a hill, and the forest is lit up for a second, alive and green, then it plunges back into darkness. My head is bent right back out of the bar and into the night. Drops of rain fall from the dark onto my face, heavy and cool. I can count every drop and feel each one trickle down my skin. Plop. Plop. Plop.

'Isn't that the guy with the spotted dick?' Jussy's voice penetrates my empty thoughts and for a moment I'm not sure I really heard it.

'Eh, Newbie, your friend's here with a local girl.'

With effort I pull my head back up and the bar and coloured lights mix in darting lines and blurry splodges. I close my eyes to steady my head. No more ganja. Not tonight.

Opening my eyes wide, the place steadies. I see him, the Liverpudlian, in a yellow Ben Sherman shirt, standing by the bar with his arm around a pretty young Indonesian girl. She looks nervous as he speaks into her ear. She smiles at what he says but tries to pull away. His hand is clasping her shoulder. He gives her a quick kiss on the lips that she tries to turn away from and he laughs. She laughs too, but it is forced.

'Someone should tell her about his condition,' says Marty as he knocks over Jussy's king.

'Fuck. You only won 'cos I'm stoned.' Jussy leans back against the balcony.

'She's probably already got whatever it is.' Kim kicks my foot with his. 'You still with us, Newbie? Looking a bit lost.'

I turn my head and I think my neck creaks. I look around to see if anyone can hear it.

It's just the joint. It's just the joint.

'Not lost,' I say, 'just contemplating.'

'Contemplating what?'

'How I'm going to tell that girl he's got a dose.' I stand up and trip on one of the cushions. Falling back onto the low rail, Kim manages to grab my arm before I tip over into the river.

'Stoned again. Sit down, man.'

'Nope. Newbie New Me has a job to do.' I take extra-large steps over the cushions to get out of my corner. 'No more thinking without action. I'm doing action without thinking. I'm action man.' I giggle as I put my hand on Julie's head to make the last step away from our table.

'What the hell are you on?' she asks.

'This man is not used to this extra-strength jungle grass.' Kim laughs. 'Got to watch this.'

I'm still giggling as I approach the Liverpudlian and the girl. No one, and I mean no one, dead ex-girlfriends and hidden split personalities included, tries to stop me.

'Alright mate,' I say in my best tribal English greeting.

'Yeah. Alright.' He pulls the girl tighter into his body. She smiles at me.

'This your girlfriend?' I ask, pointing my Bacardi and Coke at her. I look at the glass for a second and wonder how it got into my hand. I put it down on a low table next to us, where three backpackers sit.

'Do you mind?' I ask.

'No. Go ahead,' answers a dreadlocked male. What is it with dreadlocks and travellers? Perhaps I should grow some, or buy some. I giggle.

'What's so funny, mate?' asks the man from Liverpool. Liverpooooool. Ha.

'Nothing. Mate.'

'You takin' the piss or wha?'

'No. I wouldn't do tha, like. Wouldn't wanna get in yer face.' I jerk my head towards him on the last word and he flinches.

'Fuck off.' He moves the girl in front of him.

A human shield? From me? I laugh out loud. Shit. This grass works.

'Hi,' I say to the girl. '*Apa kabar*?'

'*Baik-baik*,' she answers. She says she's fine. I get the feeling I'm freaking her as much as Ben Sherman.

'How's the spots?' I ask Ben.

'Spots? What spots?' He absently scratches his crotch with his spare hand. The girl pulls out from under his arm and looks at what he's doing.

'Here spot?' The girl points at the offending area.

'No. No spot. Very big dick here. That's all.' Ben looks over the girl's head at me, eyes narrowing.

Am I about to get into my first real fight? Giggle. I'm going to lose. More giggling. I'm also aware of Kim's laughter somewhere behind me and the three backpackers inch their bums across the floor away from us. Rain has started falling in heavy, straight lines outside and the humidity has risen. Moisture fizzles on my forehead. Lightning and thunder break, one immediately after the other. Bright lights and drums.

'This is all very dramatic,' I say.

'It'll be fuckin' dramatic when I split yer fuckin' head open, eh?'

'He has spot here?' the girl asks me, still pointing at his crotch.

'That's what it looked like when I saw it dangling in the river earlier.'

'It was you naked in river.' She turns to face Ben. 'I hear from friend. She say dirty English man naked in river today. Was you?' She steps away and behind me. No more human shield. Shit.

'You're fuckin' dead, mate.' Ben takes a step forward.

'You dirty pig.' She runs past him, down the two steps that lead out of the bar and into the rain. She disappears in splashes of mud up the path.

'Well, you shouldn't go spreading that stuff about. It's not nice.' I wink at him and giggle some more.

He looks undecided for a minute and takes another half-step forward. I'm waiting for someone to talk some sense to me, but Old Me seems to be sleeping and Laura has decided to stay deceased for this one. The others must be happy to sit back and watch New Me be some sort of witty hard-man TV hero. Oh, the irony: when you stop caring about yourself you become brave.

Never mind that the others won't help. I'm an Action Man, all fuzzy hair and scars and real gripping hands, with no brain.

Ben's arm goes back and his fist is balled. I start moving my arm up but it doesn't want to move very fast. His fist is coming at me in a wide swing and I realise I should probably get out of the way, but nothing happens. My batteries must be on low. So I wait and my eyes close themselves. And I wait and I wait. I can't be that stoned. Time doesn't go that bendy, does it? Lightning flashes all pink through my closed eyelids. Thunder rumbles all around, shaking the wooden floor.

'Not here in my bar.'

I open my eyes to see who, what and why. The barman has his arm hooked over Ben's, holding it back. Ben is struggling to push him off, but the Indonesian is strong. His face is calm.

'Not in my bar.'

There is another long-haired Indonesian guy standing behind the first. He looks as if he is doing nothing more than waiting for a bus.

'OK. OK. Just let go.' Ben yanks his freed arm back. 'But this one here is fuckin' dead next time I see him.' He nods his head at me as he says this. My giggling has diminished into a smile. My eyes are jittering again and Ben is slightly out of focus.

'Please pay your bill and leave,' says the barman to Ben.

'I ain't payin'. Not if you're kicking me out. You should kick him out too.' His finger points at me. 'He started it.' The excuse of a small child. Ben's turned into a small child.

'No. You pay. You leave.' The barman turns and nods at me. 'This man helped Indah. She is my cousin.'

'Well, I ain't payin'.'

The barman steps between the two of us and faces Ben.

'You pay your bill, please.'

'No.' He steps back. 'I might come back here tonight and burn this fucking shithole.'

'Pay your bill, please.' Calm in the storm as lightning explodes over our heads.

'Fuck you.' Ben's arm is pulled back again and then swinging in its wide arc. The Indonesian doesn't move his feet, just leans back. The punch passes within an inch of his nose. He hasn't even blinked.

Ben still stands there, rebalancing his feet after a slight stumble at the punch attempt.

'People like you disappear around here,' the barman says calmly.

'Right. And places burn down.'

'People like you really disappear. One moment here, next day no sign.' They look at each other in silence for a second. 'Gone.' All the bar is watching. Lightning flashes and the sound of rain almost drowns out the thunder.

'Please pay.'

'Fuck you.' Ben turns, trips over the step from the bar as he leaves, lands in the mud, gets up and is gone down the path into the wall of rain, Sherman shirt instantly soaked. Applause from behind me.

'Thanks,' I say to the barman. I'm grateful but also disappointed I didn't get a beating. I wanted a beating.

'It's OK. He is an idiot.' he picks up my drink and hands it to me. 'We get many *bule* idiots here. I know where he stays. This place we are all close. Like family. You won't see him again. Now please go back and enjoy tonight with your friends.' With that, he and the other man, his silent partner, go back to the seats at the bar. The barman picks up the guitar by his chair and starts strumming. The other guy starts singing: 'No Woman, No Cry'.

I sit back in my corner, arms stretched along the rails, feet out in front of me.

'My hero,' says Kim.

The other three laugh.

'I need a joint after that,' says Julie.

'Yeah, that'd be nice,' I say and lean my head out into the rain. It wallops my face like a power shower. The jungle lights up every few seconds, green trees flashing on and off under lightning that scratches the length of the sky. On and off. On and off. A filling river gathering speed below. Water pouring down my face and through my hair. On. Off.

A feeling I achieved something. I meant something. I changed something. You just have to do it and it's done. It's changed.

A beating would have been nice though. Knocked Old Me out for good.

But I do feel different.
I feel new.
On. Off.
I feel stoned.

I look back at her as I go through the crowd of people. She is perched on a stool at the bar watching me, smiling. I smile back and knock into someone. I turn to apologise. A blank face looks back at me from under short-cropped hair and round head stuck on thick neck. I apologise again.

'Wanker,' *it says.*

'Sorry,' *I again say and turn sideways to slide through the gap between him and his friend.*

I keep going; the urge to pee is suddenly stronger. I make my way through the packed pub like a timid pinball trying not to bounce off anything. I push my way into the toilets and queue while the smell stings my nose and men talk in swearing sentences about women and cunts and football. Finally I arrive at a slowly emptying bowl of urine.

'There's that twat who knocked your beer.'

I carry on peeing, pretending I'm not me. The man to my right has finished and leaves. Then the blank face is there, next to me. I cut my pee short and zip up. Which is just as well as the blocked urinal is close to brimming over. As I turn, Blank's friend is waiting behind me. He knocks into my shoulder as I sidle past.

'Later,' *he says.*

I leave the toilets to laughter. My face is hot and my legs weak.

The crowd blurs past my watering eyes as I slalom my way back to Laura.

'What's the matter?' *she asks, throwing an arm over my shoulder.*

'Idiots in the toilets. I think we should go.'

My heart pounds and I'm angry at the way my body is reacting to aggression. I'm scared. I don't want to be, but I am. I can't stop it, the fear spills into my blood like an oil slick. It pollutes every vein, artery and vessel.

'Do you want to go?' *She holds my face and kisses me.*

'No. Yes. Do you mind?'

'Come on. Let's go. This place is terrible anyway.'

Someone knocks into my shoulder and I stumble against Laura.

'Sorry,' says a voice in mocking high pitch.

There he is. I feel looseness in my bowels and legs. Why am I reacting like this? Strength should be filling my muscles, not leaving them.

'Come on.' Laura is off the stool and hooking her arm through mine. 'Let's go.'

The blank-faced man is pushing up against me so that my body has Laura pinned to the bar.

'Nice girlfriend,' he says. 'Can I have a go? Then I'll let you leave.'

My throat seizes shut and my brain is incapable of creating a plan. Somewhere in a recess I will myself to deal with this. Nothing comes. I manage to open my mouth, but that is all.

'What's your problem?' Laura asks him, calm as a pond on a white-hot day.

'Your boyfriend knocked my beer. He owes me a pint. Or something else.' He winks at Laura, turns to his friend and laughs like a seagull.

'You sad little cliché of a man,' says Laura.

I almost smile at her balls, but instead grimace at the thought of where this might lead. 'I'll get you a drink if it'll make you not be such a twat.'

It should be me making snappy comments, dealing with the situation. I'm struck dumb and useless like a garden gnome. Instead of being an Alpha I'm nowhere to be found in the Greek hierarchical alphabet of male. I'm less than Zeta. I reach in my pocket and manage to hand money to Laura.

'I'll pay for it,' I croak.

My vision has become tunnelled as I focus on Laura asking and paying for a drink. My mind is cutting out Blank Face and friend. Thumping blood in my ears deafens me to words around me. Laura leaves the drink on the bar and pushes me forward, more knocking shoulders, seagull laughter, masses of people to get through. Finally out into the cold night air and two pairs of feet clipping along the road while traffic speeds around beside us. No talk. My eyes water in the winter air. Steam plumes from my mouth like a speeding locomotive.

'Useless. Fucking useless.' At last my mouth thaws. 'I should have refused. I should have stood up for you.'

I stop. Laura walks on a few steps then turns back to me.

'You are you, and that is why I love you. I don't want a man who can stand for himself in a fight. I want a man who knows all the little things that make me happy. And you know those things.'

'But you were calm. You handled it.' My hands run through my hair. 'I nearly pissed myself, for god's sake.'

She puts her arms around my waist. I pull them off.

'But I want to be able to deal with shit like that.' I think I'm going to cry. 'I wimp out. I can't even function. Fuck.'

I'm walking in a circle around the pavement. Car lights shoot back and forth beside us. The sound of engines and wheels on tarmac are like thunder.

'And that's not your fault. It's human. You couldn't help it. Your body shut down. Just instinct is all it is.'

She takes me by the arm and leads us back home. Every step brings to mind a different possible solution to what has happened, a different possible outcome; a punch here, an elbow there, a man standing next to his beautiful girlfriend being applauded, a head smashed into a urinal, a knee to a groin followed by a clever one-liner. But I am not a movie script, I am not a hero, I am me. I cannot cope with Alpha males. I cannot think quickly enough to deal with an immediate problem. I have a safety cut-out and a spine made of ice cream. I am Ice-Cream Boy. I am soft and soggy and that night I cannot make love, no matter what words, what affection, what tenderness comes from her body. It doesn't matter to her. I know. She loves me. I am sure. But I want to be more for her. She deserves so much more.

VICTIMS OF ECONOMY

'**O**ur sister was raped.'

I take a mouthful of juice and swill it around my teeth. I look from Fitri to Benny, who is chasing an ice cube around the bottom of his glass with a straw.

'That is why she is not here,' says Fitri.

I swallow my juice but my mouth still feels dry.

'Where is she?' I ask.

'In Singapore. With my mother.'

The silence is uncomfortable, at least for me. Benny has upended his glass over his mouth, and after a stubborn moment of hanging on, the ice drops. Fitri sips on her nearly full glass.

'I like mango juice,' she says.

'Me too,' I say.

'That is why we hate Indonesians. Because of what happened.'

'Why do you stay here?' I ask.

'My father has good business here, he says. He cannot have business the same in other countries.'

I can feel the floor through the beanbag; it's hard on my bottom. I wiggle and try to think of a way to lighten the moment.

'But rape isn't bad compared to other things that happened.' Fitri examines her juice. 'They used things on my friend's sister.'

'Perhaps we shouldn't talk about this now, Fitri.' I look to Benny, who is now crunching his ice.

'They put things in her.'

Fitri: fifteen, a child, still wearing her school uniform, knowing such things. I want a cigarette.

'Fitri.' Her father stands at the door. 'This is not conversation for an English lesson. Come, the lesson is over today. Children, let's go for noodles.'

I am relieved but also disappointed. Fitri needs to talk to someone. I stand and say goodbye to the kids.

'No. You come too. Meet in front. I will bring the car around.' Charles walks off around the pool with his head down.

'Cool,' says Benny, 'I'm hungry.'

'You greedy monkey. This is two dinners tonight.' Fitri stands and comes to my side. She looks at my face and smiles.

'Do not be afraid. They are good noodles where we go. My father is not angry with you.'

'I'm not…I'm not afraid,' I say, but she and Benny are leaving the games room ahead of me. I wonder how she sees I am afraid before I realise I am. There is something blunt and angry about Charles today. He must be wondering why Fitri is talking to me about her sister and rape.

I follow them to the waiting car, where Charles sits behind the wheel, cigarette hanging from his lips, squinting through the smoke straight out the windscreen. Benny climbs in beside him. Fitri and I get in the back. We all sit in silence as the gates are opened by security who check the road first, guns over their shoulders, then nod for us to drive out. It is a silent drive. Ten minutes later we pull up in a restaurant car-park under a flashing neon noodle sign.

Inside are bright white lights and white tables with red napkins and chopsticks laid out. Charles orders wine and two cokes. We order dishes. I'm not sure what I've ordered, but it looks like something with thick noodles and vegetables.

We eat. Charles says nothing. I talk to the kids about school. They ask me if I know anyone famous. Have I met Boyzone? Who is my favourite actor? James Stewart, who is that? What is my favourite film? Did I like *The Matrix*?

Charles just eats. He slurps as he sucks noodles between his teeth. He looks down at the table the whole time, taking occasional sips from the red wine.

My noodles are good; the vegetables are crisp and it's all easy to pick up with chopsticks. The wine is excellent. It coats the inside of my mouth.

We finish. Benny burps. Fitri punches his arm. I look at Charles. He is looking at the menu, but his eyes aren't moving.

'You two have ice cream,' he says to the children. 'Order what you want. Your teacher and I are going outside for a cigarette.' He dabs his mouth and stands. I do the same.

I'm trying to think if I've done wrong. I follow him out to the car park. We stand under the neon sign. It's a gentle heat tonight. Above the stars are clear and the moon is full. It reminds me of summer evenings back home, lying on the beach watching for shooting stars. The two of us lying with our arms around each other.

I offer Charles one of my Marlboros.

'Thank you,' he says.

He flicks his Zippo and lights both of our cigarettes. I smell the lighter fluid in the still air. Cars go past on the road at few-second intervals.

'My wife was also raped.' He draws long and hard on his cigarette and blows the smoke up to the night sky.

'Oh.' Oh? Is that all I can manage?

'It is alright. You do not have to say anything. I am telling you because you should know, so that when you return to your small little country that thinks it knows so much about everything, you can tell your friends about me. About the unsavoury Chinese club owner whose wife and daughter were raped by a gang of Indonesians who needed to take their anger out on someone.' He nods his head and then shakes it while he kicks little stones across the car park. 'It is the same everywhere, I know; the minority gets blamed and punished for anything the majority cannot accept as their problems.'

'I'm sorry.'

'I am sorry for you too. You have lost. I can see it.'

Charles half-turns his head towards me.

I look at my feet, nibble my bottom lip, swallow.

'I do not want to know, but if you need help, please ask me.'

'Thanks. I'm OK. Really.' I am now drawing a line in the broken asphalt with my toes.

'Yes. Yes. Of course you are.'

There is a silence. I count four cars go past. A mosquito buzzes by my ear and I flick my hand at it.

'Is that why your wife isn't here?' I ask, feeling he wants more conversation.

He grunts and nods.

'She blames me. They were taken from a taxi on the way to the airport. We could see it coming, the riots and troubles. I had to stay, but she says I should have driven her. I should have protected her.'

I look in through the restaurant window and see Fitri playing peanut wars with Benny.

'She is right. I stayed to protect my money. My fucking money.'

'I'm sure she'll come—'

'No. She won't. Never. And not my daughter, too. Never. Fitri and Benny don't know what happened to my wife. They only know about Juni. My wife is too ashamed to talk of it and to talk to me.'

'Where were Fitri and Benny when all this happened?' I ask.

'I had already sent them to their cousins in Singapore. Juni and my wife, Su-Chin, stayed here to convince me to go.'

We both flick our cigarettes across the car park. They bounce and spark across the gravel.

'And you really never heard about these riots in England?'

'Really, no.'

He shakes his head.

'I'm sorry.' I don't know if I'm apologising for the British media or expressing regret for Charles.

'Well. When you go home to England you tell your friends, and I hope they will be interested and see how easy their lives are.'

Five minutes' interest maybe, then the conversation will return to unimportant crap.

'Why do you stay here? Why not go and join your wife in Singapore?' I ask.

'She won't have me back. My business is here. I was born here. Fitri and Benny were born here. Singapore would be a strange place for us, and'—he looks sideways at me and laughs—'my money is here. My clubs make me a lot of money. My fucking money.' He shakes his head once more and lets out a long sigh.

I wonder which clubs he owns and whether he supplies the waiters with the drugs they sell. I think I know the answer.

'I will get the kids and pay. Thank you for the cigarette.' He turns and goes back into the restaurant. I look to the stars. So calm and quiet up there.

We sit with our own thoughts in the car. The stereo plays quietly, a slow Chinese song sung by a mournful-sounding woman with piano for accompaniment. We are driving back through the city so Charles can drop me at my house. I look from the window and see single women standing along the side of the road, smiling and putting one leg forward as we pass, a little calf showing.

'Pretty ladies,' I say.

Fitri laughs in the back. I turn and raise an eyebrow at her.

'They are not ladies,' she says.

'You're joking?' I look back out of the window. One blows a kiss as we pass. Very pretty and very skinny.

'She isn't joking,' says Charles. 'This is Jalan Iskandar Muda. It is full of ladyboy prostitutes. They are very pretty sometimes, but not for me—but perhaps for you? You want me to stop?'

'No. No. Not for me either.'

He looks at me.

'You are sure, because if you want—' Charles is smiling. It is nice to see. There is warmth to it.

'No. Really. Thank you.'

At the end of the street we come to some traffic lights. A woman sits in the middle of the road holding a baby wrapped in a sarong. Her eyes are dark and cheeks hollow. The baby sleeps. The woman looks up at Charles and holds her hand out, but she doesn't stand up. Charles reaches into his glove box and comes out with some notes.

Lowering his window he shakes the money at the woman. She stands and takes it from him. She nods her head and mutters, then returns to her place sitting against the traffic-light pole. The lights change and we pull off.

'That was generous of you. I thought you didn't like Indonesians.'

'How can I not like Indonesians when I am Chinese-Indonesian and this is my country? She did nothing bad to me. When I say I hate Indonesians, I do not mean it, or I try not to mean it. How can we hate an entire people just because of the actions of a few?' He shakes his head. 'I hate the few, but the few exist everywhere, no matter what their skin or nationality or religion. She is just a woman who is worse off than me.'

I look at Charles, deep-lined eyes staring at the road ahead. He has two children in the back who I can't help but like. Charles might possibly be a criminal, but I like him too.

'Pak Andy seems to think all beggars should find a job,' I say.

'Pak Andy is a pathetic little man with no business sense and no—no, character. He is a mouse.'

'I thought you were friends. That's why I'm teaching your kids.'

'No. He is repaying a debt. He is terrible at business and terrible at gambling.'

We arrive at my house and he puts the car in neutral.

'Thanks,' I say.

'Thank you. In a few weeks I am opening a new club. I want you to come to the blessing.'

'Blessing?'

'It is tradition for new businesses to be blessed by a *dukun*, to bring good luck.'

'Do-can?' I ask.

'Du-kun. *Dukun*. He is like an Indonesian medicine man, a witch doctor. He has blessed all my business premises and all are prosperous.'

'I didn't expect you to be superstitious.'

'I believe in nothing, but I am open to anything.' He stares at me again, thoughts forming behind his eyes. 'Perhaps it helps me, perhaps it doesn't, but I think you should meet him. He might help you.'

I'm not sure why a witch doctor would help me or why Charles thinks I need help, but for some reason I say, 'OK.'

'Good. Good night. Say good night, children.'

'Good night. Sweet dreams of ladyboys,' giggles Fitri.

'Watch it, Missy. Good night.' I slam the door shut and Charles is already pulling away before I have a chance to wave. I stand in the road and look to the stars again. So many shining away up there, some twinkling and others still. Are twinkling ones the planets and the others suns, or is it the other way around? I can't remember. There are also constellations I've not seen before. I never thought about the sky being different here. I should start a list: Things I Never Considered in the World. I feel my mind is breaking out of some sort of prison and seeing a new freedom it never knew existed. Everything around me is still. Even the cicadas are silent.

How can a *dukun* help me?

—*Perhaps he'll get rid of me.*

—*I thought I'd already got rid of you.*

—*You can try, baby. You can try.*

I make a noise like the screeching monkey from my balcony and go inside where Kim is staring, eyes half-closed and reddened, at the TV. He holds a joint up above his head. I take it and flop into the armchair. I smoke and don't bother passing it back. Kim is already riding the rides in the amusement park of his mind. I climb on mine along with rapists, gangsters and *dukuns*. When my dead girlfriend makes an appearance I shake her away. I picture what the *dukun* might look like to keep her out of my head: bones through the nose, rings around a lengthened neck, or a painted face. And I ask him, however he looks, 'Answer me this: how are you going to help me, Mr Dukun, or is it Dokan, or Kando? Kando. Good one. Hehe. Why they call you Kando?'

'Because I Can Do.'

'Ha, ha. Let's see if you really can, Mr Can-do *dukun*.'

BIRTHDAY PARTY

I wake up and it's there. It's in my head like a lump of lead, heavy and grey and poisonous, put in there for when I stir from sleep so I can't miss it: Laura's birthday. Old Me's already yanking the reins. I might as well let him. Laura's beside him, waiting to celebrate an ageless year. No fighting it today. No escaping or removing it or pushing it away by acting *new*. He's got me.

Not that he's really left me alone anyway; I've felt him moving around down there, pushing against my ribs. I've managed to subdue him of late, to knock him down before he's had a chance to stand up. I know he doesn't like his replacement, even though his replacement isn't fully formed yet. It's just a foetus waiting for the final touches to its features. Perhaps I'll give final complete birth to him after today. Then he can rampage without boundaries.

In the meantime, take it away, Old Me. Do your worst, just for old times' sake. I hand my body over to him and he picks it up, gets it out of bed and manages to do all the normal morning ablutions and eating and getting to work without incident.

Well done.

At work I work. In class, Johnny tries to broach sex positions, but I steer the class onto Chapter 6 – If I Had a Million Dollars. I think they can sense I'm not myself. If only they knew it's actually more a case of being myself, my old self; Old Me is settled back into the routine of being quiet and morose and is about to let Laura step forward any moment, to let her out. I can sense it. I know him so well.

Another class follows. Writing exercises. I sit at my desk and stare at my sandaled feet.

—*You don't have to do this just for me, you know.* Here she is.

—*I know, but today is just a glitch on my road to recovery.*

—*Wallow in my memory one last time?*

—*If you left me alone, that's exactly what I would be doing: one last time. I'd appreciate it if you both leave me be after this.*

—*I'll try, but I can't speak for him.*

—*That's a shame. Anyway, happy birthday.*

—*Thanks.*

—*You know I don't want to be a shit to you.*

—*I know.*

She sits on my lap and puts her arms around my neck. Her cheek touches mine.

—*I could stay like this forever,* I say.

—*So do it.*

—*Yeah. Right.*

—*You haven't said you love me for a long time.*

—*You're dead. Perhaps that's a reason.*

—*It is my birthday.*

—*You know I love you. I always love you. I love you.*

—*I love you too.*

Over Laura's shoulder a student has his hand up.

'Yes, Hendra.'

Laura nuzzles my neck, slides off my lap and leaves the class. I sniff and blink and clear my vision and go to Hendra. Once I've answered his question I move around the class, pretending to check the students' work.

I finish at nine, don't go into the staff room and instead walk out of the school. Outside Iqpal is sweeping the dry and dusty driveway.

'You not wait for car?' he asks, leaning on his broom.

'Not tonight. Tell the others I've gone, please.'

'I will. Take care, my friend.'

I smile at him. He knows I'm somewhere else. Something must be written in international language in the lines and grooves of my face. I flag down a motorbike *becak*.

'Where go, Mister?' asks the rider. He has a little leather cap on his head.

Where do I want to go? I should celebrate Laura's birthday somewhere.

—*Music?* I ask, climbing in the *becak* as she squeezes in beside me.

—*Yes. And a bar we can prop up.*

I tell the driver a hotel bar I've heard Jussy mention; small and with live music. He pulls off without checking behind. The night feels cooler as it rushes by. Two-stroke fumes are heavy in the air as usual. Cars and other *becaks* beep me and I hear the occasional 'Hey, *bule*,' as we zigzag through the traffic. The city is still busy.

'I very happy have you in my motorbike,' shouts the driver over the sound of his coughing exhaust. 'I like *bule*.'

'Good. Thank you,' I shout back. I feel like an adult in a pedal-car. My knees knock against the front rail and I have to keep my neck bent as the canopy is low. The driver sees my discomfort and pushes the canopy back. I can now sit straight. Laura rests her head on my shoulder.

'*Bule* very big. Indonesian very small,' he shouts and then laughs.

I push a smile onto my mouth. The fumes and breeze are making my eyes water. It somehow feels suitable. By the time we pull up outside the hotel bar I have to wipe moisture from my cheeks. I thank him and pay.

The hotel bar is plusher than others I've seen here, with chrome and glass tables and hidden lights shining up the walls. Girls sit alone or in groups on high chairs along one mirrored side. I know why Jussy likes this place.

—*Oh. Prostitutes,* says Laura.

—*Do you want to go somewhere else?*

—*No. It's got character.*

I go to the bar and pull out a high stool from under it. The barman says hi and smiles.

'Two double whiskies, please,' I say.

He puts them on the bar in front of me.

Two? I've gone completely mad.

—*Just drink them, numbnuts. No one's going to notice.*

I pour one glass into the other. The barman watches and I make a crazy finger swirl movement at my temple. He smiles and goes to serve a group of suited men at the other end of the bar.

—*Where's the live music?* she asks.

I look around. There's an empty stage, a few people dotted around, mostly men at tables chatting with pretty girls. The girls aren't particularly dressed up, most just wearing jeans and T-shirts, more modestly dressed than the girls in the discos.

—*I guess it's the wrong day of the week. It is a Monday,* I answer.

I put both hands around my whisky glass and slosh the large shot around.

—*Go on, have some for me.*

—*For you.*

I let it lie on my tongue for a couple of seconds then swill it around my mouth and swallow.

—*Good?* she asks.

—*Not as good as the stuff you used to buy.*

What am I doing? She's not here. I am going mad; having little conversations in my head all the time with a figment of the memory of a dead person.

—*But what if I'm not a figment?* she says. *I'm dead, alright. You've accepted that now, I know. But I mean what if I am here sitting next to you and you talk to me because you know I might be here and we're having some sort of psychic dead-to-live chat? Imagine if you ignored me and I really was here, trying to communicate with you. I'd be really pissed off.*

—*Not likely, though, is it?*

—*Not likely. No. But let me be here today. Give me that much on my birthday. Please.*

I finish the whisky without swilling; straight down with a touch of after-burn.

'Alright. Alright,' I say.

The barman looks at me.

—*Not out loud, numbnuts. Keep it all in your head, otherwise I'm going to get embarrassed and leave.*

I laugh.

—*Watch it. He'll kick you out if you get any more loopy.*

I turn the laugh into a cough and rub my head. I blow out a long breath, point at my glass and hold two fingers up at the barman. He tops us up.

—*Just today. Because I miss you. Because I fucking miss you.*

The glass blurs in front of me. I put my head on my arms on the bar.

—*Don't cry here, baby. Not now.*

She puts her arms around my neck and rests her head against mine. I can almost feel her breath in my hair.

—*Not now. Not now,* she whispers.

—*I miss you.*

'I miss you,' I sob into my arm, 'I miss you so bloody much.' The last words come out as gasps between sobs. They come out loud and into the room and I don't notice or don't care. My hands crawl over the back of my head looking for hers, but they fall through air into my hair. All I can do is pull at it, pull, pull.

Then a hand is on top of mine, warm and familiar. My other hand goes onto the top of it without looking up.

'Shhh. Do not cry.' A real voice. A living voice. Low and soft.

I look over my arm hoping for the impossible, but know it won't be.

'What is wrong?' asks Eka. 'Why cry?'

I slide my hands away from hers and sit up, wiping my eyes on my palms.

'Here.' She hands me a napkin and points to my nose. I wipe it and blow.

'Sorry. I'm sorry,' I say.

'*Tidak apa-apa*. No problem.'

She is as beautiful as the first time I saw her. Dark Indian skin and large dark eyes, bar lights reflecting in them. They're alive. Her hair falls thick over her shoulders and down her back. Laura is sitting silently, watching. Maybe.

The barman says something in Indonesian to Eka and she says something back and waves her hand at him. He moves away.

'What is wrong, crazy English man?' Eka pushes the whisky towards me. I take it and drink just a mouthful. It burns the inside of my cheeks.

—*Go on, tell her,* says Laura from the next stool, legs crossed, foot bobbing, *I dare you.*

I shake my head.

—*You're not here. You're not here, no matter how hard I try to make you here, you're not here.*

—*Are you sure? How can you be sure?*

—*I can't, but—*

'My girlfriend died a few months ago. I have trouble forgetting her,' I say.

—*Ah, so that's how it is then. Rather be with a pro than with your super-dead girlfriend. Nice. I'll be off now. See you later. Thanks for the birthday drink, numbnuts.*

I take a deep breath, swallow, widen my eyes and blink. Guilt crashes into my gut like a brick.

'I talk to her sometimes,' I say, 'but I don't think she's really listening. She says she is, but I don't think she is.'

—*Oh yes, I am. And watching everything you do.*

—*I thought you were going?*

—*Haven't made up my mind yet.*

'You are sad man. Crazy sad man. How do you know she not listens? Spirits are very clever.'

—*This girl's not as dumb as she looks.*

If I could give Laura an icy stare, I would.

Eka pulls a stool out and sits next to me, legs crossed. There is a little skin showing between the bottom of her jeans and the top of her shoes.

'I don't know. I just think that it isn't possible.'

'Many strange things possible in the world. Many many. Perhaps you should believe she there.'

—*Go on. Believe.*

'I'm going crazy believing that. Talking out loud all the time. Wanting to touch her, to feel her and not being able to. It's better I don't believe. I'm trying to get away from her. To forget her.'

—*Forget me? Huh.*

—*God. Shut up.*

'So if you don't want her spirit here, you must be strong. You must have new life.' She prods my arm on the last two words.

'Ha.'

'What funny?'

'That's exactly why I came to this country. For a new life, a new me. A New Me.' I finish my whisky and ask for the same again. 'For you?'

—*Yes, please.*

'Maybe I try this too.' She sniffs my glass, looking at me over its rim. 'Whisky?'

'Yes.'

—*Oh, don't give her my drink.*

'Please.'

I order the same for Eka.

—*Numbnuts.*

—*You still here?*

'I didn't expect to see you here,' I say, hoping Laura will take the hint.

'Sometimes here.'

'To meet men?'

She laughs.

'Yes. To meet men for money. I am bad girl.'

—*Ooooh. Slapperrrr.*

'And you told me you weren't a prostitute.'

'No, not prostitute. I just take money from men. I am beautiful, so I can.'

—*A pro, and modest with it. Charming.*

Eka sips her drink and grimaces. 'I never sleep with them first time.'

'Second?' I ask.

'Sometimes. If I like. But not for you tonight. I think you need talk tonight. You not need sex.'

I don't disagree. And nor does Laura.

'It's her...it would have been her birthday today. I haven't thought of her much for a few days, well, not that I've noticed, and then I wake this morning and the first thought: it's Laura's birthday. My day ruined.' I finish the drink. I'm not feeling drunk yet.

'Poor Mr Crazy.' Eka runs her fingers down my cheek. I jump. 'I'm sure she is happy you remember. I'm sure she miss you. Please give me cigarette.'

We smoke in silence. I can sense Laura brooding nearby. More whiskies are poured.

'You must live your life. You cannot stay in past. She understand.' She stubs her cigarette out.

—*I bloody don't.*

'That's what I'm trying to do,' I say. 'But there's a big part of me just wants to think about her and live in the past. I just wish I could go back, change something. Stop her, so she misses the bus.'

'Bus?'

—*I don't want to hear this sob story. I'm off now. Don't you dare forget the slice-of-cake rule. And if you do, don't catch anything.*

I shake my head.

'She died in an accident. She'd just got off a bus.' The words are foreign and uncomfortable as they come from my mouth.

'Do not think of past. Perhaps she will be reborn and when you are reborn perhaps you will be together again.'

'Rebirth? You believe in that?'

'Yes. I am Hindu. My ancestors came from India many years ago.' She runs her fingers through her hair, it falls through her fingertips like silk. I want to feel it too. The thought surprises me.

—*Men,* comes a voice from somewhere in the back of my skull, *you can't help thinking about nooky, can you?*

—*You're still eavesdropping, then?*

No answer.

'You talk to her again?'

'No. Yes, a little.'

'You want I go? Leave you two alone, crazy man?' She has an eyebrow raised and her full lips smile.

'No. Actually I don't. I think she may have already left. Jealousy's got the better of her.' I raise my glass and knock it against hers.

'Cheers. Here's to strange coincidences.' I down the glass again and finally my head spins.

'What is coinci… coinc…?'

'Coincidences. It means very lucky to meet you here tonight.'

'I am happy meet you. But no pom-pom tonight.'

'Sorry? Pom-pom?'

'Sex. No sex.'

'Good. I don't think my girlfriend would like it.' Good joke. I break into a mad and slightly high-pitched giggle which feels like it might become tears so I stop. Eka looks at me while I do it, but makes no comment or facial movement.

'But we go to hotel and we sleep together, yes?' One eyebrow raised.

—*What do you think?* I ask Laura, knowing full well she's still loitering.

—*Really? You want my opinion about her?*

—*Yes.*

—*Honestly and jealousy aside, I think you need solid company and whatever I may be, I can't give you that. So go on if you really must, but no pom-pom.*

—*No pom-pom.*

'What says your girlfriend,' asks Eka, looking at me from under a length of hair she is twirling between her fingers.

'Yes. She says yes.'

—*But no pom-pom.*

'But no pom-pom.'

—*Now I'm really gone. Defo. Just 'cos I want you to get a cuddle doesn't mean I want to see it. Slice-of-cake rule; no eating, remember. So behave, Ice-Cream Boy.*

—*I will.*

'Good. One more whisky.' Eka waves her empty glass under my nose.

We drink another whisky. She takes me to a cheap hotel in a back street somewhere. The guy who works at the desk calls her by her name. We go to a room. We climb into bed. She takes my clothes off. She massages me. She walks the length of my spine in bare feet.

Bones crack. With each crack tension dies. Thoughts are squashed. She takes her clothes off. I press my body close against hers. We kiss. We hold each other. We sleep together, me in her arms, my head on her breast, a landscape of beautiful skin stretched out under me, dark and smooth. She strokes my hair. I try to stay awake to take her in, but I can't. I sleep. No pom-pom.

I laugh at her and then my mind asks why she is telling such a joke; it's not funny, so why would she say such a thing.

So I ask, 'What?' and laugh again, once.

'It happened in Pilsen. The bus stopped for a break. They think she looked the wrong way.'

She is calm. How can she be if it's true?

'She looked the wrong way and then crossed.' And her voice breaks up and there is sobbing and apologising and then, 'She looked the wrong way and...'

I want her off the phone. I want it back in its cradle and I want to go back to my book and I want to return to the story and I want her off the phone so Laura can call and tell me it's a mistake because it isn't her. Of course it isn't her.

Suddenly Jane's voice is calm again.

'Are you alone?' she asks.

'Yes.'

'Can you call someone? Don't be alone. Call someone.'

'I will.' Get off the phone. Laura is trying to get through.

'OK. You will call someone? Get someone there?'

'Yes.' The phone is shaking against my ear.

'We'll call you tomorrow. I'm sorry. She looked the wrong way.'

Something is going out of my body. I can feel it leaving me. Something is leaving me.

'Take care. Don't be alone. I'm sorry.' Jane hangs up and the phone rattles against the side of my head. I put it back in its cradle and it lies peacefully, as if it never said a word.

I sit on the arm of the chair and look at my book lying face down and splayed on the seat. I'll read until Laura phones. I know she'll phone and then I can phone her mum back and tell her the mistake.

I pick the book up and my eyes scan the mass of letters on the page and they roll and move and nearly form words but then fall apart again and I can't find a sentence to start so I pick the phone up and dial and it rings and my mother answers and she is sleepy and I ask her to come and she asks what's wrong and I say Laura and she looked the wrong way and then she says my god and I'll be there soon and I put the phone back and it is still and silent again and the silence rings in my ears and something is coming up my throat and up under my skin and I don't want it to come but it has to and it pushes up beneath my face and is trapped for a second under my eyes and what is in my throat comes out of my mouth and it is dark and black and piercing and full of guilt and my soul is trying to escape and be away from this and what is under my eyes also bursts out and it is acid that burns and the cry I make has no sound but it is deafening and I am curled up on the floor and my legs writhe and my hands pull at my face and hair and still this monster flows from my mouth like bile and finally it stops and there is knocking on the door and I am not alone and my mother holds me and holds me and holds me but I am empty and she is grasping a husk.

'Come and lie on the bed and sleep,' she says, and I follow and she cradles me from behind and every time I close my eyes I see Laura look the wrong way and step out and I see her see her mistake and turn too slowly as a car hits her but it is wrong and then I picture it again and this time it's a truck and the next it's a bus and the next it's a car and each time it can't be right because it can't happen and I can't imagine Laura not being.

Laura is always.

Laura is always and she will call and I get off the bed and go back to the phone and pick it up and listen for her voice but all I hear is the long long tone and I replace the phone and check it's in its cradle and I pick it up and I hear the tone humming at me, and it hums and it hums and it hums.

POM-POM

I watch a cockroach crawling up the cracked wall, its feelers wobbling in their search for whatever it's searching for. It's a big bugger, nearly three inches long, but most of them are big buggers. I'm getting used to them, in toilets, kitchens, sometimes beds.

I can smell the mattress under me; old sweat from a thousand bodies and something musky. I can also smell Eka's sweet perfume. She lies with her back to me, curved vertebrae showing through brown skin dappled by early morning light, but her hand is in my hand. I think I should feel guilty, but nothing has happened between us and I have no one left to feel guilty towards. But it doesn't change the fact that I think I should feel guilty, even though I don't. I try to pull my hand free, but hers squeezes tighter over mine.

'Stay, Mr Crazy. You must tell me how you feel.' She rolls over to face me and now holds my hand with both of hers. Her breast feels heavy against my arm 'You feel OK?'

She is more beautiful in daylight. Her eyes look almost too large for her face and are such a dark brown that the pupils nearly blend into the irises. Although her thick black eyebrows are raised in question, there is a slight mocking to her expression.

'I am OK. I think.' I take a second to check. I do feel OK. The spine-cracking has left me feeling loose. The cuddling and holding has left me feeling calm. The weighty breast on my arm is making me feel horny.

The conversations with Laura seem misty and distant now. In today's light, sneaking in low through a crack in the faded, stained curtains, I know I didn't talk to her. How could I? Old Me must be smiling at yesterday's emotional joyride.

Well that's it. Now shut up and stay quiet and keep all that emotional claptrap rubbish with you. No more tears. No more supernatural chats. She looked the wrong way; she's dead. Now I'm getting on.

'Look better.' She is up on her elbows looking down at me, holding my hand beneath her chin. Her breast is now resting against my side. 'Your face not so...' and she scrunches her face up.

'I feel better. A new day today.' Corny but true.

'Now want pom-pom. You? Pom-pom?'

I raise my head and kiss her. Her lips are soft and moist and her tongue pushes into my mouth. My arms go around her back and she climbs on top of me and her breasts squash against my chest. And New Me slips into her and Old Me whisper-shouts 'Laura' somewhere, but New Me drowns him out by pushing his face into Eka's hair and the exotic smells within and his hands feel the silkiness of her skin and his eyes take in the mouth-watering colour of her, and Old Me is buried beneath the lust and the moment and the desperation of moving on.

We both lie there afterwards, smoking the clichéd après-sex cigarettes; a pretty damn good post-coital habit if ever there was one. I watch the smoke rise towards a crack in the ceiling. A sliver of sunlight shines through the smoke, creating a cheap laser-show effect.

I suppose I should get to work. I sigh a long breath of smoke out.

'I should get to work,' I say.

'Yes. Be happy man at work. Think of Eka, not dead girl.'

I think dead girl plagued my dreams in the night, but I'm not sure. She certainly hasn't plagued my mind since. For a fleeting moment I want to apologise to Laura for treating her so badly on her birthday, but I knock the idea away with a backward head-butt onto the pillow.

'*Ada apa*?' asks Eka, leaning across me and stubbing her cigarette out in the ashtray on the side table. She lies back down.

'Nothing. *Tidak apa-apa*.' I roll on my side so we are facing each other. '*Terima kasih*.'

'Why thank me? I like.'

'For last night. For helping. Maybe I'd be lying drunk in a gutter somewhere now if you hadn't been there.'

'I do not understand all you say.' She rubs her nose against mine. 'But I happy I help.'

'I must go.'

I give her a kiss and go the bathroom. The floor feels gritty beneath my feet so I go up on my toes. The bathroom is a traditional Indonesian *mandi*: a sort of stand-up bath next to a squat toilet. I go higher on my toes, use the squat from a standing position, then get in the *mandi* and throw scoops of cold water from a big bucket over my body. Two cockroaches the length of my index finger watch from the corner, feelers wobbling. I come out and dry myself with a towel the size of a flannel and the thickness of a hanky and I feel dirtier than before I washed.

Eka is already dressed. I'm disappointed.

'We take taxi? Your work and me my house?' she asks.

'Yes. OK.' I pull on my trousers and the rest of my clothes. I wonder if she's going to ask for money.

'You want see me again?' she asks. She climbs behind me on the bed and throws her arms around me while I try to pull on my sandals.

'Yes.' I do. I want her company. I want to look at her more. I want sex. I want more cheap dirty hotels and more spine walking. I want the life of a man who doesn't care what others think. I want to go off the British Standard Kitemark rails that I've had under me for most of my life. I want to freewheel and not worry about things getting in my way. She'll help in sending New Me in any direction he wants to take and she'll help stamp on any unwanted visitors who may turn up.

'*Bagus*. You find me on Friday night in Iguana Club.'

'I will.' I turn to kiss her but she is up and off the bed and opening the door.

'You work now. Come, Crazy.'

I'm tired.

All these moments, all these times. I'm tired. I'll sleep in this warm place. The beat of his heart is strong and calm. Sleep. For a while. Curl up with Laura down here. Hold all of her in my arms and in my mind. Sleep with her. Comfort her for the pain she feels while he finds comfort in another. While he tries to push her aside, ignore her and attempt to vainly move on from love. Console her while she has to watch him lose himself in the flesh of another. She has to bear the jealousy and the inevitability of his life without her. We will sleep together, with our moments. Close our eyes. Dreamless sleep. Long, peaceful, dark sleep.

WALNUT

The new club is right next door to Iguana. We stand there looking at it, nodding at the appearance of this new neon-signed place. The sun drizzles its heat over us. Charles is in a dark suit with a dark tie shot through with bright red swirls. His hair is slicked back. Sunglasses hide his personality. On the other side of him is a short old man whose face is made up of wrinkles joined together by peaks of leathery flesh. He reminds me of a walnut. One of his eyes is misted over milky white. He is wearing a plain brown short-sleeved shirt over a beige-and-black sarong which hangs just above sandaled leather feet. His toes are adorned with long, dirt-encrusted toenails. Over his shoulder hangs a multicoloured woven bag. I'm guessing he's the *dukun*. There is also a group of men in business suits and sunglasses behind us. Beautiful girls in short skirts and T-shirts with the name of the club on them mingle and walk up and down the street, handing out flyers and free packets of Davidoff cigarettes.

We are standing, looking up at the sign which slants up the side of the doorway, flashing its name in red, white and blue:

MEMPHIS.

'Elvis. My tribute,' says Charles to no one and everyone.

One of the suited men pats him on the back and says something in Chinese. They shake hands and Charles invites everyone to follow him into the club, which we do. The girls in short skirts are left outside to carry on promoting the chic of lung cancer and the promises of the club.

Two of Charles' armed guards from the house are acting as bouncers and push open the double doors. We gather in a small entrance foyer and Charles holds his hand up, signalling for us to wait. All sunglasses are removed and placed inside suit jackets. Charles then looks to the *dukun* and nods at him, his hand ushering the old man towards another set of double doors. Walnut Face steps forward and the bodyguards open them for him. Inside, red and green laser lights twirl, move up and down the walls and reflect and refract off mirrors and spinning glass balls hanging over a large polished and shining dance floor. Music plays quietly in the background.

Before the old man enters he pulls his shoulder bag to his front and his hand gropes around in it. Out comes a little leather pouch, as worn as his face. He pulls it open, turns it upside down and shakes sand over the threshold of the main room. While he does this he mutters some sort of chant and then he burps. I look to Charles and the others in suits to see if we're all going to smile and wink knowingly at each other and have a secret joke at the crazy old boy's expense. All I get is a wall of furrowed brows and serious expressions and some nodding of approval.

Fuck, it wasn't even an impressive burp.

The *dukun* is walking slowly into the main room, fumbling in his bag again. Charles follows a few steps behind and the rest of us shuffle in behind him like we're entering a church service or a funeral. The witch doctor has found a little bell which he holds between thick dry thumb and crooked, cracked forefinger. He tinkles it a few times in a row, chants something, tinkles, chants, tinkles, chants, all the while heading to the middle of the dance floor. Finally we're there. All gathered around him in a circle. Eyes closed, still he tinkles, chants, tinkles, chants. Green and red disco lights light up the valleys and peaks on his face, making the moment more surreal.

I don't think this guy is going to help me with my issues, as Charles seems to think. He's a fruitcake. Not that I've got any issues anyway.

—*No, of course you haven't. Otherwise you wouldn't have pom-pommed, would you?*

—*Go, please.*

The *dukun* stops in his ritual, opens his eyes and looks at me, one shining eye and the other translucent white with cataract. He keeps looking at me. I feel the others following his gaze.

—*Why is he looking at me?* I ask her.

No answer. She has already gone. Perhaps the old boy has spooked her.

I look at the ceiling, not knowing where else to put my gaze. Nice set of lighting equipment for the Third World. I must look weird, staring up there. Look back, act normal, paranoid boy. Please don't still be looking at me. Of course he won't be. Why would he? He's here for the club.

I look back. He's still looking. He nods, I think. I'm not sure. Then he closes his eyes, chants some more, breathes in, holds it and then lets out a burp that is deep and dark and almost animal-like and lasts for three seconds.

Impressive.

The bell is back in his bag and he walks to Charles. He whispers in his ear. Charles whispers in his. He whispers back again and looks across at me as he does. They both nod. Then Charles makes an announcement.

'The club is now blessed and will be open to the public from nine tonight. But please all enjoy yourselves now. There is champagne and any other drink you want, free at the bar. Please stay as long as you wish.'

The music is turned up a few dozen decibels. The small group make their way to the bar where three young men in black bowties and white shirts stand waiting to serve. I am wondering how to make my excuses and leave. I know no one except Charles and I have no interest in getting to know anyone else, but Charles comes to me, *dukun* at his side.

'What did you think of the blessing?' asks Charles.

'Very interesting. Thank you for inviting me.' My eyes are locked on Charles's face. I don't want to look at his little walnut friend. I can feel his good eye examining me, but it's like his cloudy eye is looking even deeper, sub-skin, at Old Me, making him squirm under his gaze.

'Teddy is a very talented shaman. I am very successful maybe thanks to him.'

'Very talent.' Teddy nods at Charles's shoulder; I see the movement from the corner of my eye.

'Teddy thinks you need his help.'

I feel I should look at him. I'm being rude, so I look. He is gazing up at me. One twinkling bright eye, one polluted.

'Mm. Need help.' He points his crooked finger at me.

'No. Really. I'm fine.'

The crooked finger pokes the middle of my chest. 'You,' poke, 'need,' poke, 'help.' Poke.

'No, I—'

'He says you do. So you do.' Charles looks across at his companions at the bar and raises a hand as if to say he'll be there in a second.

'Mm. Both you. Both you need Teddy help.' His finger points to my head and then to my chest again. 'Both you. Mm. And she too.' He double-taps my chest. Something like an electric shock shoots into my centre of gravity and knocks me back a step. 'Tell Charles when ready. You, you and she come and see Teddy. I help all you.'

Charles puts his arm around Teddy's bony shoulder, raises an eyebrow at me, smiles, nods and leads him away as he heads to the bar.

I breathe in quick, short bursts of air to stop from passing out. I clip-clop at a dizzy high speed across the dance floor and out into the street. I buy a pack of cigarettes from one of the girls in short skirts and walk as fast as I can away from the club, sucking in lungfuls of hot polluted air while I fumble and tear at the plastic on the cigarette pack.

We jolt to a stop. I climb out of the cramped seat of the *becak*, pull my trousers out of my sweating backside and walk off.

'Hey *bule*,' the rider shouts behind me.

'What? *Ada apa*?' I say back, sweat trickling into my eyes. I rub them.

'*Uang*. Money.' He rubs thumb and forefinger together.

'Oh, shit.' I walk back to him and fumble a couple of notes from my front pocket. 'Sorry. Stupid *bule*.' I slap myself on the forehead and hand him some notes. I haven't bothered counting; I just want to be in Mei's having a drink.

He looks at me like I'm the idiot I am and shoves the money in his shirt pocket, revs up and pulls out into traffic in a black plume of smoke. He doesn't look over his shoulder.

Teddy's walnut face is bouncing around my mind like a sped-up Atari Pong game. I can still feel where his bony finger prodded my chest. I rub the spot as I pass the compound security and quicken my pace. I have never needed a drink so badly, my mouth is bone dry, but my hand has left a wet patch on my shirt.

'Fucking *dukun*. "You, you and she." What a load of shite.' I realise I'm muttering as I step into Mei's and the two people sitting at two tables at either end of the room look at me. I stop and dither and try to decide where to sit. To my left is Barry the psycho Canadian. No way am I sitting there. To my right is Geoff the morose Mancunian. I look at one of the empty Formica tables in the middle of the room, yearning for it and its solitude, but Geoff is already beckoning me over.

I just want to be alone, but ever polite even in times of mental stress, I head to Geoff. I go via the beer fridge first, take a bottle, pop the top on the opener screwed to front of the fridge, and take a long drink. I sit opposite Geoff, who is huddled over a Bintang, staring over his glasses at Mei. I haven't noticed her until now. She is at her usual position on her stool, but today her hair is loose around her face and she is wearing sunglasses. I look outside to see if the sun is reflecting off something and into her eyes.

'It's not the sun. It's that bloody twat.' Geoff nods towards the only other customer in here.

I swig more beer. My heart is running the hundred-metre hurdles. I sit back and take a deep breath, hold it, hope my heart will slow.

Barry is staring at Mei.

'He's only been with her a couple of weeks and he's already hit her.'

Looking more closely I see a bluish-yellow mark showing out of the side of her sunglasses. She touches it with her fingers and turns her head slightly away.

'How do you know it was him?' I ask, but I know it was him too, just from having spoken to him the once. Some people leak hatred.

Geoff doesn't answer. He knows I know.

The room is silent. The heat of the day soundproofs everything with its blanket-like weight, even the whine of the beer fridge is like the hum in deaf ears.

Geoff stares from Mei to Barry, from Barry to Mei. He is leant over his beer, knuckles white where he grasps the bottle with both hands.

Mei points a remote at the large TV screen hanging on the wall. It flicks onto Sky News.

'That's new.' I say.

'Yes. He told her to buy it.' Eyes narrow as he nods towards Barry.

'Satellite.'

'Well-spotted.'

Geoff being sarcastic. Unusual.

Walnut Face pokes me in the eye. I rub it and turn my chair to see the news. Fuck off, Walnut.

'The Supreme Court has ruled against another recount in Florida, meaning George W. Bush is the president of the United States.' George W. nods and waves at a large room full of cheering people waving the Stars and Stripes.

'Put the sport on, Mei,' says Barry.

'But Mr New and Mr Geoff are watching news,' says Mei.

'Fuck those faggots. Put on the sport.'

Mei's hand shakes as she picks up the remote. She puts it back down without changing the channel.

'Mei. Sport.'

'I want news too.' She adjusts her stool towards the TV. 'I want hear about how US cheats with democracy.'

'Mei. I paid for that fucking TV, so put on what I want.'

'My bar.' She adjusts her stool again and sits upright, nodding her head. 'My bar.'

Nothing is said. From across the room I sense Barry is contemplating his masculinity and power and how to regain it in front of two lesser males. He rolls his beer bottle between his palms. I don't suppose the contemplation will last long. Soon he'll think of a way of reasserting his Alpha side or whatever the fuck it is men use as an excuse for being belligerent twats.

Geoff, on the other hand, seems to have caved in on himself. His head is so far down between sunken shoulders that his forehead is almost touching his bottle. The lesser males know they will make no clever remark or fight for superiority over the Alpha to defend the woman's honour. The woman is defending hers because the lessers don't know how to fight.

The scrape of Barry's chair on the floor is as jarring as fingernails on a blackboard. The fall of his feet across the floor is steady, not slow, not quick. I don't look his way directly, but I see unfocussed movement from the corner of my eye. Geoff's head raises enough that his eyes watch Barry's movement. Barry enters my vision; he is standing under a still-waving and self-satisfied-looking George Bush.

'You want to watch TV, you faggots, you buy your fucking own.' He reaches up and turns it off. 'And Mei, if I invest my money in this shitty business, I say who can do what in here. My money means this is our business, not just yours. Understand, Mei?'

I have turned back around to the table and face Geoff, whose head is back below his shoulders.

'Mei? Understand?' Just short of a shout.

Behind her counter Mei nods in jerky fast movements.

'Good.'

A rat scurries along the edge of the room and disappears under the beer fridge.

Barry heads back to his table and mutters, 'Fucking faggots.'

'Arsehole. Fuck you.' A whisper, then louder, 'Fuck you.'

Geoff is peering over the top of his glasses from a head still hanging low. He looks as if he hopes no one heard him, but at the same time there is a glint of something proud in his eyes. I don't turn to look at Barry but I can feel his eyes on us. New Me has been shocked into the shadows, not so *don't give a shit* after all. Old Me doesn't turn around and try to out-stare Barry; he's too busy playing face-off with his alter-ego.

'You need to watch yourself, Geoff. It is Geoff, isn't it? Geoffrey. Things can happen to a man in this country, so you just watch yourself, you Limey faggot.'

I hear a dry gulp from Geoff's throat.

'And you too, Newbie. Guess you're too fucking scared to look at me. I want you both out of here. Out of my bar.'

I'm hunting around inside trying to find the *Me* who stood up to the Liverpudlian, but he's absent; obviously only appears when stoned or mentally knackered. The rat makes a run across the floor and out of the bar.

Mei is off her stool and walking to Barry. I can hear her whisper in his ear, but don't hear what she says. He grunts. She whispers again. He grunts again.

'Alright,' he says quietly, then louder, 'lucky for you, Mei says you spend well. For faggots. So fucking stay if you must.' His footsteps cross the room. His chair scrapes again. 'Bring me another beer, Mei.'

My head and everything in it, including split personalities and eyeballs, unfreeze themselves. Geoff's face is red, and still looking down. He shakes his head.

'Can you pay my bill? I'll sort you at work next week.' Without waiting for a reply his chair is kicked back and he is gone.

'Pussy,' Barry mutters.

Enough. Enough of today and *dukuns* and expats and me. I need escape from mind games. I cross to Mei, settle up for me and Geoff, force a smile at her and say thanks. A small smile touches her lips but I can't see what's in her eyes. Then she mouths, 'Sorry.'

I smile and shake my head at her and leave her bar with my eyes fixed firmly on the outside.

'Pussy,' says Barry.

—*Pussy, says Laura, you going to let him get away with that?*

I say nothing to either of them. I want freedom. I want away from people and their pressures and needs.

I want Eka. She is no pressure, no stress. She gives, I take. She is enjoyment and a kind of peace. She is a shield of succulent flesh that wraps itself around me and lets me be the most basic of beings within her shield; a being without cognitive thought. A primal being. With her I want a succession of moments that contain nothing other than primal pleasure. And I'm going to get them.

Oh, yes I am.

Pleasure, pleasure, pleasure.

You, you and she.

Oh, shut up.

Flesh. Faces burrowing. Into necks. Into skin. Bittersweet scents. Clawing, Caressing. Pulling. Tongue trails. Gentle bites. Almost pain. Hair in lips. Bitter taste. Sweet taste. Thirst. Sobs. Cries. Sighs. Solace. Closed eyes. Stroking. Finger tracing. Softness. Chests rising, falling. Rising, falling. Slowing. Stroking. Rising. Falling. Spinning. Sleeping.

'Better?'

I mmm at Eka. I am better. Walnut Face is just an amusing event now. Rationality has returned. Eka seems to have that effect on me. The old man has crawled out from under my skin and taken his mind games and cheap tricks with him. Barry also doesn't scare me now. If Geoff wants to get involved that's up to him. It's not my business. Nothing is my business. That's not why I came here; I don't want business. I don't want involvement. Unless, of course, it suits my mood at the time, and Barry most certainly does not suit my mood. Dark, soft breasts under my cheek suit it now. Staring down the length of Eka's brown body, fingers tracing across her stomach and to her triangle of hair, the musky scent of after-sex skin, slow gentle breathing, a looseness in my shoulders and spine; all this suits now; this mood and this moment.

My mind is nearly empty again. All thoughts and anxieties flow out of my head and trickle from my ears and the corners of my eyes. They run down the sides of my cheeks and follow the curve of Eka's breasts onto the thin-sheeted bed, then briefly they puddle, soak into the mattress and join the dark and miserable thoughts of the hundreds of others before me who have sought solace in flesh and lust in this cheap and ugly hotel room.

She strokes my hair.

'I forget.' She looks at the ceiling.

'What?' I ask, my voice a croaking whisper.

'I forget. Things. Many things I don't want to think of. I forget.' A pause while her breasts rise, fall, with her breathing. 'I forget, for a while I forget. I am happy. Thank you.'

My finger traces around her belly button. For a second it isn't *her* belly button, so I close my eyes hard and kiss her nipple. It is hers again.

'Thank you, Eka. I thank you.'

MINNIE

'**S**o where you going today, man?' Johnny has to raise his voice above the sound of the rain. He flicks a cigarette at his mouth and misses. It bounces off his lip and lands in a wide rivulet of rainwater that's running across the school's forecourt. It spins and turns until it joins the torrent of water flowing down the road.

'Keep practising, Johnny.' I offer him one of mine.

The rain is relentless in its bombardment. It overwhelms roads and pavements and pours in waterfalls off shop awnings and buildings. It drums on the roof above us and thunder cracks overhead every few seconds. The day has fallen into a murky twilight. *Becak* riders have their plastic-bag-covered heads low as they pedal hard against the river that flows almost to their knees. The big four-by-fours send waves twice that height to the sides of the road as they drive on. The waves slosh up the rise on the forecourt and break over the top. Johnny and I step back towards the school entrance to avoid wet feet.

'Going to Toba with the other teachers. Just waiting for them to finish their classes.'

'Cool, man. Lake Toba is cool. Beautiful.'

'So I hear.'

Johnny is moving from foot to foot. He opens his mouth and then closes it again.

'You OK?' I ask.

'Uh. Um. Yeah.' He nods his head and looks around. We're alone outside the school. Inside, students stand behind steamed-up windows, waiting for the rain to stop before leaving.

'Actually, can I ask you something?'

'Of course.'

An old man over the street is wading knee-high through the water. Suddenly he drops and disappears up to his chest in the brief river. He swim-splashes two or three feet and then pushes himself up and out of the water as if climbing out of a well. He carries on as though nothing has happened.

'Oh man. He fell in the shit. Under the pavement is shit. What do you call it, where shit and piss goes?'

'Sewers?'

'Yeah, man. Sewers. He fell in sewer. The pavement must be missing there. Ha ha. Shitty toes now.' Johnny is nodding his head up and down in rapid movements. 'Ha ha. Shitty.'

He's probably right. Shitty toes. The sewers run under concrete slabs which make up the pavement. Every now and then one is missing, leaving a metre-wide hole. You learn to look for them when you're walking and it's dry. The holes are easy to see, but under nearly a foot of water, they're invisible.

'Lucky he did not go under. Drown in shit and piss. Ugh. That'd be shitty. Ha ha.'

'Certainly would be shitty. What did you want to ask, Johnny?'

'Uh. Yeah. So, er, you had girlfriend, yeah?'

I answer, the words nearly jam behind my teeth but I push them out, 'Yeah, I did.'

'So, you kiss her many times?'

'Yes, and other girls.' Even though we've had this conversation in class already, I still add the extra information to see his reaction again.

'Other,' he pauses, smokes, flicks something invisible off his arm, 'girls.'

'Yes.'

'And you do, you know, other stuff too?'

'What other stuff do you mean, Johnny?' I know exactly want he means but watching him squirm the words out amuses me in a Friday afternoon kind of way.

'You know. Stuff.'

'No, I don't know.'

'Yeah you do, man. You know. Stuff.'

'What, stuff like pom-pom?'

'Ha, yeah. Pom-pom. You do a lot of pom-pom with other girls?' I laugh.

'Some girls, yes.'

'So, er, you ever do it with boys too?' Johnny looks away and nervously pulls at his quiff.

'No. I haven't.' I sense something is about to come from Johnny I don't really want to hear.

'It's just that...' He looks over his shoulder at the misted faces behind the large school window. 'It's not fair, you know?'

I don't want to ask, but I have to, out of politeness to him and because I like him.

'What's not fair?'

'I'd, er—I'd, er—well, so many people pom-pom with you, it's not fair because I'd like to too.'

There is only the sound of the rain stamping its feet on the roof above us and traffic swashing through the road-river. It is the only sound for long moment, during which an immense awkwardness builds between Johnny and me like a sped-up film of a skyscraper going up. It is over when a blinding flash and simultaneous whip-crack of thunder announce that the block of concrete and steel between us is finished.

'Sorry, Johnny, but, but...' What to say? 'You wouldn't want to see me naked. It's not pretty.' What sort of a get-out is that?

'I would,' he mutters. His usual confidence is washing away with the storm.

'I'm sorry, Johnny, but I've got to go and get my bag from inside. The classes have nearly finished.' I hurry away, leaving him staring at the rain, and go into the steaming entrance of the school, pushing past moist, condensation-covered students. Any words of comfort for Johnny held at bay by a sudden, previously unknown homophobia. I'm shocked both at Johnny's advance and my inability to deal with it like the liberal-minded bloke I like to think I am.

I reach to get my bag out from under my desk and a spray of sweat drops from my forehead. The AC must be playing up. I should go back and talk to him. I will. Now. But when I step back outside, I see him duck under the canopy of a bicycle *becak* and all I can do is watch as it labours off upstream, water sloshing over the footplate, Johnny's feet getting soaked.

'Eh, Newbie.' The slap on my back is too hard.

'Kim.'

'Whassup, man? You looking drugged already.' He pushes me away from the school doors as students start to pile out.

'You know Johnny?'

'Mr Cool with the leather?'

'Yes, well, he just made a move…' I stop. No, don't. No big mouth. Not me. Johnny doesn't deserve gossip.

'On you? He made a move on you. Cool Johnny? No fucking way.'

Too late. Cocked-up again.

'No, not a move, he just asked about my sexual leanings.'

'Cool Johnny is gay. Fuck. Wait 'til the girls in school hear this one.'

'Kim. No.'

'Oh, yes.'

'No. He's a good kid. Don't.'

'Really? Why not?'

'Because it'll make me look a shit and he doesn't deserve it.'

Kim contemplates the thinning rain.

'Guess he is a kinda good guy.'

'You hate racism, Septic, remember. It's the same thing.'

He nods, looks at me, punches my arm.

'You're no fucking fun, you fucking Limey. OK. Let's get the others and get to fucking Toba, man. Need some 'shrooooooms.' The school door swings behind him as he goes back in. The pre-ordered and modern eight-seater taxi pulls in through the subsiding flow of water on the road and stops just in front of me.

Toba: out of the city. Countryside. Green. Fresh air. Space.

Kim, Marty, Jussy and Julie come out of the school door in a silent line. Kim slides the minivan door and lets the others in first, then me, and as I climb in he says, 'Gay. Ugh. Not normal, man.'

I stop, half-in and half-out. There's a glint in his eye and he pats my bum.

'Just kidding. His secret's safe with me.'

The door slides shut. Julie is double-checking the price with the driver.

'*Bagus bagus,*' she says and pats the driver on the shoulder. 'For once it's as per the quote.'

'Are we picking Naomi up?'

'She said she's not coming if you're going to be there, Newbie.'

'Oh.'

'Don't worry, man. We'd rather have you and your schizo ways than her and her dreads.'

Four hours later, after a stop at a roadside shack to buy a case of beer, talking the very easygoing driver into letting us smoke grass, sharing it with him, discussing the Ten Commandments and getting it down to five, then singing the wrong words to Dylan songs while the jungle and villages pass by unnoticed in the dark, we arrive at the already sleeping town of Parapat, on the edge of Lake Toba, somewhat dazed and very stoned.

'This picture isn't her.' Jane is sitting in the armchair. She looks like a small child who has aged too quickly. The chair towers over her like the jaws of some monster that is about to close its mouth. Her fingers stroke the edges of the photo frame. She is a small woman, but now she is even smaller. The weight of loss has pushed her down and compressed her into herself. Her red-rimmed eyes search the photo as though trying to find her place on a map, but not understanding why she can't even find a landmark.

'I have more recent photos,' I say, 'I'll send you some.'

'That would be kind. This is too old. Why don't I have any of her as she is now? Was, is, was, now?'

I have the answer, but I don't give it. Children become adults; they aren't under the care of their parents anymore. They aren't sweet and cute, they are problems, and worry, and sometimes only distant acquaintances. There is no time to photograph them when there is so much adult discussion to be made, so much disagreement and tongue-biting. The parents don't understand their children and children don't understand their parents. Everyone is too embarrassed to ask for a photo. If a photo is taken it isn't a smiling, relaxed face that is captured, it is one which is full of age and concern and vanity. It's easier and safer to look at the old photos, from a time when each was needed by the other.

Laura: vain, independent, beautiful, with a phobia of cameras.

'Is there anything else you'd like from me?' I ask.

Jane's eyes squint, then glance around the room as if it is alien to her.

'I have her clothes, I have her...' *What do I have? Now it is me who is lost. My mind goes through my apartment, through the bedside cabinet, pulling open drawers, flinging open the wardrobe and finding a winter coat and an over-sized nightshirt. It searches under the bed, slippers with holes where her big toe used to poke out. Into the kitchen, mugs, glasses, my mind pulls the kitchen drawers onto the floor. From the bottom one spills out all the detritus accumulated from broken things, spare things, things that are too good to be thrown out but too useless to be used. I kick it all across the floor. There is something, it is shining. What is it? It is broken, but it is her...*

'Necklace. I have her necklace.'

'Necklace? Which necklace?' *Jane looks at me now. Her fingers still stroke the frame.*

'It's silver. The chain's broken. It's got Minnie Mouse on it.'

'Minnie Mouse?'

'She said she used to love Minnie Mouse.'

(I used to love Minnie Mouse. My mother used to buy me Minnie Mouse stuff...)

'I used to buy her Minnie Mouse stuff all the time.'

(But then I threw most of it away, when I started secondary school)

'She threw it all away.'

(It hurt her)

'It hurt me.'

(I kept this though)

'She kept a piece?'

'Yes. I'll send it to you.'

(I keep meaning to tell my mum I've still got a bit)

'She kept it because of you.'

Her eyes search mine.

'I'd like it. Please.'

'OK.' But I want it. I want it all. I want to hold it all and feel it in my hands and against my face. I want to sleep in her nightshirt and under her coat, I want her slippers to put my hands in, to smell, I want her necklace, to feel its weight in my palm. She is my Laura. They are my things.

'My little Minnie Mouse,' whispers her mother.

'I'll bring it tomorrow.'

IN THE MOUTH
OF THE VOLCANO

Being alone is a precious thing. It gives you time to be you. No outside influences can blur your personality into one of the mishmash of personas that you subconsciously create for the people you're with; the personality you make to please the person of the moment.

I don't know who I am with these who sleep around me in this hostel room. Is it the real me, or is the real me someone who is in all those other moments, in that spinning world of moments with Laura that are sometimes so hard to grasp and which, at other times, appear without summons or desire? Or am I, the pure and base me, here only inside my head when I am alone?

As I stare at the grey ceiling of this hostel, just awake, I wish that all of today could be mine and mine alone. I want to be me without using exhausting self-control in order to smile and laugh and even just talk to these others. Others who all have issues of their own, whether they realise it or not.

Here, alone, and so grateful to be alone, the one thing I do that contradicts my need for solitude is to examine Laura's face. I pull it out of its hiding place and piece it all back together. The curl of her hair over her brow; the small, near-invisible mole above her lip, on the right side. I know it's the right side. I've heard say that when someone is no longer, it's hard to remember how they looked, or even the colour of their eyes. But I know her face. When I have these moments alone, I can put her back together and know that is exactly how she is. The light-brown flecks in her green eyes. The soft downy feel of her ear against my lips. The smell of her cheek against my nose. The hardening of her nipples against my palm. The taste of her mouth in the morning when we kiss. It is all there.

I shouldn't be thinking of her; it should be Eka I think of, with her warm and giving body and her thick dark hair and lips that are soft and violent at the same time. Perhaps I should be thinking of the nights together when our bodies blur into each other's in a ritual of forgetting all but that current sensual moment. As much as I try to move my thoughts to Eka and the sensations we feel as we melt into each other, it is still Laura who I give my mind to in these rare snippets of solitude. I know Laura knows this; that is why she isn't tormenting me with my broken promise of no pom-pom. She knows I think of her and not Eka. Infidelity of the mind is so much more damaging than infidelity of the body.

So now who am I? Is this what I have become when I am alone? A shrine to Laura. A soul desperate to be alone in order to be with my soulmate. I want me back. Not Old Me, not New Me, just me. I want me, so I can think empty thoughts that mean nothing or deep thoughts that mean so much.

I expect someone will wake soon, so I sit up and push the thin clammy sheet off me. We're all in one room together, on low-to-the-ground beds, except Jussy, who is curled up under a couple of Julie's sarongs on the floor. Not enough beds to go around.

Pulling on my shorts and T-shirt I can hear the sounds of engines and chatter coming from outside. The light coming through the thin curtains feels adolescent, as though it isn't early morning, but it's not late either. It feels about eight. I shake my sandals and put them on, then walk quietly to the door.

I like being up when others sleep; I don't have to play the interacting game.

Down the concrete stairs I go. The wall feels surprisingly cool as I run my hand along it on my descent. The light that comes in when I open the door is alive. It almost burns Laura's image off of my retinas. It is a day untouched by the heavy hand of pollution. It is crisp, clear and revitalising. The sun shines down from where it hangs on the sky and warms me. I wait in the doorway and breathe in the morning. In front of me a market is coming to life. Blue tarpaulins provide roofed cover to arrays of stands of fruit, spices and vegetables, tended by mostly older women, who sit on the ground wearing colourful rectangle-shaped headgear and vivid sarongs. Some of the women are shaking and sifting large trays of seeds, others just sit and wave flies and the growing heat away. Around them locals walk and look and weigh and smell the goods. Beyond the market the blue of Lake Toba shimmers in the sunlight. I step out of my doorway and join the scene.

I feel less conspicuous here. For once people seem more interested in the colours and buzz of the market than the plain white man. I guess it's because we're on the backpack route and whites aren't so unusual. Parapat is the port where the boat leaves for the Tuktuk Peninsula on Samosir Island, where travellers apparently relax, watch the lake, and probably smoke a lot of grass.

I wander around the market and pick up fruit I've never seen before and some I know well, but have never seen looking so mouthwatering: yellow bananas, green bananas, mangosteens, rambutans, apples, limes, tomatoes are laid out in piles on the floor, fighting for space with chillies, beans, herbs, and mushrooms. There are buckets of small dead silver fish and larger buckets with huge, live goldfish fighting for space within. I watch as one is bought and killed on the spot. There are so many stalls I don't see how people decide from which vendor they should buy. Everything looks perfect, like a living impressionist painting. Every small piece of fruit or vegetable or bean is placed precisely to make a scene to look at again and again, full of vivid colour and life.

The smell of the spices grows with the rising temperature and mingles with the sweet scent of the fruit. A day has never smelt so edible. I could bite chunks out of the air. It makes me hungry. I ask for a bag of mangosteens from a woman who smiles through red-stained teeth and head up a side street. The stalls have spilled up the narrow lane, but here are clothes and sarongs for sale, decorated with un-faded colours taken from every part of the spectrum. I sit on a wall and watch as people wander around. *Dangdut* plays from a radio somewhere. In another part of the market someone is singing and playing a guitar.

I dig my thumbnails into a mangosteen and twist it in half. The colour within the fruit bursts out at me. Purple juice splatters on my t-shirt, my fingers are stained by one of nature's most resilient dyes. I pull the fleshy white fruit from its pulpy purple cocoon and it slides into my mouth like an oyster. Sweeter than lychee. My eyes close. The sun's warmth is on my face. The day is beautiful.

'Fucking mangosteens, man. My favourite.' Kim's fingers tear out a segment of my fruit. It sits in my hand bleeding purple over my fingers.

'You're up pretty fucking early. Why didn't you wake us?' he asks while licking juice from his fingers.

There I go, born-again true me is pushed back up into the womb of pretence. Here comes the act, here comes the finest performer in the art of socialising and getting on. Here comes the character actor, the gently offensive one best suited to Kim.

'You all looked so peaceful I didn't want to disturb you. Thought I'd leave you to your morning glories and dirty dreams.' I drop the fruit on the ground.

'Fuck, did you.' Kim rubs his eyes and blinks. 'You just wanted some alone time. I don't fucking blame you. We're hard fucking going, us lot.' He pats me on the shoulder. 'Enjoy your fruit, man. It's too fucking bright for me out here. Got to shower.' He runs his hands through his hair. 'Fuck, it's going to be hot. Come find us when you done being alone, the others are just getting up. Boat's in an hour. Don't be late, lonesome boy.'

He walks back through the market nodding, laughing and saying '*Pagi*' to everyone, his brown hair flopping from side to side as he moves his head.

My actor hasn't even left his changing room. Kim sees he doesn't want to come out.

It is still a beautiful day.

—⟋⟍—

We leave Parapat on a hand-painted boat. It is green, red and blue in fading, peeling shades with a canopy over the top deck. The chairs are like metal garden chairs, painted white and screwed to the floor. There are about twenty people on this deck and more below.

I lean over the rusty handrail and watch as Parapat recedes behind us. The boat seems to glide over the clear blue-green water leaving hardly any foamy wake.

'We're on the largest volcanic lake in the world now, did you know that?' Julie is at my side, sunglasses holding her hair back. She looks relaxed today; even her hands are still, almost: only her small finger taps on the rail.

'I had heard something like that.'

'It's a hundred kilometres long and over four hundred and fifty feet deep.'

Looking down into the water I get a slight feeling of vertigo. What's at the bottom? What animals lurk down there? The child in me feels uncomfortable.

'They think it was the biggest eruption in millions of years and sent the planet into some sort of nuclear winter.'

'Maybe a volcanic winter?'

'Don't be a smart arse. Anyway, imagine if it went up now. We'd be fucked.'

'We would,' I agree.

Singing, loud and sudden, has started on a high note behind us. Three boys no taller than my waist stand in a row and are singing in complete tuneful harmony. In cut-off shorts and grubby T-shirts they look like they've come off the street, as they probably have. Their sudden and perfect voices make the rest of the boat go silent for just a few seconds. Kim, Jussy and Marty sit and watch like the three wise monkeys on a break.

When the boys finish their song they walk up and down with their hands out. Nearly everyone gives something.

As we move further onto the lake the water becomes choppier and darker blue. The hills around are green and lush but have an edge of harshness to them, presumably caused by the violence of their birth. Parapat is now a dot back on the shoreline and the size of the lake is starting to impress me. I again get a slightly queasy uncomfortable feeling from being too far from a shoreline to swim to and too high over a gaping water-filled hole that goes deeper than I can fathom.

'They're really musical on the island.'

I jump. I'd forgotten Julie was still next to me.

'Sorry. Were you somewhere else?' She tilts her head so that her eyes sneak into my vision.

'At the bottom of the lake, probably.' A shiver runs up my back.

'Kim said he thought you wanted to be alone for a bit today. Needed space.'

Kim is doing his take on an Indonesian dance for two older local ladies at the other end of the boat. Jussy and Marty are laughing at him and the ladies are clapping their hands for a beat for him. A cigarette is stuck in his mouth as he swirls around with his hands in the air.

'He said that?' I ask, lighting my own cigarette.

'He can be quite perceptive at times. So if you want me to go away just say, but I personally believe company is sometimes the best thing for people who want to be alone.'

'Jesus. The fresh air must be getting to everyone today. Making them all a little too wise and knowing,' I say. 'Sorry. That sounded wrong.'

'I'll leave you alone then. I guess he is wiser than me.' Her lip twitches and she picks up her bag at her feet.

'No, wait. Maybe you're right. I'm a little too into myself lately. Let's try your theory.'

Julie smiles and puts the bag back down.

'Don't worry. I don't want to shag you, you're definitely not my type. Too skinny for me,' she says, 'I just want us all to have a good weekend.'

I'm pleased with a hint of disappointment that she doesn't fancy me. Is the disappointment because I like her a little, or is it because my pride is hurt? Or is it because Laura won't be jealous and react? For fuck's sake, there she is again.

'Yes, let's have a good weekend.'

'And you got to try the mushrooms. They grow in water-buffalo shit, and blow your head off.' She's now hopping from foot to foot. There's the Julie I know. 'Tonight we're having mushroom tea. It's going to be mad.'

'OK.'

Twenty minutes later and the boat is cruising close to Samosir Island's shoreline. The sun is shining from a cloudless sky onto coconut trees and palms and lush green vegetation. Water, clear azure and mouth-watering to look at, laps the edge of the lake. Huts and houses poke out of the greenery and sit on the water's edge. Most of the wooden buildings have pointed roofs at the front and rear and a dip in the middle like saddles. The wood surrounds are decorated with colour carvings.

Women wash clothes at the water's edge as children run and jump in the lake. The boat passes close as it comes alongside the jetty. We wave at the kids, some of them naked, others just in their underwear.

'*Horas*,' yells Julie.

The kids yell back, '*Horas*.'

'What's that mean?' I ask.

'It's Batak for hello.'

'Batak?'

'Jeeesus. You're coming here and you don't even know about the place?'

'It's a big lake.' Should I know more?

'Yes, it's a big lake and it sits in a volcanic crater and the people who live here are called Batak, you bloody English backpacker.' She is almost annoyed, and seeing just a little of her wrath is making me shrink in my clothes. 'Batak are the people. They used to eat igno-ramuses like you.'

'No shit.'

'Yes shit. They were cannibals for ritualistic reasons up to a hundred fifty years ago.'

'Wow.' For want of a better word. But I want to fight back: 'Shouldn't that be ignorami?' I ask.

'No it shouldn't, you fuckwit.'

'Oh, OK.' I lean over the side of the boat and yell '*Horas*' in an unusually loud voice. I must be getting in holiday mood. The kids shout it back and even some of the women bent over their washing and scrubbing on the ground look and wave. It's like being in some Technicolor travel film. Scenes I've never really believed existed in places I never knew could be so vivid are burning themselves onto my mind. I know these moments will stay close to me from here on. Asia seems to have been painted with a keener brushstroke and in crisper shades than England.

We bump up against the jetty.

'Come on, let's go, imbecile.' She smacks the back of my head.

We jump off the boat as a couple of teenage boys hold it steady with ropes. There is a queue of very chilled-looking people waiting to board as we walk up the path away from the lake.

A day is passed sitting by the water, smoking grass, drinking beer. The sun is kind, not blaring, but gently dripping on us from between clouds that float across the mountains like a parade of passing zeppelins. The lake lies sleeping and calm beside us. Conversation is slow and gentle, happening between silences which fill the air around us like soft cushions. During these silences I find nothing much passes through my mind, except the slight effort of remembering where the last conversation has gone and for how long and has it in fact finished. I look around at the lake, the mountains that rise out of it, or do they fall into it, or does it creep up them? But look at the lake. So old. So wide. So deep.

'I'm going for a swim. It's a lake. It has to be swum.' Marty is up and running to the edge and pulling his T-shirt over his head as he goes. He just throws it off before he runs onto a diving board set up from the low wall. He bounces once and is gone. Into those depths. Old, old depths. Bottomless depths.

Kim takes a long drag on a joint.

'Me too.' He says through held breath. The joint goes in the ashtray, then another body to the depths.

'Come on, man,' says Jussy.

Before I have a chance to answer he is gone. Three of them, suspended over a dark abyss. What strange things look up at their legs treading water over the void?

'You not going?' Just Julie and I remain by the water's edge.

'Uh-uh. Too deep.'

'Scared of water?'

'No, just too deep. I'm scared of heights. If all the water fell out, those three would fall to their deaths.'

'If the water fell out? Fuuuck. Where would it fall?'

'Don't know. But it's too high to be swimming there.'

Julie nods, blinks and mutters, 'Yeah.'

Silent cushions are placed over our ears again. Julie stares at the lake. The vast vast deep lake. I stare. We stare. We smoke weed. Silence. For a long time? A short time?

'What the fuck did you say?'

'What?' I answer her.

'You said something about the lake. What?'

I reach in and scrape around my skull, pulling up fragments of used conversation. Lake. Water. Then other fragments that just float around my mind: Eka. Beautiful skin. Eka. Soft lips, her flesh. What did we do the other night? It was good. It was sexy. Her hair over my stomach.

'What the fuck did you say?'

'What?' I answer.

'The lake. What the fuck did you say about the lake?' She is sat forward, her elbows on her knees and eyes wide, fingers pulling a length of hair hanging down the side of her face straight, then curling it, then straight.

'The lake? What?' Her feet are tapping the ground.

Scrape my skull again. Nails scratching down the bone. *Dukun*. No not the fucking *dukun*. Get out. I squash him against my skull with my thumb. Laura. I won't squash you, and sorry I thought about Eka. It's lust and forgetting, that's all. And why not? Eh, why not?

'The lake. Tell me or I'll go fucking mad.' Julie's hair is wrapped taut around her index finger, the end has gone white.

'The lake. Oh. It's deep and high and it's too high.'

'Oh, right. Yeah.' She slumps back in her plastic chair but her hair is still cutting off circulation to her finger. I pick up the remains of another joint and relight it. Need to forget the depths, deep dark depths. Watch the zeppelins instead. Yeah. Look at them floating around. Big white floating things.

Below us the white, and here we cut through the blue. Darkness of space just above our heads, so close we can almost touch its infinity.

Laura's face is pressed up against the small plastic inner window. I sometimes worry what happens if the inner plastic cracks. Surely nothing, in which case why is it there? What if it does? Does the outside glass weaken? Does the pressure get too much, and phloomph, we're sucked through a hole smaller than my waist? Images of disaster movies flash through my mind: planes twirling, spinning, people holding on to seats being ripped out of the plane's floor while others are sucked out into the near stratosphere.

'This is time travel, you know.' She is almost whispering.

'How do you work that one out?' I lean towards her, partly to hear her answer and partly to get away from the arm that has crept across the armrest on my other side. Middle seats, bloody things. Who has the right to which rest? Instructions should be given along with the emergency evacuation pictures on the back of the seat in front. 'Please use the rest to your left and consider the person sitting next to you.' But then who gets the spare rest? Planes: hollow missiles loaded with questions.

She turns and examines her hands for a moment: small hands with long elegant fingers. A shame about the bitten-down little fingernail. Would she be she without that little ravaged digit?

'OK, we're not going far so it's not so noticeable, but we left England at two twenty. We arrive in Crete at about eight p.m. We only fly for about four hours, therefore we gain about two hours. We go forward in time by two hours. Time travel.'

'Not that simple, Missy.'

'Is.'

'Isn't.' Superior male intelligence is making a proud appearance. 'That's all just down to time zones. Every time you cross one you—'

'Don't be a condescending Ice-Cream Boy. I do know what time zones are.' She licks my face: a new habit that seems to happen every time one of us says 'ice cream'. 'If we didn't have them it wouldn't change the fact that night-time falls quicker than it does at the same moment in England.'

'Ice cream.' I hope another lick will change the subject.

'Not this time, sicko.' She sits more upright in her chair. 'If you talk to someone in New Zealand, their time is twelve hours into the future, so they're contacting someone in the past and you're talking to the future. Time travel.'

'Doesn't work.'

'Does.'

'Doesn't. If it was the future then I'd phone someone in NZ and say, "What's the lottery numbers on today's draw?" and they'd tell me, and I'd buy the ticket and then win twelve hours later. Then that'd be time travel.' I lean back in satisfaction and put my arm on top of the woman's arm from the other seat. She jumps, looks at me, tuts, and crosses her arms over her chubby tummy. I lean back towards Laura. She leans towards me, all sparkling green eyes overflowing with certainty in her belief. My confidence falters.

'Right. I break into the cockpit, yell "Get this thing moving faster or the Ice-Cream Boy gets it."' A sudden lick, I wipe it off. 'The captain puts his foot down—'

'They don't have pedals. It's not a car.'

'I know, it's a turn of phrase. Anyway, he makes the thing go faster, double-speed, treble-speed, more. And before you say anything, you male idiot, I know planes don't go that fast, but if they could.'

'OK. Get on with it.' I'm looking at her throat. A vein jumps every second or so with such force on her pale skin that for some reason my trousers stir.

'We get up to twenty-five thousand miles an hour, which puts us back in London an hour later than we left.'

'Not time travel.' My head is moving into the neck. She pushes it back.

'So I yell at the captain, "Faster, or I'm going to make Ice-Cream Boy tell you about his life."' A slow lick from under my ear up to my *eyebrow, followed by a kiss to the temple. I don't wipe this off, but I adjust my sitting so my trousers aren't so uncomfortable.*

Laura raises her dark eyebrow at me and smiles.

'Oh yeah?' she says.

'Oh yeah,' I reply, 'I love it when you talk quantum bullshit.'

'OK. So I'll continue. Fifty thousand miles an hour, we get back when we left. Seventy-five and we get back and see our plane on the runway.'

'Doesn't work.'

'Does.'

'Doesn't. It means you get back in about twenty minutes.'

'Does it? OK. Give you that. So faster and faster until you get back in a second, then faster and faster and at some point the time difference becomes a negative.'

'Doesn't work.' Confidence has not found a comfortable seat in my argument.

'And,' she adjusts in her seat as she realises a new revelation, 'the plane has passed over all the time zones with people going to bed and getting up and working at different times in each one, ahead of us and behind us, yet we arrive back before we left. Work that out. It just strengthens the belief that time as a human concept does not exist. It is not linear.'

'Have I got a week of this mental torture during this holiday?'

'All sorts of torture.'

'Good.' I kiss her neck. She kisses my cheek. We kiss lips. The woman next to me tuts.

'Time, my dear boy, not as a concept but as a dimension or an object, is always there, like the sky and the mountains and the sea.' Laura is holding the back of my neck and whispering against my ear. 'All laid out across an endless plain where it isn't known as time. You just have to travel a bit to see it all, and know where to be to soak it all up. All those moments of now that have ever been and will ever be. They're all there.'

The next few moments aren't successive, they all become one. Time is certainly not counted while kissing and holding and two-people-as-one happens. When skin melds into skin and thoughts soak into the other's. It has no length, it has no count, the convention ceases to exist while people become more than people and slip out of the universe, closer to space than to ground, nearer to infinity and timelessness than clocks and numbers. How can time travel be an impossibility when linear time doesn't exist, and all that does exist is me and her and emotion? Love at forty thousand feet: as good and mind-blowing as sex at zero feet.

GOING WITH IT

'**I** was used as a medium once.' Joanne sips from her beer and nods. She is a teacher at another school in Medan, at Toba to relax for the weekend with her husband John. Julie knows her so we've joined tables in this gently lit and wall-less restaurant. Crickets are rubbing their wings in the undergrowth. The large full moon throws a line of shimmering white across the lake's surface beyond their noise. The hills the darkest of blue under the mass of stars that decorate the sky.

'Here's a good story,' says John, small and scrawny and hen-pecked beside the tall and hippy and overbearing Joanne.

A good story. Right. Can't wait. My head pulses behind one eye, the result of grass and beer in the sun followed by a late-afternoon nap. I hope the coolness of the evening that envelops this little place by the lake will help to ease it.

'Go on, tell it.' Julie's eyes are nearly out of her head and her hands are strangling the neck of her beer bottle.

Jussy is leaning back in his seat, staring out into the darkness. Marty is leaning in, his head close to Julie's. Kim is still smoking grass and looking around the restaurant with bemused red eyes.

'Well, I went to a spiritualist meeting in Brisbane to keep a friend company and watched this woman with wild hair prance around this stage trying to find people to use her crap on. It really was a load of crap and she was a fraud, but my mate soaked it up. But this woman sitting on my other side'—she points to a spot to her left—'kept looking at me in the darkness, and every time I looked at her she didn't even look away.'

'Did she live on Lesby Avenue?' Kim sniggers and rubs his eyes.

'At the end,' Joanne carries on, 'the lights come on and this woman leans over and tells me I have the gift. I just laugh and say, "Well, if it's the same as hers, I'm giving it back." She then says that I really have the gift. That the woman on stage was a fraud. But with me, with *me*, she could feel the energy coming off me.'

John is smiling beside her, pride gushing from him. 'So she hands me and my mate a card and tells us to call her. She'd like me to help at a séance.'

'No way,' Julie's beer bottle is having its neck well and truly wrung.

'Yep. Anyway my mate is really up for seeing my powers and I'm sort of curious in a cynical way, but sort of intrigued too, so we go.'

She pauses to sip her water while Hubby nods his head. 'There's only four other people there, all wanting to talk to their dead better halves, at which point I nearly go, but this bloody woman grabs me and asks me to please stay because I really do have a gift. So I sit and the next thing she's talked me into being the host for a ghost.'

'No way,' whispers Julie. She's caught.

I want to leave. My head is worse and my patience is wearing thin. The last thing I want is another *dukun* moment.

—*So leave.*

I laugh; short and sharp and loud. The others look at me.

'Just got Kim's Lesby joke.' I wave my beer at him. 'Very good, Kim.'

Kim raises his bottle at me.

I look at my knees

—*Don't tell me you've made an appearance because this woman says she's a medium?*

—*Just thought it was time to annoy you, was all. Get you back for sleeping with little Miss Prozzy. And see how New You is getting on.*

—*New Me is fine. Having fun without you and the Ice-Cream Boy. It's been a while. I'd forgotten you.*

—*Right. As if.*

—*Anyway, I'm listening to her story.*

—*But you think stuff like that is bollocks.*

—*True. I also think you chattering away in my head is bollocks too, so right now, she is the less bollocky of my options. So shush, I missed some of her story.*

'So I'm sat in this chair and she's summoned the spirits and suddenly someone's in me. I've gone cold and can't feel my limbs and some bastard is trying to make my mouth move from within.'

'Fuuuck.' Kim is all blinking red eyes and open mouth.

'I hated it, so I took control and shouted, "No. Get out."'

'And?' Julie sucks the last dregs of life from her bottle.

'And whoever it was left and I ran from that place and never tried it again since.'

'Bullshit.' Jussy has swivelled around to join the table.

'It is not. Joanne has a gift. She senses things, don't you, Joanne.' Little hubby is rubbing wife's back.

'I can. All sorts of things. Evil or good in houses, stress in people, possessed people. I sometimes have psychic visions.' She is nodding to herself.

—*Ask her about me,* says Laura, standing behind me, hands on my shoulder.

—*Don't be ridiculous.*

'I can even sense there's something here, tonight, around this table.'

Joanne's eyes are closed and she tilts her head from side to side. 'Someone.'

—*Oooh.*

—*Shut it.*

'Oh, Joanne, no, fuck off. No.' Julie leans back in her chair and rubs her hair while she looks around the restaurant.

During the silence that follows I almost expect someone to scream. Hopefully not me. I'm willing Joanne not to look at me.

—*Look at Ice-Cream Boy.*

—*No, don't.*

—*Do.*

—*Don't.*

Before Joanne opens her eyes I'm aware of someone else standing behind me, not Laura, she seems to have suddenly cleared off. I look around. Instead of her and her green eyes and black hair and sarcasm and love, there is a man of about thirty, with tattooed arms, a shaved head, and a long pink ponytail sprouting from his shiny pate.

'Sorry, but couldn't help overhearing your conversation and just wondered if you'd mind me joining. I love these sort of stories. Got some beliefs of my own about other dimensions.' His voice is British and surprisingly well-spoken.

'Bet you have,' says Kim. 'Do share, man.'

I sneak a look at Joanne to make sure she isn't studying me, isn't getting ready to denounce me as haunted person, but she's just looking down and stroking the back of her hand.

There's a scrape of wood across stone as Pink Ponytail pulls up a chair and Julie moves round so he can squeeze in.

'That's a really cool story. I'm Derek, by the way.' His hand is offered and all shake it.

'What's your story then, man?' Kim's eyes are ready to drop from their sore-looking sockets .

'Well, I been travelling a while now.' He reaches behind his head and strokes his tail. 'Ten years. Seen nearly all of Asia, Africa, South America. I've done every continent's drugs and shit.'

My head is thumping harder.

'And I've had some weird trips, and on some of those trips I've really been places.'

Jussy yawns then apologises.

'You alright, Jussy?' Marty asks.

'Yeah, man. Just chilled and a bit bored of the drug stuff. Sorry, Derek, but heard this before. Let me guess, you've seen places that really exist, met people that really exist in these places and you could only go there after some heavy hallucinogen. Yeah?'

An unusually vocal moment for Jussy.

'Yes. That's it. But it was real and I've been there a few times.'

Kim is giggling and bangs his head on the table.

'Fuuuck. Take me there.'

For a moment we all look at Kim. He looks back at us through slow-moving eyes.

'What?'

'Think you need to slow down on the grass, Kimbo.' I say.

'Who the fuck are you to tell me that? Don't fucking tell me what to do.' The sudden aggression tenses everyone around the table for a second and I have no reply.

Julie tells him to chill.

'I am fucking chilled. You lot fucking chill. Fuck.' He shakes his head, swigs his beer and laughs. 'Everyone suddenly wants to mother me, fuck. Get on with your story.'

'OK man.' Derek swallows then coughs. 'So, yeah, I took some LSD or something and I literally flew out from my body and where I was, right out over the town, and I could see everything clearly below me, houses and trees and cars, and then out over the sea, then I landed really gently on this green grassy island and met some really nice people. It was, I know it sounds weird, just a really warm friendly place. Then I just took off and floated back to me, opened my eyes and knew I'd really been somewhere. Somewhere real, but not on this Earth.'

'I've heard of those places too,' says Joanne. 'I believe in them. Lots of drug users believe they have really gone somewhere out of our time and dimension.'

'Really?' I ask. Why have I asked that? Don't even consider it to be true, you idiot. But what if it is? It isn't.

—*What if it is?*

—*It isn't.*

—*Time: fields and fields of moments. Or maybe islands and islands of moments, where you can hop from one and onto another.*

I whack my forehead with my hand and the smacking sound makes me jump more than the pain.

'Jesus, Newbie.' This is Marty. I nearly forgot he was there. In fact I nearly forgot everyone was there. 'What're you doing?'

'Mosquito. On my head. Squashed it.' I pretend to rub something off my hand.

'I sense something in you.'

Oh shit, no.

Joanne is up and standing behind me before I can move my chair back and leave. I can smell patchouli on her.

'Stress. You are stressed and troubled.'

'Er, no. Just a headache. That's all.'

'I can help.'

'No really.'

'I won't touch you. Wait. I promise I can make you feel better.'

'Yeah. Go on. Exorcise Newbie.' Kim bangs his bottle on the table.

'Really. I practise healing.'

Healing and a medium. What a girl.

'It will help. Just relax your shoulders and keep your head still.'

—*Go on. Open your mind, numbnuts.*

Laura laughs and it rolls around my head like a dropped cymbal in a hall.

I let Joanne do her thing. Her open palms are just a couple of inches from each of my temples. The smell of patchouli is stronger. She slowly moves her hands in little circles.

'Close your eyes.'

I do. I can't not. I don't want to protest too much. The table is silent and everyone is watching. The silence only breaks when Kim mutters something under his breath every few seconds.

'Relax. Just feel the warmth. Can you feel the warmth?'

I can feel the warmth. Her hands are giving off warmth. And it's soaking into my head. Little warm spots.

Nice.

Tension is going from all over my body. It's actually nice.

'Just let it go. Feel my energy.' Patchouli, all herbal and fresh, getting stronger, weaker, stronger, weaker with each little rotation.

Nice. Really nice. Don't stop. My headache's slipping away like ice down a sink.

—*There. See. Don't knock it 'til you've tried it.* Laura smiles gently somewhere. Her face just visible in the shadows.

Joanne takes her hands slowly away, but the warmth is still there, fading, like the last ember in a fire. My headache gone.

'How's that?' Joanne slides back into her seat next to smiling, proud husband.

I just nod and smile.

'There. See. Don't knock it 'til you've tried it,' she says.

My mouth opens, nothing comes out.

'I told you I sense all sorts of things.' She winks and smiles. 'All sorts of things.'

'This is exactly why I asked to join you lot.' Derek is now alternating between stroking his bald head and his ponytail. 'Love meeting people like you lot.'

I'm pleased he speaks. The attention is off me, although Joanne's eyes meet mine for another second. She gives me another smile, a secret smile, that no one else sees, and I smile back.

I'm losing it.

I take a sip and it tastes like mud. It looks like lots of little turds in a glass of hot water.

'Don't you like it?' Julie is sitting next to me, licking her lips after taking a large mouthful of hers. She chews on one of the little brown lumps.

'Tastes like mud, looks like poo.'

A ball plonks down a hole on the pool table in the corner of the bar. Kim bangs his cue on the floor.

'Oh yes. Watch out, Paul Newman.' He lines up the next ball, brings his arm back and thwacks it. The ball bounces from cushion to cushion, sending most of the other balls it hits into a whirling frenzy that ends with the target ball coming to rest just by the top corner pocket. The Batak Indonesian he's playing with smiles. Teeth protrude from his tight lips at a forty-five degree angle. His hair is held back by a red bandanna and his eyes bulge out almost as far as his teeth. He eyes the notes on the edge of the table as if they are all already his. I understand why as he takes his shot, pots a ball, then another, then another. Kim looks on, nursing his cup of mushroom tea like it's a cup of bedtime cocoa.

'Have some more.' Julie is holding my tea in front of me. 'It's an acquired taste, but the results are stunning.'

I examine the dark mushrooms piled up in my glass. I have no one to answer to, no one to preach to me.

—*What about me?*

Ignoring her, I gulp a mouthful and feel three slimy objects slip into my mouth.

—*Go on then. Swallow. I'm intrigued to see what happens to you.*

I swirl them around, give them a quick chew and swallow. They slide down my throat like shitty oysters. I hope the mud taste is the mushrooms and not mud.

'They grow in water-buffalo shit, you know. That's why they're so potent.'

Julie takes another swig of the strange solid drink.

—*Mm. Nice. Bet you feel good.*

I close my eyes and will her to leave. For a moment she is fully formed and visible behind my eyelids. Smiling and beautiful, alive and floating there. I clamp my eyes shut until she becomes a blot of dark colours and then blackness. That was easy.

When I open my eyes the room is blurry for a second and then clears to a more vivid place. The colours seem a little more, what, colourful? Kim and the Batak are setting up another frame. Marty and one of Batak's friends have joined them to play doubles. Jussy is chatting to a very short girl with a large head up at the bamboo bar. Pink Ponytail has been left behind in the restaurant with Psychic Jo and adoring husband to discuss the afterlife and out-of-body balls. I'm happy they aren't here, in this less backpacky bar away from the lake. Other people sit around, chatting in their little groups, becoming more there as I watch.

'Bloody hell.' Julie has slouched back in her chair with her feet up under her. Her elbow is touching mine. I'm sitting back with my feet up on the little wooden table in front of us.

'What?'

'This is working quick.'

'It is. Is it?'

There is no more talk while we watch Kim and Marty lose another frame. The Bataks aren't smiling or laughing, just taking the money like it's theirs. Watching from over here is like watching a film. The characters are so obvious; two stupid tourists being taken for a ride by two locals who have seen idiots like them in here every night, getting stoned and playing like amateurs and handing over money like it's nothing more than paper.

'His teeth are getting bigger.' Julie's finger waggles at Bandana Batak.

She's right. How the hell is that happening?

'That's cannibals for you. Big fucking teeth getting ready for the kill.'

I look to Julie and then back to Batak. Those teeth are definitely sticking out more. Heading for ninety degrees rather than forty-five. And his eyes…

'And his eyes, they're bulging more.'

Julie leans forward and squints.

'Shit. They are. Shit.' Her mouth hangs open.

'Do you think his ancestors really ate people?' Batak looks down the end of his cue as he bends over the table, but his eyes aren't on the ball, they're on me, bulging at me. He grins and his teeth are more pointed, like a shark's.

'Tell me it's the mushrooms.' I look at my glass. Half empty. Half full? Can't be bothered with that discussion. Have another gobful, take away the argument and the psychoanalysis. Mud, mud, glorious mud. Mud pies, little me in the back garden eating my mud pies. No wonder I was sick. Gritty mud in my teeth. Scrunch scrunch.

'It is the 'shrooms. Just go with it. It gets more amusing.' Julie is alternating between raising one eyebrow and then the other.

'You exercising?'

'What?'

'Eyebrows. You exercising your eyebrows?'

'No.' Up, down, up, down, left up, right up, down together. 'Why?'

'Thought you were.'

'Weirdo.'

Kim is suddenly in my face. How did he get here from over there so quickly?

'We're going. These guys have fleeced us. Going to the lake to watch the stars do their thing. Coming?'

'Did they eat anything?' asks Julie. 'Have you checked your fingers?'

Kim checks his fingers. Marty checks his behind Kim.

'Why would they eat my fingers?'

''Cos they got the teeth for it. Skin-tearing teeth. Rip your face off in one peel, like a satsuma.'

Kim blinks at us, says something that has been slowed down somehow to indecipherable and walks slowly out of the bar. It takes about half an hour.

'See you later.' Marty is still there, looking at us both, some Cheshire-cat smart-arse condescending smirk on his face. 'You two are gone already.'

'Not me.' say I.

'Oh yes you are. You never done these before, have you, Newbie?'

What? Done what?

'Just go with it. Time's going to go bendy and slow and fast and if things get bad, just go with it. The bad bits will pass. And make sure you watch the star show.' He laughs and walks away. He shakes hands for an hour with the Batak.

Check your fingers. Check your fucking fingers.

Julie is laughing next to me, her head on my shoulder.

'What?'

'This is fucking great. Good 'shrooms. Good fucking 'shrooms.'

Am I really stoned already? Is stoned the word for mushroom stoned? Is this a trip? I've never tripped before. Have some more mud. Good mud.

'You two look stoned.' A man in front of us. A big bulk of a man. Who's this?

'Can I join you?' The bulk sits.

'Who's this?' I ask Julie.

She shakes her head and shrugs and eyebrow-exercises all at the same time.

Whoever he is, he's got black hair, white skin and a red eye. Why has he got a red eye?

'Why have you got a red eye?' asks Julie.

'It's an infection. Picked it up in Penang.'

'Why have you got a flat head?' she asks.

'Eh?'

She's right. He's getting a flat head. Fuck it's flattening out. And… and…

'You got bolts.' I point at either side of his neck. 'Bolts. Why have you got bolts?'

'I haven't got bolts.'

But he has, and as I watch they get larger and his head gets flatter and his other eyes turns red.

Julie whispers in my ear, 'Don't tell him. He doesn't know. He's changing and he doesn't know.'

'Oh.' I start laughing. I look at the flat-head man. How can he not know? He's turned into the Monster. Bolts. What are the bolts for? Would they really keep a head on? I think about grabbing one and twisting but decide not to. Julie's laughter is right in my ear. Tears are running down her face.

'He doesn't know. Poor bloke. And we're laughing at him.'

I'm laughing more too. I've caught it off Julie. I laugh tears. Happy tears. Happiness shooting up from my stomach. Julie laughs. I look at Frankenstein and he's gone.

'He's gone. Looking for a little girl,' snorts Julie. 'Fuck. No other fucker can see all this. Just us.' We sit there laughing, legs curling up, cheeks wet, muddy mouths. She's my friend. She can see what I see. I can see what she sees. How cool is that?

Teary watery vision. Big skin-ripping teeth, bulging eyes stare from across the room. I laugh more.

'We should go. He's hungry,' I blurt into Julie's creased-up face.

'Yeah. Fuck, drink up and we go. Go let's go. Yeah. Come on. Go.'

Stumbling feet. More mud. A spaceman's slow walk across the bar to leave. Jussy waves to us. I wave back, a big slow arc of a wave. Jussy winks and turns back to big-head girl. Bulging eyes everywhere. Wolves circling. Come on, feet; faster. Out. Night and cool. Insects screeching in the grass. Julie's hand through my arm. One foot in front of the other. And again. And again. This is taking forever. The lake was never this far. One foot, then the other. Slowly. Come on. Before sunrise.

One foot.

The other.

One foot.

The other.

The path is dark, but things start shooting around in the corners of my eyes. Bright white lines like comets. I look around and up. The stars are still, but then one suddenly streaks across the night sky like a comet, leaving a long shining trail. Then another.

'The stars are falling.'

'Dancing,' she says, 'they're dancing.'

Finally we turn off the lane and follow a path down some steps and between the blocks of buildings that make up our hotel. Down the steps, down down down. So many of them. How can the lake be down such a steep hill? I'm at the bottom and sitting in a chair, plastic chair, white plastic, rough edges around the arms. I run my fingers along the rough bits, pick at the loose bits. This bit won't come off. Twist it. Pull it. Ah. It's free.

'Fucking Newbie. Fucking Newbie.' Kim is sitting opposite. His moonlit head is shaking, wobbling, blurring.

'What?' How can a word take so long to say? Whaaaaaaaaaaaaatttt.

'Newbie. Newbie be tripping.' Kim is rocking on his chair. No he's not. He's still. No, he's rocking. No, my head's rocking. Keep still. Stop moving head. You'll wake the dead.

'Ha haaa.'

'You OK?' Julie rubs my arm. I push it off. Too close. In my air.

'Wake the dead. Funny one.' I rub my arm. It's hot from Julie's hand. She's too hot. I'm too cold?

Silence. The lake is dark. An endless black crater just feet away. Silent and black and deep and still. All around black. Mountains pushing down with blackness. Breathe in. Deep breath. I'm high. That's all, just high. I spin back to normality. Everyone's clear; Julie is tapping her knees with clumped-together fingers. Kim is looking from me to Julie. His eyes wide and watery. One second on each of us. God, he's gone, not me, he's wasted, not me. Am I? Splashing from the lake. My head spins again. No, don't go again. Stay here. Stay straight. Marty comes out of the black, dripping black, black eyes in the blackness. Oily black tar running off his body.

'Great swim. Great. Go on. Jump in. Lie on your back and watch the laser show. Bloody awesome.' He falls on his behind in front of us.

Laser show? The stars. I look. I'm spinning. Then I'm not. The stars shoot here, there, crossing over each other. None of them stay still. Trails of thin light scar the night sky. I jerk my head in every direction trying to follow them. I never knew they did this.

'I never knew they did this.'

'Mushrooms, man. Make you see it all as it really is.' Kim's face is skyward. Eyes dart around.

Is that true? Is this as it really is? Is this the real world?

Get a grip. Get a grip get a grip get a grip. Heart beats in my ears every ten seconds. Too slow. It's too slow. Speed up heart. Speed up. It just gets louder.

Get a grip getagripgetagrip.

Everything's back. The stars are still. My heart is silent in my ears. Thank you. I don't like this high. The other three are back in focus. Back to looking real, but mad. Julie tapping and still doing that eyebrow thing, Marty cross-legged smiling at the sky like an alien spacecraft is landing. Kim bulging eyes. He's talking to himself. Smoking a joint, lit up by the lights of the hotel path, a dark deep mass behind him. But I'm back. I stand.

'I'm going to—' My heart. Thump. Where's the next thump. Where is it? I'm slipping again. Where is that thump? Fuck, my heart's stopped.

'My fucking heart's stopped.' I claw my chest.

'Relax. It's still there, beating. Bendy time, remember.' Who said that? I look from Marty to Kim to Julie. Back to Marty.

'Bendy,' Marty says. 'Just go with it. Don't panic.'

I sit again. Shut my eyes. Stars are too much. Too much shooting light.

'Joint.' A bullet between my eyes. I open them. Kim's massive finger is prodding me. Some orange light is shooting around next to it. 'Joint. Take it. Calm you down.'

I grab the orange light and turn it away so it faces Kim. Strong on my throat. Thump goes my heart. Thumpthumpthump. I give the orange light back. It leaves a trail in the dark. Close my eyes again. Orange trail burnt into them. It moves and wavers and streaks and then fades.

'You having a bad one?' Marty's voice from the dark.

'Leave him. He's OK. Aren't you?' Hot hand rubbing my arm.

'Newbie, Newbie. Bad trippin.'

Bad trippin'? Me? Don't say that. Shit, what's a bad trip? Will I come out of it? Sometimes people don't, they just go mad and stay there, in a mad place. My mouth waters. Swallow. Swallow it away. No vomit. Don't say vomit. You say vomit you vomit. No vomit. Thump. A tap is on in my mouth. Thump. I can feel it through my chest. Vomit. No. No vomit. Hate vomit. Hot hand. Burning my arm. Get up. Plastic chair caught in my feet. Scrabbling on the floor. Get up. Kim laughing. Fuck you, Septic. Fucking idiot. Stars rain laser fallout on me. My eyes hurt. Thump. My body shakes with the force. Get away. Get away from these things. I can calm on my own. Need quiet. Get away. Climb the steps. One. Two three. Thump. Four. Watery mouth.

Sit. Breathe in. Breathe out. You'll be OK. Away from them. Small stick people by the lake. Can't hear them now. Calm down. Come back. I'm coming back. I can grasp normality. Got it. I lean back on the step, put my hands behind me for support. Idiots. Idiot. It's soft behind me. But isn't it concrete? I look at my hand. It's sinking into the step, into the grey concrete. I try to pull it out, but suction is holding it there, like I'm stuck in mud. Pull. Pull. Pullpull-pull. It's out. But shit. My other hand is sinking too. I pull it out and the concrete makes a sucking sound as the vacuum where my hand was is filled.

'It's a bad trip, man.' Marty is suddenly next to me. His features are wobbling and the lines of him are blurred. He's half night, half man.

'Yeah. The steps. Trying to suck me in.'

'Just a bad trip. Go with it. Don't stress. It'll pass.'

I realise I've leant back again. My hand is in up to its wrist.

'Go with it. The comedown's great. This bit will pass.' He's smiling like fucking Gandhi.

'Thanks, Marty.' I turn my hand in front of my face. At least the concrete doesn't stick to me. But Marty, you're too close. I want alone. Alone. My mouth waters.

'I promise you'll get out of it soon.'

'Thanks, Marty,' I say. I swallow, fight the need to puke, 'But please just piss off.' I spit.

Gandhi smile doesn't fade.

'OK. No worries. We're down there if you need us.' Marty points back to the blackness and the two white things lurking on its edge. Then he is suddenly down there with them.

Right. Come back. Come on. Come back. It's just a trip. You won't puke. You'll be right as rain. I chant straightness at myself, and after half an hour, an hour, four hours, whatever, I feel a warmth spread across me as the concrete becomes solid and the stars slow down to a stop. I wait and make sure I'm not going to slide again. I count my heartbeats, regular, often, no time delay. I stare at the sky, willing the stars to move. They wobble a little, and shimmy, but no laser show. Is this a comedown? Thank God. Thank God.

Blackness is becoming dark blue in places. Mountains are silhouetted against it. Stars become faint against the changing colour of the sky.

I'm lying on the steps. Hard edges poke my back and behind my calves. Have I been sleeping? I sit up and the world skews for a moment, then levels out.

'Come on down. It's beautiful down here.'

I look to the voice. Just two stick people huddled together by the lake, sitting on the ground. I stand and walk down to them. My feet are light, my chest is relaxed. I feel the need for company.

'Come sit here.' Julie pats the ground beside her. She is wrapped in a blanket she shares with Marty. It's draped over their shoulders.

I sit and she pulls the blanket, taking some off Marty, and throws it over my shoulders. Her arm goes around my waist. I lean into her and put my arm around her. Marty's arm is already there but he doesn't move his and I don't move mine.

'You better now?' asks Marty.

'Yes. Much. Sorry about that.'

'No worries. Been there myself.'

'Where's Kim?' I ask.

'He suddenly faded. I think he went to bed.'

'How long was I up there?'

'Don't know. Doesn't matter,' says Julie. Her head rests on Marty's shoulder. 'Let's just watch this sunrise.'

We do. The dark blue becomes lighter. The black of the mountains becomes another shade of blue. The lake yet another. Everything is shades of blue. No other colour exists.

'Would you just fucking look at that?' Marty smiles at the view. A silent view undergoing a slow slow change. 'Beautiful.'

The mountains surround us. As they awake they grow bigger and bolder, showing their strength. The stars are fading to nothing. The blues keep changing. Cobalt, indigo, azure. The sun is still buried under the rock somewhere, slowly nearing the surface as all the other hues of its spectrum have yet to filter through this coming morning.

Marty is up and walks to the edge of the lake. Julie adjusts the blanket so I have more of it. The weight of her head is comfort on my shoulder. I tighten my grip on her waist. Tingling warmth spreads over my body, from my stomach down to my groin to a stretchy feeling in my toes and up through my chest and along my shoulders. It passes to Julie and the same passes from her to me. It's not sexual, or maybe it is, or is it just friendship, or is it some psychic knowing and enjoyment of this moment together?

'Fucking just look at that.' Marty is on the end of the diving board, standing over the dark blue of the lake, holding both hands up to the mountains, the sky, the power of the world. 'Isn't it the most beautiful fucking thing you ever saw?'

'Yes, Marty, beautiful.' Julie speaks from my shoulder and sighs. Her hand is on my knee. I look at her face and her eyebrows are still. Her hand is calm on my leg.

'Is this what a comedown always feels like?' My head rests on hers. I can smell apples.

'This is a good one. This is a good sunrise and an amazing place. And you two are pretty fucking great too.' She squeezes my knee. 'I feel so close to you two right now.'

'Would you just look at this view? Come on. Join me out here. It's even better.' He has become all the shades of the morning. He has become part of this day. Standing on the board suspended between an ancient lake and an even more ancient sky and in front of hunks of beauty hewed by the violence of countless millennia ago.

I get up. I want to be a part of this. I pull Julie by her hand and we shimmy along the diving board. It's only just wider than the length of my feet but we all manage to huddle at the end, gently bouncing above the stillness of the water. The world is silent in expectation of the coming morning. We hold onto each other for support, arms around each other, Julie's head between mine and Marty's chests. He smiles at me, wide and happy and blissful. I smile back.—

'Just look at it,' he says, 'just fucking look at it.'

I do. And I look and I look and I look, until finally most of the blues have gone, and the lake has become the lake, the mountains green mountains, and the sun has clambered up to a place just above the peaks to tell us tiredness must win, and comedowns must end.

I'm the first to break away.

'Don't go. It's still beautiful.'

Julie falls into the space I took. It reminds me of sliding into the warm part of the bed when Laura's just got out. Both of Marty's arms are around Julie and hers are around him.

'It is still beautiful. And it was great and the best and worst night almost of my life. But you two enjoy now. I'm off to sleep.' I walk up the steps towards my room.

'Good night,' mutters a sleepy Julie.

'Good morning. *Selamat pagiiii*,' I say. As I get to the top of the slope next to the door to my room I look back and watch as they walk together, wrapped in the blanket, towards Julie's room.

Right choice. I think. I'm happy to climb into bed alone, be calm and warm and tingling by myself.

The photos are tumbling again. I catch one and turn it round in my hand. It is blank. I drop it and catch another. Blank. Another. Blank. Why am I catching them? What do I want them for? I can't remember, but I must see something. There is something I must remember. What is it? I reach out with both hands. The air is filled with them; a blizzard of photos. I grab two handfuls and look at each one. Nothing.

'Keep trying.' A voice from somewhere. Who was it? 'Keep trying.' I put a hand to my mouth. My lips move. 'Keep trying.'

More. I grasp more. Paper scrunched in my fists. Blank empty paper. It shouldn't be blank. What should I be seeing? One is falling from high up. Twisting and twirling amongst a thousand other spinning, empty photos. But this one has something on it. What is it? I jump to try to catch it, but it's just out of my reach. It spins. Is it a face? A face? But it spins too fast. I must get it. A face appearing so quickly then disappearing on the turn. I jump. I have it. I turn it around in my hand. It's a mash of melting colours, running off the paper and over my fingers, leaving the glossy paper blank. Blank. Just blank. Too late.

MEAT OR VEG?

Geoff takes three long strides into the staffroom, sits in his chair, pulls it close to his desk, puts his head down.

'You alright?' I ask. I admire the interlocking squares I've just drawn on my blank lesson plan and contemplate where to start shading in.

'He's just sacked me.'

'What?'

'Pak Andy. Just sacked me for this.' He looks up and shows us a shiner, puffy and dark blue. 'I was just coming in and he saw me as I went past his office.'

'He can't do that.' Julie swings around from her desk in her swivel chair.

'Of course he can. No rules over here.' Marty is standing next to her. He squeezes Julie's shoulder. She wheels her chair a few inches away from him.

'For having a black eye. I told you he was a cunt.'

'Apparently it scares the students and I'm bringing the school into disrepute. But I've got a month.' Geoff touches the black blue around his half-closed eye.

'How did you get it?' I ask.

'How do you think? That Canadian bastard at Mei's.'

'What? Barry?' asks Julie.

'Yes. Don't ask why.'

I draw a spiral next to the blocks and lines doodled on my lesson plan.

'But you still had six months left on your contract.' Marty sidles along to follow Julie's chair.

'He's giving me a month to save up for my exit visa. He says he won't pay it as I breached the contract.'

'Hold on.' Julie stands and steps across the room and sits in Kim's chair. 'You haven't been given a contract, so how can you breach it?'

'You try arguing that with him. Anyway, I don't want to talk about it.'

'Why did Barry hit you?' Marty asks but is looking across at Julie, something hurt in his eyes.

'I was in Mei's on Saturday night while you lot were getting high at Toba. I got drunk on my own and told him to lay off Mei. He was having a right go at her in front of the customers.'

'Good for you.' Julie is nodding at him.

'Not really. He whacked me. I ran out like a girl, then I expect he took more out on her.'

I get up and head for the door.

'Where are you going?' Geoff asks, but I don't answer. New Me, who appears to be getting on nicely with forgetting his wimpy predecessor and all his issues lately, has his superhero clothes on, but as he gets to the door Kim knocks into him on the way in.

'Whoa, slow Newbie.'

'Excuse me Kim.'

'If you're going to speak to Pak, stop right there.' He walks me back a few steps with his hands on my shoulders.

'Why?'

'He just pulled me in as Geoff came out. He says anyone who stands up for him will be out the door straight away and won't get his month's notice. Geoff will lose his too. And no exit taxes paid by him.'

Do I care? So I lose my job? Is it a big deal?

'He can't do that. He knows most of us haven't enough for the tax.' Julie is up and stomping across the room with her arms crossed.

Exit tax. Good point. I don't have enough. Geoff probably does, but why should he pay it? Sit down and think this one out. It's not my battle after all. I look at my knees.

'Don't worry about it, guys. My fault. My problem,' says Geoff.

'That's a beauty, Geoff.' Kim leans in and examines the eye. 'Oh man. Standing up for Mei again?'

'Someone has to,' snaps Geoff. 'Anyway, I'm going up to prepare my class.' Geoff nods to himself, picks up his books, and heads to his class. The rest of us nod to each other, pick up our books, and head to our classes.

The day doesn't improve. Once the class has arrived there's a hole the size of China in the group.

'Anyone seen Johnny?'

There's a lot of shaking heads and one or two negative mutterings.

'OK. Perhaps he's ill. What shall we talk about today, then?' I walk around the horseshoe of tables expecting prompts.

Silence.

'Any questions about my life, England, anything?'

Everyone is looking at their desks. The class has lost its ringleader.

Oh shit. And I've got nothing prepared. The photocopies are just for show for Pak and the staff. I haven't had to plan for this lot since day one.

'So today, at last we can have a normal lesson, yes?' says Franz, the serious boy.

'Ah, yes. Of course. Page—er.' I fumble through the course book and feel heat spreading across my face. Lucky dip. 'Chapter Seven. Reading exercise: The Royal Wedding. Read it then answer the questions.'

There are a few sighs as the pages turn, but at least three of the students sit up straight, pick up pens and start making notes as they read. There are some serious learners here. My body feels strange on me as I shrink yet further into it.

—◊—

Eka's hands work their way down my back, squeezing and kneading and pulling as they go. My face is buried in the pillow. The smell of stale sweat and damp, almost hidden by perfumed washing powder, fills my nose.

'What will your friend do?' Knuckles rotate in the small of my back.

I open my mouth to answer and get a mouthful of musky pillow case. I turn my head to one side.

'Knowing Geoff, probably work the month then leave quietly. Then we all carry on and he's forgotten in a week.'

'Not nice.' A palm thwacks my left bum cheek.

'Ow. What was that for?'

'Because you are friend. You must help him.'

'He's not my friend. None of them are my friends.'

Thwack across my other cheek.

'If they not your friends, I not your friend too. You care for nobody?'

All hand contact leaves my body. I can feel her sitting upright as the weight shifts on the back of my legs.

'You are my friend. I don't talk to them. They know nothing about me. You know a lot.' I argue.

'They do not know about your ghost girl? They do not know you are crazy man?' The weight shifts again as she reaches for a cigarette and then I jump as she places a cold ashtray on my back.

'They probably think I'm a little crazy, but no one knows about, about her.' I try to move so I can sit up, but Eka pushes my head back down.

'No move. I'm talking and smoking, so you not to move.' She bounces up and down on me once to make sure I get the message. 'You stupid, you know?'

'Oh? Why's that? Can you give me a cigarette, please?'

'No. Because they like you. They invite you, who they never know a few months ago, to join at Toba and Bukit and in bars. They make you friend, but you say they are not friends. You not a nice crazy man.'

From the angle my head is turned I can see into the bathroom. A small green gecko clings to the wall above the squat, eavesdropping. I wonder what he makes of it all.

'OK. You're right. Maybe they are my friends and maybe I like them, I'm not sure, but how can I help Geoff?'

Her hand is in front of my lips holding the cigarette there.

'Go on. You get nicer. You allowed one smoke.'

I suck on it while she holds it between her fingers. I smell cheap moisturiser and tobacco. Then she takes it away.

'You help him is all. I don't know how. He your friend, not mine.'

She rolls off my legs and lies down next to me. Her naked breasts fall towards her sides. I sigh at the beauty of her. What is she to me? It's not love, I know that. She is a sounding board, someone to tell my pathetic woes to, someone who is mine and not connected to anything else. She is my release and my fantasy. She is my sanity too.

'Promise you will help him.' She turns her face to mine. Black eyes framed by curling soft black hair. Thick lips that pass on wise advice. Does she know what she is, what she could be in the other half of the world? Men would fight for her, any job would be hers. Her life would be easy. But instead she sells herself when she needs and befriends a strange *bule* man with a dead ex who lurks somewhere under his skin and makes surprise appearances at the strangest of times. Although I wonder if Laura has finally had enough of my forced personality change and disappeared; I've never known her be so quiet. I'm pleased. I'm sad. I'm empty. I'm lonely.

'You think of her again.'

'No. I don't.' I roll onto my back so she can't see my eyes.

'You think of her. I know. It's OK, crazy man. One day I find rich normal *bule* and you never see me after. OK?'

'OK.' I go up on an elbow and look at her face. Now she looks away. 'And it will happen. You are so very beautiful and very clever. Any man would be happy to have you.'

'But not you? You not happy to have me?' She continues looking away. Perhaps she's watching the gecko too.

'I don't "want" anyone. But you are my friend, my best friend here.'

'So that is good. And you must help your friends.'

'I know. I must.'

I kiss her but she doesn't kiss back. An unusual moment. Is Eka actually pissed off at me? Suddenly she is up.

'I hungry. We go for food.'

She walks on tiptoes to the *mandi*. A long, dark, perfect form. She disappears and I hear her scoop up water and throw it over herself. The gecko scrambles up the wall. I reach over and get a cigarette. The smoke hangs motionless in the heat.

She is perfect. Why is she stuck here? How did that happen? Just one of those people born unlucky. Made even more unlucky by the fact that had she been born a few thousand miles away, she would be living at the other end of the social scale. Perhaps I should take her with me. Fly her back to England, parade her beauty around the streets, make her my little Eliza Doolittle. But I won't. Selfish as I am, I know it would change her. I don't want her changed. And I don't want anyone anyway. What I have lost is irreplaceable. Because of that I don't see that I could ever love her, and she should be loved, although something tells me she never will be. In some ways I want her all for me and me alone, but in others I don't want her at all. We aren't meant to be together. I think she knows that.

—*So not only are you forgetting the slice-of-cake rule, you're becoming a chauvinistic twat.*

—*Why now, Laura? Why do you come now?*

—*I've had to watch you with this girl. Be ignored while you bury yourself in her sex. Use her for your own selfish needs. Well, I feel responsible. If it wasn't for me she wouldn't be falling for my Ice-Cream Boy. Because of me she's going to be heartbroken and abused by you. I'm trying to be your conscience.*

—*You lost that right when you died.*

—*I didn't ask for it.*

—*I know. I'm sorry. But I didn't ask for what you left me.*

—*Do you have any idea how I feel? How I feel when you sleep with this beautiful girl? When you do it without love, but with anger. And it's my fault. Do you know how sad this makes me feel?*

—*I'm sorry, Laura. I'm sorry. I just need to forget you, and with her, it happens. Just for a short while the pain is gone. Without that break, that rest, I will break. I'll shatter.*

—*Man up. Just man up and deal with me.*

—*Don't you think I would if I could?*

I'm aware the pillow is getting wet around my face. Tears are running down my cheeks. What am I doing?

'Leave me be. Please fucking leave me alone,' I shout to the room and the gecko and the crazy voice that can't be.

'Come here, Crazy. Stop talking to her. Come here,' comes a voice from the *mandi*.

I swing my legs off the bed onto the dusty floor, take a long drag on the cigarette and let the smoke out in a sigh before stubbing it out. Geoff and his black eye flash across my mind. He's got balls, more than either of me. I smile. I will help him. I just need to think how.

'Come, before I angry.'

But my dead girlfriend, her wishes and my conscience lose. Eka brings sanity of a type. I'm not ready to break. Not yet.

I don't bother tip-toeing. Trying to stay clean here is a lost cause. Flat feet plop across the dusty shed skin of people unknown, limbs of dead insects, and dirt walked in by rodents. I walk to the naked beauty waiting with a bucket of cold water in the blue-tiled room. Even when she throws scoopfuls of water over me, lathers me, rinses me and leaves me shivering in the icy cold fluid of the *mandi*, the dirt still sticks to my soles.

I look at the plates of food laid out on the plastic tablecloth. A fly buzzes from a dish of boiled rice and then lands on a fried chicken thigh. Eka picks the thigh up and the fly buzzes onto the next dish. There are about eight more for it to taste. They have all been placed on our table by the open-shirted waiter. They are dishes from the window display where they've been sweating in the heat and been walked on by countless more flies. There is no one else in this small eatery and I wonder how long the food has been sitting there.

'Eat.' She tears a strip off the thigh.

'It's all meat. I don't eat meat.'

'That not meat.' She points at the rice. 'That not meat.' She points at boiled eggs in a yellow sauce. 'That not meat.' She points at something wrapped in leaves. 'But no matter because today you eat meat. Man eat meat. Chicken die to be eat, so you eat. You,' her finger is now directed at me, between the eyes, 'eat.'

Those massive eyes of hers accuse me of everything; being a coward, being untrue to my friends, being untrue to her, being untrue to me, and a lot of other things that I don't know I'm guilty of, but no doubt, without a shadow, I am.

'That looks like cow.' I point at a dish of brown flesh.

'It is. You can eat, but I don't eat. I am Hindu.'

'I know and that's my point; you won't eat it, so why must I?'

'Because you think you are good, but you are not. You have no goodness for others, you have no...' She chews the chicken slowly while her mind hunts for the word. I get it first.

'Principles?'

'Principles? Maybe. Is principles goodness in life? Care for things? Belief in gods? '

'Yes. Maybe. But not the god bit.'

'So you can eat meat. You not care for things, not care for animals, not care for friends, you no principles. You only care for your problems. So eat meat.'

She waves the chicken in front of my face. The fly buzzes around it trying to get on.

'Eat.' She waves it again. 'And it is *enak enak*. Tasty.'

Have my principles gone? What were they to begin with? Vegetarian because of what? Pacifist? Really? In this age where everyone has guns and everyone has an alleged cause to fight, is there room for pacifism? And what about treating people with respect? So few people deserve respect. Don't they?

Do I still care about these things? About animal welfare? About wars being fought for oil and water and fuck anyone who lives in the vicinity? Have I ever cared? Have I just been a bullshitter, because having principles is cool?

'Padang food very tasty food. Special from Sumatra. Very spicy.'
She brings me back from my internal soliloquy. 'Eat chicken, Mr
Crazy Chicken.'

I smell the spices and chilli coming off it. Why not eat it? What
do I care for a chicken? What do I care for anything? Laura has
gone. I have no real love for this girl sitting opposite; no love for me;
no love for anyone. Why not eat the bird?

—*Go on, eat the bird, dickless.*

—*Great. So you're suddenly back and joining sides with the mad
Hindu, are you?*

—*I'm saying nothing. I'm dead. The bird's dead. What does any
of it matter?*

I look at the other dishes on the table, at all the various parts
of cows and sheep and chicken marinated in all sorts of spices and
herbs.

—*Do what the hell you want. That's why you're here. Care for
nothing and no one anymore. Hurt who you want. Eat that little
chick-chick-chick-chick-chicken.*

Eka is holding it so close to my mouth I can almost taste it. No
meat for eight years; why not have it now? What does any of it
matter?

'It matters,' I say and push Eka's hand away and pick up a stuffed
cassava leaf. It tastes good and chilli heat sears my mouth. I take a
gulp of water from a smeared glass.

Eka nods and smiles and a hand strokes my face, but not Eka's.
Hers still hold the chicken.

—*Still got some cares, then, Ice-Cream Boy.*

I nod and smile back at Eka.

'First you help friends, you help people you can. Then you help
her. You help crazy dead girl who still loves you.'

—*I think I'm beyond help, but she has a point. You could try.*

I nod again.

'I care for you, Eka.'

'No you not. Shut up and eat.'

I pick up an egg and take a bite. More mouth burning. My head is on fire.

'Egg is animal,' she says.

'I'm vegetarian, not vegan,' I say through the pain. The inside of my mouth is near blistering. 'I'm not that crazy.'

STATIVE
AND ACTIVE

itri is dangling her feet in the pool while Benny floats tummy-side down on a gently turning airbed in the middle. His arms are drooped over the front and slowly rotate in the water. Although guards still patrol around outside these walls, the rest of the house is silent and empty. I feel more like a babysitter than a teacher. My feet swing in the water next to Fitri's.

'Does your father miss your mother and sister?'

'Sometimes you English people are really stupid.'

'I guess we are. But how do you know he misses them?'

'He is my father. Yes he is big boss man too, but first he is my father.'

'Your mother's name is Su-chin, isn't it?'

'Yes. Why?'

'I just want to make sure I've got it right. It makes someone more of a person, more human and real, when you know their name.'

'Please don't mention her again. It makes me sad.'

'OK.' I steer back to the straight and narrow. 'What's the past participle of drive?'

Fitri looks at me, all open eyes and open mouth.

'Well, I am being paid to teach you English.'

'But I know nearly all in English.'

'Nearly everything. You know nearly everything in English.'

She kicks me under the water.

'Benny,' she shouts, 'what is the past participle of drive?'

'Driven,' he shouts back.

'Even he knows. We don't need lessons.'

'So why not ask your father to take you to Singapore to meet your mum?' She doesn't want to learn, fine. I'll spin it back into dangerous bends.

'He is too proud. Too busy. Too scared. And I think my mother will not talk to him.'

Something tickles my knee, and before I see what it is, I flick my hand across it. A small moth flitters off my skin and lands in the water. Leaning forward I try to pluck it out, but the mini-waves from my waggling legs push it out of my reach. It flutters a little more, wings weighted with water, then it's still. Guilt prickles me like nettles. We both stare at the moth for a long moment.

'You should ask him.' I pull my eyes away from the death and look at Fitri's profile. 'You should tell him to go with you. It hurts him all the time. He needs resolution.'

'I know.' The only sound is the gentle lapping of water around the pool edge and the faint hum of traffic from outside the house.

'Can you use stative verbs in the continuous?'

'OK, Mr Teacher. What is a stative verb?'

Benny shouts from his plastic lily pad, 'A verb like, like, hate, love. It describes a state. My sister is sooo stupid. And you cannot use in continuous.'

'Is he right?' she whispers to me.

I nod.

'Little shit.'

'Fitri, where do you get this language?'

'American TV. We cannot see kissing, it is all cut out, but we can hear all the bad words in the world.' She picks the can up from beside her. 'So I cannot say "I am loving this Coke"?'

'No. You can't. Love should be permanent and not short-lived. Not just this moment. You don't love one thing one day and not the next.'

She nods.

'But language is always changing and no doubt one day someone, or some big company or something, will create a slogan and change the rules overnight. Then everyone will go around saying "I'm loving you right now" or some such bullshit.'

'You are right, love should be for always. And watch *your* language.'

'Sorry. That's exactly why you should convince your dad to see your mum.'

Fitri is about to say something more when the sound of the front door slamming reverberates around the house. Shoes clip-clop in a regular fast beat across the tiled floor. Charles appears by the pool in business trousers and short-sleeved white shirt. He looks at us for a moment through a smoke haze wafting from the cigarette clamped between tight lips. He takes it from his mouth.

'These English lessons are becoming very relaxed. Maybe I pay you too much, Englishman.' He leans against the wall and stares some more.

'I've learnt a lot today, Father,' says Fitri, 'about stative verbs and love.'

'Love? Huh. That can't be taught in day. It can't be taught in a lifetime.' He sighs and pushes himself off the wall.

'Do you have time for me to ask you something after the lesson, Charles?' I ask.

'Yes. Come and talk now. My lazy children can wait for you.'

I stand up and wet feet marks follow me into the main room. I look back at the trail I have made. They are already disappearing in the heat.

Charles goes to the fridge and takes two Heinekens out. I'd forgotten other beers existed in this land of Bintang and Anker. Europe survives without me. It still makes its own beer, still extends its prying tentacles searching for the smallest of profit into the faraway reaches of the rest of the world. I'd prefer a Bintang but I take the Heineken with thanks.

Charles flicks the TV on and we each sit in an armchair. He reaches for the video remote and a Manchester United–Arsenal game comes on.

'Mr Beckham relaxes me. He is the best thing from your country.'

'Something of a god in this country,' I say.

'Yes. The only Western god most of these Indonesians are will-ing to accept.'

I pull the ring from my beer and take a swig.

'So what do you want to ask me?' He sits back in his chair and puts his feet on the table. He sighs and wiggles in his chair as though try-ing to achieve comfort, then takes his feet off and sits upright again.

'Are you OK?' I ask.

'Yes. Just tired. Is that what you wanted to know?'

'No. I'd like your help with something.'

He nods and keeps watching the match.

'It's actually to help a friend of mine.'

'If you ask for my help, you know I will want something in return.'

I nod. 'I thought you might.'

But I have no idea what. Different possibilities shoot through my mind: free lessons, sell drugs to my students, give him money, lots of money. I have always wondered why he wanted me to teach his kids.

'First you tell me what you want.'

'Right.' So I do. He listens and nods. He doesn't interrupt. I tell him my idea of how he can help, and when I have finished he looks at me.

'Why do you need me? You should do this on your own. And why do it anyway?'

'Because I want to. I don't want to sit back and hear about these things anymore and do nothing. And I want your help because I don't want to risk screwing it up on my own. I'm just not physically up to it.'

Charles snorts.

'That is maybe true, but if you are mentally adequate, you can do it alone. Trust me, I know about these things. I am not a strong man, but people think I am. Reputation is my biggest muscle.'

'I don't have that reputation.'

'Are you sure? You are a little mystery to most, I think; that is a kind of reputation on its own.'

'I just don't want to mess up.'

On the TV Beckham hits one off the post, but Charles expresses no emotion. His dark eyes don't brighten at the near miss.

'OK. So tell me where and when and it will happen. Although why you assume I can help with such a thing I do not know.' A slight glimmer of something in his eyes at this, maybe humour, as he peers sideways at me.

'Thank you. Is tomorrow night too soon?'

He shakes his head.

'Now, what you must do for me.'

What will it be?

—*I go for the drug-selling, myself. Or maybe sexual pleasure to one of his business partners.*

—*I hadn't thought of that one.*

—*Mafioso, numbnuts. It's going to be gruesome.*

'Your mind is elsewhere,' cuts in Charles, 'your eyes have gone away.'

'Sorry. It happens.'

—*Stop making it happen, will you.*

She seems to take notice.

'You remember Teddy?'

Oh shit.

'The witch doctor?'

'The *dukun*. You will see him. He will find out where your eyes and mind go and he will help you.' He takes a long swig from his beer and then burps. 'Excuse me. Too much gas in this piss.'

I think I would have preferred the drug-selling rather than the *dukun*.

'But that doesn't help you,' I say, hoping for a way out.

'But it makes me happy. Teddy says he can help you, then he can help you.'

'So why doesn't he help you with your problem?'

Charles shifts in his seat and the faintest of redness touches his cheeks.

'Because I have told him not to and his power isn't that strong. And do not mention it again.' He looks at me and this time holds my gaze for an uncomfortable time. Some sort of warning passes unspoken, and then he looks back to the football. My heart beats heavy in my chest.

'You will meet the *dukun*. I will ask him where and when and you will go there.'

'OK. But it won't help me either.'

'Why? Because you don't need help?'

'Exactly.'

Charles laughs suddenly and loudly.

'There are so many things wound up in your body, between your shoulders, down in your insides, swirling around your fragile skull, I can almost hear them. You need help, believe me.'

I think about telling him he is wrong or that he also has the same symptoms, but decide against it. Instead I thank him and walk back to the pool where Fitri still dangles her feet and drinks her Coke and Benny snores on his floating mattress.

I sit quietly between Julie and Marty, like a piece of paper slid between two electrical contacts. Remove me and sparks might fly.

Mei's is busy tonight; we teachers, the usual lot, all present, albeit quieter and gloomier than normal and taking up the long table near the beer fridge. Also present are Barry and his gang: an unpleasant fifty-something German with a big moustache and his beautiful yet sad-looking twenty-something Indonesian wife beside him. With them an English retired businessman who changes allegiances in Mei's every week or so and no one seems to mind because he is a man who expresses little opinion. In the far corner sits a group of six Indonesian men, and over all watches Mei from her place behind the counter. Her slips of paper for each drink taken for each table are impaled on the spike in front of her.

'You should go over and whack him, man.' Kim's hair is sticking out at all angles, as though he's just got up. 'I fucking would if I were you. Fucking whack him.'

'No you wouldn't. You're as pussy as the rest of us, Kim. Just slightly more stoned.' Jussy wipes condensation down his bottle so it pools on the table.

'I am not stoned.' Kim sits more upright in his chair.

'You're never fucking straight, Kim. We all know it.' Julie gives an unnatural shake of her head and blinks.

'I think you're talking about yourself there, Jooolie. You're constantly twitching and fiddling like a fucking, a fucking twitchy English bitch on drugs.'

'Kim, watch your mouth.' Quiet yet surprisingly firm from Marty.

Julie sighs.

'Hey, everyone fucking gang up on the Yank, why don't you?'

'We're not ganging up,' says Julie.

'You are. You fucking are.' Kim runs his hands through his messy mop of hair, then laughs. 'Finding out who my friends are. Fuuuck.'

'You're getting paranoid, Kim. Have a break from the grass, dude.' Jussy flicks his little pool of water, sending a small spray across the table.

'Fuuuck. Even the homeboy has turned.'

'Like I said, Kim, paranoid.'

I look over to Geoff, who is sitting unnoticed amongst us while the others debate their paranoia and addictions. He is sitting with his back to Mei and turned slightly sideways in his chair, presumably to avoid catching Barry's eyes.

'You alright, Geoff?' I ask.

'What?' he comes back from somewhere. 'Yeah, fine.' He looks at me but his eyes wander over my left shoulder to Barry's table, where they linger, then move back to the bottle on the table in front of him.

The others sit silent for a moment to let fingers tap glass, hands run through hair and cabin fevers grow. I can feel the static growing around me as whatever is going on with Julie and Marty builds unspoken like a thunderstorm waiting to crack.

Something is building in me too, as I look at the clock behind Mei. The hands have moved on as though the universe has just bent and we've lost half an hour to the blackness of time warps and wormholes. I've been hoping they'd be here by now, but I'm also pleased they aren't. No doubt now, as I wait and watch the clock, time will change its mind and make things move slowly in the sludge of this uncomfortable night.

'What's the matter with the faggot table tonight?' Barry must be able to feel whatever it is emanating from our group. 'Did someone break a nail?'

The only one of us to make a sound is Kim, a sort of guffaw verging on a donkey bray, followed by an agreement. 'Yes, this is a fucking faggot table tonight. Fucking twitching miserable Brits, a love-struck Aussie and a Montana moron.'

We all just stare. I look for the hairline crack that must be running through Kim's head somewhere. Jungle ganja breaking a good mind.

Jussy just shakes his head at Kim, Julie's hand grasps her Bintang as though she is about to swing it at him, and Marty's face moves through various expressions as he probably tries to think of something to impress Julie and belittle Kim. Nothing leaves his mouth. Geoff is the only one who doesn't react.

I, on the other hand, am dealing with the other I, the other me, only I'm not sure which one is which anymore. There's something trying to pull me up and out of my seat and punch Barry straight in the face. There's another force keeping me stuck to the chair. Images of the bar in England, quaking in my shoes, being useless in the face of aggression, swirl around inside me. Thoughts of New Me facing up to the Ben Sherman shirt at Bukit Lawang mix in the mucky mental soup. Who am I to be tonight? I know who I want to be, but being afraid is the most crippling of afflictions.

I look to the clock. It now struggles to move on. Time hangs off its arms like weights.

They will be here soon, but I wish they were here, now, in this moment.

—Why wait?

Just what I need now to add to my schizoid confusion.

—Why wait? You've got it in you. You froze once and that was OK. You learn from it. You have learnt. You weren't scared of that Liverpudlian.

—I was stoned. It wasn't even me, either of me.

—*It was. Your mind was just free to let your body do what it wanted.*

—*I'll get pummelled. Or pee myself. Or both. Or I'll just get tongue-tied and laughed at and end up looking a twat.*

—*What do you care? What happened to the new you? Don't give a shit, remember? Do whatever, say whatever, take no prisoners.*

That is true. She has a point. What's happened to that?

—*Perhaps I can't change, at the end of the day.*

—*Misery? Loss? Poor little boy with dead girlfriend? Nothing matters? What happened to what I made you? You mean I died for no reason? Or perhaps your little Indian girlfriend, what's her name, Eka? Perhaps she's having more of an effect on you than you realise.*

—*Oh shut up. She's nothing compared to what you were. And you, you just died. That's it exactly. Died with no consideration for me.*

—*I didn't do it deliberately. I just did it. I just forgot people drive on the other side of the road there. That's all. So, yes, I died with no consideration for you. I was in too much pain to consider you. It hurt too much. It hurt. I considered me and shuffled off this mortal coil because it just hurt too much. Any idea how that felt? That much pain? Ever considered that, Ice-Cream Boy?*

I try to blank my mind from her. It fails. She always manages to get in there.

—*I didn't think so. So go ahead, give my death some reason. Grow some and go and tell that Canadian woman-beater what a shit he is.*

Big slow footsteps, heavy behind me. Chair legs scrape back across the tiles. One, two, three heavy bodies sit on creaking wooden chairs. It's like I can see out of the back of my head. It's a Western, the gunslingers have walked in and the piano stops playing, poker players stare with forgotten hands, and the barman moves the expensive bottles off the shelves. Sort of. At least everyone's staring at whoever's sitting behind me, but Mei's most expensive bottles are all in the fridge and are all the same price, there is no piano, and this is a no-gambling country. But the effect is still close enough.

I shift in my seat to look behind me. I recognise two of them as Charles' guards and the other I've seen loitering in the Iguana. Here they are. The cavalry.

—*Lucky you. Don't need your balls after all. There's six the size of coconuts just behind you.*

—*Well, I'll do the talking. They'll do the muscle bit.*

My confidence has grown. The moment is here and I can change the whole mood of the evening. Newbie will save the day, with a little help from his friends.

Whispers cross the room from Barry's table, followed by laughter.

'You packed your bags yet, faggot boy?' The Canadian voice kills the silence and my Western movie metaphor; they don't know the muscle is my backup.

—*Go on. Be Clint Eastwood. Clean up this town.*

'Oh, shut the fuck up.' The words come out loud and angry and unexpected. So much for internal conversations.

'Oh, one of the girls is menstruating.' More laughter from across the room. Mei presses the remote to turn the TV on, perhaps in some hope of calming the room.

'What you doing?' asks Julie in a hushed voice, while others stare at me.

Three large bodies give off heat behind me.

—*Feel lucky, punk?*

—*Not really, but bugger it.*

I stand. I turn.

'Look out, Barry. He'll kill with his verb tenses.' The German strokes a large moustache that lies across a puffy, moist face, and looks to his wife, who stays expressionless. Barry sits back in his chair and smirks. Biceps I've never noticed before pour out from under his T-shirt sleeves.

I look to Charles's guards and although they are looking nowhere in particular, my balls grow. The opposite of the expected shrinkage.

It's like the mushrooms have kicked in again as I walk across the bar. Ten steps that feel like an hour each. During not one minute of one of those hours do I think about sitting back down, running or fainting. What's the worst that can happen?

—*You could die.*

—*If that's the worst, then I welcome it.*

—*Liar.*

—*I miss you, and this here, this moment, is nothing. This is what I want. I want nothing else to care about. I'm not scared of dying.*

—*Easy to say with backup.*

'Can you, Barry'—my finger, strangely steady, points at him—'please keep your mouth shut when we are in this bar?' I'm by their table. The three of them are turned towards me. German's wife goes to the toilet.

'Sit back down, son,' says the Englishman, wobbling on his fence.

'No, not yet.'

'Come and sit down,' says Julie from behind me. Marty mutters agreement.

'Fucking Newbie is back on form. Yeah. Go get him, Newbie.'

Sighs and then silence again after Kim's input.

I wait, expecting to hear the sound of chair legs scraping tiles as three strong Chinese make their move. But no. Just more silence.

Just as well. I'd do this anyway. With or without them.

—*Brave and all lack of self-care, I am impressed. But you're going to get creamed, Ice-Cream Boy.*

—*It'll do me good. Might even wake me up. Now hush.*

'And I'd like you to apologise to my friend Geoff.'

Barry shakes his head and with each shake the smirk widens.

'Anything else? Fag.' Hate pours from him like piss from a burst colostomy bag.

'Stop hitting Mei.'

He stands up, his chair flies and skids across the floor on its back.

'You…' Glasses leave his face and are placed on the table. Squidgy little eyes. People look different when you see them for the first time without glasses. They look lost.

'Me what? Faggot?' I use his favourite word. 'Haven't you got any other insults in that ape head?'

He stutters for a second and blinks.

'Pussy.' He spits it out, but there's not a lot of venom to his attempted strike.

I laugh. Something strange is going on.

—*You're not backing down, numbnuts. Keep it up. He's floundering.*

'Now first, say sorry to Geoff.'

'Fuck that.' Barry takes a step to the side of the table.

I hear a chair move behind me. No, not now. I don't want the help now. I want the battering. I want to feel and I want to bleed.

'Apologise.' A voice from behind. An Australian voice.

Barry squints as he looks behind me at Marty, like he's trying to read a distant road sign. More chairs scrape across Mei's tiled floor.

'Yeah. Apologise, dude. And apologise to Mei, too, on your way out.' These aren't Chinese voices. That one is from Montana.

I look behind. Marty, Jussy and Julie are standing. Kim has both hands running through his hair and Geoff, although still seated, is almost smiling at the beer bottle he holds. Kim pulls his hands out of his mop.

'Fuck it, Newbie. I'm with you. Fucking apologise, Barry. You dick.' He stands and pops a cigarette in his mouth and lights it. 'I fucking love this country.' Then he giggles like a four-year-old.

The Oriental backup have heads turned away, watching football on the TV like it's the only thing happening in the room.

Sweat patches are spreading out across Barry's tight-fitting T-shirt.

'Fuck you, faggot.' He steps part way around the table.

'Apologise, Barry.' A female voice, so far unheard.

He stops again and looks at Mei, who has come out from behind her counter. In her hand is a baseball bat. This is turning into the best film I've seen.

'Get back behind the counter, Mei. I'll deal with you later.'

'No. You apologise. Then you leave. You not come back, Barry.'

'Get back behind the fucking counter, Mei, before I put you there.'

There's a cry from the Chinese muscle table. Reflex action means we all look.

'Sorry. But Chelsea score,' says the one in the middle. 'You please carry on.' He waves his hand in a general sweeping motion to indicate the rest of us and looks back to the screen.

I'm smiling.

—*You're weird.*

—*Not as weird as you. You're completely inexplicable.*

'You attempt to put her anywhere, and I'll put you in the hospital.'

—*Did I just say that?*

—*Corny.*

—*Sorry.*

'I'm with him on that, Barry,' says the British businessman as he falls off the fence and lands on his feet, on the side of the righteous and messed-up.

'You lay one finger on her and I'll take that baseball bat to you. Business interests will be forgotten.'

Barry looks at him and his facial muscles twitch as though he has just stood on a nail.

—*He's going to say "et tu, Brute?" now.*

—*He hasn't the brains.*

He looks to the German for backup, who looks around the room and does a quick mental calculation. His eyes linger on Mei, run up and down the bat, pass back to me, his mouth turns up, a nod, back to Barry.

'*Ja*, fuck you, man. You are a dick.'

'But I own this bar. You lot get the fuck out before…'

'Before what? You take on everyone in here? I'm playing with the idea that we do all leave, except for Mei, the baseball bat, and you.' I turn. 'You'd be happy with that, wouldn't you, Mei?'

She nods, her eyes thin and focussed on her prey, lips drawn tight.

'I like much. But most I like is Barry sign me my bar back, and then never come again here.'

'I think it is possible.' British businessman gets businesslike. 'As it's part my money you've invested here, Barry. And since you've invested, the profits seem to be suffering, so I'm pulling out. We'll have the contracts ready next week, won't we, Barry?'

Barry rubs watery eyes. A lost and scared and lonely boy. He replaces his glasses, then removes them again as if he doesn't like what he sees, mutters something that might be an attempt at being defiant, but only sounds like 'faggot,' and he starts walking out.

'What about the apology, Barry?'

—*And still you persevere.*

—*Now I've started…*

Barry stops with his back to the room. Shoulders rise slowly.

'Now, Barry. To Geoff and Mei.'

Barry turns, and as he does so his head sags as though his body is exhausted from carrying the weight of it and the rubbish held within. He is running on emergency power only. Geoff, however, has had a recharge bolt shot up his arse and gets up, puts his arm through Mei's and leads her to where Barry stands.

'Mei first, please, Barry.'

A momentary flash of anger lights Barry's eyes as they meet Geoff's, but when they see whatever is there, the light goes out and they move on to Mei, but not her eyes, they rest on a point just below her mouth.

'I'm sorry, Mei.' His shoulders slump. 'Really.'

Really? Genuine remorse?

Mei stands with straight back, chin up.

Barry looks back to Geoff, but before a word leaves his mouth, Geoff's fist is shooting through the air. It hits his chin, carries on, pushing with the wound-up tension of a released coil, sending Barry's head back on his shoulders, causing the rest of his body not to fly backwards but to collapse almost silently to the floor. His hands don't have time to even attempt to break the fall. He is creased up on the tiles like a feeble foal freshly dropped from its mother's rear. Then his hands find ground, push up slowly until he is standing on legs that wobble like the same newborn foal and, without another word, he staggers from the bar.

'Bugger the apology,' says Geoff, 'that felt better.'

'You have free beer, Mr Geoff. And you too, Mr Newbie.' Mei surveys her kingdom and subjects like a queen. 'All of you. Free beer.'

'Fuckin' A.' says Kim.

'But only one.'

The Chinese backup, who haven't backed up anything, stand and throw notes on the table. 'Not for us, thank you. The football was very good. Liverpool win.' And they leave.

'Who were they?' asks Marty.

I watch their dark-jacketed backs disappear into the night outside.

'Passing trade, I guess. And who,' I say to Geoff, who examines his knuckles with a smile I never knew could fit on his face, 'are you?'

'A happy man,' he laughs. 'And thanks for that very surreal and satisfying moment.'

The British businessman downs his beer and raises his eyebrows to the German, whose wife checks the room for blood and guts as she comes back from the toilet.

'Come on, Erich. Let's leave this lot to their not-so-faggotty ways.' He pats me on the back as he goes. 'Well done. I never really liked him.' And they too are gone.

—*Want to go get a drink somewhere quiet?* she asks.

—*Yes. I do.*

—*You've grown a nice set. I knew they were there somewhere. I always knew that.*

Despite the noise of laughing and celebration and of protest at my wanting to depart from Mei's, we leave together, hand in hand, stepping out into the warm enveloping night, where people are as invisible as ghosts.

We lie in the grass of the housing-compound playing field together and look to stars and constellations. I hold her hand. She holds mine. Our mouths are still as our lives together speed through our minds. I am plugged into her and memory and moments flow between us in powerful currents. There are things she remembers clearly that only lurk in the dark, dusty areas of my brain. They are cleaned off and brought into the light thanks to her. Important moments to her. Important moments to me. Some match, some don't. But they are all equal here. We are one under this foreign sky. One life created by moments we share.

Lightning soundlessly cracks the clear sky. It starts near the horizon on the right and spiders across the night, shattering its wholeness in less than a second.

—*Not a cloud to be seen.*

—*Anvil lightning, I do believe, she says, smug in her complete lack of smugness.*

—*How do you know so much?*

—*Because I'm me. It's probably travelled from a storm cloud miles away.*

It does it again, spidering across the sky at such a speed that it's nearly impossible to follow its journey.

—*Wow.*

—*Don't see them like this back home.*

—*Clouds will roll over in a few minutes, then it's going to pour down.*

—*We should move.*

—*Why? Scared we might get hit and die? Because I'm already dead, remember.*

She leans over my face and blows in my eyes. I blink. Then she kisses me, forcing her tongue between my lips.

—*If only all dead people were like you.*

—*Over her shoulder I see the blackness of a cloud bank rolling over the top of the houses that encircle the playing field. Another bolt escapes, lighting up the cloud and shining through Laura so that she disappears in the light. I blink. I blink again.*

She is gone. You idiot, she's gone because she isn't real. Control this madness. Control it.

—*If that's the case, how come you now know about anvil lightning?*

She is lying beside me again, as solid as the trees and houses around us.

—*Subconscious memory. I learnt it at school and it's been lurking in the recesses ever since.*

—*Could be.*

—*But I hope it's because you are here.*

—*I am. And so is the rain.*

Big, heavy drops arrive, random and far apart, landing on us and around us. But we lie there, more drops slowly filling the spaces between the first, until I am blinking water from my eyes.

—*Let's go clubbing. Celebrate the coming together of Old Me and New Me. Celebrate the birth of a don't-give-shit hero.*

—*Sounds good to me. To both of me.*

I laugh.

We run from the field and the compound to the main street, where we flag down a taxi. By the time we are in, I am soaked. Laura is dry. I ignore the possible meaning.

SEASICK

'**I** hear you did a good show,' Charles says into the bowl as he
sucks in a mouthful of noodles from his soup.

'Yes, it seemed to do the trick.' I decide his way of eating
is better than mine, as I have splatters of sauce over the front of my
T-shirt. Trying to eat noodles with dignity doesn't work. I bend my
head low down over my bowl and slurp up too. Inelegant, but it isn't
a social issue here. Get those noodles in no matter what noise you
make. And why not?

'So now you must do your part of the deal.'

Cars crawl past outside the window. I squint as white sunlight
reflects off them.

'But your men didn't do anything.'

'Exactly what I told them. Only if you were being killed would
they step in. I am an excellent judge of people, and there is something in you, or perhaps not in you, that I knew would deal with the
problem without too much help. '

'I'm a coward, so I don't know what you saw.'

'It's what I didn't see. Something is missing in you, and when
people aren't whole, they get on and do what they must without
worry for themselves.'

'Like you.'

Charles nods, then slurps up the last of the noodles. He dabs his
mouth with a fine handkerchief he pulls from the inside of his
jacket, then his hand goes to the pocket on the other side and he

pulls out a small, worn, black book. He flicks through some pages, eyes squinting, until he finds what he is looking for.

'On Tuesday you must be in Lampuuk near Banda Aceh. Teddy will meet you at the next cove north from Lampuuk beach during the afternoon. You will do everything he says.' He closes the black book and puts it on the table next to his coffee.

'Why?' I dig around under the thick black coffee with a tea-spoon, looking for condensed milk. I manage to recover some. This is the taste of Indonesia. Strong thick coffee and sweet milk.

'Because he will help you replace the missing bit of you.'

'If you're so sure, why don't you use him? Use him to help you and Su-Chin sort out your problems.'

'Because Su-Chin does not want to be helped. She does not want me.' He lights a cigarette and rubs his eyes. 'And I respect her for that. I am not good for her.'

'Well, I think—'

'I do not care what you think. It is not your business, so do not talk about her again.'

My mouth opens to tell him that I'm not his business either, but I yank the words back down from the top of my throat. He can't help his wife, so he wants to help me. Although why me, I'm not sure. Maybe he just wants to help anyone.

'Neither you nor Teddy know my problems. I'll do what you want, but you can't help me either. It's impossible.' I move my packet of cigarettes on the table around like I'm thinking chess moves, then I take one out and light it. I draw in the smoke and hold it, let it burn my lungs, get in my veins, do its business, before blowing it from my nose in two long straight grey lines.

'Teddy sees you have problems. You are like a glass man to him; you can't hide anything from him.'

I study him for once, stare at him like he stares at people. Look at the straightness of his mouth, into the lines around his eyes and the darkness within them. He looks back and for the first time we hold each other's gaze as equals. His pupils seem to quiver for a moment and then they break away from me. They scan the room as if searching for something.

'Excuse me.' He gets up and heads to the toilets.

I blink, move the cigarette pack around the table with index finger again, until it nudges Charles's notebook. The notebook that holds the details of my future appointment and, as he normally keeps it close to his chest, probably details of many of his appointments, meetings and, perhaps, contacts.

I look over my shoulder: waiter scribbling a couple's order, people dotted around the high-class restaurant slurping noodles, a corridor leading to toilets. No one paying *bule* any attention; that's one thing about expensive places, the Westerner is left alone.

I flip the book around to face me and flick through its pages. Chinese characters everywhere and no order or headings to pages. But at the back, just as I am about to replace it as I found it, a page of numbers, each one preceded by characters. The numbers look like phone numbers, and some have international prefixes. Quickly checking behind me again, I reach into my school bag and pull out a scrap of paper and a pen and scrawl any number that starts with 00. I scrawl quickly and copy ten numbers. I fold the paper and slide it into my shirt pocket with the pen and then return the notebook to where it was. Five seconds later Charles returns and sits. His hand goes to the book and puts it back in his jacket.

'You have been running while I was in the bathroom?'

My eyes can't meet his. I force a laugh.

'Why do you say that?'

'You have sweat on your face.'

'It's hot.'

'There is air conditioning.'

'Perhaps it's the thought of Teddy and his voodoo.'

'You will see it is not voodoo. But you will see. You have no excuse for not going.'

'But Tuesday is only three days away. My teach—'

'I must see Pak Andy later today. I will tell him you must have time off. Do not worry about him. His debt has made him my bitch.' He manages one of his almost-smiles at this. I manage a whole one.

'Your American English is really good.'

'I thought this phrase was universal English.'

'It probably is, but it started in the States, I'm sure.'

'Most things do these days. Most things do.' He stands up and looks down at me. 'Go there. Lampuuk. That is almost the last thing I want you to do.'

'Almost? What else?' I prepare for the drug-dealing bit, or the smuggling, or whatever strange something this man is going to ask of me.

'Pay the bill. It is your turn.' He leaves without another word, steps out into the heat in his black suit, sun reflecting off slicked-back hair. I watch through the window as a car pulls up beside him. He climbs in and is gone.

I ask for the bill, wondering if I have enough cash on me.

'No bill,' says the waiter, stern-faced and polite. 'Always free here for Mr Charles.'

I put a generous tip on the table and leave, confused, guilty for looking at his book. There is a grumbling in my stomach. I feel something else. Excitement? No, but something. Tingling. Perhaps about this meeting with Teddy, maybe about travelling to Banda Aceh, or maybe about the numbers in my pocket.

Or is it about Laura? This is all to do with Laura. Everything: my confusion, my situation, my unhappiness, my anger. My anger at myself for hoping again, for letting her in when she doesn't exist. For the other night I spent with her in the storm. And why does she only come when she feels like it?

Yes, why does she only come when I don't expect her? The self-ish, selfish bitch. I wince at the word and for using it for her, but fuck, she's ruined me. I don't know who I am now. One minute strong and confident and somehow sort of happy, and the next mis-erable and alone. She has made me mad. Clinically mad. Bitch.

I don't believe it's possible, but I hope Teddy will sort me out, rid me of her. Give me a reason to carry on and maybe enjoy life again. I am suddenly feeling empty, gut-twisting empty; I haven't even got Old Me or New Me down there; I'm not sure who or what I am any-more. I'm rubbing my head, aware that a dull throb is behind my eyes. I walk down the street, the busy, hot, stinking street where dust sticks to me and everyone watches me. Watches the foreigner.

The strange man who is so big and awkward-looking. Out of place like an elephant in a field of sheep.

She just fucks with me. Plays with me. She died and now all she does is mess with my head. And that is not what Laura was. Laura was understanding, wise, kind. Alive. Whoever it is that comes to me now, it is not the Laura I know. It is a Laura changed by death, made bitter and hurtful.

Fuck, it's so hot today. The traffic is so noisy and the smell of rotting rubbish burns my nose. Getting so deep up my nostrils I won't be able to get rid of it. It will stick like the stench of vomit. And the throbbing behind my eyes has started to spread through my head.

'Well, fuck you, Laura. If you don't come now to discuss this, fuck you.'

I wait for a response.

'Exactly. Point made. I fucking miss you, and when I really want to see you, you don't come.' *Bule*, big, awkward, talking to himself. What do I care?

Ah, is that her next to me? I sense her as I walk along the pavement. But when I look, she isn't there.

I miss my old girlfriend. 'My solid, funny, annoying girlfriend.' My lips are moving while I walk. I'm willing her to come to me, but with each step I take, she still doesn't appear, and I grow angrier.

'Don't give a shit. Don't give a shit. Don't give a shit.' Each time louder. I shout the last and people around me stare. 'Don't give a shit.' Suddenly I run into the road, forcing a motor *becak* to stop. Sunlight is scalding my eyes, giving strength to the fire that now burns in my head.

'Crazy *bule*,' the driver yells and before he has time to do or say anything else, while taxis and yellow buses beep horns behind him, I jump in his sidecar with such a force that it nearly overbalances him and the bike.

'Hotel Garuda,' I tell him. It's the only place I can think of to dull my head, to dampen the burn in my skull and to get pissed up in the afternoon. And I want to get pissed up.

I am pissed up. The skull pain has been numbed by drinks at Garuda. But I've moved on from there. I stumble through the doors at Memphis into a world of spinning lights and forced deafness. A thumping, repetitive drumming hits my ears like a boxer punching and punching them. It's a different assault to the headache. This repetition aids the numbness. It feels good. I'm looking at everything as though through coloured sweet-wrappers. Everything is crinkly and unclear and yet vivid. And I'm angry. The bitch still hasn't made an appearance. One day she's all over me like life was never whacked out of her and the next she's roadkill, dead and empty and rotting.

Well what about me, you cow? Getting my hopes up for something that's impossible. Pretending you never died, just so that you can break me apart again when you want. Make me crazy and force me to run away and live in this other world just to get over you. And then you follow me here and mess with me so I can't move on. I can't change.

You fucking BITCH.

'Whisky and Coke.' The wallop with which my chest hits the bar as I fall against it knocks the words out. I reach between my legs, fumble behind me and pull a stool up while the barman does as he's told. He places the drink on the bar and I throw a note next to it. Spinning around on my stool I scan the room like a broken CCTV camera. The image is shaky and nothing is in focus but the camera manages to go from left to right without falling off its mount.

Is that Charles? Come on, turn around. Black suit, black hair. Nope. Not Charles. Your club, but you wouldn't be seen dead here of a night. Not your thing, eh Charlie boy?

I move from the stool and collapse onto a chair by the dance floor, being oh so careful with my glass as I put it on the table. There are only a few people shimmering around the place at various tables and in darkened corners and only one person swirling in their psychedelic secret garden on the dance floor. She is *bule*. Light-brown hair flops over her face and she moves like some hippy chick from Woodstock. Her dancing seems familiar.

'Still not coming for me then, ickle Laura?' I ask the room, not caring if anyone sees me talking. They can't hear me above this hammering wall of sound that's wrapped around me. 'Eh, I said not coming then?'

Silence in the thunder. Is that an oxymoron? Who knows? Who cares?

Closing my eyes I sip on my whisky and amuse myself with the slight dizzying of my mind. There is a hand on my neck and a warm breath of unheard words next to my ear.

'Ah, you couldn't resist, could you?'

I open my eyes to see Laura. But it isn't her. This face is familiar but too close for me to see all its features and complete the jigsaw. I put my hand just below her neck and push back. The face falls together under the mess of brown hair.

'Ha. Julie.'

'Ha. Newbie.' She pulls a chair up next to mine and leans in close again, mouth millimetres from enveloping my ear. She smells of sweat and coconut.

'Didn't recognise you swirling around out there.'

'What you doing here, hero man?'

'Getting fuck-faced mostly.' I wave my glass at her.

'Feeling down? What is it with you? What's your story? Tell me for once.'

'Nah. It'd make your brain explode.'

'I think that's already happening.' She laughs and shakes her head around to prove it. 'Go on.'

'Nope.' I'm not sure why I don't want to tell her. Scared? Not sure what will happen once the weight of it falls from my mouth again? Just too drunk to get my tongue around it? Anyway, 'Nope, nope, nope.'

'Well how about some medicine then? It's got to be about nine. And it's Saturday night. And I, too, wish to get fuck-faced.'

'Why? What's your story then? Marty been too much?'

She touches her nose with her index finger, then points it at me.

'Spot on. Marty's a fucking pillow on my face, suffocating me. I wish he'd give me a fucking break. Know what I mean?'

'Oh. Is that my fault? Leaving you two alone together at Toba?'

'Nah. Would have happened eventually. You obviously weren't going to shag me, so he was the next choice.' She punches my arm and sniggers. 'Not really. Like I said, you're too fucking skinny, man. Too delicate.'

'Let's get medicine.'

'Well, alrighty then.' She puts her hand up and calls over a waiter. Five minutes later he's handing us little blue pills from under his apron.

'These look different,' Julie says as she turns one over in her hand.

The waiter leans down to talk to her. Green laser lights descend in lines through foggy dry ice to the floor. She nods and gets close enough to eat my ear.

'Says they're the same *obat* to the usual, but changed the colour. Do the same shit.'

'Whatever,' I say and throw the pill to the back of my throat.

'Let's dance these bastards up.' Julie pulls me by the arm to a stormy ship's deck of a dance floor where we sway from side to side and a strange seasickness starts to work its way up my legs.

I try to stamp it away. Banging feet on the floor. One of them clicks like wood on wood. Ha, a wooden leg. I am Long John Silver. She is my first mate. I salute her. We dance a shanty. The ship pitches on a swell. I stumble across the deck and hold on to the rails. The ship rights herself. The lights are flashing all around. We're in a storm, me hearties. I hang on to my first mate and shout in her ear over the clap of thunder, 'No frigging in the rigging.' She looks at me, eyes wide, and then laughs a hearty sailor's laugh.

'Aye aye, Cap'n."

What's that coming through the wind and rain and lightning? A dark and dusky girl. She is a beauty. Must be from a nearby island. She talks to my first mate and first mate nods. First mate hands me over. Dusky beauty leads me to a seat below decks. Out of the storm.

'What you do, Crazy?'

Ah, native girl knows the lingo. And a familiar voice. A soft hand strokes my cheek. Familiar touch too.

'Aha, Princess Eka. What are ye doing on my ship?'

'So now you crazy pirate. I think you take very strong *obat*. I get you water.'

'Water? There be nothing here but water.' I laugh as I look to the sea and don't find it.

A bottle is put in my hands.

'Drink.'

I drink. I drink it all. Feel it flowing down and down inside, cooling. It feels like a long time since something so pure passed my lips. I blink at the lightning in the night sky. It flashes a few more times until it turns back into spinning wheels of bulbs and strobes and lasers.

'I'm fucked.'

'Yes, you are. And you look very bad. You should go home.'

'I like fucked.' Suddenly my stomach burns. I cradle it with both arms. Sweat drips off my head onto my trouser legs.

'I think you sick.'

'Just fucked...' I get up and stagger to the toilets. Where are the toilets? Everything is suddenly banging at my back door to be let out. But toilets? I don't know where they are. Can't see the signs for the lights. I stagger and bounce from table to wall to table. Another hand is on my arm, strong and guiding. It is a man. From where? Where do I know him from? 'Where do I know you from?'

He doesn't answer but suddenly I am pushed into a small room and there, oh yes, there is a toilet. A sit-on one. God bless progress. Trousers just make it to thighs and bum to seat and the trapdoor bursts open to a raucous cheer and clapping and a sigh.

When it's all over, I walk back to Eka, who is talking with Julie. Sweat stings in my eyes.

I sit and the room moves around me.

'How you doing?' Julie asks, wide eyes unblinking at me.

'Want more fucked.'

'No,' says Eka.

'Yes,' says I.

'I'm up for it,' says Julie and raises an arm at the waiter.

Eka tuts and crosses her arms under her breasts.

'You have beautiful breasts.'

She tuts again and wiggles her arms under them.

'You sick. You need bed.'

'No. A sick man needs medicine and here comes mine now.'

The waiter slides another blue pill out from his apron and Julie and I tilt our heads back. I want to be on my boat again or to be some other strange place. Sick or not. I want out of reality.

Kiss Eka on the head. Here's the hand waving, hip gyrating again. Julie's hair thrown around. Things are coursing through me, a thick viscous fluid through my veins. Under my skin. Burning under the surface. I shake my head, my body, not sure if I want to make it more or less. I don't care. My face is liquid, flowing off my skull, leaving bone bare. Laser lights reflect off my bone. Dancing crazy skeleton. I feel my face and bone so cold. Rub it. Feels weird. Weird cold wet bone.

—*OK. Enough.*

Ah, at last the bitch.

Her voice inside my head, above the thundering music.

I spin around to see her, but here is Eka. Hands on my hands, pulling them away from my face. Her lips move and head shakes.

'What?' I ask. Trying to pull my hands free to touch my face again.

—*Enough. Come away from here. You need sleep, Ice-Cream Boy.*

Eka's mouth says the words, but it's not Eka.

'How? What?'

I lean in close to her, stare deep in to her eyes.

'Eh, Crazy. Come. You wet everywhere. Come.'

I blink and it's Laura staring into my eyes.

'Come. I give massage to help sleep.' Eka's voice. Laura's lips.

'Fuck going on?' I grab Laura by the top of her arms. 'Fuck you doing?'

'*Ado. Ado.* Hurt me. Stop.' Laura's face is creased. I let go. Eka again.

—*You tripping, boy.* Laura behind me.

I spin to see Julie there smiling wide-eyed.

—*Go on. Go off with your little girlie.*

—*Laura, just be you, damn it. Don't fuck with me.*

—*You're fucking with you.*

Behind me again, I spin and only Laura is there, lights dancing over her white linen top, her jeans, her black eyelashes, her beautiful nose and pale skin and darker than black eyebrows and she is there and she says,

—*I love you, idiot. Don't kill yourself. It sucks here in my world. Stop tripping and wandering and messing about and start living.*

I hug her. Hold her close. Her cool skin on my hot. So cool. But she feels wrong. Her breasts too large against me, hair too thick. I pull away and Eka is there.

'Come,' she says and new water flows down my face. Salt water everywhere. I taste the sea again. I'm all at sea.

'Susu. Sweet milk. Drink. Susu.'

Warm glass against my lips and sweetness almost washes the bitterness away. I keep my eyes closed. So much easier with them closed.

—*Come on, drink the milk. Poor sick numbnuts.*

I wish I could block my ears. My hot ears. Or is it her voice in my head? My thumping, full head. They can't both be here, Old Me and her. Are they best friends now? So hot. Is this what dying feels like?

—*It hurts more than this. A fast, sweet pain that cuts through like blades.*

'Come, Crazy. You not die. Just fever. Sleep.'

Softness of skin on cheek. Soft-skinned pillows. A hand stroking my hair.

—*Sleep, baby. Sleep.*

'Sleep.'

—*Sleep.*

ROLLING, BREAKING, ROLLING

'What day is it?'

'Monday.'

'What? Shit.' I sit up and my head is whacked by an invisible baseball bat. 'Shit.' I lay back down to avoid more hits. 'I need to get a bus.'

Eka pushes a bottle of water against my lips.

'No. You do not.'

'I do. I have to meet a *dukun*. In Aceh.'

Eka stands up. She is naked. Her hair falls down across her breasts, perfectly placed by gravity and nature to cover her nipples. She is beautiful.

'*Dukun*? To get rid of her?' She waves a hand around the room. What room I don't know. 'She was here a lot. You talk to her too much. Maybe he get rid of her. She should go. She not good for you.'

'Yes she is.' I think again. 'No she's not. I don't know. Where am I?'

'Hotel. Do not worry. You were very sick. I look after you. Not her. She make you bad. I care you. '

'Thank you.'

'You still sick. You should stay.'

'I promised Charles I would go. It was the deal.'

'And I think you need special medicine from special doctor. Perhaps he is right. So you go to *dukun*. Go wash now and get ready. I help.' She yanks the soggy sheet off my naked body. 'You too thin,' she says, looking down at me. 'You should eat meat.'

I should probably just eat.

This feels familiar. A familiarity that I don't like, a sign of Western comforts. The bus is modern, not like most I've seen here. Even the windows are tinted. It idles next to us.

'Take care, Crazy. *Dukun* sometimes good *dukun*, sometimes bad, sometimes lie.' She is stunning. Jeans tight around her legs like a second skin and a batik shirt the colour of light coffee, highlighting her natural beauty and skin tone.

You could have been somebody. You should have been somebody.

I force a smile for her.

'Here are pills for head.' She taps me in the centre of mine, where there is still a gentle throb. Although gentle is a stupid word to describe a headache.

'Thank you.' I hold her hand and she pulls it away.

'Not on street.' She runs her hand through her hair and I remember how it feels. 'People don't like see affection.'

'Thanks for being a good nurse.'

'Not nurse. Doctor. Now go.' She blows me a kiss. 'Go. Be careful. Fix your ghost.'

I board the bus and air conditioning hits me, drying the still-fevered sweat as it seeps from my pores. The seats are all fully reclining with a blanket folded on each. Unexpected luxury. I sit in my seat and look for Eka from the window, but she is gone.

Lying back, sweat prickles up on my forehead, beating the conditioning. I pull the blanket up over my head, close my eyes, and spin slightly. And then I'm gone.

The restless night passes in half-consciousness, flashes and slits of light cutting through the darkness. I peer from the window in one of the flashes. A checkpoint. A man peers back at me, machine gun over a shoulder. Aceh? The border? Probably. The bus is waved on. Eyes close and darkness floods in. A flash of light again and I see flames burning, reflecting in water. Oil rigs? Burning ships? Dragons? My mouth feels like blotting paper, but I have no energy to reach for my water. Blanket back over my head. My eyelids fall closed. Images flash through my mind, all forgotten as soon as they pass.

Then blackness and nothing. Peace and complete sleep. Like death should be.

'Eh, man. Wake up. Banda is here.' Blackness is wrenched from behind my eyes with the blanket. I try to yank it back but someone is stronger.

'No more sleep. End stop. Terminus, man.' The driver is nearly straddling me. He throws the blanket over the seat behind him.

'Alright. Alright.' I blink away the night and day slashes its way in. My face feels stiff so I rub it and dry salt sticks to my palms. Christ, I must have been sweating rivers, but now I feel almost normal.

'Off bus. Come on, man. Off bus.'

I pick up my bag and stagger down the aisle on legs deprived of blood and movement for too long. My fitful sleep has lasted the whole journey, about ten hours, maybe. I remember the oilfields and border but the rest is just the nothing of deep, deep sleep. My body is almost creaking with dried sweat.

I step down from the bus into a bustling, noisy and parched-dry square. People are walking in all directions around parked and moving buses. The square is alive with colour and the smell of ripe and overripe fruit. The near-invisible film of exhaust taints the air. The heat is stifling and the sun is falling on my head like hot hailstones.

It must be the start of the day. People still have energy. I'm centre of attention again. Taxi drivers surround me on the dusty road.

'Come, come. I take you to Pulau Weh. I take you to boat for Pulau Weh,' says one of three drivers jostling for my business. They are all in grubby trousers which hang above their ankles and sandaled, dusty feet. Two wear wool hats and one a baseball cap. How can they still be standing in this heat?

'No. No taxi. Go. Leave me alone. Go.'

'No, come, mister. Taxi now.'

'No. I want coffee.'

'Come.' One of them is tugging at my shirt. 'My taxi here.'

'NO.' I yank my arm away

That shuts them up.

'I don't want taxi, I want coffee. *Kopi susu. Mengerti*?'

'Ah. *Kopi*,' says one of them, the baseball cap. '*Mengerti*. Understand good.'

'*Dari kopi susu*?' I ask in a quiet voice, rubbing my dry eyes.

'*Disini*.' The scrawny hand of Baseball Cap points to a building just in front of us with a wonky table and two feeble-looking chairs outside.

'Thank you.' I sit at the table. The taxi driver stands next to me while the two with winter hats wander off kicking up dust.

'No taxi. I don't need now.'

'OK. No problem. *Tidak apa-apa*. I wait you *kopi*.'

'No. Look. I don't want taxi. OK? No Pulau Weh. No ferry. Lampuuk, OK. I will take bus. Now go.'

The owner of the one-tabled coffee shop moves a dusty old Coca-Cola umbrella so that the sun doesn't kill me.

'I wait. Take you where you want.' He adjusts his sweat- lined cap.

'OK,' I sigh. 'Please sit.' If you can't beat them and all that. 'Have a *kopi*.' I point at the other spare chair. The café is full with its two customers and I give up. A crowd has started loitering near us, so I decide it's best just to be calm, drink *kopi*, and take his taxi. I'm risking being late for Teddy anyway, although I have no idea what the time is, and my fuzzy brain isn't even sure of the day of the week. I'd ask Laura, but she must be off in a sulk somewhere. I'm starting to think she is jealous of Eka. No contest, Laura. You're a part of me that Eka could never be. You're like an amputated limb; you're gone but you still itch like mad.

No. Even that won't raise a conversation.

Lampuuk Beach is at the end of a path which passes through sand dunes and occasional palm trees. I walk past a never-completed hotel of grey concrete walls with gaping holes where doors and windows should have been. It never made it past the first floor. A childish stick drawing of a naked woman with fuzzy genitals and big breasts is daubed on one of the walls. Next to it is written, 'Fuck me. I am British whore.'

There is a whumping sound every few seconds that grows louder with each step. I follow the path around a grass-mottled dune and stop. The noise comes from massive waves which rise and curl and crash into the shoreline. The beach runs off to the left and gently curves round to a point about half a mile away. I can see fishing boats bobbing on the shoreline in calmer waters at the farthest point. To my right is a high rock outcrop that must divide this beach and the one where I'm due to meet Teddy. The outcrop is steep and high and full of caves and jagged holes. High waves break in white frothy curls around its base.

I walk further onto the beach, and to my left, set back a little on the brow of sand dunes, is a row of three bamboo-built restaurants and a few huts. Three sleepy white people sit in the shade under a bamboo shelter in the restaurant nearest me, reading books and staring out to sea. A hand-painted sign saying 'Jack's Bungalows' hangs from weathered rope attached to the bamboo roof.

My stomach suddenly takes a turn again and a slight cramp kicks me. I decide Jack's will do. It's the nearest.

The *bules* nod and say hi, but I get the feeling they aren't happy to see another of their race. I can understand that. They've come a long way to this tip of Indonesia to escape the West and its people.

Behind the bar-cum-reception counter is a young Indonesian who introduces himself as Jack. He has long curly hair and a permanent smile. I tell him I need a room and he takes me to a hut that is set slightly further back, but still has a sea view. It has an uneven balcony and a hammock strung across it. Laura is lying in the hammock, eyes closed, smiling. She's wearing a bikini that she wears in other moments on other less-exotic beaches, when stones explain the layout of time and death is happy being ignored.

'You like it?' asks the smiling Jack.

'Very much,' I say, looking at the very clever girl in the hammock, whose fingers of one hand are placed in the top of her bikini bottom.

My gut suddenly churns and I bend over. Sweat is on my forehead again.

'You OK, man?'

'Yeah,' I moan, 'just getting over something. Where's the…?'

'Over there.' He nods to a wooden outbuilding. 'And the wash place is the well, just in there.' He points to a chest-high walled enclosure. 'Use bucket from well. No soap in well, OK? It pollutes the water.'

'OK.' And I run to the wooden loo and am overjoyed when I see it is one I can sit on and not squat over. My body lets go. A mouse sitting in the rafters watches without comment, just twitches his nose, as well he might.

—You really aren't well.

—Because I have the squits and a temperature or because my super-dead girlfriend is lying in my hammock?

—Possibly both. Although I know I'm here, so therefore I exist, which means the squits is your biggest problem.

I place my hand over her stomach, which quivers.

—Mmm.

—Don't tell me you can feel that?

—OK, I won't.

—I'm not going to shag a dead person.

—OK. But your touch feels good.

—I'm not touching you.

This is crazy. I take my hand away and look to the sea rolling and crashing relentlessly onto the beach.

—Ever wonder where all that energy comes from? she asks.

She has turned her head to the sea.

—The moon, wind, turning of the earth, I reply.

—And ever wonder where all that *energy comes from?*

I look back to her and shake my head.

—All I wonder is where all your energy went. All your life force. I say.

—I'm still here.

—No, you're not. You've gone. All you are is some electric spark fluttering around my brain, fucking me up.

—Am I?

—*Yes.*

—*All those moments are still there, numbnuts. They're all still there and I'm in every one, still with you. All lying there waiting to be found.*

There is an Indonesian family playing in the sea. Mother covered from head to toe in clothing, but still in the water up to her waist. Dad is bouncing a toddler up and down at the water's shallow edge.

—*You really want to see this* dukun?

—*I've got to. I promised Charles.*

My head does a sudden turn and my mouth goes watery. I can feel sickness rising.

—*Do you really want to? He might magic me away.*

—*You're not here anyway, so…*

I swallow the excess water and shake my head.

—*Want to be fixed, do you? So you can go off and be an angry New You with a massive chip on his shoulder for the girl he lost?*

Wumph. Wumph. Wumph. Three waves collapse in on themselves, heavy and slow and powerful, before I answer.

—*No. I don't want to be fixed. I just want it all back. All those moments with you. And all the moments we never had. I want them back. I don't want this hurting teasing you give me now.*

Laura sighs and puts an arm over her eyes. I go to touch her but I can't. All I feel is the rough cloth of the hammock. I'm so tired.

—*It's nearly time you went, then. Go see the magic man. Let's hope I'm waiting for you when you get back and he hasn't ghost-busted me away.*

—*I love you, Laura.*

—*I love you more.*

—*Not possible.*

I look down at her and she is gone. There is just a hammock, torn and stained. Pain, intense and raw, jumps up behind my eyes, and I turn just in time to vomit over the side of the balcony. My hands hold on to the wooden rail and it wobbles with each spasm of my stomach. When my body has finally finished doing its thing, I rinse my mouth with water. I go to find smiling Jack and ask him where the path to the next beach is. He points to a gap through some ferns that grow at the rocky outcrop's base.

'You OK, my friend?' he asks, the smile giving way to a look of concern. 'You not look so good.'

'I'm good, thanks. Small headache from a long journey. I'm just going for a walk. Clear my head. *Jalan jalan.*'

'OK. Take it easy. *Jalan jalan* is good for a man with troubles.' He nods at me and winks, then the smile is back and he starts wiping the glasses on his bamboo counter. 'Eh, anyone want a drink?' he shouts to his three residents in the shade. They are all grunts and pleases.

'Eh, man. You want fish with us tonight? Fresh fish I catch this morning?' Jack asks me as I start walking away.

My stomach wants nothing at the moment. Not even to think about fish.

'I'll let you know later. Is that OK?'

'Yeah. OK. No what what. Happy *jalan jalan.*'

The path leads around the land side of the outcrop. It is overgrown and hard to follow in places. It takes me through a grove of coconut trees, then along a small fenced-off area with a solitary water buffalo in it.

'Hello, water buffalo.' My throat hurts. 'Seen any witch doctors in these parts?'

He looks at me, ring through his wet nose, as though considering whether he has. He looks away without comment.

The path carries on; grasses and ferns tickle my bare legs as I try to follow the thin indentation through the undergrowth. I'm mostly in the shade here. My head feels better, but someone with a small hammer still taps the back of my eyeballs with each step. My heart is also beating hard in my chest. Hard and fast and uneven.

Why am I going through this for some crazy old walnut? Why is he so interested in me? Jesus Christ, I'm bloody mad. Why am I here? Even in this country? I should have just stayed in England. Got on with life. Things would have got better. I'd have met someone else. Life would have become normal.

I shake my head and my eyes nearly fall out. Nothing would ever have been normal. I'd just be a different mad.

The path starts widening out and turning sandy again. The sound of the sea beating the land returns and then the path spits me out onto a cove. It is about six hundred metres long and enclosed on both sides: the rocky outcrop to my left and a hill covered in trees and bushes to my right. A thick line of driftwood curves along with the beach. At the rocky outcrop the waves are breaking with double the size and force of the waves on the other beach. They spit white foam as they curl and crash on to the point.

There is no old man. There is nobody. I am alone here.

I wander to the water's edge. Sweat runs down my cheeks and around my eyes, but I can feel the heat drying it quickly. I'm not in the shade here and I can feel the sun searing my flesh. I throw handfuls of seawater over my head. God, it feels good. I'd attempt a swim but the waves are too big and I feel too weak. They'd smash me to pieces or drag me out to sea.

Or perhaps that's the way to go. Perhaps that's why the *dukun* wanted me here. Sacrifice me to the sea for some strange spell of his.

I kick my sandals off and step into the water. I can feel it pulling me backwards and forwards as the waves break just a few metres in front of me. This is a strong old boy, this sea. Been pulling people in and under since its birth. I step in a little more. It's knocking my knees, trying to push me over and then it'll have me. Eat me up and turn my bones to driftwood.

I stand here in the sea, feeling its power, listening to its booming voice, while the sun bastes me with its heat from the eternal white-blue of a cloudless sky for a long moment, or string of moments. Staring at a horizon which leads onto other horizons. Horizons which continue all the way around the world until they come up behind me and poke me in the back.

I smell something. Burning wood. Smoke floats around me. I turn. Walnut Teddy is sitting cross-legged on the beach. Little coloured bag over his shoulder and a small fire burning in front of him. A small metal pot sits in the flames. His one good eye is looking at me, his one cloudy eye seeing me.

He smiles and pats the sand next to him. Feeling too exhausted and ill to protest, I leave the sea and sit where he tells me. I watch the hairs dry on my legs, waiting for him to make the next move.

'You have fever,' he tells me.

'Yes.'

'I have something for you to help one of your sickness.' Teddy fumbles in his bag of tricks.

One of my sickness? Crazy old nut. I wonder what he'll pull out. Am I about to go on one of those Jim Morrison in the desert find-myself trips?

'Somewhere here.' He is still fumbling, the creases even deeper around his face as he frowns. 'Ah.'

Snake's head? Bottle of gnat's piss?

'Take one very four hours.'

A blister pack of pills.

'Oh. Thanks.' I pop one and swig it back with water he also gives me.

'It will help with stomach and fever a little, but of course bad drugs you must sweat out. I tell Charles he should not sell bad drugs at club, but he like his money.' Walnut laughs and punches my shoulder. 'But he is good man in other ways. And he likes you and you have problems. So I help.'

I peer at the tarnished pot and see that about a cupful's worth of watery liquid is starting to bubble in it. There are broken pieces of leaf in it.

Laura leans over my shoulder to take a look.

—*Mmmmmm. Yummy.*

'Tea?' I ask.

'Special tea.'

Aha. Here is the 'find yourself' trip.

Teddy fumbles in his bag again.

Laura sits next to him and rubs sand from her feet. She's still wearing her bikini. I chew my lip and swallow.

'It just needs one more ingredient.' His hand brings out some brown nuts. 'Areca nuts. Some people call betel nuts.' He smiles a wide smile and shows me his red-stained teeth. 'I like very much. Very good for many things.'

He pops them in his mouth, chews them for a second or two, smiles again, and then spits them into the potion. I'm not so sure drinking that is going to improve my stomach. I might leave after all.

—*Perhaps you should. That's going to taste awful. And I don't want him to disappear me for good.*

'Now we smoke and wait.' He pulls a long pre-rolled joint out of his bag. He sniffs it like a cigar and then puts it between his gritted red teeth and grins.

I decide to stay.

—*He won't disappear you. I'm just humouring the old walnut. You're too much in my head to be disappeared.*

—*I hope you're right.*

—*I don't know what I hope.*

He pulls a piece of burning driftwood from the flames and lights the reefer. A pungent puff wafts into my face.

'Here,' he says while holding a lungful down.

'Thanks.' I draw on it and cough. 'Whoa, Teddy.'

'Good shit, as you *bules* say, ya?'

'Ya.' There isn't one strand of tobacco in it. Just pure grass from the jungle. I take another drag.

He is nodding away, watching the fire. His smoky eye nearest me. I wonder what things it can see.

He smiles at me and winks. Then he turns towards Laura and nods. She raises an eyebrow and there is a fleeting glint of fear in her eyes.

—*No way can he see me, right?*

—*Of course he can't. You're in my head. You don't exist. You're not even on the beach.*

—*You think. Then how come the sand's burning my bum?*

I don't know what I think. I don't want to think.

Teddy looks away from Laura and into the flames.

'Not matter how many wrong turns a man take, he end up every time where he should be.' Sudden wisdom from my new friend. 'You have taken many wrong turns, but you will end up in the right place, the right moment. And so will your demons.'

'My demons?'

'You know who I mean.'

—Is he talking about me?

—He's just playing with my mind, that's all. Relax.

—I can't. He's freaking me. I'm going for a walk.

I watch as she walks along the beach towards the trees that line it. There are no footprints in the sand behind her.

He looks at me, eyes study my head. 'No, no. Your brain will shrivel in this heat.' He pulls a square of coloured old batik cloth out from where it is tucked into his woven belt, shakes it out and puts it over my head.

I offer the joint back to him. He shakes his head. Fair enough. I carry on with it.

Laura is studying the leaves and trees. She looks like she's spotted something in them and leans in. Then she parts a big fern, looks back towards us, and steps into the forest.

Something moves in my chest.

'When you get in car, or on bus, or plane, you travel away from some place. You think that place has gone? You think you can't get back there?' He pokes me in the side. 'Eh? You think it is "poof"?' Now he opens his hands in the air like a magician. 'Gone?'

'Er.' Fuck. Both his eyes have clouded up. Ganja. Strong ganja is all it is.

'Tell me? Is it gone?'

I look to the forest to see if Laura has come back out. She hasn't. I open my mouth but he cuts me off.

'No. It is still there. You can take another bus, plane or drive car back there. No problem. Maybe the ticket costs more, or there is diversion on road. Maybe how you get there has changed, but the place has not. ' He nods his head and is silent again. 'Like time, my friend. Like time.'

I look at the potion steaming in the fire. This mad old walnut must have gone to the same school as Laura. I picture them sitting at desks next to each other, studying quantum physics.

Walnut in school uniform. I giggle.

'Mmm. Get high. Good. Time for drink.' He puts his hands into the smouldering fire and lifts his dish up with bare hands. He puts it quickly down on the sand and blows his fingers.

'Shit. Is hot.'

'Of course it is. It's a fire.' I giggle more.

He stirs the potion with a stick and mutters some words I don't understand, then he scoops up some sand and throws it in my face.

'Ow. Fuck.' I shake my head and blink my eyes. For the first time I notice my headache has gone.

'Shh. Drink.' He pulls the cloth off my head and uses it to pick up the soup.

'No thanks.'

'Drink. It is sweet. Drink slowly. But leave a little.' His eyes narrow and he stares out to sea, as if trying to find something under its surface. 'While you drink, listen to the great water, watch the waves. Rolling. Breaking. Rolling.'

I sniff the liquid. It smells of sweet berries and cardamom and something musky, like the weed I'm smoking. Oh, the weed I'm smoking. I look at its black-brown and glowing end and take a long last drag on it. I push it into the sand and take a sip of the soup, or whatever it is. It is sweet, slightly sickly, but I like it.

'Rolling. Breaking. Rolling. Look.' His scrawny dirty finger points out to the sea. 'The waves.'

Is this going to be the trip? Is he going to mind-fuck me? Oh well. I sip more and more, watching the rolling, breaking, rolling waves. White foam spilling. Blue. Emerald green. Azure. The colours of the unseen world beneath.

'Rolling. Breaking. Rolling. The wave, she comes in, she goes out, hiding under the next wave as she comes in. All of them rolling, breaking, rolling, over each other, then back out to great ocean. But they will return again in another time, or on another shore.'

My eyes are becoming heavy. My fingers and toes tingle and quiver where stress is leaving me. Down my arms and legs and out of my fingers and toes.

'Rolling. Breaking. Rolling.'

If only Laura were here. If only she…

'Forward and backward. Rolling. Breaking. Rolling. Retreating under the next.'

If only she what?

'The places we have come from are still there. They are still there. We just have to find them.'

Laura. She is still where? Where is she? Why have I come here, without her?

I can't remember. But it's alright. I'm not scared. My Laura. Somewhere. Still somewhere. In some moment.

'Rolling. Breaking…'

My eyes are drooping. The warm dish is still in my hand, nearly empty.

Relaxed. I am so relax—

'Buuuuuurrrrrrrrrppppppppp.' The sound is deep and guttural and comes from the depths of Teddy.

I jump.

'Bloody hell, Teddy.'

He is up on his bent old legs.

'It is nearly finished, now give me the dish before you drink it all. You greedy Westerners always drink up all that is offered to you. And sometimes all that isn't.'

I hand it up to him and he carries it into the sea. He wades in up to his thighs. I watch as the waves smash down in front of him. I'm amazed his flamingo legs can handle the force. I stand unsteady but ready to rescue him. I can tell he is saying something to the sea, but I can't hear over the crashing of the waves, which have become bigger, more violent.

Teddy throws the metal dish into a collapsing wave. It swallows it whole. He rubs his hands then holds them open-palmed up to the sky and says more words, unheard in the roar of the sea. He turns and starts to wade back. Suddenly he loses his footing and falls over in the shallower water. I splash out to him, but he holds up a hand.

'I am good. No what what.'

Dripping, he stands next to me, and we stare at the sea together. I admire its strength, but don't quite understand its power.

'It is done. Go home, my friend. Go and return to the old places. See what is still there. Waiting for you.' He looks sideways at me and winks with his one cloudy eye. 'Good luck.'

He squeezes my shoulder and walks back to the fire, kicks sand over it, picks up his bag and wanders along the beach towards the hill and trees at the far end. Bent legs and scrawny arms hanging out of colourful clothes. I watch until he clambers into the foliage, like an orang-utan, and disappears.

The sea has calmed again. And so have I. I'm not high, either. I'm not anything. I'm not Old Me. I'm not New Me, I'm just me, and relaxed and happy about it. Calm and happy. I try to think about why I would be any other way and I'm not sure.

And why isn't Laura here?

Because she's dead. Isn't she? She was on a bus and she…

She what?

What?

She is dead. By a car. But she arrived, too. Didn't she? I remember her calling me from Prague. To say she arrived.

No, her mother's phone call. She is dead. Dead. Of course she is. She is dead. I know she is dead.

What has that old fool of a walnut done to me? I must be high. I must be. But I feel so alive. I'm so vivid and clear. I am here.

Mad fool. Mad drugs.

But there is something else. Itching up the notches of my spine and in the curls of my stomach. And I think, but I'm not sure, that it is hope.

TYING THINGS UP

'I finish today.'

Pak Andy nods.

'You're going to pay me everything I'm owed.'

'Yes.' Something on his desk seems to have his attention. I see more of his bald patch than his face. 'I will also pay exit tax.'

'Thank you, Andy. I'll pick the cash up at the end of class today.' I stand up and with my hand on the door handle I say, 'You will treat the other teachers with respect, Andy. Yes?'

'Yes.'

'And also Iqpal. He is a good man.'

'Yes.'

'Because they are my friends. And you know who my other friend is?'

'Yes.'

'Take care, Andy. Thanks for the job.'

I close the door on his bald head and feel a little sad for him. He's going to be Charles' bitch for a long time.

I enter a full staffroom.

'Hey. Newbie returns.' Kim gets up and smacks me on the back. 'Thought you'd been eaten by the drug monster somewhere. Last seen leaving Memphis with a beautiful Indian girl and off your face, I heard.'

'That was five days ago,' says Julie. She hugs me. 'That *obat* was strong shit. We've been worried.'

'I'm OK. Just had to shoot off for a couple of days.'

'Up to your nuts in curry sauce?' Jussy sniggers at his own filth.

'Justin, you get worse,' says Marty.

'All I'll tell you lot is, Mei's for a farewell drink on Friday.'

'Whoa. What?' Kim's mouth shows how wide it can go.

'Yep. Bye-byes all round. In the meantime I'm off to class. See you later.' I laugh and trot up the stairs to my room, leaving a room full of 'no ways' and 'fucks' behind.

I enter the class and put my irrelevant lesson plan on the desk.

'There you all are.' I scan the room with a wide smile across my face. Johnny is in his usual seat, looking embarrassed and awkward, leaning forward over his desk, Jimmy Dean hair swinging in front of his eyes.

'Sorry I missed you on Monday. Who was your teacher?'

'Mr Geoff. He did good lesson about past tenses.' My arch-enemy, the serious Ferdi.

'It was boring,' says Johnny. 'Finished time, blah blah, unfinished time, blah blah.'

'Got to agree with you, Johnny. Especially as there's no such thing as finished time.'

'Of course there is,' says Ferdi, 'I ate my dinner yesterday, it is finished.'

'No it's not. It's still waiting for you to eat it.' Sod it. I'm going to mess with minds; it's my last day with them.

'What? You are crazy.' Ferdi shifts about in his seat and shakes his head.

'What did you have, Ferdi?'

'*Nasi goreng.*'

'Was it good?'

'It was OK.'

'What's your favourite food?'

'*Martabak.*'

'Oh yeah. I love *martabak* too. Well you could have that yesterday if you want.'

'What?'

There is laughter from around the class and a couple of 'crazy sir' comments.

'The past is still there. And you can live it any way you want. You just have to get there, and when you do, you can eat something different.'

Johnny sits back in his chair and whistles.

'Eh, teacher. I said some crazy stuff in the past. You say I can change that?' He studies his fingers, but sneaks a look from under his eyebrows.

'If you can find that moment, then yes. But perhaps you don't have to change anything you said.'

There is a pause from Johnny.

'Whatever you said, Johnny. It was you that said it, and it was probably true, but maybe you just said it to the wrong person. So don't change it. Just accept it and don't worry. Make sure if you say it again, it's to the right person.' *Dukun* seems to have worked some wise magic shit on me too. 'You are you, Johnny, and everyone likes you for that. Perhaps the person you said these things to feels bad for running off and not saying anything when he could.'

There is silence in the class while they try to work out what the hell we are talking about.

Johnny's finger trails an invisible pattern around the desktop; he nods and says, 'So you mean what I said is no problem?'

'I can't imagine anything you say being a problem. You're a good guy, Johnny, and one day someone, the right person, will see that.'

'Thanks, boss.' Awkward silence scratches around the walls of the room.

Change-the-subject time.

'So what does anyone want to discuss today, for this, our last lesson together?'

I wait while the noise dies down. My eyes water at the response.

'What do you mean last lesson?' demands Johnny.

'You cannot go,' says Jenny. 'No other teacher talks to us like you.'

'That's probably because they want to teach you what they're supposed to be teaching. Not how evil and corrupt and immoral my world is.'

'And sexy.' Johnny is being Johnny, and his audience applaud with laughter.

'Sexy maybe. But sometimes subtle sexy is better.'

'Subtle?' asks another student.

'Not here,' I hold my hand in front of my face, 'not in your face like this, too close, but maybe over here,' I move my hand behind my ear, 'where no one can see, or maybe just a little glimpse. Subtle.'

'This country is too subtle,' says Jenny, and most of the class make a sound of agreement.

I nod. 'Maybe.'

My stomach flutters. Sudden clarity from nowhere; in two days I fly home.

In two days I find out how crazy I am.

'We will miss you, sir.' This is from Jenny again.

'Why you going man?' asks Johnny. 'You not like Indonesian or Chinese pussy?'

Oohs and aahs of disgust and laughter mean I can't answer for a second.

'Johnny. Bad boy. You shouldn't say that. That, that rudeness is something you should change if you get the chance. At least only use it where it's suitable.'

I sit at my desk. Has it all really changed? I have new memories of old moments. My past is changing in my mind. But old memories, old moments are still there too. Two versions of everything. Old moments hiding under the rolling-in waves of new ones. Perhaps my mind has split down the middle. Perhaps I can't handle the truth anymore and my brain is making its own history. Drugs have done their work. Or perhaps time has bent or split, perhaps the moments have been changed. Laura doesn't visit anymore and the moments rolling and turning in my head tell me why. I'm just not sure if I should believe them. But in this world, where we have come to be, where things of minuscule intricacies and immense beauty exist together without true explanation or reason, why shouldn't I? Why shouldn't it be possible that previous time still exists, and therefore can still be acted on, changed and replanned? If I've been somewhere before, then when I revisit I take a different route, I might find that maybe the place has had a facelift, a paint job, an improvement. Surely that should be possible in all facets, dimensions and ways of life. If you strongly want to believe it is possible, then believe it. Believe it. Make it true.

Just listen to me; mad as a hatter.

'So you don't like?'

'Sorry. I, er, was just thinking of something.'

'Very good, very polite,' says Ferdi. His skill at sarcasm is coming along nicely. 'I have had enough. *Have had.* That is present perfect tense. We use it to talk about the past when it is connected to the present. The past lessons to now have been bad and so is this one. I have had enough. I will complain and now I go.' He scoops his books up and stuffs them into his bag. 'Goodbye and please return to your stupid country. You very bad teacher.'

We watch him leave in silence. When the door has closed there is a little more silence, then Johnny says something in Indonesian for the benefit of both native ethnicities in the room, but with the exclusion of mine.

'What did you say?'

'What is this on woman?' He points between his legs.

'I'm not falling for that.'

'No. Not for sex, for insult.'

Several words go through my mind, but I hit on the one that I think is the equivalent to what he might want to say.

'Twat.' I say.

'He is a twat,' says Johnny.

Laughter.

The class have their useful word of the week.

'Twat,' they all repeat.

'So anyway, boss, why leave? Why leave us?'

'Why? Because I just miss home. I need to go home. I'm scared of it, but I must go home.' I blink away my blurred vision. 'I need to find out if the past is finished past or if it is still there, waiting.'

'Well then, you better go I guess. Good luck, man,' says Johnny, 'good luck.'

'And good luck to you too, Johnny. Good luck to all of you.'

'See you then, Iqpal.'

'*Selamat*. Have a good journey home.' He has paused in squirting cleaner on the outside windows. 'I think you happy now.'

'You think?' I look at the traffic moving up and down the road. 'I'll miss it. The colours and the smells, the *becaks*, the coffee and the heat.'

'No. You miss this? No. Your country is paradise, I think.'

'Paradise? I don't think so. This is closer to paradise.'

'No. Here is poor and no money, disease and dirty and many problems. Your country I have seen on TV. It is paradise. Beautiful houses and women with white skin and you are all rich.'

'You can't always believe the TV.'

'But it must be better than here.' He idly rubs a patch of glass with his cloth and his voice quietens while the glass squeaks. 'It must be.'

'Iqpal.' I squeeze his shoulder. I feel a little condescending doing it, but I want to touch him to show him some warmth. For some reason I feel his life will not be a good one. 'Take care. I'll remember you.'

'You also take care. Come and visit.'

'I will try. I want to.'

'And bring me present. Bring a watch. You have good watches in England I know. Beckham and Bond wear them. Bring me a watch.'

'I will. OK. *Selamat*, Iqpal.'

'*Selamat*.'

I walk away from him and English World school for the last time. I flag down a bicycle *becak*. As it pulls away I watch Iqpal, standing with a spray bottle in one hand and a cloth in the other. We watch each other until he disappears behind the wall of colours of the street.

'Where you go, mister?' asks the pedalling taxi man.

'The Medan School, please.'

'OK.' He pushes hard down on his pedals and we pick up speed. I look to the front as we swerve in and out of the traffic, my rider pushing other *becaks* away with his hands and feet as we move along under the heavy sky of yet another hot afternoon. In and out of the traffic. Hot, hot day. My eyes are dry from the dust and air. I close them. Just for a moment. My mind sees its chance and wanders, looking in the darkness, going to the furthest corners, digging about, turning over moments like playing cards, looking for the ace. Turn. Turn. Turnturnturnturn.

She stuffs a slice of her pizza into my mouth. All cheese. As she pulls it out a long string of it flops onto my chin.

'Messy.' She leans across and sucks it off.

'You realise the nearest sea is going to be eight hundred miles away?' We watch the small curls of water on a gentle sea lap at the stones. Moonlight making them silver.

'Yep.' She moves the pizza box off my lap and lies down, resting her head there.

'You know I love you, don't you.' She picks up my hand and lays it on her soft hair. 'Stroke, please.'

'I do.'

'You love me.'

'I do.'

'You know there's a world out there?'

'I do.'

The sea hisses with the rhythm of a slow high-hat as it plays on the beach.

'I don't want anyone else. Ever.' She nestles her head against my crotch. 'Never ever.'

'Where is this leading?'

'I want to be me for a year.'

'You're always you.' Something squeezes the pieces around my heart.

'I know. But I just want to be me. As an experiment. Just me. And be somewhere where I know no one and see how I do. Just me. On my own. Without help.'

My hand slows and pauses in its stroking. The feeling is creeping up my throat, tightening on my neck.

'A year. Not even that. Nine months. I'll be back in nine months and then I'll find you and shag your brains out and ask you to marry

me and have kids and die happy.' She kisses my thigh through my jeans. 'But to do that, I want to be a sole explorer. I want to make my own opinions about things. I want a little last time as a single cell, before I divide into a double cell. I'm not splitting up with you. I just don't want to talk to you for nine months, or see you, or any of my friends or family. I want to survive on my own, just to prove I can.'

'Not splitting up with me?'

'Nope.'

'But no contact after you get on the bus tomorrow?'

'Nope.'

'One phone call. Let me know you arrived safely.'

'OK. One phone call.'

'Nine months? That's too long.'

'No it's not. You can't count time, remember. It's just a human way of labelling something beyond them. Look at cats as a cute, cuddly example. They don't have days or months or years. They just are, without restriction.'

'Cats, huh? I guess I have never seen one with a watch.'

'Exactly. And you could use that lump of moments and go somewhere. Why don't you do some alone time somewhere new?'

'Why don't I?'

There's a question: why don't I?

Why don't I?

Why...

The *becak* bumps over a kerb.

What is that memory? What is that moment? Is it a moment? Is it a lie? What is it? I must keep this hope. I must. Because if it is a lie, a brainwashing put there by black magic and drugs, then I am mad. And that is the end of me. Or if...

IF

Teddy has helped me find a new path back to be in the right moment, then life is wondrous, the world is always inexplicable, and I am an overjoyed, jubilant man.

IF

'Here is school.' He stops pedalling and we freewheel to a stop in the dusty road. A thin powdery haze rises up around my feet.

Naomi is sitting on a bench outside. Her face turned towards the sun, puffing thoughtfully on a cigarette. She doesn't see me getting out of the *becak*.

I pay the rider and walk to her, pulling my cigarettes out of my pocket.

Try not to question the moment or my sanity. Just go with it. You're doing fine.

Sitting on the bench next to her, I light my cigarette and watch her while she still looks skyward. She is a good-looking girl who just wanted to show me around. She didn't deserve my attack, my bitterness at everything.

'I'm sorry.'

Her shoulders twitch and she turns her head quickly to me.

'Shit. You made me jump.'

'Sorry for that too.' My toes are white with dust.

'After all these months you finally come to apologise?'

'Pretty much. Yes.'

'Well, you can eff off.' She squashes her cigarette under her foot. 'Too late.'

'Wait, Naomi. Really. You didn't deserve what I said. I've been a little crazy of late.'

'I was good to you. Nice to you. And you were an asshole to me for no reason.' She is standing, her face screwed up with anger. 'You upset me and since then I've had to avoid you and that group of misfits from your school. I was embarrassed, angry and annoyed that I let you get away with it.'

'I'm a tosser. I was a tosser.' I stand too and try to move my face into her vision so she can see I mean it. 'I'm leaving in two days and I just wanted you to know I feel bad about it.'

'Well, too late. Have a good journey and don't come back. Brit prick.'

She takes wide steps around me and heads up the path to her school.

I wasn't expecting that. Apology not accepted. Probably quite rightly not. But it hurts. As I flag another *becak*, I feel a knot in my gut that I know will be there for a while, as a reminder to think twice before going selfish and 'don't give a shit'. Just because I might not give a shit, doesn't mean everyone else doesn't. Everyone else might give a very big shit.

COCKROACH HOCKEY

The guards let me into the house and close the door behind me. I slide my shoes off and look around the room. At first I think no one is there, the kitchen area is clean and there is just a bowl of ripe-smelling fruit sitting on the long worktop. The TV is off, giving Mr Beckham a break, and I can hear no splashing from the pool. New furniture poses by the TV: two big leather armchairs, one with its back to me. I wander into the room and reach for a mangosteen in the bowl.

'It is theft if you do not ask.' A body-less voice. 'This chair is very big. I might slide down the back of it and never get out.'

'How did you know I was taking some fruit?' I walk around the chair and Charles is sitting there with his arms on the rests, fingers stretched out on the leather.

'Always make sure you can see what's behind you, especially if you have enemies.' His points to the large TV screen. 'I still watch it even when it isn't on.'

I see my shape in its black screen.

'Please have a mangosteen, but don't get juice on my furniture.'

'Thanks.' I take one and twist it, breaking the skin. 'I'll miss these.'

'Ah. So Teddy helped you make a decision?'

'Maybe. Or maybe he's just screwed me up even more.' I sit in the chair opposite Charles. 'Nice chairs. A lot of dead animal.'

'Imported from Europe. They are cold and sticky.' He runs his palm up and down on the leather arm a few times. 'I do not like them.'

'Have you seen Teddy?' I ask.

'No. But you look better. Something has changed in you.'

'Yes there's a big crack running through my head here'—I run a finger across the top of my head and down the back—'and all my common sense and sanity is dripping out of it.'

Charles smiles.

'Teddy will do that to a man,' he says. 'Just remember, I never said I believe if what he does is real or just superstition, but he is a wise old man.'

'Anyway, thank you.'

'For what?'

'For seeing something in me that needed help. Thank you.'

'This a very strange world. I live in one part of it that is a lifetime away from yours. I live in a place of tragedies, both man-made and natural. Your country is a place of soft padding and half-truths where your biggest tragedies are holes in the road and rain in summer. You are ruled by ignorance taught by your government and media.'

I wonder why he has suddenly sparked into a soliloquy, perhaps it has been rehearsed; his farewell speech.

'But now you can go back and remember that the belief in magic still exists here. That it is a country where small children are forced to sell cigarettes through the night and others are sent out to sea to fish on platforms that they can't get off until someone comes to get them. That there are tribes in parts of Indonesia that will still eat the hearts of their enemies because they believe it will give them strength. That if a volcano explodes it is a bad omen.' Charles pauses and strokes the cold leather on the arm of his chair.

'I helped you so that you could see the world is not all polished and clean and rational. This is a place where smoking isn't bad for you, where tobacco companies hand cigarettes out free on the street using campaigns that they used in your world in the sixties. This is a place that is not educated, that has morals of the highest standard and also of the lowest. Your world and this world do not mix so well, but if both were better informed about the other, perhaps they would start to understand each other.'

'I understand all that, Charles. I've seen some of it and it's shocked me, but can I ask you one thing, and please don't get angry?'

'I know what your question is.'

'You do?'

'Yes.' He looks to the blank TV screen. 'Why do I do what I do? Why do I promote the smoking in my clubs and why do I sell drugs and allow prostitution?'

I nod. 'Pretty much.'

'Because I can. I am a businessman and people everywhere are stupid and someone will always take advantage. Sometimes governments, sometimes businessmen. What is the difference? I am a businessman. I feel better that it is me and not someone else.'

'Perhaps governments and businessmen should take responsibility for their actions. Perhaps then changes might happen.'

He studies me, those eyes slit to almost closing.

'You are naïve.'

'Perhaps.'

'And I thought you like my drugs.'

I laugh. 'I do.'

'So keep your Western hypocritical opinions to yourself.' He stands and smiles an unusually wide smile. 'And go and teach my children your oh-so-important language.'

'Thanks again, Charles.'

'No problem. What I just said I mean. But please remember that mostly I wanted Teddy to see you because I like you.'

'Mm. OK.'

'They should be in the games room. Fitri will be sad. She also likes you.' He goes to the front door and slips his shoes on. 'When is your flight?'

'Saturday at ten in the morning.'

'I will pick you up at eight. No argument.'

'None made. See you then.'

—ɯ—

Fitri wipes her eyes.

'Why must you go?'

'You remember the time I cried?'

'Yes.'

'Well, I have to go because of that. I've had enough crying and I hope to find out the world is more flexible than we think.'

'Flexible?' she asks. She lies back in the bean bag and sighs.

'Bendy. Easy to bend. Changeable.'

'This world is not bendy,' she says, now with eyes closed. 'It is hard and straight and cannot be changed.'

'Big cockroach.' Benny is up and out of his beanbag. He runs to the corner of the room, gets a broom and runs to the other corner. 'Really big.'

Fitri sits up and opens her reddened eyes.

'Such a stupid boy. It is his new game. He calls it cockroach hockey.'

'Watch this,' says Benny as he slides his foot close to the resting creature.

The cockroach is a long one, about seven centimetres. Benny flicks it on its back with a knock from his toe. The roach's countless legs are scrabbling in the air. Benny runs to the door and opens it. The pool is glistening in the quickly fading sunlight outside. He runs back and uses the broom to move the cockroach away from the wall. He holds the broom back like a hockey player about to strike a puck.

'Ready.' He eyes the open door. 'GO.' He whacks it. It flies across the tiled floor, through the door, across the outside patio and plops into the pool. Benny holds the broom above his head and dances in a circle. 'Aaaah. He scores.'

'Idiot,' says Fitri.

'Got to watch it swim.' He dashes out the door and kneels by the pool, watching the immortal cockroach backstroke.

'Why do you think the world is so unbendy?' I ask Fitri.

She looks up at me like an animal caught in barbed wire and says, 'Because my father will always be sad. Nothing will bring my parents together. This country will always hate us. My little brother will always be an idiot. And friends will never stay long.' She throws herself back in the beanbag. 'That is why.'

Benny runs back in, looks around the room, sees a small plastic box with toys in and empties them on the floor. Then he is gone again with the empty box.

'What if your mother at least started talking to your father again? Would that make a difference? Perhaps if your sister came to visit?'

'It is impossible.' Then there is a pause before she suddenly sits up. 'Isn't it?'

'I feel something might happen. I'm not sure, but…' I smile at her.

'You've done something.'

'Now how would I do that? And even if I had, it might not amount to anything, but there again, it might.'

Fitri studies me hard and I see her father in her eyes. The intensity, the unnerving ability to see beneath the surface of people. This girl is never going to stay in this country. Her life will not be inflexible. She has the wisdom and strength in her to go anywhere and do anything.

'If you have managed something, my teacher, I will come and find you one day and kiss you.'

'Like I say, what could I have done?'

She leans across and grabs my head in her hands and puts her lips on my cheek.

'That was just in case I cannot find you. I know it is bad, but I wanted to.'

'Well, thank you. But maybe you kissed me for doing nothing.' I wink at her. 'I hope whatever I have or haven't done helps a little.'

'Well, thank you, for maybe or maybe not trying.' Her cheeks are now red to match her eyes.

'But I'll tell you one more thing, young Fitri.'

'What, old teacher?'

'I definitely can't do anything about the idiot brother.' I nod to the door as Benny comes back in carrying the box, which is now dripping water over the floor.

'He will not die. Even if I push him under water, he keeps living.' Benny sits down carefully on his beanbag, still holding the box. 'Look.' He holds the box near to Fitri and she peers in.

'There is nothing—'

His arms move in a quick blur. The water pours off her head and face as Benny runs screaming and laughing from the room, dropping the now-empty container on the floor. She is up and running after him, yelling in Hokkien as she goes.

I am left alone in the room. I look around at the big plasma TV on the wall, the pool table, the piles of games in the corner and the two beanbags with indentations of children in. The room is filled with loneliness. I suddenly don't want to leave these two even though I know I will; I must. But my heart breaks for them, locked up in a house guarded by men with guns in a country that looks on them as outsiders. I just hope I have helped. I just hope that what I have done will work for the better in some way.

I get up and go outside to the pool. I can hear small voices yelling somewhere in the house.

'Fitri. Benny.' I call. 'I have to go.'

They come running.

Fitri hugs me. Benny watches.

'Fitri,' he says. 'Dad will be mad if he sees you do that.'

'It's OK, Benny. None of us are going to tell him, are we?' I say.

'No, we aren't,' says Fitri from my chest, now soggy from her wet hair.

Benny holds his hand out. I shake it.

'It is still wrong,' he says. 'But I will not tell him. Goodbye, teacher.'

'Goodbye, Benny.'

Fitri squeezes and her words are lost in my shirt.

'Goodbye, Fitri.' I peel her off me, hold her by the shoulders and smile.

She looks up at me and smiles back.

'Everything is bendy. Everything. If it seems that it isn't, you just have to learn to bend it.' Those are my last words to Fitri.

She nods.

They watch me as I put on my shoes and leave the house. As I walk across the security area the caged dogs bark and the men with guns swing them around into ready position at their fronts. I wait while the gate slides open with an electric hum and one of the guards quickly checks the road before I walk out. The two children hold hands and wave from under an almost-dark sky as the gates close in front of them, like stage curtains. The gates shut with a metallic click. The humming stops. Crickets chirp away at each other in the still of the coming humid night.

CRACKED
OR FIXED

A *new moment. It spins out of the darkness like a flaming torch
falling towards me. I catch it. I look into its light. There I am.
I see me, reading and rereading the same line. The phone is
there beside me. It is ringing.*

I put my book down.

'Hey.' Comes the voice at the other end.

Tension slides down my back into a pool on the floor.

'I don't know why, but I was expecting you not to call.'

'Why not?'

'I don't know. I don't know.' This isn't right. But it is right.

'You OK, Ice-Cream Boy?'

'Yes. So you made it?'

'I made it.'

*The light flickers around the moment. The stage darkens, a scene
change, then the lights come up again. I am rereading the same line
once more. The phone again. It is ringing.*

I put my book down.

I listen to the earpiece.

'There was an accident. She's dead.'

*Sickness in my gut. Tears sting my eyes. Which is it? Which moment
is real? Which is happening? Are they both there, like stones lying next
to each other, slightly different, but side by side? Which one do I pick?*

How do I pick the right one and put it in my bag, so I never lose it? How do I know it isn't just my mind that has cracked and not time?

'I do not want to meet your *bule* friends.'

Her back is straight, head held high on her slender neck. The made bed a brilliant white background to her skin, like a cup of sweet coffee on a clean white tablecloth.

'I'd like you to meet them. Let them meet you. See how special you are.' Condescension has somehow tainted my compliment.

'Ha. I so special you leave me. So special you no want pom-pom now with me. You leave me to find ghost. I very special and stupid prostitute, yes.' It isn't a question, but a statement that she makes. One she agrees with by nodding her head.

Leaning awkwardly forward from my bamboo chair, placed in front of the bed at just the right distance for discussion, not intimacy, I try to clasp the hands that lie like nesting birds in her lap. They fly the nest before I can catch them.

'No, Eka, please. I have never thought of you as a prostitute. And how can I when I have never paid you? I think of you only as a wise and lovely friend.'

'And you have good sex with me.'

'Very good.'

'And you pay taxi and food and hotels.'

'Yes, I do.'

'And you pay too much. *Banyak-banyak*.'

'Maybe. Yes.'

'So I prostitute.'

'No. Anyway, listen. I want to explain.' I sit back and stare at the ceiling. 'Something has happened in here.' I tap the offending spot next to my eye. 'Maybe I have become crazy.'

'Huh. Already crazy.'

'Yes, and now maybe more. I don't know. Or maybe the *dukun* has done something very impossible and special to my world.'

Eka grunts something.

'But I cannot have sex with you again. Something is different in me. I must go home.'

'You think she lives again?'

'I think maybe she never died. Not now.'

'But maybe she did.'

'Maybe she did.'

'*Dukun* clever. Not that clever. She dead. She is only ghost now.'

Her head has dropped forward, losing its nobility, and thick hair hangs down over one side of her face. The birds have returned to their nest in her lap. I lean forward and capture them in my hands. They are lifeless.

'I don't know, Eka. I don't know and I'm scared I'm crazy.' My fingers stroke the hidden rough palms of her hands. The feel of them fills my eyes with water. 'I'm scared things will be as they were when I left England, that she is dead, that I will still be alone. Just me without her.'

'And I am scared she will be there. I am scared of this *dukun* bad magic. I am scared for my crazy *bule*.' The birds escape my grip and fly around my neck. She pulls me onto the bed and overbalances me so that we are lying, arms wrapped around each other, my face in her hair and nose against her cheek.

'You come back here if she still dead. You come back to your Eka.' Her strength is surprising as she holds me tight, her breasts squashed against me and legs wrapped around the back of my knees. I breathe in her skin, concentrate on the softness of her hair against my face, so I'll always remember it. I wonder how much I will miss her.

Wet lips press hard and angry against mine while I'm held there in some wondrous mantrap, and then I'm released. The birds fly again. She thrusts me away with hands of cold stone. Her legs untangle themselves and spin through the air so that the movement carries her off the side of the bed and into standing position in one swift motion.

'Now go. Go, you crazy *bule*.' A bag is thrown over a shoulder covered by a sheer satin shirt. Silky calves pour out of a leopard-pattern skirt like mocha waterfalls. Hair is thrown back from her face and she smiles, big eyes shining like dark water in moonlight.

'You go say bye your friends then go find ghost lady. Think of me sometimes. Think of girl who lives in another world, who wants to meet nice man to look after. Think of me. I think I will always be here. Always looking for nice man.'

'I will think of you.' I stand and try to hold her again. Some sort of sadness urging me on to comfort her. Or maybe to comfort me. 'And you will find—'

A thrust against my chest sends me back onto the bed.

'Shut up. I go. I have good time at Iguana. Bye, Crazy.'

She moves with speed and grace across the room and is gone. Eka has become a moment, an exhibition of moments in my mind's gallery, and I will never see her in another moment that isn't already hanging there.

The bed is sadness. I jump off it and leave, shutting the door on the lonely room. I breathe in the early evening smells of chilli and noodles and rubbish and walk away from the backstreet hotel that will never hold my body again.

I hold the pebble in my hand, feeling its weight, its age, its permanence. I sniff it. The smell of an English beach still lingers on its surface. From that near-insignificant scent come images of a small seaside town, the smell of fish and chips, suntan oil, seaweed and salt. I pass it from one hand to the other, then slide it back into the pocket of my almost-full backpack, its top still undone. A blue-and-white batik shirt trying to escape it.

'Fuuuuuuccck, man. You not really going, are you?' The crown of Kim's head pokes over the back of his armchair. Pungent sweet-smelling smoke hangs in the air around him like a cloud around a mountaintop.

'Yep. I am. Eight in the morning I be gooonne muffa fucka.'

'Well then, sit down and have one last joint with me man.' He points at the chair next to him. 'Sammo going to do some karate shit on the TV in a minute.'

Sammo is eyeing two thugs in black suits on the TV, looking ready to fight.

I take the joint from Kim, wonder for a smallest of wonders if it's a good idea the night before I fly, and then decide what the fuck, there's no way I'm not waking up to get that flight tomorrow. The taste is sickly sweet and scratches my throat like a cheese grater. I cough so hard I have to close my eyes to keep them from flying out onto my cheeks.

'Hehe. New stuff, fresh from Aceh. Fucking good yeah?'

'Yeah.' More coughing. 'This is one to go out on.'

'Can I just tell you one thing, Newbie,' Kim flicks his hair back so he can stare me full-faced. 'Not once did you buy the fucking ganja, man.'

His stare is long and hard and serious.

'Ah, yes. You're right.' He's right. I'm so wrapped up in myself I just take the weed supply as a rightful payback for a shitty life. 'Sorry, Kim.'

He bites on his bottom lip and nods.

'Fucking Brit. Wouldn't have expected it any other way. Fucking tight Brits.'

The silence hangs almost as heavy and heady as the smoke. I'm not sure for how long we sit that way, and with me still holding the joint, not sure whether I can suck on it again or not. It's strong and already I'm not sure how quickly moments are passing by.

A laugh pushes through his closed mouth, a large lip-farting laugh, spraying wetness through the haze.

'Fuuuuuuccck, man. Fucking got you.' He leans forward and whacks my knee. 'I don't fucking care. Been good sharing with you. I know you're fucked up, and if I helped in aiding your fucked-uppiness or recovery, I'm fucking pleased, you Brit fuck.'

Please don't tell me you love me, man.

'Don't worry, I won't tell you I love you, man. I know you Brits hate that American shit, but I do like you, Newbie. I'm going miss you and your hero shit.'

He's shoots the TV dead with the remote and is up by the door, banging any unwelcome creatures out of his deck shoes before slipping them on.

'Let's get you to Mei's and get you fucked up for your journey home.'

I don't tell him that I think I'm already fucked up in more ways than one, and instead get my shoes on and follow the giggling, muttering American out of the house.

We sit at our usual table.

The next time they are all here I won't be. In some future moment someone new will be with them. Here for his or her own reasons, wondering what this group of mish-mashed nationalities and mental states is all about. Watching for the first time what I now watch for the final time: Julie's fingers tap dancing on the table top, Marty stealing sideways glances at her while she looks and laughs in every direction but his. Jussy slouching in his chair, quiet except for the occasional smutty interjection. Geoff sitting on my right, upright and confident, a newfound strength, or perhaps his long-lost old self, back in his body, smiling every now and then at Mei who sits confident and radiant behind her counter, surveying her newly returned kingdom of expats, local businessmen and drunk, lost teachers. Kim sitting to my left, alternating between paranoia and expletive-filled exclamations about my sudden and imminent departure. And cockroaches sitting in lines along the edges of the room and under fridges and under any other recently unmoved object, listening to us in their arrogant and superior way, knowing full well that they are better, stronger and more resilient to life and its senseless beatings than we are.

We chatter, reminisce, laugh and irritate each other, while in my mind, where other voices now are silent, there is space for me to picture a possible scene: a reunion, holding and kissing and smelling and feeling. Perhaps at a bus stop while the driver waits impatiently for us to remove her case from its belly, or in a train station while people jostle past us unaware that the impossible has happened, or outside that ice-cream kiosk on the seafront, crying into each other's necks while seagulls circle above, seeing us just as a part of the theatre of life that scurries around below them.

I nod and talk and ask about their plans and they ask about mine. I don't tell them about the why and how and my crazy hopes. I will find a job, a house, a girl to marry, I say. I don't say I have shifted the pebbles of time and the past is always the present and the dead haven't died. I don't tell them new memories have mixed with old and that ghosts have left the afterlife for the living. I don't tell them of my hope that witch doctors can do magic and that I prefer believing that to accepting my mind has cracked.

I am too excited to be here. I want to sleep so time does another of its mind-bending tricks and hours pass in a closing of the eyes and morning comes sooner. But I stay. These are my friends. I am Me. I am no longer trying too hard to be cold. I like them and I will respect them. So I stay. I drink more beer until the name of the day changes and I finally feel I have stayed enough and say my farewells. They say no, let's go to Iguana and I say no, and they say no, come on, but my nos have it and I shake hands, I hug and smack backs. Mei cries quietly and squeezes my hand while her other hand is held in Geoff's and he thanks me. Marty says stay in touch and Jussy just says see you, man. Kim sticks a clove cigarette in my mouth and tells me to leave fucking quietly in the morning because he's going to be fucked and I tell him to take it easy on the grass and he asks what the fuck I mean and I say nothing and hug him again. Julie says she'll walk part way home with me 'cos her house is on the way and she needs sleep too and I say OK and Marty's stare is suddenly heavy on me and I look at him and gently shake my head and he smiles a weak and worried smile which fades as Julie takes my hand and we step from Mei's into the moonlit, star-filled night.

'You sure you want to go?' she asks.

'I am.' Her hand feels heavy and strange in mine. I keep my grip loose.

'Don't worry. I'm not going to shag you.'

'I wouldn't let you.'

'Oh, if I started on you, you'd let me.' Her finger tickles in the inside of my palm.

I wouldn't. Not while there is a chance for miracles.

'Anyway, you arrogant man, I don't want to shag you. I'm still reeling from my shag with Marty.'

'Not good, then?' I pull my cigarettes from my pocket and we both light one. These I'm not giving up until I see her. I think she'll laugh at my attempt at rebellion. I suddenly wonder, if this turns out to be the miracle Teddy thinks he's performed, will I tell Laura about it all? Will I tell her she is dead in another moment? Will I tell her a witch doctor has changed and bent the course of the universe just so we can be together? Then suddenly there is clarity that I am mad. I must be. I will never talk to her again because she is dead and I am a loon.

'Alright, Newbie?' Julie has stopped and stands in front of me, the light of a full moon shining on her face.

'Not really sure.'

'What is it with you? What's your story?'

The sounds of the hot night are all around: the insects rubbing knees in the grass along the side of the road, traffic going along just outside the housing compound and somewhere a dog barking.

'It's a long and strange one, Julie, and I think it ends in madness.'

'You're not mad.'

'No?'

'Not completely. I'm mad, so I can tell.' She puts on a little hysteric laugh. 'So tell me.'

'I came here because my girlfriend died. And I'm going back because I think now she hasn't.'

'Aha. I take it back. You are mad.'

'I have memories I never had before, but I also have memories that I've always had. Memories of her death. And now also memories of her alive. Alive when she is dead.'

'You been taking drugs I've never heard of?'

We arrive at her house and sit on the white wall that encloses it. A mango tree hangs over us, the full moon's light falling through its leaves and dappling us in its glow.

'Nope. But I have been seeing witch doctors.' I tell Julie about the beach, about Walnut, about Laura, about everything. I wonder why

I choose now to tell her, and why her. Perhaps it's just that I will never see her again, and I want her, them, my friends, to know what I was about. To know that something magical, or something tragic, has happened in Medan and they have been a part of it.

We light more cigarettes and look to the sky.

'A lot of those stars are dead now. But we can still see them,' she says. 'And I've got to tell you, Newbie. I think your Laura's dead, but maybe she's still shining away for the moment inside you somewhere. It's just so hard for you to conceive that. In the same way we can't conceive the size of space and that some of that up there doesn't exist anymore. You can't conceive she's gone because she's so alive in your mind. You think she's still there.'

'I'm nuts, then.'

'Not necessarily. Just heartbroken and hopeful.'

'Anyway, I'm going back and staying hopeful until the last moment.'

'Hokey dokey. Respect that. It won't happen, though, 'cos it's too weird, but weird shit happens, so perhaps it might.' She laughs.

'Talking of weird shit, what about you and Marty then?'

'Best sex of my life.'

'And you're ignoring him.'

'Oh yes. Because how fucking dare he. How dare he be so fucking good and nice and loving.'

I let the silence be my question.

'I'm scared is what.'

'He's nuts about you.'

'I know.'

'So give him a chance. Stop being hard on yourself for whatever ghosts are bugging you.'

She sucks long and hard on her cigarette and then taps out a quick succession of Morse code on her knee with her fingers.

'Just 'cos you told me your story, doesn't mean I'm going to tell you mine.'

'I don't want to hear it. But Marty does.'

'Don't fuck with my mind, Newbie. I was actually planning on shagging you tonight to get back at him for being so bloody, so bloody…' she sweeps her hair back and looks to the moon for her words, 'magnificent.'

'Wow. Big word.'

'Big man.' She laughs and I join her. 'I don't want to fuck him up.'

'Then don't. Easy.'

'Oh, you just have to mess with all of us, don't you? Like it's some mission you're on before you go.'

She kisses me on the cheek, hops off the wall and slaps her thigh a few times.

'Right. Cheers, Newbie. Good luck with the ghost.'

'Thanks, Julie.' I slide off the wall. 'Just go grab him. No luck needed. He's a good bloke.'

'I'm a screwed-up woman. My story would blow his head off.'

'He's that in love with you, his head's already mush.'

'That's true. Right then. Bye. Take care.' She throws her arms around me and holds me tight, clamping my arms to my side so I can't hug back. Then a big wet kiss to my cheek and I'm released to the night. 'Thanks.'

I watch her walk up the short path to her house, fumble keys into the lock and mutter to herself, then she turns, purses her lips and blows a kiss and a wink and she's gone.

I stand alone in the street, my farewells all done but one. The stars above taunt me into a guessing game of which of them are still there and which have gone. Forever. But they all shine so bright, I can't believe any of them are dead.

I watch the ceiling, lying naked and wanting sleep, my sheet crumpled on the floor. But all I can do is count the days of this month. Over and over. Checking, double-checking. My flight is today. Today is July thirtieth. It says so on my ticket. July thirtieth. I arrive in England on July thirtieth, at about five in the afternoon. My head calculates time differences, flying times, double-checking today. Rolling the number and month around and around in my skull. July thirtieth in England. Today is the day I find out. Today I'll be mad or blessed. Today is the day I live. Or I die.

A new moment is born into my brain.

July thirtieth.

'July thirtieth?' I ask.

'Yep. I'll email you on July thirtieth to tell you when I'll come back.'

'July thirtieth.'

'Yes.' Her hand moves down over my stomach, which trembles, then down under the cover where it rests on me.

'Try not to let too many other hands do this.'

'Don't worry. I won't.' The warmth from her palm spreads across the area.

'But one slight flaw is that you don't know how to use email,' she says.

'I'll learn. Just while it's popular and cheaper than letters. We'll all be back to pen and paper in a few years. And as for those mobile phone bricks, I'll definitely never have one of those, so don't bother setting that up for me. Just a fad for the new century.'

'OK. So no mobiles, I'm with you on that. But you don't have an email address.'

'Oh. That's a point.'

'And I thought you were a clever boy.'

'Always cleverer than you, little girl.'

Her hand squeezes and I yelp.

'Don't be a condescending Ice-Cream Boy.' She doesn't loosen the grip.

'Please. Stop. I'm sorry.'

'Really?'

'Really. Aaah. Thank you.'

'Icecreamlover@spacemail.com. All one word.'

I raise my eyebrows at her.

'Your new email. It'll be up and running in about eight and a half months. Password will be Mivvi6969.'

'Eh?'

'I'll open you an account just before I come back. An account just for me to contact you when I'm ready. Just check it on July thirtieth.'

'You're nuts.'

'Very possibly.' She squeezes between my legs again. 'Your nuts.'

'Ha ha.'

'What's the password?'

'Mivvi6969?'

'Correct. Figured even you could remember that one.'

'Cheeky.'

My hand reaches down her back and gently slaps her beautifully cool rear.

'Mmm mm.'

'You drive me mad.'

She takes my hand and holds it against her skin.

'Why not set it up earlier?' I say, seeing a way of staying in touch and keeping an eye on her.

'Nope. It'll be ready for July thirtieth. That's the only contact you're getting. I don't want you writing to me and I don't want to be tempted to write to you. And I'm not telling you my address.'

'You've thought of it all.' I shake my head, 'Fuck, Laura. I know you'll come back to me, but it's going to be the most painful few months of my life.'

She leans up and kisses me, her hand sliding back under the covers.

'You'll enjoy it too. A little holiday from your Laura. Just make sure you're there when I get back.'

'You know I'll be there. No matter what.'

'I know. And so will I. Nothing will stop me. Nothing.'

TIME TRAVEL

I'll miss these early mornings. Uninterrupted blue sky tinged by white. The heat of the day not yet smothering the city. The sound of the call to prayer from first light still echoing around my mind.

I close the front door as gently as possible behind me, hoping not to wake Kim. We've said our goodbyes and there is no need to repeat them.

I stand by the gate feeling the sun waking up on my face. My backpack leans against the tree and together we wait for Charles. A small bird flits around within my ribcage.

The sound of an engine rides the air. The Range Rover crawls along the road. Charles is sitting behind the wheel, window down, cigarette and sunglasses stuck to his face.

'Good morning.' The cigarette bobs up and down in his mouth.

'Morning.' Backpack hoisted over my shoulder, I open the gate and then close it gently behind me. Kim's window is open behind the mosquito mesh and I decide to say one more farewell after all.

'Take it easy, Kim.'

'Fuuuuccck. You woke me, man.' The voice comes from the darkness within. I hear a lighter click and then, 'Have a good *jalan* home, man. A good *jalan* fucking *jalan*.'

I throw my bag in the back of the car and climb in next to Charles.

Charles sits in silence, lighting another cigarette with its predecessor as we drive out of the compound and weave our way across
the city to the airport. I see deepened lines around his eyes at the
edge of his sunglasses. His jaw is clenched and white knuckles grip
the steering wheel. He doesn't speak. Whatever is held in his mind
doesn't know how to get out. There is some sort of energy sparking
off his body. I'm not sure if it's positive or negative.

Yellow buses and *becaks* are overtaken on both sides. The car
slews about like a skateboard on a slalom.

I swallow and ask Charles if he is alright.

He clears his throat twice before speaking.

'I told you that some things cannot be changed. I don't want
some things changed.'

I take a deep breath but say nothing. He also stays silent for a
moment, while his words are put carefully together.

'But you try to change them.' Knuckles go whiter.

I wonder if the steering wheel will snap.

'I am angry.'

I look ahead at the road to check we are heading to the airport.
I have no idea. Perhaps I have badly misread Charles and done the
wrong thing. Perhaps he now has other plans for me.

'I am angry because I know I should have made that phone call
a long time ago. The phone call you made.' His hand leaves the
steering wheel, squeezes my thigh, slaps it and returns to the wheel.
'Thank you.'

The tightness in my stomach loosens. 'Have you heard something?'

'She called me last night. It was very difficult. But she called and
we have spoken about things. About the children. About possibilities for the future.' Charles removes his sunglasses and rubs his
eyes. 'She told me you called her. She told me you were worried
about the children and about me.' Sunglasses replaced on face.
'Thank you for doing something I was too scared to do.'

I lean back against my door and smile. I look at this man who
does so many questionable things, but yet is as fragile and scared as

the rest of us. He deals drugs, has prostitutes in his club, turns a blind eye to promiscuity, but he is also a loving father, husband and friend. It might be morally wrong for him to be all that together, but that is what he is. And what do I really know about morals?

'I can't judge you, Charles. I don't want to. Not when you come from a world so different to mine. And who am I to judge anyone? All I know, wrong or right, is that I like you. And you have great children.' I look from the window. The city passes by for the last time. 'I really just wanted to help all of you. Fitri and Benny as much as, if not more, than you.'

'They will be seeing their mother and sister soon. Su-Chin won't come here, but I will be taking them to Singapore next month. I haven't told them yet.'

I wish I could be there when Fitri hears this, hugging her dad, then me. Her face lighting up and the corners of her mouth twitching with near laughter at the news. I'd like to see this very much. But I'd like to see Laura more. More than anything. As I think of her I wait in case she has anything to say. But no. She has stopped haunting my mind. Please, please, please let that be because she's walking around the square in Prague, taking the city in for one last time before she boards her bus to come home. Or maybe she is already on the bus. Maybe she's already home.

In England it is only two in the morning. Today I'll get her email. Or not.

I punch and kick reality away. Smack it in the face. I can't afford to be realistic. I should check if that email account has been set up before I leave, to see if the address even exists. No. I'll do it after my flight. Not now, I don't want the pain of finding out everything is still the same. I'll endure the hope, the possibility, for as long as possible.

'So how many numbers did you have to try first out of my little black book before you got the right one?' he asks.

'Oh. Just a few.'

'It must have cost a lot in calls.'

'A bit. But it doesn't matter. You've changed my life, so I wanted to change yours.'

'Well, let us hope we have both helped the other for the better.'

We look out of our respective windows and I do hope. I think he also does. I think we both hope during that peaceful interlude in our farewell drive.

The street stalls and roadside shacks slide past. Noodle sellers, sugarcane juice and coffee stands already have groups of people under their canopies, hiding from the sun, smoking cigarettes and playing chess. We pull up at traffic lights and three boys, no more than twelve years old and dressed in dark-stained open shirts and barefooted, work their way along the waiting cars, hands cupped to the windows. One comes to my side as the other arrives at Charles's. In my front pocket I have my last small roll of rupiah notes. I pull it out and hand it to the boy on my side. He looks down at it in his hands, as though he has caught some beautiful creature there.

'Thank you mister. Thankyouthankyou.'

'*Tidak apa-apa*,' I say through the closing gap of my window as Charles pulls off with the changing lights.

'You are too generous. Someone will probably steal it from him.'

'But maybe they won't. And it wasn't so much. Worth nearly nothing in English money. Not even worth me changing it at the airport.' I suddenly remember the cigarette seller from outside the club, the boy with big, tired eyes.

'Charles, can I ask one more thing?'

He smiles. 'Go on.'

'Please can you do something to help the boys who sell cigarettes outside your clubs?'

'They are nothing to do with me. They are run by street mafia gangs. I do not work with them.'

The car swings off the main road and turns into the airport's potholed car park.

'But can you?'

'Some things cannot be changed. In poor places children will always be abused in this way and worse. People will starve. Rubbish will be left on the streets to rot and for rats and beggars to eat. The rich will always use these truths for their own gains. They will learn to make excuses for themselves for not doing the right thing, for not changing things. I know because I am the same.' He pulls up in front of the airport building and switches off the engine. With it the AC whirrs down and the temperature starts to rise. 'I never want to be poor. I never want for my children to need for things. They never will. I will make sure of this. People will always do things that others don't approve of, but if it keeps them and their family safe, why should they care?'

'I'm just asking about some small boys on your street, nothing more. Please keep an eye on them. Can't you just do that? Keep an eye on them?'

'Alright, I will keep an eye on them, but you must do something for them too. You must let people know that they are here. Tell them about the shit things you have seen here.' He pats my leg again. 'Tell them the good things too, but don't forget them, the poor cigarette boys who make your Western countries so much money. Tell your friends and keep telling them.'

He sweeps his sunglasses off his face and his hand is held out before I have time to say any more. Our relationship is in its final moments.

'Have a good journey. And thanks again for what you have done.'

'Thank you, Charles.' I hold his hand and his stare.

'Let us hope Teddy is not just a crazy old man.' He winks at me.

'If he is or isn't, it's good to have hope. Even if it's in the impossible.'

'Impossible happens.' His other hand covers our joined hands. 'As you have proved to me. Su-chin talking to me again was an impossible idea, but it isn't now.'

A last hard squeeze and my hand is dropped. The stare lasts a moment longer and I see some light flash briefly, brightly, in his narrow dark eyes. He swings back around in his seat, sunglasses go back on his face, hands grip the wheel, he squints frontwards.

'Goodbye. Good luck.' The engine is juddering again. Sunlight reflects off the bonnet as cool air blows across my face.

'Goodbye, Charles.'

Across the zones. Time speeds up in the white bullet cutting through the blue. Cutting the sky like a scalpel. Moments push together, squash up. The Indian Ocean glitters seven miles below. Next sea becomes land. Dubai shimmers on the approach. Bags are unloaded and loaded into a different plane. Lifting again. Dubai fades behind. Cutting through the air once more, defying the turn of the world. Europe passes below. A small strip of sea. England. Londoners and their tick-tock lives await.

Descending through cloud. Shaking us back to reality, back to the current. Here it comes. London: grey, wet, sick, only aware of itself.

Tires scar the runway with black. Nearly fifteen hours of travelling. Time on the clock has only changed by nine. It is early evening. July thirtieth.

I have stopped trying to picture the meeting. I have stopped trying to work out how it could be, if it is to be. I have even slept, and then I have been awake with streamers flying around in my stomach, a marching band striding across my chest, beating drums and blowing trumpets. I have been breathless. My head has almost spun on its shoulders.

An electronic *ding-dong*. People are standing, swinging bags from overhead lockers, standing too soon, impatient, staring in the same direction at the back of heads, all waiting for the stale air to be released from this sealed container. Waiting to stream out, to walk like a gigantic creature to the passport gates, where one by one, each person will be separated off from the mass and given permission to get on with their planned lives, or turned away, forbidden entry to the land of false hope and feeble promises.

I will live my hope, false or not. I will. It cannot be any other way.

I want to rush, want to climb over their stupid heads, jump from the plane to the tarmac and run to the building, smash through the glass doors, vault the passport control and hammer the keys on a computer, but I wait. I wait.

'Mivvi6969. Mivvi6969.' Only I can hear the words that come from my lips like baby breaths.

Finally I stand on legs of rotten wood. They are near numb and seem to bend in strange directions and quiver and to want to snap under my weight as I walk. I hang on to the end of the long creature which winds down the steps from the plane and slithers down tubes and along corridors. It grows as more people join it from other passageways. I am no longer at the tail, I am in the middle, being pushed along. The creature has stopped rushing. It now shuffles forward in little movements of its infinite feet.

Up ahead passport signs tell the creature how it is to divide.

I follow the line in front, controlling myself, telling my muscles to relax. Don't push. Don't rush. This moment will move on and you will be on the other side of the passport control very soon. Very soon. Then just your bag to collect, and then through the sliding doors and into the nearest internet café. A few taps on a keyboard, the log-in screen will appear. Type it in, *icecreamlover@spacemail. com*. Was that it? Was it? Fuck. Was it?

Of course it was. It was. You know it was. Calm. Stay calm.

Just three people between me and the expressionless man in the passport uniform.

Mivvi6969.

Smutty girl. God, I miss you.

Be there.

Press Enter.

Wait for the page to load. I can wait. I will wait and watch. It will load.

And look for the messages. There will be a message. She has sent me a message. She has. She has. She has. She must have. God, she must have.

Certainty and uncertainty swirl around inside me.

I must be certain. It is my only option. Laura cannot die again. It is impossible. It would be a joke. A big, sick joke that would destroy me. She will not be dead again. The email will be there.

I force an unsure smile as I stand in front of the passport man. He has a moustache, brown and straight, like it's drawn on in quick downward movements. Blue eyes. Lines around them. I hand my passport to him. The eyes fix on the open page. Then on me. The moustache doesn't move. Doesn't twitch.

Hurry up. Please hurry up. This moment is stuck. It isn't moving on.

'Where have you been?'

'What? Oh.' My throat is dry. The drumming of my heart carries along arteries into my neck and my legs and hands like someone banging on heating pipes. I can feel it in my temples.

HURRY UP.

'Indonesia.'

'Have you been gone long?' Eyes don't blink.

'A while. I've been gone a while.'

Please, please, please. I close my eyes. I can see a computer screen behind my eyelids.

One message.

Laura.

—*Come get me, Ice-Cream Boy.*

'But I'm back now.'

The moustache twitches. The corners of lips turn under the brown hair. The eyes narrow.

'Interesting name, Mr Wells.'

Oh, come on.

'Yes, my father had a thing for science fiction and time travel. He thought the initials would be funny.'

Science fiction. It's not science fiction. It's possible. It is.

'Harper Gregory Wells. A good name.'

'Thanks.'

Give me my passport and let me go.

'I read *The Time Machine*, too. I can remember a bit. Now let me think.'

Oh please, do I have to. Come on, you idiot.

'What was it.' He peers to the ceiling. 'Ah, yes. "There are really four dimensions, three which we call the three planes of Space, and a fourth, Time." I always liked that one, the thought of time as a dimension.'

I look at him and a smile turns the corners of his moustache. Then it's gone. He hands me my passport.

'Welcome back, Mr Wells.'

'Thank you. It's good to be back.'

And I'm through.

And running.

ACKNOWLEDGEMENTS

Thanks to Sian for being honest and giving some bonzer suggestions.

That's it.

The Tuttle Story:
"Books to Span the East and West"

Many people are surprised to learn that the world's leading publisher of books on Asia had humble beginnings in the tiny American state of Vermont. The company's founder, Charles E. Tuttle, belonged to a New England family steeped in publishing.

Tuttle's father was a noted antiquarian book dealer in Rutland, Vermont. Young Charles honed his knowledge of the trade working in the family bookstore, and later in the rare books section of Columbia University Library. His passion for beautiful books—old and new—never wavered throughout his long career as a bookseller and publisher.

After graduating from Harvard, Tuttle enlisted in the military and in 1945 was sent to Tokyo to work on General Douglas MacArthur's staff. He was tasked with helping to revive the Japanese publishing industry, which had been utterly devastated by the war. After his tour of duty was completed, he left the military, married a talented and beautiful singer, Reiko Chiba, and in 1948 began several successful business ventures.

To his astonishment, Tuttle discovered that postwar Tokyo was actually a book-lover's paradise. He befriended dealers in the Kanda district and began supplying rare Japanese editions to American libraries. He also imported American books to sell to the thousands of GIs stationed in Japan. By 1949, Tuttle's business was thriving, and he opened Tokyo's very first English-language bookstore in the Takashimaya Department Store in Nihonbashi, to great success. Two years later, he began publishing books to fulfill the growing interest of foreigners in all things Asian.

Though a westerner, Tuttle was hugely instrumental in bringing a knowledge of Japan and Asia to a world hungry for information about the East. By the time of his death in 1993, he had published over 6,000 books on Asian culture, history and art—a legacy honored by Emperor Hirohito in 1983 with the "Order of the Sacred Treasure," the highest honor Japan can bestow upon a non-Japanese.

The Tuttle company today maintains an active backlist of some 1,500 titles, many of which have been continuously in print since the 1950s and 1960s—a great testament to Charles Tuttle's skill as a publisher. More than 60 years after its founding, Tuttle Publishing is more active today than at any time in its history, still inspired by Charles Tuttle's core mission—to publish fine books to span the East and West and provide a greater understanding of each.